**Acclaim for
Paul Johnston's
Matt Wells novels...**

THE DEATH LIST

"If you like your crime fiction cosy, comforting and safe,
for God's sake buy another book!"
—Mark Billingham

"Very gripping, very frightening stuff…. Though a good
bit darker, will remind readers of James Grippando or even
Donald Westlake in his serious mode."
—*Booklist*

"Morbidly inventive."
—*Kirkus Reviews*

"His masterpiece novel…the plotting is paranoid, the
action is authentic, the characters are convincing, and the
denouement is devastating. It's an absolute ripper."
—Quintin Jardine

"Impossible to put down and a fantastic read.
Another author to add to the not to be missed list."
—*Crime Squad*

"A thrilling, blackly funny read."
—John Connolly

"A ferocious thriller."
—*The Observer*

D1111660

THE SOUL COLLECTOR

"Johnston does an expert job in this extraordinary mixture of police procedural, head-banging vigilante lit.... Great stuff."
—*The Guardian*

"Captivating."
—*Daily Mirror*

"Clever in all the right ways: its plotting is a little out of the box with its mixture of all things serial killers; a touch of Golden Age puzzle solving (Colin Dexter would approve); a large dose of machismo bravado, and the emotional exploration of fledgling love."
—Mike Stotter

"A heady brew...the action is relentless."
—*Times Online*

MAPS OF HELL

"A superb action-packed thriller. Mindful of *The Manchurian Candidate* and *The Prisoner*, only much more graphic...."
—*The Mystery Gazette*

"Frantic and engaging.... Johnston has captured Matt's fear and confusion in a way that's so vivid it's almost palpable... Begin your journey into the mind of one of the most creative—and criminally under the radar—thriller writers working today."
—*Savannah Morning News / Savannah Now*

"Harrowing... At times explicitly violent, it's never gratuitous."
—*RT Book Reviews* [4 stars]

THE NAMELESS
DEAD

PAUL JOHNSTON

MIRA®

If you purchased this book without a cover you should be aware that this book is stolen property. It was reported as "unsold and destroyed" to the publisher, and neither the author nor the publisher has received any payment for this "stripped book."

MIRA

Recycling programs for this product may not exist in your area.

ISBN-13: 978-0-7783-2950-3

THE NAMELESS DEAD

Copyright © 2011 by Paul Johnston

All rights reserved. Except for use in any review, the reproduction or utilization of this work in whole or in part in any form by any electronic, mechanical or other means, now known or hereafter invented, including xerography, photocopying and recording, or in any information storage or retrieval system, is forbidden without the written permission of the publisher, MIRA Books, 225 Duncan Mill Road, Don Mills, Ontario, Canada M3B 3K9.

This is a work of fiction. Names, characters, places and incidents are either the product of the author's imagination or are used fictitiously, and any resemblance to actual persons, living or dead, business establishments, events or locales is entirely coincidental.

MIRA and the Star Colophon are trademarks used under license and registered in Australia, New Zealand, Philippines, United States Patent and Trademark Office and in other countries.

For questions and comments about the quality of this book, please contact us at Customer_eCare@Harlequin.ca.

www.MIRABooks.com

Printed in U.S.A.

To John Hamilton,
last of the old breed

Long is the way
And hard, that out of Hell leads up to Light.
—Milton, *Paradise Lost*

Prologue

Two degrees above freezing, and people's breath was rising over their heads like souls en route to another dimension. It was after 9:00 p.m. and the shops in Greenwich Village were still open, even if customers with money to spend were scarcer than beat cops near an actual crime.

Laurie Antoinette Simpson came out of the subway at Christopher Street-Sheridan Square and headed down Grove Street toward her apartment. Gasoline fumes hung in the air and burned her throat. She pulled the cashmere scarf that her mother had given her for her thirty-fourth birthday over her mouth, but that only impeded her breathing. She needed to get back to jogging. The problem was that the legal practice she had established in Harlem was swamped with civil rights cases, many of them involving immigrants. She no longer had time to produce the articles about extremist organizations that had made her name when she was still in her twenties.

'Hey, Laurie.'

She smiled at the young man with the straggly beard, who was leaning against a wall. 'Cousin Sam, how are you? I thought you went to Brooklyn.'

'Nah, nothing doing over there. Too much competition.'

'And there isn't around here?'

He shrugged. 'People know me. Hey, you need anything?'

'No, thanks. You got somewhere to sleep?'

'Yeah, I'm okay.'

'Those clothes could do with a wash. What have you been lying in?'

Cousin Sam peered at the stains on his threadbare Levi's as if he was seeing them for the first time. 'I don't know, Laurie. Maybe I—'

'Save it,' she said, raising a hand. 'Come around on Sunday afternoon and I'll wash them for you.'

'Hey, thanks.' He looked over her shoulder. 'Gotta go. Customers.'

'Don't rip them off,' she said, watching his skinny frame weave between the cars. Time was, she'd have preached him a sermon about the dangers of drug use, but she knew that was pointless. Keeping him clean was the best she could do, that and being thankful that he wasn't really her cousin, with all his problems.

Shouting reached her from farther down the street. Two black youths, all Converse All-Stars and baggy denim, were being ejected from a music store. As she passed, Laurie heard the shop owner say they were lucky he wasn't calling the cops. Between curses, the young men claimed they hadn't done anything. She was about to take their side when one of them pulled a switchblade.

'Knife, Andy!' she shouted.

The troublemakers looked around at her, giving the shop owner time to grab a baseball bat. After exchanging glances, the young men took to their heels and disappeared around the corner ahead.

'Thanks, Laurie,' said the overweight man with a ponytail. 'Those assholes asked to see my Bob Marley bootlegs. I barely managed to hold on when they tried to grab 'em.'

'Times are hard, Andy.'

'You got that right. Got time for a drink? I have some ten-year-old Calvados.'

'Tempting, but I'll pass. I'm in court first thing.'

She continued down the street, keeping her eyes off the antique furniture store. She had paid the weird Frenchman who ran it plenty when she moved into her apartment. Nineteenth-century European fittings and expensive spirits had been her only weaknesses in recent years. Her mother was forever needling her to spend more on her appearance. She had such beautiful features, how did she expect to get a man if she let herself turn into an old maid? What was she doing in the Village when she could be on the Upper West Side? Her father would happily buy her a place and it was much more convenient for work, though why Laurie insisted on helping people who couldn't pay was beyond her.

The truth was, Laurie had no interest in moving closer to her parents. Her father was a property developer with a beach house in the Hamptons and a ski lodge in Aspen, but he had never been interested in her and would never even speak to her if her mother didn't hand him the phone.

Neither did she have any desire to find another man.

She stopped and looked up and down the street. It had been several months since Wendell had appeared to her, and over a year since she had last run after a tall black man and embarrassed herself by grabbing his arm and saying her dead lover's name. Wendell and she had been together for eight years. Sometimes she could remember every detail about him and the things they had done together, but more and more she could hardly recall his face without help. She only kept one photograph of him on the wall in her apartment because it hurt almost as much to see his sweet smile and perfect skin as it would to banish him from her mind's eye. But suddenly she felt a strong desire to see his features again and extended her stride.

Six years since he had been taken by leukemia. Would she finally be able to look at the photo without tears? The prospect made her heart beat faster, as if she was going to meet her lover in the flesh following a long separation.

Laurie turned the key in the lock and went quickly up the stairs—there was no elevator in the converted family house. She felt the breath catch in her throat, aware that her feet were heavy on the steps. She really did need to get a fitness program organized. Filling her lungs, she opened the pair of locks and went inside. There was an unusual smell, something chemical, but she hardly noticed it, so eager was she to lay eyes on Wendell. She flicked on the light, shucking her coat and throwing off her scarf. Then she stepped toward the dining room door, her heart hammering.

There was a wide smile on Laurie Simpson's face as she walked into the knife that killed her. The last thing she saw, and it hurt much more than the blade slicing through her abdomen, was the red swastika that had been sprayed over Wendell's face. She opened her mouth to let out a cry of anguish, but no sound came as she went to join her beloved.

One

A healthy mind in a healthy body—yeah, right. A crow cawed, then took off with a rattle of wings from the trees on my left. The sounds were immediately swallowed by the sodden vegetation and chill damp air. I came round the bend in the path and sprinted toward the timber wall. I'd been over it so often recently that I knew exactly where the hand and toeholds were. That didn't stop me getting more splinters in my fingertips. After I was over, I ran to the rope slide. That added to the abrasions on my palms. Now there was only the long stretch to the finish. My knee had started to ache from its old injuries, but I reckoned it would hold out. Since I had started doing the circuit, my body had found numerous ways to show its displeasure at being treated like a delinquent at boot camp. Which, of course, is what I was. There weren't so many twinges as there had been at the start. The winter air hadn't helped when I was given the go-ahead to use the course a couple of weeks back. It could have been worse. I'd been told that this part of Illinois could easily have had snow and been freezing cold by now.

I pressed the button on my watch—one of the few personal possessions I'd been allowed to keep—as I crossed the line in the ground. Twenty-two minutes and sixteen-point-six seconds. I bent over, hands on my knees, and tried to get my breathing under control.

'Not bad.'

I looked up. 'Close to my best time,' I said between gasps.

The tall individual in green vest and thigh-hugging shorts gave me an indulgent smile. 'Like I say, not bad.' He paused. 'For a civilian.'

'Uh-huh. What's your record, Superman?'

The soldier dropped to the ground and started doing push-ups at a frightening rate. 'You don't want to know,' he replied, his breathing still regular.

'No, seriously.'

He glanced up at me and grinned. 'How serious do you wanna get, friend?'

'However serious you like.' I knew I was asking for trouble, but life had been dull of late.

'How about this?' the soldier said, still doing rapid push-ups. 'We race the circuit and then I tell you my best time. Oh, and the loser buys a case of beer.'

I went for it. The man in green had well-toned muscles all over and his height gave him a monster stride. I took him at the start, but by the end I was about fifty yards behind, my thighs and lungs on fire.

'Make it Bud,' he said, his sculpted chest hardly rising.

'Can't,' I eventually managed to reply.

He gave me the eye. 'Ain't no can't about it.'

'Sorry,' I said, wiping my mouth. 'I'm not allowed in the canteen.'

He was unconvinced. 'Who are you? Even the FBI can buy shit there.'

The camp was shared by the army and the Justice Department, and no doubt what he said was true. There were different rules for me, though. I pulled up the right leg of my tracksuit so he could see the tracking cuff. 'Do I look like a Fed?'

The soldier took in the device. He looked at the stubble on my face and my less-than-perfectly-groomed hair. 'You don't sound like one, either. Shit, you're that foreign prisoner we ain't supposed to talk to.'

I extended my hand. 'Matt Wells.'

He took the hand dubiously. 'Where you from, Mr. Wells?'

'Call me Matt. I'm from London, England.'

'Is that so?' he said, reclaiming his hand rapidly.

'Now you know why I can't buy that beer. Not only am I barred from the canteen, but I haven't got any money.'

'Aw, forget it,' the soldier said. 'Way I hear it, you got other things to worry about.'

'True enough.'

He gave me a hostile look. 'You really try to kill—'

'Well, if you count that I was brainwashed. They're working on getting me back to normal.' I didn't know how much had been made public about us. We had only been allowed newspapers in the last week, and the internet was still off limits. 'Seems to be working. That's why I'm allowed out here unsupervised.'

'Apart from that thing on your ankle,' he said, with a lopsided grin. 'I heard about you. Your wife was involved, too, yeah?'

'Partner. Karen's due to give birth in the next couple of weeks.'

'Hey, congratulations.' He relaxed, but not much. 'I mean, good luck when the time comes.'

'Thanks. Everything seems to be going fine.'

'Great.' The soldier glanced at his watch. 'I'd better be getting back. See you around, man.'

'Hey,' I called after him. 'What about the beer?'

'Forget it.'

'What's your name?' I shouted, feeling like the kid in the playground with no friends.

'Jerome,' he yelled, over his shoulder. 'Quincy Jerome.'

I watched him run off. I didn't know his rank or unit. The troops in the camp had obviously been told to treat us like pariahs. Which, to any normal person, was nothing less than we deserved.

I went back to the apartment we'd been given, and whined.

'Don't worry about it,' Karen said, her hands resting lightly on the prominent bulge in her abdomen. 'What did you imagine would be said about us? We tried to kill the President and a member of his cabinet, remember? That was hardly going to endear us to anyone, especially not soldiers. He *is* their commander in chief.' She grimaced. 'Your son's kicking like mad again. I might have known he'd be a rugby player.'

I went over and put my hand next to hers, then kissed her on the lips. There certainly was a lot of activity down below. 'Of course, rugby league players don't kick the ball nearly as much as those union tossers.'

'No, you just kick the opposition.' Although she'd

been taken into custody with me after trying to kill the justice secretary in FBI headquarters and then the President in the Washington National Cathedral a couple of months back, her stern manner was that of the detective chief superintendent in the London Metropolitan Police she technically still was. 'That's enough about rugby, Matt. You haven't played for years.'

She was right. This was the first time in months that I'd even remembered the sport I played as an amateur for most of my adult life. The imminent arrival of my first male child had resulted in a revision of my priorities.

'Haven't you got a clinic this afternoon?' Karen asked. Her own sessions with the psychologists and neurologists had been suspended until after the birth.

'Oh, joy…' In fact, the treatment was becoming less arduous. At the beginning we'd been badly affected by the drugs we were given, Karen in particular finding it difficult to eat and sleep. I'd been worried that the baby would suffer an adverse reaction, but the experts assured us that wasn't on the cards. There had been long hours wired up to an overhead machine that reminded me of the device used by the Nazi twins back in their camp in Maine. I'd wondered if the so-called 'reverse indoctrination' would result in me singing the 'Star-Spangled Banner' and demanding a box of doughnuts for breakfast. The effects must have been more subtle, as I had now remembered a lot about myself and kept insisting on Oxford marmalade for my toast—not that I got it.

'What are they doing?' Karen asked. Her face was fuller than before and she looked a picture of health, her lustrous blond hair tied back in a chiffon. 'Still trying out triggers?'

I nodded. The Rothmann twins had programmed their subjects to go into attack mode when they heard certain words. One of them, 'Barbarossa,' had been the default trigger that activated a large number of people in the cathedral during a veterans' ceremony attended by senior government members. But each subject also had personal triggers that affected only them. The one I fell prey to back then was 'Goethe' and the experts had succeeded in deprogramming my brain from responding to it, which was just as well as it had made me zero in on the most powerful man on the planet with murder in my heart. There might still have been other triggers lurking in my subconscious, so hours were spent each week bombarding me with words, most of them German. I had reacted to two other triggers so far—'Landshut,' the name of a town, and 'zugzwang,' a chess move—they had also been dealt with. For the FBI, the worry was that Jack Thomson, aka Heinz Rothmann, had escaped capture despite my best efforts, and he might succeed in contacting me and activating a trigger—hence no internet and no contact with the outside world.

Karen was looking dispirited. 'They're never going to let us out of this place.'

I took her hand. 'Don't worry, I'm doing my best to drive them crazy. Soon they'll be paying us to leave.'

She let out a sob. 'I never…I never imagined our son would be born in a secure facility, attended by army doctors.'

I put my arm round her shoulders. 'It doesn't matter where he's born.' I kissed her cheek. 'All that matters is that you both come through all right and that he's healthy.' I nudged her gently. 'Besides, you'll have a room of your own with hot and cold running midwives.'

Karen looked away. 'We tried to kill the President, Matt,' she said, her voice pitched low to elude the listening devices. 'Even if they give us a trial, we aren't going to be let off and sent home.'

She had a point. Although people from the British Embassy had visited a few times, we hadn't been allowed to see lawyers. When I complained, I was told we could either stay where we were or join the general population in separate federal prisons. I certainly wasn't going to allow our son to be born in a prison infirmary without me present, so I shut up. The fact was, we were better off being deprogrammed in the camp. Peter Sebastian, the FBI homicide chief with responsibility for us, said the Justice Department had no desire to drag us through the courts, citing not only my assistance with the authorities, but the political desire not to have a sensational trial that would overshadow the President's entire domestic agenda. But they had to be sure we no longer posed a danger, and that stage hadn't yet been reached. As usual, the British government had been completely craven and had caved in to American pressure, even though Karen was a high-ranking and decorated police officer. So much for the special relationship between the two countries.

Karen's eyes were wet. 'It isn't fair. He deserves better.'

I felt my son kick against the palm of my hand. 'Of course he does,' I said softly. 'Especially since his names are going to be Mick and Keith.'

That earned me an elbow in the gut.

'I told you, Matt,' Karen said, a smile playing on her lips. 'No wrinkled Rolling Stones' names. It's Algernon or nothing.'

I laughed and brought my mouth close to her bulge. 'Hey, Nothing!' I called. 'Stop kicking your mum!'

Her elbow made contact again before I could get away.

Later on, I went to the FBI's version of Franken-stein's laboratory. It smelled as bad as usual: of dubious chemical compounds, half-finished plates of food from the canteen, and apprehension, though I may have been responsible for the last.

'Good afternoon, Mr. Wells.'

I nodded to the elderly scientist. Dr. Rivers wasn't a bad type, but he was over-keen on formality. Despite the fact that I'd told him weeks ago to use my first name, he stuck to my surname. Maybe he thought that would reinforce my comprehension of what I really was—a British crime novelist who had got involved with more killers than was good for his health, rather than the mindless pawn of Nazi conspirators.

'Today we will try some new triggers that the com-puter has thrown up, if you don't mind.' Rivers led me to the secure room. It had armored glass windows on all sides and the only furniture was a chair bolted to the middle of the floor. At least they weren't chaining me to a bed anymore—that had got very tedious. Now I was free to walk around in the room.

I sat and watched as electrodes were attached to my head and body. The wires ran to a transmitter that was hooked onto the pocket of my orange jumpsuit. Then the glass door closed behind the doctor and his technician, bolts shooting into their sockets with a loud *thunk*. My legs twitched as tedium gripped me. Things only got interesting when we came across a trigger, but that hadn't happened for a couple of weeks. I was still on edge—the experience was weirder than smoking camel dung.

'Ready, Mr. Wells?' Dr. Rivers's voice came through a speaker above the door. He had taken up his usual position behind a bank of screens.

I raised a hand.

'Matthew Wells, session number twenty-seven, December fifth, 1612 hours,' the scientist said for the recording. He paused, and then started reading out the list of words slowly.

'Faden.' He paused again, waiting to see if I metamorphosed into a psycho killer. Nothing.

'Eggenfelden.' Ditto.

'Kinski.' Zilch.

And so the list went on. I sometimes tried to guess what the unfamiliar words meant, but I'd never studied German so I remained generally clueless. It was often hard even to discern which ones were proper names.

'Alexanderplatz.'

That was easier. I had the impression there had been some important Nazi offices in the Berlin square of that name. Since I remained in control of myself, the Rothmanns obviously hadn't deemed it worthy of use.

My mind began to drift. Rivers didn't protest when that happened; in fact, he'd told me at the start of the process that it was probably better if I didn't concentrate on what was said. So I let my thoughts wander. Inevitably I found myself thinking about Karen. She was right. We might well be kept in the camp indefinitely; it might become our personal Guantanamo Bay,

Illinois-style—we'd only been told which state we were in after a week had elapsed. There had been no sign of the therapy ending. For prisoners, we were comfortable enough. We had a fairly decent apartment and wholesome food provided but were under constant surveillance, with cameras and microphones in every room. The tracking cuff had only recently been taken off Karen's swollen ankle. Given her condition, she was hardly going to make a dash for freedom—not that the high, razor-wired fences could be scaled, even by someone as fit and long-legged as Quincy Jerome.

There was only one thing to be said for our enforced stay. It meant that the woman who had sworn to kill me couldn't get to us. Sara Robbins, my former lover, had turned out to be the sister of a ruthless serial executioner who called himself the White Devil. He tried to frame me for his crimes, and, after his death, Sara took up the baton, murdering one of my closest friends and nearly doing in my ex-wife Caro and our daughter Lucy. Sara had made herself into an even more lethal executioner than her brother and it wasn't long after the attempt on the President's life that she'd sent me a message—helpfully passed on by the Feds, who were monitoring my email—saying that she was looking forward to catching up with me.

'Bismarck,' said Rivers.

'Too obvious,' I said, shaking my head.

The doctor raised his hands, a look of irritation on his thin face. 'Please don't interrupt, Mr. Wells,' he said, with a cough. 'Or make smart comments. Krankenhaus.'

I was tempted to recommend that he get his throat looked at in a *krankenhaus*. The word had come up in a pub quiz years ago and I had guessed it meant 'lunatic asylum' rather than 'hospital.' That really would have been too suggestive, considering the Rothmann's father had worked at the Auschwitz krankenhaus. I was so busy damping down a sudden flare of anger about what the Nazi bastards had done to millions of innocent people, let alone Karen and me, that the next word took me by complete surprise.

'Fontane.'

Immediately I felt the hairs rise all over my body.

The conscious part of me seemed to disconnect and rise upward like a spirit. I watched from above as my corporeal self leapt to its feet and started roaring incomprehensibly. Running to the door, trying to break out, I felt no pain as my shoulder repeatedly crashed into the glass.

Somewhere in the distance a voice was speaking, telling me to breathe deeply and calm myself, reminding me to use the calming techniques I had been taught. With concentration, they had some effect. Eventually I returned to my body, which stopped raging and stepped back from the door. I found myself confused and gasping for breath. I kept hearing words I couldn't understand, words barked out in a harsh voice, and I looked around desperately for a way out. I knew the idea behind these triggers was to provoke different reactions. Some drove subjects to acts of extreme violence at specific targets, others to covert intelligence gathering, or communication with superiors via phone numbers or email addresses previously inaccessible to their memory. This had been one of the violent reactions, but I didn't have any target in mind. I also knew what would happen next. When Dr. Rivers was satisfied that my condition had stabilized, there would be a puff of gas from a pipe in the ceiling and I would be rendered unconscious.

Before the darkness took me, I found myself wondering who or what 'Fontane' was.

Two

Peter Sebastian, Director of the FBI's violent crime unit, was not a happy man. In the last week his hitherto stellar career (apart from the jolt at Washington National Cathedral) was beginning to turn to excrement.

First, there had been the murder in Manhattan: civil rights lawyer Laurie Simpson found decapitated in her apartment, her innards piled on a dresser above which a large red swastika had been sprayed. Her head had been carefully positioned upside down in the toilet bowl. Examination of the wounds suggested that a large, but by no means unusual, knife, probably manufactured for the hunting market, had been used, while the paint was a very common brand. The CSIs had discovered minimal signs of a forced entry—the killer had picked two complex but fairly standard locks, but there were no foot- or fingerprints and no significant fibers or other traces. NYPD detectives were following up on Ms. Simpson's professional activities—the legal practice in Harlem had been vandalized by far-right extremists more than once, and she had written some strongly worded antifascist pamphlets when she was younger. The fact that her dead black lover's face had been at the center of the swastika seemed to point indisputably to racist motivations.

Now Sebastian was standing outside a lakeside house in Michigan, listening to the harsh cries of birds that he could neither see nor identify and looking at the darkening surface of water that would take a man's life in minutes. He shivered in the late afternoon gloom, hoping against his professional experience that the dead man was not the second in a series. He had heard enough on the phone from the local sheriff to suggest that the same killer could be responsible, but he wasn't going to draw any conclusions till he had scoped the scene. The CSIs had finished earlier, but the supervisor was on hand to give a report. On Sebastian's specific request, the body had been left in situ. December on the shores of Lake Huron meant that decay would be slow and the gas boiler in the house had not been turned on.

'Sir?' Sebastian's assistant, Special Agent Arthur Bimsdale, a twenty-eight-year-old so fresh-faced he could still have been at junior high school, handed him pairs of overshoes and latex gloves, as well as a white protective suit.

When they were ready, the detective in charge, a heavily-built man by the name of John Jamieson who smelled strongly of sweat, took them inside the house. It was in a state of disrepair, the paint flaking and the wood distressed.

'No sign of forced entry,' the big man said, looking round. 'There were no tire tracks in the driveway apart from the vic's truck. And no recent footprints around the house except the vic's.'

'So we have a ghost.' The smile on Arthur Bimsdale's lips froze when he caught Sebastian's eye. 'Sorry, sir.'

In the living room they were joined by the senior CSI, a blonde woman with a heavily lined face.

'Traces?' Sebastian asked.

'We're analyzing,' she replied. 'Nothing that stands up and begs for attention.'

'Prints?'

'Comparisons are underway. Most of what we've got so far belongs to the victim.' She shook her head. 'A killer this organized would have been wearing gloves.'

Sebastian turned to the detective and noticed that a single hair nearly an inch long curled from the policeman's left ear. 'Witnesses?'

Jamieson shook his head. 'As you can see, there aren't many houses in the vicinity, and it's quiet up here during the week.'

Peter Sebastian looked around the room. It was furnished by what must have been original pieces dating from the fifties, many of them in poor condition. The floral wallpaper was faded and the curtains frayed. There were piles of CDs, books and newspapers around the floor. The juxtaposition of old and recent objects struck the FBI man.

'The place used to belong to the vic's aunt,' Detective Jamieson continued. 'She died early last year and he took it over. Guess he didn't have time to do any refurbishments.'

'Has the dead man been positively identified?'

'Well, not officially. Seeing as the body's still here and…how we found it. But the sheriff knew him.' The detective bit his lip. 'So did I. Met him once at a charity disco.'

Sebastian's nostrils flared. 'That's another reason to show respect by using the man's name.'

Points of red appeared on Jamieson's cheeks. 'You're right.' He looked down. 'As far as I'm concerned, the body is definitely Sterling Anson's.'

The FBI man nodded. He had never liked the way law enforcement professionals deprived the dead of their personal identity by calling them 'vics.' It was a professional issue. If you kept in mind that people were unique individuals, you were more likely to nail their killers.

'I understand Mr. Anson was quite a celebrity in these parts,' he said, softening his tone.

The detective nodded. 'Everyone in Detroit knew of him. Most people thought he was a great guy, but he did have his enemies. Someone tried to burn down the radio station when his show was on air a couple of years ago.'

'Those fucking Nazis,' the CSI put in. 'After that, they called in the next time he was broadcasting live and said they'd get him sooner or later.'

Sebastian turned to Jamieson, who nodded. 'It was a public phone and no witnesses came forward. We never caught them.'

'And you don't have any idea of their identities?'

'No, we don't.'

'After all this time.' The senior FBI man let several seconds pass to register his disapproval.

'The thing is,' Jamieson said, 'he used to talk about the threats he got on air rather than reporting them to us. If he was telling the truth, there must have been dozens of them.'

'All right, Detective, let's see what you've got.'

They moved into the hall and toward the stairs. According to the briefing Bimsdale had prepared on the Bureau plane from Washington, Sterling Anson was a Howard Stern look-alike whose nightly talk show knocked lumps off anyone who demonstrated racist tendencies. He never hesitated to name names, and several companies had fired staff displaying prejudice. Businesses run by bigots had been harassed out of business. Anson was an obvious target for retaliation, even though he had never suffered personal physical attack. Until now.

'I didn't see any alarm system,' Bimsdale said.

Jamieson shook his head as he led them to the second floor. 'Seems he was too fearless for his own good.'

On the landing, where the metallic smell of blood was pervasive, the CSI stepped forward. 'This isn't pretty,' she said, her hand on the first door to the right.

Peter Sebastian leaned forward and took in the badge on her chest. 'Don't worry, Martine. We've seen it all before.' When the CSI looked at Bimsdale, who swallowed nervously, he amended his statement. 'Well, I have,' said his boss.

He followed the woman inside and immediately regretted his bravado. It was true that he had witnessed the worst that the country's murderers could provide, but the scene by Lake Huron was a real eye-opener.

'We think the killer may have been let into the house by the vic…by Mr. Anson,' the detective said.

Peter Sebastian's eyes were fixed on what remained of the talk show host. 'Why's that?' Bending down, he lifted the cover of a plastic container on the rug below the suspended body. Two blood-drenched eyes stared up at him.

'Like I said,' Jamieson said, after a long pause, 'there's no sign of a break-in.'

'But that's not all,' the CSI said, pointing to the curved piece of rolled steel from which Anson was hanging head-down. 'There are traces of blood on the hook in the beam.'

Sebastian looked around at the congealing slick on the floor. There were spatters on the walls, too. 'So his throat was cut before the hook was attached up there? You think that suggests the killer didn't gain prior entry?'

The detective nodded. 'The medical examiner said that Anson took a blow to the back of the head that would have knocked him out.'

The senior FBI man looked up at him. 'Is it likely that a man with a history of threats would have opened the door to a stranger?'

Jamieson frowned. 'If it was a stranger. We're checking with his family and friends. His wife, who's Chinese-American, said he was careful at their place in the city—they've got two small kids—but up here he was less concerned.'

Sebastian and Arthur Bimsdale got as close as they could to the hanging man, the younger agent visibly shaken. Sterling Anson, a Caucasian in his early forties, was naked, the ends of his long brown hair dipped in his blood. The wound across his throat was wide and clean-edged. Apart from the removal of his eyes, his chest and abdomen had been mutilated. He had been cut from groin to sternum, with another incision running across the belly button.

'It's inverted,' Sebastian murmured, glancing at his assistant. 'If he was standing the right way up, the cross would be upside down.'

Jamieson was immediately alert. 'You seen something like this before?'

'Not exactly,' the FBI man replied, turning to the CSI. 'Has anything been drawn or written in the house? Anything in red?'

The blonde woman shook her head. 'What were you expecting?'

Sebastian didn't answer. The swastika in Laurie Simpson's apartment had been kept from the media to avoid copycat actions. 'Have you been through all the rooms?'

The woman looked at Jamieson and raised an eyebrow. 'We know our jobs, sir,' she said, her chin jutting.

'Not suggesting you don't. But this killer strikes me as highly devious.' He turned to Bimsdale. 'Arthur, you go with Martine here and check downstairs. Lift all the rugs, take all the pictures down.'

'No stone unturned,' said the young agent earnestly.

Peter Sebastian watched them go and then looked at the detective. 'We're going to do this floor together. Have you got a camera?'

Jamieson nodded, his expression stony. 'Why would the murderer hide something when he left his victim in full view?'

The FBI man gave a humorless smile. 'Two pretty dubious assumptions behind that question. First, just because Sterling Anson was made a display of doesn't mean the killer wasn't subtle in other ways. Second, you just classified that individual as male. Why?'

The detective rubbed the back of his head. 'It would have taken some strength to haul him up there,' he said, looking at the beam. 'Even though he wasn't the biggest of men.'

'And there are no women strong enough to do so?'

Jamieson raised his shoulders, but he looked unconvinced.

Peter Sebastian ran his eye around the room again. As with the first floor, the furniture was old and the décor in tatters. There were several reproductions of artworks on the wall, but his attention was immediately attracted by an amateurish painting of Martin Luther King above a bookcase. He stepped over, his heart pounding, as he realized that the other frames were all slightly awry, while the doctor was perfectly aligned.

'Take some shots,' he said to Jamieson, and when several angles had been photographed, he reached out and took the painting down. The wall behind was unmarked.

'Damn,' he said, under his breath. Then he turned the frame around and got an immediate adrenaline rush. Two inches high and painted twice in red was the letter *S*—jagged and fraught with the weight of history.

'Shit,' said the detective, 'Is that what I think it is?'

'If you're thinking that those letters form the initials of the SS, Adolf Hitler's elite guard, then the answer is affirmative.'

'So some neo-Nazi bastards did get him.'

Sebastian didn't reply. He wasn't worried about *neo*-Nazis; his concern was over the son of a genuine Nazi—Heinz Rothmann, responsible for the failed plot to kill the President in the autumn. He stepped out of the room after giving Sterling Anson's body a last look. It wasn't just that Rothmann junior saw himself as a real Nazi. He had also resurrected the Antichurch of Lucifer Triumphant, a vicious cult that included among its rituals human sacrifice—with the victim suspended from an inverted cross, throat cut and eyes put out. The problem was, Heinz Rothmann had disappeared more successfully than a firefly at midday.

'Where are you going?' John Jamieson asked.

'The bathroom.'

The detective joined him in the run-down room. He knew the CSIs would have found anything obvious. The FBI man was on his knees, his head close to the floorboards. Then he groaned and reached for a pink, knitted toilet-roll holder on top of the cistern.

'Camera,' he ordered.

Jamieson fired off some shots, then watched in horror as the cover was removed. A human tongue, Sterling Anson's chief weapon against fascists and racists, had been placed inside the cardboard tube.

The sole Master of the Antichurch of Lucifer Triumphant looked up from the couch, displacing the surgical gown that had been placed around his shoulders. Southern sunlight was streaming in through the windows in the roof and dust motes swarmed in the beams. He remembered the Latin poet his father had made him read as a teenager, the only non-German writer the old man had ever cared for. For him, Lucretius was a master, who had raised science above the arts. He alone had shown the glory of creation and the futility of fearing death. Atoms were the basis of all things, as Democritus had proved, and all things could be changed by adjusting molecular structure. Even dust consisted of atoms. And dust, as everyone knew no matter what they purported to believe, was what human beings ultimately came to—unless you consigned yourself to the Lord Beneath the Earth.

'I'm ready, Mr....Master.'

Heinz Rothmann, formerly known as Jack Thomson, and now the possessor of seven alternative identities, glanced at the gaunt man in faded surgical scrubs. 'Is that you, Doctor? The last person who kept me waiting was sent to clean the snake cages.' He gave an empty smile. 'While the creatures were still in them.'

The doctor wiped the sweat from his brow. 'Are you sure you won't have an anesthetic, Master?' He avoided looking directly at the man with the striking aquiline nose. The Master must have once been handsome, but the way his hair had been cut—short at the sides and back like the Führer's—gave him a bestial look.

'I am sure. Proceed.'

As the scalpel cut into his face, Rothmann felt the blood course hot over his cheek, but there was no pain. The conditioning program that his sister had developed just before death had been completed and was a success. Those who believed wholeheartedly that the world could be cleansed by the genius of the Führer felt no physical pain—only regret that the great man had not been able to complete his work.

'It's over,' the doctor said, stepping back. He picked

up a mirror and held it in front of the Master, swabbing the blood from the wound.

'Very good,' Rothmann said, his eyes narrowed. 'But my father had dueling scars on both cheeks. Proceed.'

As the second cut was made, he thought about Matthew Wells. Where was he?

He needed to find him. After his sister's death, Rothmann had thought only of avenging her, but more recently he had realized that he needed him alive. The problem was, nobody knew where he was.

The Master nodded as the doctor showed him the second wound. Wells wasn't the only problem he had. The murders in New York and Michigan concerned him. There was something going that was unacceptable.

It was time the Antichurch took control.

Three

I came round in the infirmary, my head pounding from the drugs that had been pumped into my system.

'Ah, the return of the prodigal,' said Dr. Rivers, checking a monitor.

'Return of the guinea pig, more like,' I mumbled, trying to reach for the glass of water on the commode and finding that, as usual, my arms and legs had been secured.

'Come, come, Mr. Wells. You fought that trigger very successfully.'

'Didn't seem that way to me.' I licked my dry lips. 'When are you going to stop using that knockout gas? It isn't as if I can escape.'

He gave me a reproachful look. 'It isn't a question of escape. It's essential that the trigger is rendered completely ineffectual, and that I can only do when you are unconscious.'

'So, Doc, has the treatment worked this time?'

'Let's see,' he said drily. 'Ready?'

I took a deep breath and dropped into the defense zone I had learnt.

'Fontane.'

I felt a momentary buzz, but nothing more. 'Okay, you can unbuckle me.'

Rivers shook his head. 'You know the protocol, Mr. Wells. We wait for ten minutes in case of—'

'Delayed reaction,' I said, closing my eyes. This was always the dullest part of the procedure. 'What does Fontane mean?' I asked, to pass the time.

'Who rather than what,' the doctor replied. 'Theodore Fontane was a major nineteenth-century German novelist.'

'Never heard of him,' I muttered, mildly embarrassed by my ignorance. Even though I'd studied English literature at college, my knowledge of foreign writers was negligible. Being a crime writer didn't help. I spent most of my reading time on the competition, and not much of it was translated from German. 'So did the Nazis approve of this Fontane?'

Rivers shrugged. 'I rather doubt it. He was some kind of early Modernist—too refined for them, I imagine.'

'Oh, I get it. A double bluff by the Rothmanns.'

He nodded. 'It wouldn't be the first time.'

An earlier trigger had been 'von Stauffenberg,' the man behind the bomb plot that nearly cost Hitler his life in 1944. The Rothmanns were cunning as hell. They had no qualms about using words abominable to the Nazis.

When the ten minutes were up, Dr. Rivers called in an orderly. I was released from my bonds, the big man remaining in the room while the scientist finished writing up his notes.

'All right, Mr. Wells, that's it for today.'

'How did I do, Doc?' I asked, rubbing my ankles.

Rivers peered at me though the thick lenses of his glasses. 'A perfectly adequate response,' he said. 'You still cannot control the post-traumatic rage that being confined here has exacerbated, but that is within the parameters. It would be interesting to monitor your reactions in the open, but I rather doubt Mr. Sebastian would sanction that.'

I felt another flare of anger when I heard the FBI man's name. 'Maybe in five years,' I said, heading for the door.

The gorilla came with me as far as our rooms. Despite the ten-minute delay precaution, Rivers and his team would be watching me carefully over the coming hours, just in case. Such a lengthy response time had happened once before. I had broken my fingernails on the window locks trying to get out. Afterward, I was thankful I hadn't hurt Karen—she managed to take refuge in the closet and I was eventually restrained by a quartet of soldiers in body armor. It was possible that I had been programmed not to injure another Rothmann subject, as Karen had been, but she wasn't taking any chances. Her own reactions to triggers had been less overtly aggressive and she became even more docile as the pregnancy advanced.

Peter Sebastian was the scumbag responsible for our continued incarceration. Although he knew that, without me, the Rothmann conspiracy would have been even more devastating for the U.S., he wouldn't cut us any slack. He had visited the camp once a week, though it was nearly ten days since we'd last seen him, always pretending he was our friend because he was a law enforcement colleague of Karen's. I knew better. Dr. Rivers had recommended we be given access to internet and television, arguing that cutting us off from the world was no longer beneficial to our treatment. Sebastian had rejected that and we were going stir-crazy— especially Karen, who wasn't able to make as much use of the outdoor facilities as I was. Of course, Sebastian might have been taking orders from the justice secretary or even the White House, but in any event he was definitely the scheming type and was probably using us to further his career.

Still, I was pretty good at scheming myself. If that was the way he wanted to play the game, I would be happy to take him on.

The killer called Abaddon—according to the Book of Revelation, 'the angel of the bottomless pit'—was drinking a latte in a café near Faneuil Hall, central Boston. It was five in the afternoon and the winter gloom was interspersed with Christmas lights and the glare from shops whose owners anxiously awaited potential customers. The newspapers were full of stories about unemployment, Chapter Eleven filings and bankers' bonuses. The assassin's funds were mostly in offshore accounts, so the state of the economy was of minimal interest.

Coverage of the two murders so far had been disappointing. The authorities were keeping quiet about the Nazi angle and only a couple of writers, both online bloggers, had made much of the fact that the victims were both supporters of liberal causes. Laurie Simpson, the Greenwich Village resident, had been acclaimed

as 'a tireless worker for human rights and social justice' by one of the geeks, while the other had been
full of compliments for the Detroit radio host Sterling
Anson, saying that he'd brought numerous hate groups
and racist factions to the attention of the authorities.

The other element missing from reports were the
details of how the victims had been dispatched and
disfigured. Abaddon wasn't surprised by that, though
the people picking up the tab were apparently unhappy.
Earlier that day there had been a message from the assassin's broker on the secure bulletin board they used.
Double the money was on offer if the next victim was
displayed in a public place. Abaddon had agreed, but
needed an extra couple of days to come up with a
plan.

There were some favorable aspects about the target.
Rhoda Rabinovich was even smaller than Sterling
Anson. According to her medical records, she weighed
only ninety-four pounds and was less than five feet two
inches in height. On the other hand, she worked for a
Massachusetts state senator, a Democrat with heavy
support from the Jewish community, and she was hardly
ever on her own, despite the fact she was single and
lived alone. However, the briefing had given some help
and Abaddon had been careful to research the locations
and work up a convincing appearance.

The target had an office in a block near City Hall and
she was always there in the early evenings on weekdays.
Abaddon, unconcerned about witnesses because of the
disguise, headed over there without delay. The black
leather briefcase wasn't just a stage prop. Inside it were
a combat knife, rope and other equipment. Apart from

the building's security team, there was no one guarding Ms. Rabinovich. The other office staff would have left by now and all the assassin had to worry about was voters—they would be more interested in their Christmas shopping, even if they spent less than usual, than in bellyaching to the senatorial aide. Nodding at the uniformed man in the entrance hall, Abaddon took the elevator to the fifth floor, two below the target's office. After checking the vicinity—a young woman carrying files hurried past without even raising her eyes—the assassin went up the stairs and looked through the glass in the fire door on the seventh floor. No one passed in the corridor beyond.

Abaddon made it to Rhoda Rabinovich's office without encountering anyone. The outer door was unlocked and the receptionist's desk was tidy. The assassin went up to the inner door and listened intently. There were no sounds at all from within. Patting the Glock 17 semi-automatic pistol in the belt holding up gray suit pants, Abaddon knocked and entered.

A woman in a white blouse sat behind a large desk, head resting on her crossed arms.

Abaddon coughed quietly when Rhoda Rabinovich didn't move. That had no effect.

'Excuse me?' the killer tried. 'Ms. Rabinovich?'

This time, the woman raised her head, but it was a slow process that seemed to take a huge amount of energy. 'What…what is it?'

'I'm sorry,' Abaddon said, smiling widely. 'Are you unwell?'

'Am I…' Rhoda Rabinovich broke off and let out a shrill laugh. 'Oh, no, I'm just fine. I'm…' The words stopped and were replaced by a long, low cry that seemed to contain all the pain in the world.

'Can I help?' Abaddon asked, feeling unusually uncomfortable.

'Oh, I don't think so. I...'

The killer watched as the target leaned forward again onto her arms, her weeping partially smothered. But the head, with its wreath of lustrous black curls, came back up before any advantage could be taken.

'You see...' the woman said, wiping her forearm across her eyes and smearing makeup onto the fabric. 'You see, the senator...the senator has decided that I am too old for him. That little...little bitch who only left Vassar last year is much more to his taste.' She laughed bitterly, then choked and started crying again.

Abaddon knew from the briefing that Rhoda Rabinovich was thirty-six, which was hardly old. She also had a forty-inch bust and lips that must have done a lot to keep her employer's chin up over the years. None of which was relevant right now.

Ms. Rabinovich watched unperturbed as the killer stepped closer.

'I like...I like your mustache, young man,' she said, with an attempt at levity. 'Are you a fan of Groucho Marx?'

Abaddon stopped at the desk, right hand on the Glock's grip inside the suit jacket. 'No, I'm not, lady. I'm a fan of Joseph Stalin.'

The woman's hands flew to her mouth. 'Oh, that... that will never do. Democrats abhor dictators.' She grabbed a paper cup and swallowed a mouthful of the contents. 'I'm sorry, would you like some? It's vodka and…and orange.'

'No, thanks,' Abaddon said, leaning forward.

'But it…it doesn't do anything,' Rhoda Rabinovich said. 'It's useless. It's…it's over.' Then she stood up, her hands scrabbling in the desk drawer.

The killer watched in astonishment as the woman pulled out what looked like a novelty paper knife and thrust it deep into her chest.

'That fucker…' she gasped. 'He brought…me this piece of…shit back from…Spain.' Her eyes widened and she fell forward on the desk with a crash.

Abaddon was surprised, but not enough to forget what was to be done. The window frame looked secure, and the desk would be a good counterweight. Going back to the briefcase, the killer took out a black spray can, then pulled the painting of autumn in New England from the wall opposite the windows and set to work. It wasn't long before the shape of a black cross with the equal sides narrowing toward the center appeared on the wall, the white paint providing good contrast. Using a second can, this one red, Abaddon added the words *Mein* and *Kampf* on either side of the Iron Cross. Then the killer stripped Rhoda Rabinovich of all her clothes, leaving the knife embedded between her remarkable breasts, and wrote the required words with a red indelible marker pen, the first on her belly and the second on her back.

After putting the spray cans and pen back in the briefcase, Abaddon tied one end of the rope from the briefcase tightly around her neck and the other to the desk leg. The precalculated length seemed to be right.

The locks on the windows were easy to disengage. Cold air blew in from the Atlantic. The killer took a shorter piece of rope and attached it to the handle of the sliding window, then lifted Rhoda Rabinovich up to the ledge and stood her against the vertical part of the frame. Her high heels remained on the floor. Then Abaddon took out the combat knife and ran the blade across the rope—a cut had been made previously, but it felt like the victim was even lighter than the briefing had said. Perhaps she had lost weight because of how the faithless senator had treated her. Such is troubled love.

Leaving the office lights on, Abaddon stood at the door listening, and then unlocked it, pistol at the ready. There was no one around. The assassin opened the door beyond the receptionist's desk and dropped the victim's clothes in the toilet. After exiting the office, it took just over a minute to go down the stairs and exit the building, the Glock out of sight. Abaddon was near City Hall when the first scream rang out.

The killer turned, suppressing a smile. This was working out even better than expected. A woman in the square had noticed the naked figure in the window even before Rhoda Rabinovich fell. The only question now was, would her head stay on or not? Either way was acceptable to the killer's employers.

More screams echoed around the concrete walls, and suddenly they went up in pitch. Heading away, Abaddon glanced back and saw the senator's aide and former lover plummet earthward after the partially severed cord gave way. Then the carefully measured length of thicker rope broke her fall. Her head stayed attached to the rest of her body, which swung slowly from side to side like a grotesque pendulum. There was no way the details of this murder would be kept from the media.

The assassin walked swiftly on, smiling under the bristling mustache, as the clocks of Boston's many churches started to sound the hour.

Never send to know for whom the bell tolls, she thought, piqued that the victim had done the best part of the job.

Four

Karen was lying on the sofa with a blanket over her. Her eyes opened.

'Sorry. Go back to sleep.'

'It's all right,' she murmured. 'Your son's finally stopped doing somersaults. Kiss?'

I went over and gave her what she wanted. As her time came closer, she had become more insecure, something I would never have expected when she had been the stern, driven detective. I was doing the best I could to support her, but she really needed to be in familiar surroundings so she could nest and prepare herself. Bastard Sebastian.

'How was it?' she asked, taking my hand.

'Okay.'

Karen wasn't buying that. 'You had a hit, didn't you?'

I glanced away. The last thing she needed now was to worry about me.

She squeezed my hand. 'I'm a big girl, Matt,' she said, pulling me closer with surprising strength. 'We've talked about this. We'll get through it together. You tell me what happens to you and vice versa. That's the deal.' She tugged me downward and kissed me on the lips.

I felt my eyes dampen. Karen had been kidnapped by the Rothmanns earlier in her pregnancy and the fuckers had put her through the brainwashing process. No one knew what effects the drugs and machines would have had on our son, even though both Rivers and the obstetrics team expressed confidence for his health, at least on the surface.

'Don't worry, my love,' she said, putting her lips to my eyes. 'We're doing fine, all three of us. You'll see. We'll beat this. We'll beat them all.'

I leant against her and felt the bump where our son was sleeping under my abdomen. God, I loved Karen. Without her, I wouldn't have got this far in the therapy.

She laughed, her breath tickling my ear. 'Now go and get me a sandwich, male slave. I'm ravenous.'

I went into the kitchen. The camp staff had been bringing us the makings of all our meals since Karen first refused to eat the food that came on covered plates from the mess hall. I put together some ham and cheese sandwiches and took them back to the living room. Then, my voice low, I told her about the trigger. I didn't say the word out loud in case she had been programmed with it, too—Rivers would follow that up after she'd given birth.

We had just finished eating when the doorbell rang. Although the Feds could have walked in any time they liked, they preserved the fiction that our quarters were private, despite the cameras and microphones. I opened up.

'Hi, Matt.' Special Agent Julie Simms, a nondescript woman in her late thirties, was one of the FBI team.

She handed me an envelope. 'Enjoy,' she said, turning away.

'What is it?' Karen asked.

I ran my eyes down the communication and laughed. 'It's from Peter Sebastian.' I handed over the sheet of official paper. 'Progress at last.'

'My God, he's giving you unarmed combat sessions even though he knows how dangerous you can be?'

'It's about time I got back into shape. You know what this means?'

'We're going to get out,' she said breathlessly.

'I reckon so. He knows that Sara will come after me, so he wants to get me back to full fitness.'

Karen's face fell. 'In that case, he should be giving you a small arms refresher course, too.'

I knew that wasn't likely, given that we were still finding triggers in our minds. There could have been hundreds of others, even though I had escaped from the Rothmanns' camp before the conditioning—what they delightfully referred to as 'coffining'—was complete. But that wasn't what was worrying me. The idea that crazy Sara might be on my tail when our son was a tiny baby horrified me, as did the fact that I was partially responsible for the threat. If only she'd been killed alongside her sick brother...

I knew what I would have to do when we were released—find her before she got to us, and deal with her once and for all. I would never forgive myself if something happened to the woman I loved and our son.

'Matt,' Karen said, 'I don't want to think about the Soul Collector.' She never called Sara by her real name. 'Come here.'

I sat down on the rug by the sofa and took her hand.

Karen gave a shy smile. 'I…I want to talk about the baby's name.'

I remembered the lack of progress the last time we'd done that. 'Are you sure? Maybe we should wait till after he's here.'

There was a flash of anger in her eyes. 'What, now you're superstitious?'

'No, of course not. I take it Algernon's out of favor.'

She ignored that. 'I don't know. You'll probably hate my idea.'

'No, I won't. Try me.'

She took a deep breath. 'Magnus.'

I liked it immediately. 'You know what it means?' I'd always been fascinated by names and had several books about them.

She shrugged. 'It's Latin, isn't it?'

I nodded. 'Magnus means big.'

Karen laughed. 'Really? Like father, like son.'

'Ha.' Suddenly I knew the time was right, although I hadn't been planning it. I shifted onto my knees, her hand still in mine. 'Karen Oaten,' I said, as formally as I could. 'Will you do me the enormous honor of marrying me?'

She looked like she had been struck by several bolts of lightning. For what seemed like a long time, she was unable to speak. Then she managed the words I'd been hoping I'd hear. 'Oh, Matt. Of course I will.'

We kissed for an even longer time.

And then the doorbell rang again.

'Shit,' I said, after our lips had parted.

'Don't go,' Karen whispered.

'They'll only use the passkey. I won't be a second.'

I got a surprise when I opened the door.

'Sergeant Quincy Jerome, 182nd Airborne Division,' said the familiar figure, this time wearing full fatigues, cap, belt and gleaming black boots. 'I've been assigned to work up your unarmed combat skills, Mr. Wells.'

'You couldn't have picked a worse time.'

'Go!' Karen called. 'I want to let the good news sink in.'

Quincy gave me a quizzical look. 'It's good news that I'm going to be at the…give you a rigorous workout?'

I smiled. 'I'm less of a civilian than you think.' I went to change my clothes.

Sergeant Quincy Jerome beat the crap out of me. Or rather, he would have done if we'd been fighting for real. As it was, I still had pains in places I'd forgotten existed. We started with judo. I was a black belt, but Quincy was several dans better than me. Then we boxed for a while. My stamina wasn't too bad—I'd been running and doing exercises every day for the past two weeks. That was the best that could be said of my performance in the ring. He was taller and his reach was longer: I hardly landed a punch on his head guard, never mind his body. The fact that I used to train with an ex-paratrooper and SAS man didn't do me any good; Dave, the meanest bastard I ever saw in a fight, would have had trouble with the sergeant.

Jesus, Dave. Sara had killed him in cold blood. And that was my biggest secret and motivation—my lust for revenge was just as great as hers.

The sergeant folded his arms and shook his head. 'You're softer than a marshmallow, friend.' He slapped me on the back. 'Come on, it's time to get wet.'

We spent some time going after each other in the pool. After I'd swallowed most of it without laying more than a fingertip on him, we called it a day. I dragged myself out of the water and staggered to a bench.

'Actually,' Quincy said, standing in front of me, 'I've seen worse.' He laughed. 'At a grade school.'

I gave him the finger without looking up.

'Joking,' he said. 'For a civilian, your grasp of the basics isn't bad. Give me a week and I'll knock you into shape.'

'That's what I'm afraid of,' I said, finally getting my breathing under a modicum of control.

He grinned. 'Same time tomorrow?'

'Sadist.'

That got me a heavy punch on the shoulder.

Peter Sebastian looked down at the gray waters of the Potomac as the Bureau driver crossed it on their way into Washington D.C. The flight from Boston had been delayed and he was going to be late for his meeting with the Director. Not far downstream, the Nazi Heinz Rothmann had last been seen on his boat, heading toward this same Potomac. Matt Wells had done what he could to stop the madman, but it hadn't been enough. No body had been found and Rothmann had survived, the FBI man was certain of that—survived to start anew with a murderous campaign against the people who hated everything he lived for.

'Sir?'

Sebastian glanced at Arthur Bimsdale. The young agent was like a puppy desperate to please. At least you didn't have to worry about hidden depths with him— what you saw was very definitely what you got. That made a change from Sebastian's last assistant, who had played him for several kinds of fool.

'What is it?'

'Well,' Bimsdale said, flicking through the pages of his notebook, 'I was wondering how we'll be handling the media with this latest killing. There's no chance of keeping most of the details under wraps.'

'Considering the poor woman was blowing naked in the wind in front of half of Boston until the paramedics arrived, that is a reasonable conclusion.'

The agent's cheeks reddened. 'Em, yes. So, shall I give the Massachusetts detectives details of the earlier killings?'

'Do nothing of the kind.'

'But they're already asking—'

'Let them ask. We don't have to answer.' A thought struck Sebastian. 'Have you told the people working on the other killings not to volunteer information to Boston?'

Arthur Bimsdale nodded. 'I thought that would be advisable until you told me otherwise.'

Sebastian was impressed, not that he showed it. He had lined another agent up to assist him, but Bimsdale had been foisted on him by the deputy director of personnel. Apparently he came highly recommended by the special agent in charge in Butte, Montana. J. Edgar Hoover, who used to exile incompetents there, would be rotating in his grave.

'Keep it that way until I do tell you otherwise.'

'Yes, sir.' The young man looked at him earnestly. 'Do you think it's the same killer in all three cases?'

'Yes.'

The abrupt answer seemed to surprise Bimsdale. 'What about the differences in the M.O.s?'

The senior man shook his head. 'We've been over this before. The specifics may vary, but the general picture is the same every time. The victims were all involved in activities that could be construed as anti-Nazi, and all three were killed in ways that relate to the rituals of the Antichurch.'

Arthur Bimsdale looked unconvinced. 'Yes, sir, I've looked at the archive material, such as it is. I have to say, I don't find it hugely convincing.' His manner was that of a nitpicking student in a philosophy seminar.

'Oh, really?' Sebastian said, giving him an icy look. 'One of the core rites of the Antichurch of Lucifer Triumphant was human sacrifice. The chosen ones were suspended from an inverted cross before their throats were cut. Then their eyes were put out. Does that sound at all familiar?'

Bimsdale was unaffected by his boss's sarcasm. 'First of all, the Antichurch only operated in the state of Maine—none of these killings took place there. The records also show it was eradicated in the 1850s. I don't understand why an obscure and highly localized cult should be relevant, especially considering that there was no direct reference to it at the scenes.'

Peter Sebastian turned away and looked at the lights in the center of the capital. In a few minutes he would be in the executive elevator that led to the Director's office. He didn't need a debate about the killings right now. Then again, honing his case on a callow subordinate might be beneficial.

'As I've told you more than once, *Arthur*,' he said, using the young agent's first name to induce a bogus sense of camaraderie, 'the Antichurch of Lucifer Triumphant was recently revived by Heinz Rothmann and his sister to give their Nazi movement a religious component. They calculated, quite correctly in my view, that Americans had to be engaged on the spiritual dimension before they would accept a political agenda.'

'But human sacrifice?' Bimsdale was unable to conceal his horror.

'Is that so strange? Millions of our fellow citizens believe that Armageddon is almost upon us, you know, the battle in which scores of people are going to die horribly.'

'Really, sir, that's nothing more than a myth,' the young agent said dismissively.

'Is that right?' Peter Sebastian caught his assistant's eye. 'Tell me, Arthur, what's your faith?'

'I'm an Episcopalian.'

'From Philadelphia, as I remember. And you studied sociology and criminology at Yale?'

'Among other subjects, yes.'

'Have you spent much time in the Bible Belt? Or the deep South?'

The young man shook his head. 'My family has a holiday place in Vermont.'

'But you came across fundamentalist Christians in Montana, I'm guessing. Fundamentalist Christians with some worrying political beliefs.'

Bimsdale nodded, looking uncomfortable.

'That's what I mean. There are enough frightening

people with beliefs related to human sacrifice even before you go anywhere near cults like the Antichurch, never mind Nazis.'

'All right, sir, I can accept that. But what about the differences in the M.O.s? Victim one was decapitated and disemboweled. Victim two was hung upside down—but then his eyes were removed, unlike the previous victim's. And number three was stabbed before being hung from a window.'

Sebastian had turned away, his eyes fixed on the Washington Monument. 'You're forgetting several significant points.'

'With respect, sir, I'm not. Nazi slogans and/or insignia were found at every scene, and all the victims were engaged in activities that could be construed as anti-Nazi—or at least pro-minorities and liberal. But there's been no specific reference to these Rothmann people, nor to the Antichurch. It's all very circumstantial.'

Sebastian looked round. 'What, your detective skills require that Rothmann leaves his fingerprints at every scene?'

'No, sir,' Bimsdale said, less deferentially. 'In any case, the lack of trace evidence suggests that an experienced professional carried out the murders.'

'An experienced professional hired by Rothmann.'

'Maybe.'

Peter Sebastian sighed. 'Look, the M.O.s are not so different. True, Laurie Simpson's head was removed, but that's a form of throat cutting, isn't it? And that poor woman in Boston had a rope put round her neck—again, the throat.'

'What about the postmortem mutilation of the first two victims?' Bimsdale demanded, holding up his yellow pencil like a teacher questioning a pupil.

'The records suggest that the Antichurch faithful tore apart the victims of human sacrifices.'

Bimsdale nodded. 'But there's nothing about organs being placed in or near the vicinity of toilets.'

Sebastian groaned. 'Like all those indoor toilets in nineteenth-century Maine? Come on, Arthur, you've heard of metaphors, haven't you?'

'The victims' head and tongue put where fecal matter goes? I see the rationale, sir, but it's hardly an established methodology, even amongst fascists and Satanists.'

Sebastian was tempted to pull rank on his assistant, but he restrained himself. If his case struck a lowly agent as being flawed, what would the notoriously acerbic Director think of it? Then again, the Director had shown a personal interest in the murders from the start, and he'd been keen on a meeting even before his head of violent crime had been obliged to go to Boston.

The thing was, whatever the Bureau's manuals said, investigating murder wasn't only about collecting and collating evidence. You had to go by your gut as well, and Peter Sebastian's had been telling him from the moment he saw the swastika above the heaped innards in Greenwich Village that Rothmann was pulling the strings, even though he'd still hedged that conclusion until the house on Lake Huron.

The question was, what to do? Given the distance between the various scenes and the skills demonstrated by the killer, it would be impossible to predict who and where the next victim would be—and he was sure there would be more. They could either sit back and let the bastard run with it until they nailed him, or launch a preemptive strike. Convincing the Director to go with the latter would be a hell of a job, he knew. But at least he had a card up his sleeve: the former Rothmann subject Matt Wells.

Five

Back in our apartment, Karen was sitting at the table. She looked up at me and laughed. 'Oh, dear. Was the nasty man a handful?'

I managed to bite my tongue. 'What have you got there?'

'A very nice laptop,' she replied. 'With full internet access. Julie Simms brought it round. There's a note from Peter Sebastian, saying it's time we rejoined the real world.'

I looked at the screen. Karen was on the Metropolitan Police website, reading emails. 'Should you be doing that?'

'Officially, as I've just discovered, I'm on maternity leave. They haven't blocked access to my in-box, so I'm contacting my team.'

I stepped out of range. 'Will they remember who you are?'

'Ha, ha, Matt.'

I'd almost forgotten how attached she was to her job. They'd have to fire her to get rid of her, and they'd be reluctant to do that, both on legal grounds and because she was a highly effective detective. They probably hadn't bothered to block her correspondence because Sebastian had told them she didn't have internet access. Which raised an interesting question. Why had he suddenly authorized that, on the same day I'd been given unarmed combat training? Something was changing in the way the U.S. authorities regarded us.

I had a long shower, which helped the aches and pains a bit. What state would I be in after a week of this? Not that I was going to give Quincy Jerome the satisfaction of scaring me off. I needed to be in the best possible shape in case we were let out. It wouldn't take Sara long to catch up with us. She had ears and eyes all over the place.

When I emerged, I found Karen in the kitchen. She was grilling pork chops, though her own regular evening meal consisted of peanut butter on brown bread.

'You don't have to do that,' I said, encircling her girth with my arms. 'You need all your strength to make those horrible sandwiches.'

That got me two elbows in the midriff, and they hurt a lot more than before Quincy had put me through the grinder.

'Aren't peanuts supposed to be dangerous for small children?'

'After they're born, idiot. I don't know, I act like the good housewife cooking your dinner and all I get is mockery.'

I didn't want to tire her out with a bout of verbal sparring that would end in inevitable victory for me, so I let that go. We ate and retired to the sofa. She fell asleep not long afterward, so I went over to the computer, flexing my fingers. It was weeks since I'd typed. There was another problem. Would I be able to remember all the passwords for the firewalls I'd set up to keep Sara out of my life? As it turned out, my memory worked fine, suggesting that Dr. Rivers was right about the conditioning wearing off.

I managed to dredge up the email addresses of my family and friends from my memory as well and sent them all messages, hoping that Sebastian's team wouldn't censor them. My family had been advised by the Foreign Office that Karen and I were well but out of contact until further notice—the press hadn't been given the details of our involvement in the cathedral action.

My in-box was full of unread messages. Over a year before, I'd instituted a daily reporting regime to ensure Sara didn't pick us off one by one. My mother and thirteen-year-old daughter Lucy were frantic in their earliest messages. Even my ex-wife Caroline, Lucy's mother, was fairly concerned. My closest friends had also been climbing the walls, convinced that the Soul Collector had made a move when they didn't hear from me for so long. It was good to reassure them personally that we were well, not that I could tell them anything specific. I didn't think we'd be allowed visitors anyway.

I thought about Sara. In the past she'd managed to access all my various communication systems, though more recently I'd had a high-level security system applied to my computers and phones. Even if she used other methods to find me, she'd struggle to get into the camp. On walks around the place, I'd noticed a very large amount of razor wire, as well as sophisticated monitoring gear of all kinds; and large numbers of personnel, both in FBI jackets and army camouflage gear, all toting firearms. Which reminded me, if we were heading toward release, I'd need some time on a firing range. Even back in the U.K., with its zero tolerance policy toward handguns, I'd managed to equip myself with pistols. We'd have no chance against Sara without them.

I leaned back in the uncomfortable chair. Maybe Peter Sebastian wasn't really planning on cutting us loose. He only knew about the Soul Collector by reputation, but he'd had experience of what Heinz Rothmann and his brainwashed mob could do with guns. With Rothmann still out there, Karen and I were targets if we were going to be staying in the U.S. until we were sent for trial—if that ever happened. Could it be that the Americans and the Brits had done a deal and we were going to be allowed home? Given what Karen and I had tried to do to the President, I didn't think that was very likely.

When I looked up again from the computer, I noticed it was after midnight. I woke Karen up and walked her to bed. She was only semiconscious, but she managed to press my hand against her abdomen and kiss me before sleep swallowed her up again. I stood watching her, a stupid smile on my face. Then I remembered how it had been when Lucy was newly born—never more than an hour of sleep at a time, deafening wails, the endless changing of diapers. Soon I'd be going through that again. I had never thought I would, but the prospect didn't induce panic. To my amazement, I was actually looking forward to it. How old would Magnus have to be before I could get him his first rugby ball?

I went out and made a jug of coffee, then spent the

next three hours getting in touch with people and surfing the web. Nothing earth-shattering seemed to have happened in the weeks since we'd been out of circulation—the usual earthquakes, changes of government, wars. There had been a string of grisly murders across the U.S.—Peter Sebastian, who was in charge of the FBI investigation, was quoted as saying that the fact the victims were involved in human rights activities and Democratic politics was not necessarily significant. Go, Peter, go. Asshole.

I diverted myself by checking the rugby league scores. My old club, the South London Bison, had lost their last four games. That put everything into perspective. I needed to get back there and do some coaching.

Eventually my eyes started to close of their own accord. I found myself checking my email in-box before logging off, as I always used to do—it seemed plenty of old habits had survived the brainwashing process. The second I took in the new message in bold, I sat up like an electric eel had brushed me.

So, Matt, how are you? You must have gone to ground, I can't find you anywhere. I've been busy—blood, lots of it, and enough pain to make a torturer squirm in jealousy—which is why I haven't been bombarding you with messages like a sick schoolgirl. I'm sick, no doubt you'd say, but a schoolgirl? Well, you remember what I was like in bed, don't you? How's Karen, by the way? Not up to much in the sex department these days, I shouldn't think, getting fat and such. Have you become a father again yet? I do hope that doesn't cramp your style. I won't let it cramp mine...

Anyway, keep well, Matt. I will find you and only one of us will walk away from that happy reunion. Did you ever come across that Thomson/ Rothmann character again? I heard that he'd escaped, despite what one of your pet detectives in Washington D.C. called your 'brave and selfless efforts.' You really must be more ruthless. It's essential in this line of work.

Remember this: you brought about my brother's death, you killed my sister. I'm going to slaughter you and everyone you love, not necessarily in that order.

In the name of our beloved and most glorious White Devil,

S.C.

The Soul Collector. Sara. I sat back, my heart thundering and my palms damp. The bitch. If I hadn't been sure before, now I knew—nobody was safe, not Karen, not our son, nobody. The only way for us to survive was for me to kill my ex-lover. And the only way to do that was to offer myself as bait. But to do so, I needed to get out of the camp.

I was going to have to do whatever it took and, as my crazed ex-lover said, I would have to be ruthless— a rock; tougher and sharper than steel.

I needed more time with Quincy Jerome.

The woman was of average height and build, only the lightness of her movements suggesting that she maintained a high level of physical fitness. She wore a pale blue tracksuit and a green baseball cap with the single word *Irish* on the peak. Any passersby on the street in Astoria who tried to make out her features had little luck. She used no makeup and her features apart from the high cheekbones were unremarkable. A ponytail of auburn hair sprouted from the back of her cap and the unusually bright winter sun brought the color out.

'Hey, doll, you want to feel my olives?'

The woman stopped and looked back at the stall-holder. He was short and swarthy, a slack smile on his lips. Olives in various shades of green and black were arrayed in large plastic trays.

The man tried again. 'Just for you, from Kalamata with love.'

A plane taking off from nearby La Guardia roared above them.

'What's that?' the stallholder said, leaning forward.

'I said, your olives look beautiful, but I hate the taste.' The woman's voice was even and only marginally accented.

'Hey, where you from?' the man said, still eager despite the fading prospect of a sale.

'Oh, here and there,' replied the woman, her eyes invisible beneath the peak of her cap. 'How about you?'

'Astoria born and bred,' he replied proudly. 'My family's from Greece.'

The woman smiled. 'Land of brave heroes and tragic wives,' she said, her voice hardening. 'If memory serves, Queen Clytemnestra killed Agamemnon in the bath.' She stepped forward, raising her hands as if she was brandishing a weapon. 'With an ax.'

The stallholder took an involuntary step backward.

'Crazy *poutana!*' he yelled, as she disappeared into the crowd on the sidewalk.

The woman didn't know Greek, but she could guess what the word meant. In a way, the fool was right. She was a whore, selling her services to whichever client paid most. But she didn't open her legs for them. She... how did Havi, the guy who brokered her jobs, put it? She put people's problems to sleep. That was quite poetic, even though Havi, a preening Puerto Rican who doubled as a Wall Street economist, wouldn't know a poem from a postmodernist.

She was here in Queens to put a certain problem to sleep. It was a low-profile job, but she liked to kick back occasionally with something simple. There wasn't much money in it, but that didn't matter—she was making enough on the big contracts to retire in a few years. Not that she had any longing to duck out of the world she had slipped into so easily. The work was an addiction, but one with no side effects—as long as you weren't in possession of a conscience.

The street she was looking for was off Ditmars Boulevard. The building was in reasonable condition and the vehicles parked by the curb were recent models, a mixture of family cars and SUVs. The red BMW Roadster stuck out like a thumb that had been caught in its door. She knew who its owner was. Besides, Havi had told her that the target always slept late and the presence of the car suggested his information was, as usual, correct. Glancing down the street in both directions and confirming there was no one nearby, the woman worked the lock. She was inside in under thirty seconds.

The lobby smelled of lemon cleaning fluid and dope.

She subdued a sneeze and headed upstairs, her sneakers making no sound on the carpeted steps. Jimmy Vlastos's apartment was on the third floor. He had made a lot of money from a coke deal and had bought the whole building without a mortgage—officially with money given by his father, a ship owner. When she got to his door, the woman slid her right hand under her belt and took out the custom-made switchblade. The blade glinted in the light from the cupola.

It took slightly longer to open these locks. The question was, had the target applied the chain? Negative. Either he wasn't in after all or he'd forgotten after a long night in his cousin's club. She slipped inside and closed the door quietly behind her.

The apartment was a blaze of glass and stainless steel, the drapes open to admit the sun. There were magazines all over the place, women in minimal clothing displaying their charms in positions that must have been agony for more than a few seconds. The musty smell from an ashtray full of roaches was cut by something sweet and mildly rotten. A bottle of Southern Comfort had spilled its contents onto an ugly purple rug.

The woman headed for the bedroom, extending the hand that held the well-honed plastic blade. She knew which door it was from the plan Havi had sent. Although it was closed, the sound of snoring announced that the resident was, indeed, present. She gripped the handle and turned it, her shoulder against the paneling. Then she was betrayed.

As the door opened, the hinges let out a loud screech. The woman moved forward quickly, but the man in the bed was instantly alert. He leveled a snub-nosed revolver at her before she was halfway across the varnished wood floor.

'Who the hell are you?' Vlastos demanded, his gun hand steady.

The woman slowly lowered the knife to her hip. 'I'm dropping this, okay?'

'You do that, bitch,' Vlastos said, his eyes boring into hers. 'That's better. Now answer the fucking question. Who are you?' Keeping the gun aimed at her chest, he pulled aside the quilt and stood up. He was naked.

'Nice weapon,' the woman said, flicking her eyes toward his groin.

'Quit playing around. Take off that cap. Slowly.'

She complied, letting it fall to the floor beside the switchblade.

'Now take your top off.'

So much for not getting distracted, the woman thought. She raised her hands to her neck and pulled the zipper down. Then she shucked the tracksuit jacket off.

Jimmy Vlastos eyed her breasts, which were accentuated by a tight white T-shirt. 'Who are you working for?'

The woman smiled. 'You don't want to know.'

'Don't fuck with me, bitch!'

The smile widened. 'I didn't come here to fuck with you, Jimmy,' she said, though her sultry gaze suggested the verb had some relevance.

'You were going to gut me with that blade, *poutana*.'

She shook her head. 'No, I wasn't. Honestly.' Suddenly she was pleading, her right hand raised toward him. 'Please, I'm not a killer. I'm a—'

Vlastos's eyes had followed the hand, which meant

that he didn't see the Ruger semiautomatic that she'd pulled from behind her back until it was too late. The silencer swallowed the sound of the shot. The spit was immediately followed by a loud crack as the 7.65 millimeter Parabellum bullet ricocheted off the barrel of Vlastos's revolver and ripped it from his grasp.

'Shit!' he gasped, as his hand flew back.

The woman was holding the pistol in both hands now, the muzzle trained on his chest. 'On your knees!' She kicked the revolver under the bed. 'Now!'

Jimmy Vlastos did as he was told, his eyes locked on the Ruger. 'Where did you learn to shoot like that? You had the blade in your right hand.'

'So I'm a woman and I'm ambidextrous. Get over it, asshole.'

He stared up at her. 'So finish it,' he said, his voice cracking. 'But before you do it, tell me who's paying you.'

'I told you, that's not for you to know.' She smiled, but there was no warmth in it. 'If you find out, I'll have to kill you.'

Furrows appeared on Vlastos's brow.

'That's right.' The woman trained the pistol on the center of his face. 'I'm not going to kill you.'

'So what the hell are you here for?'

The woman stepped backward, holding her aim, and picked up the knife. 'I've got some information for you. If you hadn't pulled that gun on me, we'd have got along fine.'

'Gimme a break. You came in packing.'

'How was I to know if you were on your own or not?'

He looked dubious. 'What good would a knife have been if there were two of us?'

She laughed. 'Do you want to see how good I am with it?'

Jimmy Vlastos sat back on his heels and tried out a grin. 'Not right now.'

'Smart decision. All right, listen up. Your cousin Eleftheria.'

Vlastos tensed immediately. 'What about her? Do you know something?'

'I know that she's eleven and she was raped last summer.'

He stared at her morosely. 'So?'

'I know who did it.'

There was a snort of disbelief. 'How the fuck would you know anything? It was dark—even Ria didn't see him.'

'But he boasted about it later.'

'*What?*' Vlastos's expression was a mixture of disgust and rage. 'Tell me his name.'

'Alonso Larengo.'

'Fuck! Alonso? He's my business partner, he's a friend of the family.'

'The kind of partner and friend nobody needs.' The woman reached the door and lowered her pistol. 'We're done.'

'Wait! That's it? You don't want nothing in return?'

She shook her head. 'Even drug dealers are entitled to deal with child abusers.'

'How do I know you're on the level and this isn't some play to screw with my Colombian connection?'

'Well, I suggest you take Mr. Larengo to a darkened room and ask him if what I told you is true. I find pincers and wire cutters useful in such cases.'

'I'll bet you do, lady. Can I give you something for your trouble?'

The woman turned away. 'Just stay off my tail. If I hear you behind me, I'll empty my clip into your Roadster.' She glanced back. 'I've got another one for you, if necessary.'

Back on Ditmars Boulevard, the woman headed for the subway. Seagulls were shrieking above the buildings, flying in from Rikers Island, with its teeming prison, and the strait between Queens and Manhattan that was called Hell Gate. Her broker Havi wouldn't be impressed by what she'd done—she'd been contracted to kill Vlastos, but she had decided that the rapist Larengo should be punished. The Colombians would give Havi a hard time, but she thought Vlastos would survive. Larengo had crossed a line.

She felt an unusual lightness of spirit, although that did nothing to alleviate the ache in her upper back that had appeared a few weeks back. She had painkillers at home. What would her ex-lover Matt Wells think if he heard the dreaded Soul Collector had just righted a wrong that was beyond the normal reach of justice, and that she was pleased she'd done it?

Sometimes the line between good and evil was as blurred as a charcoal drawing in the rain.

Six

A week passed and we started gearing up for the birth. Karen seemed fine, though she got tired very quickly. She looked magnificent, like a galleon with the wind in every sail, as she moved around our rooms. Judging by the size of her bulge, my son was going to live up to his name. I was still having daily sessions with Quincy Jerome and, when pressed, he agreed that I was making progress. My body disagreed. I had more bruises than a linebacker—*American* football was the only sport I could get on the TV set we'd been provided with—but my fitness was definitely improving. I spent a lot of time on the internet, catching up with old contacts and, as much to see if there was any censorship going on, searching for traces of Heinz Rothmann and my lethal ex-lover Sara Robbins. None of the sites I logged on to were blocked by the Feds, nor did I find anything about the pair except out-of-date media reports.

We were sitting watching a romantic comedy—not my choice—after dinner one evening, when Karen let out a groan.

'What is it?' I asked, immediately panic-stricken.

She grimaced and then smiled. 'Calm down, Matt. I'm supposed to be the nervous one.' She ran a hand over her abdomen. 'Oh, you little swine. Stop doing that. It hurts.'

'You aren't having contractions, are you?'

'I don't think so.' She squeezed my hand. 'I have a feeling it won't be long, though.'

I fetched her a glass of water and she gradually got back to normal.

'Do you want me to call the health center?' I asked.

Karen shook her head. 'It's okay. Things are calming down.' Then she swallowed hard and her eyes filled with tears.

'What is it, my love?' I said, putting my arm round her shoulders.

'Oh, nothing,' she said, sobbing. 'It's just…it's just I'm so happy…to be having our son.…' She blinked and looked into my eyes. 'I'd never have done this if it wasn't for you.'

I laughed. 'You got that right. Remember how it started?'

She inserted her elbow under my arm. 'Don't make a joke of it, Matt. I…I've never felt so happy.'

It was infectious. I felt tears in my eyes. 'Neither have I,' I said, kissing her. 'Neither have I.'

Karen slept unusually deeply that night, and so did I; no nightmares or blood-lathered memories, and no Sara. Despite all the bullshit—the kidnapping, the conditioning, the Rothmanns' conspiracy, being held in this Spartan camp for weeks—the imminent arrival of our son was all that mattered; that and Karen keeping well.

In the morning we had breakfast together and I went off for a session in the pool with Quincy. I'd asked him to see if he could arrange some time on the shooting range, thinking that perhaps he'd be able to swing it with his superiors, but that didn't work out. I knew who I could blame for that.

And when I got back to our rooms, there he was—Peter Sebastian, sitting at the table, in front of our laptop.

'Where's Karen?' I asked, looking around the living room.

The FBI man raised his hand. 'Good to see you, too, Matt.' He gave me a tight smile. 'Don't worry, she's lying down in the bedroom.'

I took a deep breath. I had got to the stage that anything to do with Karen provoked unease, or, rather, blind panic.

'Sorry,' I said, going over to shake his hand. 'Though I don't know why. You're the reason we're still stuck here. Karen should be in a proper hospital.'

Sebastian raised an eyebrow. 'Where Sara Robbins could get to her?'

I wasn't letting him get away with that. 'I guess I assumed the mighty FBI would be able to protect us outside of the camp.'

'Cool it, Matt,' he said, closing the laptop. 'You know she'll get excellent care here.'

I circled the table, unwilling to sit down with him.

'What's up?' he asked.

'Have you got kids?'

'Sure. They're both at college now.'

'You remember what it was like when they were born?'

Sebastian smiled weakly. 'Not much. I was on duty both times. That was when I was working undercover in L.A.'

'Really?' I was interested because he'd never said much about his past. 'What were you pretending to be? A junkie?'

'Nice,' he said, with a subdued chuckle. 'Actually, I *was* supposed to have a coke habit. No, the Bureau was investigating links between a Hollywood studio and organized crime. I was a writer with a hot script about the Mob.'

'Who wrote it?'

'Not me, obviously. We found some washed-up script editor and kept him in booze for a month.'

'The romance of the writing life.'

He looked up at me. 'Why aren't *you* spending your days writing a book about your experiences?'

Further proof that we were being watched around the clock. I let it go. 'Because they haven't ended yet, Peter.' I sat down opposite him. 'When are you going to let us go from this shit-hole?'

He looked around the room. 'I've seen worse.' He put his hand on the computer. 'What do you think of this? I haven't heard any thank-yous.'

'Screw you. When we can walk out the gates of this concentration camp, I might consider thanking you. Until then, you can swivel.' I raised my leg and pointed at the tracking unit. 'What am I? A common criminal?'

Sebastian's expression was blank. 'Many Americans would say you're something a lot worse than that if they knew. Going after the President wasn't the best move you ever made.'

'So put us on trial. You know any decent lawyer will argue we didn't know what we were doing.'

'Are you sure you want to risk that? Karen will be nursing your son. Do you want her to do that in court, with the TV cameras running? Do you really think you can win a trial against the President? Even my word wouldn't be enough.'

'Of course not.' I looked away. 'I appreciate the computer and the combat training.'

'How's that going? Sergeant Jerome comes highly recommended.' He smiled. 'Shame you can't get him to smash the tracking unit on your ankle for you.'

I'd made a few unsuccessful attempts to put my leg in the way of Quincy's unrestrained kicks. He'd always managed to pull out in time.

'Haven't you got anything better to do than watch me all day long?'

'I do. So Special Agent Simms and her team watch for me.'

'Oh, great.' I wondered if there was a camera in the bathroom—I hadn't been able to spot one. The idea of the asexual Simms watching me in there was strangely disturbing. 'So what's going on, Peter? You're getting me back to full fitness, you're letting us communicate with the outside world. Are we going to get out soon?'

He stared at me. 'I don't know, Matt. There may be some movement in Justice's position. The birth should help.'

'How about Doc Rivers's reports? He says I'm making good progress with the deconditioning.'

'Why do you think I'm down here, Matt? I'll be talking to him later. I might even look in on a session.'

That didn't fill me with hope. If another trigger kicked in...

'How about some firearms practice?' I asked, putting the pressure back on him. 'You know I'll need it if we get out.'

'Will you? Whatever you think, I reckon the Bureau's quite capable of protecting you and yours from the so-called Soul Collector.'

'Touché,' I said, shaking my head. Getting round Sebastian was about as easy as spearing mosquitoes.

'I'm working on things.' He stood up. 'I'll see you again before I go back to D.C.'

'Hey,' I said, as he walked to the door. 'You never told me what happened when you were undercover in L.A.'

The FBI man looked round. 'That's classified.' He paused. 'What the hell? You're almost family now. Put it this way—the studio went out of business and the Mob lost five soldiers.'

'You're some tough guy,' I said. 'How many special agents breathed their last?'

'That really is classified,' Sebastian said, slamming the door behind him.

Arthur Bimsdale was watching Sergeant Quincy Jerome instruct some very raw-looking army recruits in the basics of self-defense. There were regular thuds as they hit the padded floor of the dojo; none of them managed to lay a hand on the big man.

'Why don't you give it a shot?'

The special agent turned and saw that his boss had sat down behind him on the tiered benches. 'Em, I don't think that would be a good idea, sir.'

'Don't you?' Peter Sebastian gave the tight smile that always appeared when he wanted to put the squeeze on a subordinate. 'What's the matter? Forgotten everything you learned at Quantico?'

'No, sir. It's just that I wouldn't like to put him in the hospital.'

Sebastian's eyes opened wide. 'Very good, Arthur. Maybe you have got a spine after all.' He frowned. 'I'd still like you to challenge the sergeant.'

Bimsdale knew there was no point in further resistance. He'd already taken a chance by answering his boss back. He waited patiently till the squad was dismissed, then made his way over to the mat without looking at Sebastian.

'Excuse me, Sergeant, could I challenge you?'

Quincy Jerome looked at him dubiously. 'Who exactly are you, son?'

Bimsdale explained.

'Okay, Arthur. How do you want to do this?'

Bimsdale had taken off his suit jacket and shoes, and placed his pistol and shoulder holster carefully on the floor. 'I don't suppose you'd let me throw you and then pretend you got concussed?'

'You don't suppose right,' the sergeant said, with a laugh. 'You FBI dudes are really something.' He stepped back quickly as Bimsdale launched a high kick at his throat.

The contest lasted longer than Sebastian had expected. He knew from his assistant's file that the young man had done well on every module at Quantico, but he assumed he'd been putting on a show for the examiners. After twenty minutes, during which Bimsdale almost put Jerome down several times, he walked over to the dojo.

'All right, gentlemen,' he said, clapping his hands.

Both combatants were breathing heavily and Arthur Bimsdale's tie had come undone.

'You've made your point,' Sebastian said to his assistant. 'Go and have a shower, then meet me at the science block.'

'Yes, sir,' Bimsdale said, voice louder than usual.

'So, Sergeant,' Peter Sebastian said when they were alone, 'what do you think?'

Quincy Jerome wiped his forehead with his forearm. 'Not bad for a Bureau guy.'

'Not Bimsdale. How's Matt Wells coming along?'

The sergeant grinned. 'Sorry,' he said unconvincingly. 'Yeah, Wells is in pretty good shape. Someone taught him some useful moves.'

'Any sign of him losing control of himself?'

'You mean like some kind of robotic fighting machine?'

'That's exactly what I mean, Sergeant.'

'Nope. He gets into the zone well and stays pretty cool.'

Sebastian considered the reply. 'All right. Give him daily sessions at the range from tomorrow.'

'Just pistol, or rifle, too?'

'Both. And Sergeant? Make sure he knows that at least two weapons will be trained on him all the time he's armed.'

As Sebastian walked away, Quincy Jerome wondered, not for the first time, exactly what kind of game was being played around him.

* * *

Bimsdale was alone in Rivers's office when his boss arrived.

'Impressive, Arthur,' Sebastian said. 'You're wasted working for me. You should be in a field office, leading the charge.'

'Not me, sir,' the young man replied. 'I can learn so much from you.'

His superior gave him a questioning look. 'Tell me, how does fighting square with your Episcopalian principles? Your file says you shot a man in Montana.'

Bimsdale nodded. 'He was threatening to execute a hostage.'

'So you killed him and got a reprimand for excessive use of your weapon.'

'The hostage was an eight-year-old boy, sir. He'd been…'

Sebastian raised his hand. 'I read the file, remember. I asked about your religious beliefs.'

The young agent held his superior's gaze. 'So did the recruitment board. I told them that being an Episcopalian would affect my performance only in positive ways.'

'What does that mean?' Sebastian asked, as the door opened.

'Ah, there you are,' Rivers said. His glasses were perched on his bald head and he had a sheaf of papers under his arm. 'All's well in Washington, I hope.'

Sebastian nodded, glancing back at his assistant as if to say that their discussion would be resumed. 'Bring us up to speed on the subject Matt Wells, please, Doctor.'

The scientist sat down at his untidy desk and tried

to find a space for the papers he was carrying. 'Matt Wells,' he said, as if the name was unfamiliar. 'Yes, yes, Matt Wells.' He dug out a laptop and opened it, then pulled his glasses down. 'Indeed,' he said, peering at the screen. 'Response to the latest trigger was good, definitely improved on the previous one. Evidence of deep conditioning minimal.' The doctor looked up. 'Of course, you realize that the very nature of such conditioning militates against us finding traces of its presence.'

Sebastian nodded. 'And your drug regime?'

'Substantially curtailed now. The effects became counterproductive as the subject gained more conscious control over his reactions to triggers.'

'So Wells is functioning like a normal human being again?'

Rivers considered that. 'What is normal, I wonder? According to the report you provided, the subject's behavior prior to what happened in the cathedral was largely rational.'

'That was what made the attacks on the President by him and Karen Oaten so disturbing. They were impossible to predict.'

'And you are wondering whether they still have it in them to behave like that.'

'Of course. That's what all this is about, no?'

The scientist pursed his lips. 'To be frank, I don't know. I'd say it was unlikely, given the treatment both have received, but I can give no guarantee. Of course, we have treated the female subject less intensively because of the pregnancy.'

'Would you say allowing Matt Wells to shoot on the range was a risk?' Sebastian asked.

'Undoubtedly, but probably a small one.'

'Just as well. I've already authorized it.'

Arthur Bimsdale looked shocked. 'Did you, sir?'

'Yes, I did, Special Agent. I'm sorry, should I have asked your permission?'

There was an awkward silence.

'All right, Doctor,' Sebastian continued. 'Two final questions. Has your treatment in any way compromised Karen Oaten's chances of giving birth successfully?'

Rivers sniffed. 'Considering the state she was in when she arrived, I'd say it's remarkable that she's done as well as she has.'

'Which is hardly an answer, but never mind. Two, is Matt Wells capable of functioning reliably outside the camp?'

This time the scientist was taken aback. 'I was led to understand that the therapy was open-ended.'

'Nothing's forever, Doctor,' Sebastian said, getting to his feet. 'This time I'll need a clear answer.'

Rivers pushed his glasses back onto his cranium and stared at the two men. 'I'll give you your answer. No, I do not think he would be reliable in the outside world and I will take every possible step to see that he remains here.'

With that, Peter Sebastian headed for the door.

Seven

One had a Mossberg shotgun and the other a Smith & Wesson Sigma pistol, but I tried to blank them out, the soldiers who were covering me. Quincy Jerome was standing behind them, carrying an M4 carbine. There was only one thing to do. I pulled down my ear protectors.

I took aim at the target that had started to move toward me up the lane of the range. It had been nearly two months since I'd fired a shot, but I remembered the training Dave had given me. I had taken up the correct stance, feet apart and legs bent at the knee, and was holding the Glock 17 in a doublehanded grip. I took a breath and fired off nine shots, a second between each one.

The target kept on coming, stopping a yard in front of me.

'Suck on that, Quincy,' I said, looking over my shoulder.

The big man strode up. 'Shee-it. You're even better with a moving target. Everything in the inner head ring and five, no, six, nose shots.' He clapped me on the shoulder. 'You don't need no refresher course, man.'

He didn't know about Sara. She was a better shot than I.

'How about some rifle shooting?' I asked. When he'd showed up at our place earlier on and told me that the range had been approved, he hadn't specified which weapons I'd be able to use. I hadn't pressed him, but had tried to find out who had given the okay. He didn't say Sebastian's name, but he did nod when I mentioned the Bureau. Although it hadn't struck me at the time, I wondered about that now. Did the army take orders from the FBI? It didn't seem likely, even though they shared the camp. Presumably Sebastian had gone to a senior officer.

'All right, Mr. Wells,' Quincy said, the formality for the benefit of the two other soldiers. 'Let's go see what we can find you.'

What we found was a Colt M16A4. As it happened, I had fired an M16 after I escaped from the Rothmanns' camp, but I wasn't going to bring that up. I reckoned the better I performed, the more likely Peter Sebastian would be to sanction our release, though that raised another question. If I was expected to use pistols and rifles, it was unlikely we'd be sent back to the U.K. Surely we weren't going to be cut loose in the U.S.? Sara would have a field day.

Quincy took me and the others to the open-air range. 'All right, Mr. Wells,' he said, 'you've got a thousand-yard lane in front of you.' He checked with his binoculars. 'The target is currently at 500 yards. Give me five shots there. Then we'll go back a hundred yards each time till we hit 1000. Five shots at each stop, okay?' He handed me a thirty-round magazine.

As soon as I slapped it home, I felt the other soldiers

tense. I grinned at them and got down on the ground, resting the rifle on a sandbag. There were no telescopic sights, but I'd trained without them so I wasn't worried. I pulled down my ear protectors again and got into the zone, breathing steadily.

Before I knew it, the magazine was empty and there was a dull ache in my right shoulder. By the time I got to my feet, Quincy had scoped the target.

'Very funny, motherfucker,' he said, this time paying no attention to the men behind him.

I tried not to laugh. 'I thought you'd like it.'

He handed me the binoculars. I was impressed. Although the legs were a bit uneven, I'd managed to shoot a decent outline of the human form around the charging infantryman image on the target. The oversize heart that I'd put on the chest was unmistakable.

'What was that Woody Allen film?' I asked. 'There was a loudmouthed black sergeant in that, too.'

Quincy Jerome gave me the eye big-time.

'I remember. *Love and Death*.'

'Asshole,' said the big man.

The other soldiers only just succeeded in keeping their faces straight.

I decided to move things along. 'Can I have a go with the shotgun now?' I asked, pointing at the Mossberg.

'No, Mr. Wells, you cannot,' Quincy said, relieving me of the M16. 'That isn't included in your program.' He turned away. 'I just decided.'

I found Karen on the sofa, the laptop on her chest.

'Guess what?' I said, after I'd kissed her.

She gave me a languid glance. 'You shot a perfect score?'

'More or less,' I replied, deflated. Then I had a worrying thought. Could my ability with the firearms have something to do with the Rothmanns' conditioning? I had been a reasonable shot in the past, but I'd never done anything like I had on the range today. Maybe the same went for my unarmed combat skills. It wasn't unlikely. The Rothmanns had trained people to become top-class warriors, as the mayhem in the cathedral in Washington had shown. Then an even worse idea came to me. What if the combat skills, lurking deep in my subconscious, actually freed up more trigger words formerly hidden? I decided not to share those fears with Karen.

Her due date was still a few days away, but the obstetrician had told us the baby could come any time. She preferred to be horizontal, even though the doctor recommended that she keep active, and she lost her breath easily. She hadn't said anything, but I knew she was wishing things would get underway. Still, first babies were often latecomers—I remembered that from my daughter Lucy, nearly a week overdue.

'What are you looking at?'

She pursed her lips. 'Have you read about these murders?'

I shouldn't have been surprised. Karen was a homicide detective at heart, despite the fact that she'd been working on financial crime before the kidnapping, and she wouldn't let a little thing like childbirth distract her from her calling. I had seen the stories, which had become a lot more high profile with the poor woman in Boston, who had been stripped naked, defenestrated and daubed with the title of Adolf Hitler's repulsive book.

'The FBI isn't confirming anything, but some reporters think there are now three in a series with hate crimes elements.'

'The others being in Manhattan and north of Detroit.'

'I might have known you'd be keeping up-to-date. Do you think the bastard Heinz Rothmann's behind them?'

'It's not beyond the realm of possibility. There could easily be another brainwashed killer out there.' Before the attack on the President, there had been a series of so-called 'occult killings' in Washington D.C., which were linked to the Rothmanns. There was no guarantee that all the conditioned subjects had been caught at the National Cathedral.

Karen closed the laptop and shifted her bulk gingerly. 'Don't you think it's odd that Peter Sebastian is here rather than at his desk at FBI headquarters?'

'Did he say something to you?'

'Not about the murders, no. He was very interested in you, though.'

'What do you mean?'

'Oh, how you were getting on with Dr. Rivers and Sergeant Jerome, that kind of thing.'

Concern stirred in my gut. Then I saw how tired she was, her eyes drooping.

'Screw Sebastian.' I squeezed her hand. 'Let's get you to bed.'

'Oh, no you don't. You've forgotten something.'

I stared at her. It wasn't her birthday—that was in March. I couldn't think what she meant. 'Er, is it the anniversary of your first murder case?'

She leaned forward with surprising speed and grabbed my nose between her thumb and forefinger.

'Ow!' I pulled free. 'First time we had…I mean, made love?' I asked desperately.

'No!' she said, laughing. 'Come here.'

I moved cautiously back into her range.

'Here.' She patted her chest.

I laid my head there.

'Bloody men.' Her voice vibrated into my body. 'Was I dreaming, or did you really ask me to marry you?'

'Of course I—'

'I know you did, Matt,' she said, her tone lighter. 'Don't you think we should fix a day?'

I raised my head. 'I though you wanted to wait until after Magnus arrives.'

'I did. But I've changed my mind.'

I laughed. 'Bloody women.'

'Thirty days after he's born,' she said. 'No matter what.'

I wondered if she knew what she was asking, given everything that could happen. In the end, it was easier to agree. I had no qualms about marrying her.

'Thank you, Matt.' Her face was wreathed in smiles. 'Now I've got something to look forward to after all the pain and screaming.'

I kissed her. 'Don't worry, it'll be fine.'

Karen seized my nose again. 'There's one more thing.'

'What?' I said, doing a passable imitation of a duck.

'Where's my engagement ring, you tightfisted bastard?'

I was saved by the doorbell. Peter Sebastian was standing outside with his baby-faced sidekick Bimsdale.

'*What?*'

'Charming,' Sebastian said, his expression hardening. 'I need you to come with us.'

'I'm helping Karen to bed.'

'This is nonnegotiable, Matt.'

I was tempted to slam the door in his face, but I had a favor to ask.

'I'm all right,' Karen said.

I grabbed my jacket and went out into the cold.

'What's the big deal?'

'Rivers' came the reply. 'He needs an extra session of trigger identification every day. Starting now.'

Was it Rivers who wanted that or Sebastian himself? I let the thought go and concentrated on my number one priority.

'Okay, but you owe me.'

The FBI men looked at me curiously.

'Do you know any good jewelers?'

Doctor Jack Notaro had been sculling on the Schuylkill River. Despite the chill of the December morning, he enjoyed himself greatly. It was still dark when he left his apartment north of the university to run to the boathouse, but by the time he lifted the long craft onto the water, a gray dawn was permeating Philadelphia, blurring the lights of the buildings on the eastern shore.

Jack spent an hour alternately pitting himself against the current and feeling the thin hull race along with the flow. He remembered early mornings on the Isis in Oxford, the college eight which he stroked being put through its paces before the bumping races. Worcester had been head of the river in both Hilary and Trinity terms, and he'd been approached to try out for the Blue boat. He declined the chance of rowing against

Cambridge on the Thames, even though he had dreamed about it. Work had to take priority in the second year of his post-graduate degree—that was a requirement of his scholarship. Besides, it was either give up competitive rowing or cut back on his dalliances with the university's most eye-catching women. The first form of physical activity stood no chance.

Sitting in his office in the University of Philadelphia later that morning, Jack didn't regret the choice he'd made. He knew himself too well. There were only two serious interests in his life—women and researching the full horror of fascism in Italy during the Second World War. Thirty-five now, his muscular six-foot-three frame and rugged looks still attracted more doe-eyed female post-graduates than he could handle. He drew the line at undergraduates—too much like jailbait. He managed his workload well, despite the distractions. His books and articles had been well received, except by the odd right-wing academic and the usual crazy extremist groups. He was hoping to make full professor in a year or two, and generally life was good. Even his mother, eighty-eight and as spirited as ever, had got off his case, accepting that he wasn't going to get married any time soon.

The rest of the day went well. His current girl, a willowy third-year PhD student from New York named Alicia Finn, had dropped by on her way to the airport. She was attending a conference in San Francisco on gender representations in war writing and would be away for five days. Jack gave her something to remember him by: he locked his door, pulled down her panties and took her from behind over his desk. After she left, he found that she had deposited a pool of saliva on his copy of Michaelis's *Mussolini and the Jews*. That made him smile.

Jack Notaro got back to his apartment on 38th Street around seven. He was in a rush to get showered and changed. He was meeting Professor Norma Winston, the head of the history faculty, for dinner at an Italian restaurant in the Old City and he didn't want to be late. He had high hopes of gaining her support for his latest research project. He also reckoned there was a good chance of getting her into the sack. Although Norma was in her fifties, her recent divorce had turned her into a sex machine. She had a thing for even younger men, but Jack was still betting on himself to score.

That was why he didn't notice that the drapes in the living room had been drawn shut, or that a hook had been inserted into the ceiling. He did see the brief-case that was open on the dining table but, a second later, lost contact with his senses and surrendered to the eternal dark.

Eight

After a display of reluctance, Peter Sebastian agreed to buy the ring. I told him I'd email him the description and cost. The problem was that neither I nor Karen had any source of funds—the Justice Department had frozen our credit cards and bank accounts. Sebastian said he would look into the situation, but in the meantime would pay for the ring himself. I was impressed.

'So what about these murders?' I asked, as we approached the labs, our feet ringing out on the icy paving stones.

The Fed played dumb.

His assistant craned his head forward to look at me in the orange light from the lamps overhead. 'Which murders, Mr. Wells?'

'Those three hate crime killings,' I said. 'Do you need me to list the victims' names and locations?'

'You can't expect us to talk about ongoing investigations,' Bimsdale said, glancing at his boss.

'Even when they might be connected to Heinz Rothmann?'

'What makes you say that?' Sebastian demanded.

'Do you have many other suspects?'

'As Arthur here said, we're not going to discuss that.' Sebastian upped his pace.

'Touchy, isn't he?' I said to Bimsdale.

'You couldn't possibly expect me to comment.'

I got the impression that the young agent was less of a fool than he looked. I was also intrigued by his boss's reluctance to talk about the murders. It didn't square with his continued interest in Karen and me.

By the time we caught up, Sebastian was on his cell phone.

'Where? All right, I'll fly there immediately. Describe the scene.' His eyes narrowed. 'Shit. Keep me advised and inform local law enforcement that we're on our way.' He ended the call and turned to Bimsdale. 'Come on, we're going to the airport.'

'So soon,' I said.

Sebastian gave me a sharp look. 'Dr. Rivers is waiting for you. I'll be in touch.'

'Where has the Nazi murderer struck this time?'

'Philadelphia, if you must know,' he said, moving away.

'I'll be looking out for you on the news,' I called after them.

I hadn't seen Sebastian so spooked since Washington National Cathedral.

'Ah, there you are, Mr. Wells,' said Rivers, after a white-coated young woman opened the door of his office. 'This is Dr. Brown.'

I looked at her and tried not to laugh. She had ice-blond hair tied into a bun, and a complexion so pale that blue veins were visible around her eyes and jawline.

'Hello.' I stuck out my hand. 'I'm Matt.'

Dr. Brown stared at my paw as if vicious claws might be concealed beneath the skin. Her grip was cool and firm.

'Matt,' I repeated. 'Not Wells.'

'My first name is Alexandra.' She gave me a thin smile. 'You can call me Dr. Brown.'

This time I did laugh. 'Fair enough. I'll win you round in the end.'

Rivers stood up. It occurred to me that I had no idea what his first name was. Red? Running?

'It's Lester,' he supplied, as if he'd read my thoughts. 'I'm not fond of it. Shall we proceed?'

'My finger is twitching on the trigger.'

'Very droll, Mr. Wells, but inappropriate. Dr. Brown will explain what we have in store for you.'

I looked at the woman in white. She opened the silver file she was carrying and started to talk, her voice curiously breathless.

'The Brown Disassociation Process makes use of advanced neuropharmacology, music and language, all calibrated to the individual patient, to induce a state of deep tranquility. The patient's responses are used to establish an even more profound condition of disassociation, during which data stored in parts of the subconscious beyond all alternate forms of artificial access can be brought to the surface. Such data can subsequently be replaced—'

'You're going to brainwash me again,' I said, stepping forward.

The gorilla in camouflage gear watching through the open door made a similar movement, raising a Taser.

Rivers brushed past me. 'It's all right, Wayne. Please.'

It wasn't the first time I'd noticed the scientist's distaste for weapons. It didn't stop him using words to attack me in the glass room.

Dr. Brown stood motionless, her lips tightly pressed together.

'Well, you are, aren't you?' I reiterated.

'Certainly not, Mr. Wells.'

'Matt.'

She looked uncomfortable for a few seconds. 'Oh, very well. Matt. I have carefully reviewed Dr. Rivers's records and am confident that the treatment I have mapped out for you will be both safe and effective.'

'I see. And how many patients have benefited from this safe and effective treatment, Alexandra?'

She glanced at Rivers.

'Dr. Brown's process is groundbreaking,' he said, flapping his hands. 'It has been extensively tested on computer models—'

'But I'm the first human being... Jesus, now I really am a guinea pig.'

The scientists looked at each other.

'I suppose you could put it like that,' Rivers said. 'We really must push on, Mr. Wells.'

'I thought I was making good progress with the trigger identification.'

'Yes, yes. Indeed you are. But...'

'Peter Sebastian has told you to speed things up.'

'Certainly not,' he said angrily. 'I can assure you that I have given Dr. Brown's process detailed consideration. I make the decisions here.'

'Well, that's a relief. I don't suppose I can ask for a second opinion?'

'I've already given one,' Dr. Brown said, a faint smile on her lips. 'You're the ideal subject for this exper—process.' The slip brought spots of red to her pallid cheeks.

Rivers stepped closer. 'Mr. Wells, you must appreciate your position. Ms. Oaten's access to the *full* resources of the medical center is conditional on your compliance with our requests.'

The bald bastard. He and Sebastian had me over a barrel.

'All right,' I said, after a long pause. 'Lester.'

'You must approach the procedure calmly and with your mind at ease,' Dr. Brown said, handing the file to me. 'Sign at the bottom of the first two pages, please.'

I didn't bother to read the text. They would do what they wanted whether I played along or not. Maybe I was being too suspicious. Anything that removed the residue of the Rothmanns' conditioning had to be a good thing.

'Thank you. This way, please.'

I followed the blonde doctor into a different glass room, this one with a hospital bed on it. Thick leather straps dangled down from it.

I lay down reluctantly. 'Is this going to hurt, Alexandra?'

'You more than me,' she replied, as the gorilla fastened the straps.

'Great. Would you like to talk me through your process?'

She started attaching electrodes to my forehead and chest.

'It's very straightforward. A cocktail of drugs will be injected and then your brain will be stimulated in ways too complex for you to understand. All you need to do is relax.'

'Right.' I felt less than reassured. 'Two more questions. How long is this going to take?'

'You'll be back in your quarters by morning. Don't worry, Ms. Oaten has been informed.'

'Uh-huh. Tell me, will I be the same person when you've finished with me?'

Alexandra Brown smiled, this time with some warmth. 'Better, Mr. Wells. I guarantee you'll be a better person.'

'What if I don't want to be better?'

She ignored that. 'Deep breath, please, as the needle goes in. Very good.'

'Hey, I hardly even felt…'

Major Andrew 'Slim' Carstens had commanded the City of Philadelphia Police Homicide Division for four years, but he had never seen anything like this. As soon as he'd been advised of the scene in the apartment north of the university, he had driven straight there. He'd been present for three hours and had decided to deal with the FBI people himself. A mobile command unit had been stationed on the street and he had taken refuge there as soon as he could. Just after 11:00 p.m., two men in dark suits were ushered into the trailer.

'Andy,' Peter Sebastian said, extending his hand. 'How are you keeping?'

Carstens stood up. 'Pretty good. Until tonight.'

Sebastian nodded. 'I hear it's a bad one. This is Special Agent Arthur Bimsdale. He watches my back.'

'I'm sure you don't need that.' The major had met Sebastian several times over the years during high-profile cases and at law enforcement conferences. He didn't much like him.

'You coming with us?' Sebastian asked, as a uniformed officer handed him a bag containing protective garments.

'Yup. Let's see what the CSIs have turned up in the last hour.'

'I gather the dead man has been identified,' the senior FBI man said, as they headed for the three-story building.

The major nodded. 'Dr. Jack Notaro, history professor at the University of Pennsylvania down the street.'

'What did he specialize in?'

'Italian fascism, apparently.'

Sebastian gave him a sideways look.

'Who found the body?' Bimsdale asked.

'One of his girlfriends, Alicia Finn,' Andy Carstens replied. 'She was also one of his post-grad students. You can't talk to her, I'm afraid. She had to be sedated. She was meant to be on a flight to San Francisco, but she missed it and came back.'

'*One* of his girlfriends?' Sebastian said, as they took the stairs to the second floor.

Carstens looked over his shoulder. 'The neighbors told my guys that he had plenty—most of them young and pretty.'

Bimsdale cleared his throat. 'These days most universities have regulations preventing faculty mixing with the student body.'

'Nicely put, son,' the major said. 'I'm guessing Dr. Jack didn't pay those regulations much attention.'

White-suited technicians were working on the door and frame. They stood aside to let the trio enter the apartment.

'Jesus,' Sebastian said, his eyes widening.

The body of a tall and well-built man was suspended by the ankles from a hook in the ceiling. He was naked and the points of his fingers were touching the wooden floor. The entire body was covered in so much blood that it was hard to discern at first that its eye sockets were empty.

'The medical examiner reckons he was knocked out by a heavy blow to the front of his head,' Carstens said, shaking his head. 'Then what you can see took place, probably postmortem.'

Bimsdale squatted down and examined the floor. 'The blood looks like it was painted on.'

'You're right, son. There are marks from a three-inch brush on both body and floor.' The major pointed to the table behind the corpse. 'We think the victim's throat was cut after he was strung up. The killer probably lifted him onto the table before attaching him to the hook, then bled him into the basin over there.' He pointed to a red plastic container at the far wall.

'Must be strong,' Bimsdale said. 'Unless there was more than one of them.'

'There are footprints that don't match the victim's, size nine Reeboks.'

'Meaning we have an individual with average-size feet, if it's a male,' Sebastian said. 'And oversize biceps. Any other traces?'

Carstens shook his head. 'Smudged fingerprints. Obviously wearing gloves.'

'Witnesses?' Bimsdale asked.

'None so far.'

'Let's concentrate on the body and the scene right now, Special Agent,' Sebastian said, looking around the living room.

'You need to see this,' Carstens said, going to the rear of the body. He pointed to two gaping holes, one on each side of the lower back. 'The killer took his kidneys.'

Arthur Bimsdale craned forward.

'He hasn't seen that kind of mutilation before,' Sebastian explained.

'One of the victims of the Occult Killer in D.C. had his kidneys removed, didn't he?' the major said softly.

Sebastian shook his head. 'No, his kidneys were skewered, but they were left in situ.'

'Still, could there be a connection?'

'Too early to say, Andy. So the killer took both eyes and kidneys?'

The major nodded.

'Where's the bathroom?' Sebastian went in the direction Carstens pointed, stepping around a CSI who was examining a sheepskin rug.

Another technician, this one female, was standing in the bath and bagging hair samples.

'Have you checked the toilet?' the FBI man asked.

'It's gleaming,' the woman replied. 'The vic must have had a cleaner.'

Sebastian raised an eyebrow at her and headed for the bedroom beyond. The main feature was a king-size bed, covered by a quilt with what looked like a Native American design. The walls and other surfaces were not marked with blood or any other obvious sign of the killer's presence.

'This scene is different from the others,' Sebastian said quietly, when he rejoined his assistant in the living room.

'No Nazi words or symbols?' Bimsdale asked.

'No. And no body parts in the bathroom. I wonder why.'

'It isn't unheard of for killers to change their M.O.'

'Thank you, Special Agent, I'll bear that in mind.'

Andy Carstens bit back on a smile as he came up to them. Sebastian's tongue had always been sharp and he'd been on the wrong side of it more than once. He'd also been outsmarted, but he was damn sure that wasn't going to happen again.

'Have you looked behind all the paintings and posters?' Sebastian asked.

The major nodded. 'Nothing doing. The Nazi connection was kinda public in the Boston murder, wasn't it?'

Sebastian nodded.

'Maybe we'll find something in daylight,' Bimsdale suggested.

The older men looked at each other.

'Obviously you'll want anything of that sort to be kept under wraps,' Carstens said to Sebastian.

'Won't you, too?'

The homicide chief nodded. 'I'll get extra people on the streets at first light.'

'Make sure they cover any evidence up rather than destroy it,' Sebastian said.

Andy Carstens didn't like his tone, but refrained

from comment. Peter Sebastian had been known to screw local law enforcement over big-time.

'Do you want joint command?'

Sebastian shook his head. 'We'll stay in the background, at least for now. Special Agent Bimsdale will keep in touch with your people.'

The major was surprised, though he didn't show it. Since when did the FBI stand back in a case like this? he asked himself. Then he thought about the potential consequences. If the killer was hard to catch, there was nothing but failure and opprobrium in store for the officer in charge of the investigation. Which meant two things. Slim Andy needed to keep a close eye on the Bureau's head of violent crime. And it was time he did some serious delegation himself.

Nine

There was a flash of white light and I came round. Doctors Brown and Rivers huddled at the foot of the bed. I let them confer for a while, my mouth and lips drier than raisins. Finally they noticed that my eyes were open.

'You're awake!' Rivers's face was unusually animated.

I looked at his colleague. Alexandra Brown's cheeks were glowing and her eyes were bright.

'Fantastic, Matt,' she said, gripping my forearm. 'You did really well.'

I was glad she was happy, but I was still tied down and desperate for a drink. I looked pointedly at the cup on the bedside table.

'Undo the straps,' I gasped, after I'd been given water through a straw.

They glanced at each other.

'Not yet,' Rivers said. 'Dr. Brown's protocol is that we must wait an hour.'

'Wonderful. So what happened? I heard music, the Who, I think, then I was falling…'

'I'll need you to tell me everything you can,' the

woman said. 'But the results I have so far are very encouraging. Your readings are better than I ever expected.' She was like a schoolgirl with a new crush, though not on a human, but a process.

'Calm down, Alex,' I said.

She shot me a look that was slightly less icy than normal. 'Excuse me. I've been working on this for a long time.'

'Good for you. Just tell me what it means for me.'

'Very well.' She went back to efficient-scientist mode. 'It's difficult to describe for the layman. Basically we tapped into the deepest levels of your memory. Much of the data will need extensive analysis before its significance can be established. The process caused you to speak numerous words in German that we think were triggers. The reverse-conditioning action that I have built into the procedure means that those words will no longer provoke you into predetermined courses of action.'

'Try me.'

She looked at Dr. Rivers, who nodded. They went over to the bank of screens at the foot of the bed.

'Blaue Reiter,' she said.

I felt absolutely nothing.

'Remarkable,' Rivers said. 'Quite remarkable.'

'Machtergreifung.'

The same again.

'Wohlauf.'

Ditto, and so on. In every case, I remained completely unaffected. That was unlike the sessions I'd had with Rivers, when I always had to fight the triggers' effects consciously, with varying degrees of success.

'Congratulations, Dr. Brown,' Rivers said, gripping

her hand. If he hadn't been such a dry old stick I'd have bet on him inviting her for a candlelit dinner when we were done.

'That isn't all, Mr. Wells,' the female scientist said, levels of formality in the lab now fully restored. 'You also gave certain information that I think will interest our FBI colleagues substantially.'

'What information?'

'Please, Mr. Wells,' Rivers said. 'You can't expect us to share classified material with you.'

'Classified material? You just said it came from me. Why can't I know what it is?'

He was looking uncomfortable. 'Those are the rules.'

Dr. Brown was getting excited again. 'Are you sure you have no recollection of what you said?'

I shook my head. 'I fell for a long time. After that, I found myself walking through a forest, and then crossing a river on a small boat. There was smoke in the air and I heard voices, a lot of them crying. I went through a ruined city, but there was no one around. Just more voices…' The scene seemed familiar, but I couldn't place it.

'That's very gratifying,' Dr. Brown said.

'What do you mean?'

'The "katabasis" was induced by my process,' she said proudly.

I found my bearings. It so happened that I knew what the term meant—a descent, specifically to the Underworld. When I was at college studying English, I did a project on the literary tradition of such journeys. I'd always been fascinated by the depiction of hell in Milton's *Paradise Lost*. That had led me in all sorts of strange directions: from Wilfred Owen's subterranean First World War trench poems, to the trips to the death god's realm described by Homer and Virgil, to the urban wastelands of T.S. Eliot. I'd brought in works of art, too—ancient vases and sculptures showing Charon and Cerberus, visions of demonic horror by Hieronymus Bosch and Peter Brueghel, Rodin's sculpted *Gates of Hell*. The fact that the Rothmann conspiracy had involved a satanic cult called the Antichurch of Lucifer Triumphant and had previously spawned a killer who left maps of hell attached to the victims meant that the literary and artistic traditions had extra significance for me, no matter what Alexandra Brown's drugs and other methods of suggestion had brought out.

'So you did brainwash me.'

She gave me an imperious look. 'Certainly not. My process is directed toward the extraction of material from subjects, not the insertion of predetermined stimuli. The emphasis is on making use of structures already present. Do you have some knowledge of underworld voyages?'

'You've read my file. My whole life has been one of those recently. What about the triggers?'

'What about them?' said Rivers.

'Wakey, wakey, Lester. Do you think Alex here's process has nailed them all?'

'Please don't call me that,' the pale woman said.

'How about Sandra? Or Lexie?'

'Please, Mr. Wells.' She was irritated. One-nil to me.

'Probably,' Rivers said, in a low voice.

'Is that a scientific term?' I asked.

'Unfortunately it is,' he replied. 'We have now identified a total of one hundred and seven trigger words and phrases. The likelihood is that there are few, if any, remaining.'

'It'll only take one,' I said, remembering the murders in the cathedral. That shut them up.

Eventually they loosed my bonds and let me go. My legs were unsteady and there was a vile metallic taste in my mouth. Dr. Brown said those side effects would soon disappear. I hoped the same could be said for any psychological effects of her process.

On my way out of the lab, to my surprise, I saw that it was after four in the morning. The gorilla had been told to escort me all the way back to our apartment. I managed not to screw with him by turning into a werewolf on the way. Karen was awake, but drowsy, so I kissed her and lay down beside her.

'What happened?'

'They told you I'd be late, didn't they?'

'Yes. What was Rivers doing?'

'He's got a new sidekick. Dr. Alexandra 'I'm Pale Because I Only Come Out at Night' Brown. She's not only a grade-one weirdo, but she's got a process.'

'That sounds worrying.'

I gave her a rundown, wondering if she'd be put through it after she'd given birth. Were the drugs safe? Then I felt myself heading rapidly toward sleep's Niagara Falls. I managed to kiss her again before my barrel went into the watery void. My last thoughts were: what exactly was in Dr. Brown's pharmaceutical cocktail? And was I about to set off on a trip to hell?

I woke up with a clear head and serious hunger, having had no dinner the previous evening. It was nearly noon. Karen was encamped on the sofa, watching a kids' cartoon on TV.

'I'm getting in training,' she said.

'Yeah, we'll be seeing a lot of those in the next few years. How do you feel?'

'All right, I suppose. My appetite seems to have gone walkabout.'

'So you don't fancy a full English?'

She gave me a foxy smile. 'As in breakfast? No, thanks.'

'Sexual innuendo at this time in the morning? Shame on you, Karen Oaten.'

'Why don't you try "Karen Wells"?'

'Because I know you'll keep your own name. That's who you are in the Met.'

'Work isn't everything, Matt.'

'I never thought I'd hear you say that.'

She took my hand and put it on her bulge. 'We've got someone else to think about now. Magnus Oliver Wells.'

'Where did "Oliver" come from?'

'My grandfather on my mother's side. I liked him.'

'Okay.' There were worse names. Like Heinz. Or Sebastian. 'I'm ravenous. Do you mind if I stuff my face?'

Karen shook her head, then pulled me closer, her eyes suddenly damp. 'Don't ever leave me, Matt.'

'Of course I won't. What's got into you?'

'Nothing. It's an emotional time. Now go and have your grease feast.'

When I came back with a plateful of eggs, bacon and sausage, I sat at the table. Karen had drifted off to sleep, so I left the cartoon and found a news channel.

I was halfway through a mouthful of food when I heard the announcer's voice get serious.

'In the City of Brotherly Love, a gruesome discovery,' said the over-made-up woman with huge hair. 'TV stations, including our own, were directed by anonymous calls to a disused factory in North Philadelphia. There, the crews found human organs said to come from murdered university professor Jack Notaro. His body was…'

The pictures showed a scrum of cameramen and reporters around a police line.

I watched as a tall man wearing a senior officer's insignia on his uniform jacket and cap inserted himself between two street cops. Microphones were immediately directed at him, like arrows on their way to Saint Sebastian. Which made me wonder where the FBI man with that surname was. I was sure this was where he and Bimsdale had flown off to last night. The caption read Major Andrew Carstens, Philadelphia Homicide Chief.

The reporters were baying like wolves. It wasn't often they got to make the headlines in their own story. A particularly pushy type, an oxlike man with carefully sculpted facial hair, got his question in first.

'Major, will you confirm what was found?'

The policeman gave him a weary look. 'As I think you know, Wayne, a human eye and kidney were located in the building behind me.'

'By the crew from WZNT News,' the reporter said proudly.

'Major!' yelled another reporter, this one Chinese and almost as tall as the cop. 'Major, what about the

Nazi objects that were with the organs? Are they linked to the murders in other cities?'

Carstens looked reluctant to answer. I wasn't surprised. Peter Sebastian had probably fitted an explosive device to his backside. If he strayed onto the FBI's patch, his colon would be well and truly irrigated. This was looking bad. Rothmann and his group of extremist thugs had to be involved.

Eventually the major went on, confining himself to stating that a copy of *Mein Kampf,* a Nazi flag and an SS dagger had been arranged around the eye and kidney. There were also Waffen-SS marching songs playing on a boom box.

I pushed the plate away, no longer interested in food. The camera was panning around the crowd, then zooming in on individual members of the public. These were the ghouls who rushed to rubberneck at crime scenes, the gorier the better. That was when I saw him, the shithead. He was wearing a beard—probably false—and had a woolen hat pulled down to his ears, but I recognized his ratlike features immediately. It was Gordy Lister, one of Heinz Rothmann's sidekicks. In Washington before the slaughter at the cathedral, we'd made the mistake of letting him go before we knew just how important he was. Here he was, right back in the frame.

I picked up the phone—it only connected to our FBI minders—and told Julie Simms to get Sebastian on the line as quickly as she could. It wasn't only Alexandra Brown who could make significant discoveries.

Ten

Special Agent Arthur Bimsdale was perplexed. Back in his hometown for the first time since he had been posted to Washington six months ago, he had never seen Philadelphia in a worse light—even on the autumn day that his parents, killed in a car crash three years ago, had been laid to rest in the Episcopalian cemetery. It was then that he had questioned his faith for the first, but certainly not the last, time.

It didn't help that it was winter and the city's prevalent color was gray, in a plethora of merging shades, but there was more to his feeling of disquiet than that. A sensitive person would have put it down to his proximity to death, in the forms of Jack Notaro and his predecessors in recent weeks. That didn't apply to Bimsdale. He might have looked like the Yale scholar he once was, but his few friends knew he had a stainless steel backbone. There was no question that the behavior of the local media had been horrifying—a school of barracuda would have shown more respect to the professor's mutilated corpse. No, the root of the problem was that his boss, Peter Sebastian, had chosen Philadelphia as the place where he finally showed his true colors.

And those, Bimsdale reflected as he hurriedly downed a cheesesteak at a stall near the university, were blacker than a pirate's heart. He had suspected from the beginning that Sebastian saw him as a lightweight. His boss had read his personnel file, but quoted only selectively from it. In fact, the special agent in charge at the Butte, Montana, field office had given Bimsdale the best report he'd ever signed off on, commending in particular his aptitude for handling violent crime and his diligence in nailing the most hard-nosed felons. Sebastian seemed unimpressed by that. Arthur knew that his previous assistant was in jail, and he couldn't understand what he was doing wrong. Maybe his boss had been romantically attached to the mysterious Dana Maltravers.

But all that was in the past. The fact was that Bimsdale hadn't dropped the ball in the brief period they'd been working together. He had acted as the link between Sebastian and the Bureau's investigators, both at the Hoover Building and in field offices, as well as dealing with local homicide teams. He had written reports, often in his boss's name. Sebastian read and signed them, but he had never given him one word of praise. He even kept the media off Sebastian's back, which had been quite some job since the career of 'Hitler's Hitman,' as the killer was now called by the press, had started in Greenwich Village. Just remembering what information had been made public and what had been restricted in each case required an elephantine memory.

None of that really mattered. Arthur Bimsdale would have been having the time of his life. If his boss had kept him in the loop, he'd have been walking on air. But that wasn't happening. The worst thing was that Peter Sebastian kept quiet about the details of earlier cases, particularly those which involved the Washington 'Occult Killer' and were confined to restricted files. Bimsdale suspected those murders were connected to the Rothmann conspiracy that had targeted the President, but Sebastian refused to discuss that angle. Most of what Arthur had learned, he'd found on the internet. What kind of a way was that to run a high-profile investigation? In fact, the violent crime unit wasn't even running it—the day-to-day homicide work was being carried out by local detectives. That seemed like an abrogation of responsibility.

And then there was the question of Matt Wells. Why had Sebastian suddenly started visiting the British writer so regularly? Why did he spend so much time on those visits closeted with Dr. Rivers, whose career in mind control had been characterized as 'highly dubious' by several researchers and bloggers? Now Matt Wells was doing combat training and firearms practice. What kind of a way was that to treat a prisoner with dubious legal status, one that had tried to kill the President?

Arthur Bimsdale threw the remains of his lunch into a garbage bin. He was going to spend the afternoon in the University of Pennsylvania library, seeing if Jack Notaro had written anything that could have provoked his killer. Meanwhile, his boss had returned to D.C., for a meeting with the Director. At least that showed he had top-level support.

If it were up to Arthur, he'd have busted Peter Sebastian's hindmost region to Guam, never mind Butte, Montana.

I heard several clicks on the line.

'Hello? Sebastian?'

'No, this is Special Agent Bimsdale. Who's this?'

'Matt Wells. Listen, I need to talk to him urgently. Is he there?'

'I'm afraid not. Can I help?'

I thought about that. Obviously Sebastian wasn't taking calls. I didn't have any option but to talk to his worryingly young-looking bagman.

'All right. Are you familiar with the name Gordy Lister?'

There was a pause. 'Wasn't he involved in the Rothmann case?'

At least he'd done his homework. 'Correct. He was the scumbag's fixer on the *Star Reporter*.'

'And he was allowed to remain at liberty.'

'Thanks for pointing that out, Arthur. Not one of our better calls at the time. The thing is, I just saw him.'

'What? At the camp?'

'No, you idiot. On the TV. He's at the back of the crowd at the scene where the professor's organs were found.'

'Really? Give me a description.'

I did so. 'Are you there?'

'Yes. Stay on the line.'

The TV was no longer showing the live feed from Philadelphia, so I could only follow what was happening on the phone. I heard raised voices—one of which seemed to call the special agent 'fuckface'. Bimsdale responded with, 'Coming through'. He wasn't so dumb though—he wasn't shouting, so Lister might not realize he was being approached. I zapped from channel to channel, but there was nothing relevant, not even on the 24-hour news stations.

Eventually I heard Bimsdale's voice again.

'I don't see him, Mr. Wells.' He was breathing heavily.

'Shit. Are you sure?'

'I'm standing on a newspaper dispenser.' That would have made his tall figure stick out like a lighthouse, but it sounded like it was too late for caution. 'No. I'm sorry, Mr. Wells, he must have gone.'

'Circulate the description among the cops.'

'Okay. I can do better than that. I'll get hold of the TV footage. He's bound to show up on at least one channel.' He paused. 'If he really was here.'

'I'm telling you, it was him.'

'He was wearing a beard, you said.'

'Yeah, it could have been fake.'

'So how did you recognize him?'

I sighed. 'I don't know, Arthur, I just did. It was something about his manner. Lister's a shifty bastard and that was what I picked up on.'

'All right, Mr. Wells, I'll do what I can. The problem is, if his beard was a false one, he could easily have jettisoned it to aid his disappearance.'

He was right. Lister could also have dumped the overcoat he was wearing, or turned it inside out, and he could easily have dispensed with the woolen hat.

I signed off and thought about what Lister's presence might mean. Could he be 'Hitler's Hitman?' I'd had some run-ins with him and he had played the tough guy, but he usually made sure he had big men present to look after him. I couldn't see Gordy, who was skinny and below average height, hoisting a body as bulky as Jack Notaro's onto a hook in the ceiling, nor could I see him killing people and cutting them to pieces.

So what was he doing at the scene? He was taking a hell of a risk, despite the disguise. He would have known that law enforcement often checked TV footage for suspicious individuals. What was so important that he had shown up in Philadelphia? Had Rothmann sent him? I was pretty sure that Lister would have hooked up with his boss after he disappeared. But if the Nazi was behind the murders, why would he risk incriminating himself and his underground organization by sending Lister to the locus? I was certain he was still scheming, no doubt having changed the name of his armed force from the North American National Revival, also known as the North American Nazi Revival, and no doubt still manipulating the Antichurch of Lucifer Triumphant. Details of the M.O.s had been scanty, presumably because Sebastian had censored the reports, but it seemed to me that the satanic cult's sacrificial ritual might be being copied in the stringing up and mutilation of the victims. On the other hand, Heinz Rothmann was a subtle operator, at least until his plans came to fruition. These murders were about as subtle as a cockroach in a cup of coffee.

Karen moved her bulk on the sofa. 'What's going on?'

'Nothing.' I hurriedly turned the TV off. 'I thought you were asleep.'

'I was. Who were you talking to?'

'What? Oh, Quincy Jerome. Just arranging a run.' I didn't want her to know about the latest murder, and especially not about Gordy Lister. She hadn't met him, but she knew who he was. The idea of her going into labor with him in mind was not appealing. Then again, the process might not start for days. Keeping the news from her would be impossible now we had internet and TV access.

'How about some music?' she said, hands on her bulge. 'There's a whole lot of kicking going on down here.'

I turned on the CD player. Julie Simms brought fresh disks from the camp library every week. I'd managed to get her to steer clear of garbage pop and concentrate on rock and folk. She was obviously a classical fan; there were always a couple of orchestral pieces in the bag.

The Manic Street Preachers blasted out. I'd forgotten that I'd left the CD in. They weren't a top class band as far as I was concerned, but I couldn't fault the sentiments of what was playing now—'I You Tolerate This, Then Your Children Will Be Next.'

'No!' Karen cried. 'Too raucous. Do you want your son to shake his way out of me?'

'Sorry.' I ejected the disk and put on one of Julie's. A swathe of gentle strings and what sounded like a harpsichord filled the room.

'That's better. What is it?'

I looked at the box. 'Monteverdi.'

'Mmm, it's nice. Come over here.'

I did as I was told.

'I feel…funny,' Karen said, taking my hand.

I was instantly alert. 'Is it beginning?'

'I don't think so. It's just…it's just that I'm afraid, Matt.' She let out a sob.

I pressed myself against her. 'Don't be silly. You're my strong woman, you can stand up to anything.'

'I don't think I can. I keep…I keep thinking about what the Rothmanns did to me. What if the baby's damaged? What if I can't act like a proper mother?'

I squeezed her hands. 'You've had plenty of tests. Nothing's wrong with the boy. Or with you.'

'How do you know?' she demanded, pulling her hands away. 'Rivers is still dredging triggers out of you and I've had much less treatment. What if some function of the conditioning is activated when I give birth? What if they designed the process to keep female subjects childless? That isn't so unlikely. They wouldn't want their robot soldiers to be distracted by kids—'

'Karen, Karen,' I said, wiping her brow. 'Calm down. Take some deep breaths.' I did that and she eventually followed suit. 'That's better. You know you mustn't get overwrought. It's bad for junior.'

'Don't call him that. He's Magnus Oliver—Magnus Oliver Wells.'

'That's right, darling.' I repeated the names. 'He's desperate to see us, so you have to look your best.' I handed her a box of tissues.

'I'm sorry, Matt. Sometimes it gets too much for me.'

'I don't believe that for a second. You're just trying to make me sorry for you so that I'll make your lunch.'

She laughed. 'I don't want anything to eat.'

'Aren't you supposed to keep your strength up?'

'Look at me. I've got enough blubber reserves to sink a whaling ship.'

'Rubbish. You're the most attractive woman in the camp.'

She raised an eyebrow at that admittedly less than ringing endorsement. The average female soldier's looks were forbidding and Julie Simms was no Venus de Milo, though she did have a full set of limbs.

'Matt, don't go out today.'

'Okay,' I said, alert to her tone again. 'I think Rivers is expecting me in the evening, though.'

'Let's see if we get that far,' she said, closing her eyes.

I took the phone into the bedroom and called the medical center. The midwife said everything was ready and there was nothing else to do, so I cut the connection. I felt useless, a spare part. I went back into the living room and turned the music down. Monteverdi was surprisingly pleasant, but the lack of guitars was a problem for me. I was going to make sure Magnus Oliver Wells had a working knowledge of classic rock music before he went to school.

There were certain things a father had to do for his son.

The boy was between two and three years old. His legs were short and bowed, in a pair of clean and well-pressed corduroy trousers. The black leather boots had been polished, but were now spattered with Central Park mud—the Filipina nanny wasn't quick enough to stop him dashing onto the grass and under the trees. He screamed with delight every time she came after him, his cheeks red and his blue eyes sparkling. The last time the woman approached, he pulled off his woolen hat and threw it in her face. That earned him a stern talking-to and he started to sniffle as he was led back to the path.

Sara Robbins watched from behind a wider tree trunk than most. The day was milder than its predecessors, but there was still a bite in the wind. The water in the reservoir looked chill, low waves sweeping across its surface. As she walked out of the cover, she felt the plastic switchblade in the pocket of her Levi's. She always had it with her, not least because it wasn't picked up by metal detectors.

As the little boy walked past, trying to tug his hand away from the Filipina's, Sara threw the ball she'd bought in his direction. The nanny looked round and stared at her suspiciously. Scott smiled at Sara and then ran to retrieve the ball.

'Tana,' said the boy, pointing at the picture of the steam engine on the ball.

'Thomas?' Sara said. 'That's right, it's Thomas.'

'Come, Scott,' the nanny said firmly. 'We do not talk to strangers.'

Sara ignored her, kneeling down beside the boy. 'Your name's Scott? My brother's called Scott.' She viewed that as a white lie.

The Filipina pulled on her charge's arm. 'Come on. Mummy will be angry.'

'Oh, for heaven's sake,' Sara said. 'I've got kids myself.'

The nanny looked around the area of grass. 'So where are they, Mrs.?'

Sara laughed hollowly. 'Where are they? Visiting Granny.' She pointed to the ball. 'Would you like to have Thomas?'

The little boy nodded avidly. 'Tana. Scott love Tana.'

'Come on now,' the Filipina said, glaring at Sara. 'Or I call police.'

'Because I gave him a ball? Are you insane?'

'No. You are insane person.' The nanny tugged hard at the boy's arm.

'You're hurting him,' Sara said, standing up and grabbing the woman's wrist. 'Let go.'

The Filipina's face clenched in pain and she quickly released Scott's hand.

'That's better,' Sara said. 'Are you all right, darling?'

The boy smiled. 'Tana.'

Sara ran her fingertips down his cheek. 'Have fun. I have to go now. Bye-bye.' She looked at the nanny. 'Don't you dare hurt him again.'

The trembling Filipina dropped her gaze.

Sara Robbins walked into the trees, and then started to jog away. That was stupid, she said to herself. What were you doing? Your brother wasn't called Scott and you don't have children. What's the matter with you?

When she got to Museum Mile, she hailed a cab and sat back in the seat, her breathing ragged. She knew herself too well to be under any illusions. She had never had the slightest desire to have children, but now Matt Wells was about to become a father again. That was getting to her. She had no idea whether the child was a boy or a girl, but for some reason that she couldn't fathom, she was interested.

This was changing her, and that wasn't good. Something that she couldn't control was happening to her, something that was making her see the world differently.

The Soul Collector had to find her former lover urgently.

It was as if he had unknowingly infected himself with a disease that would change him irrevocably.

Whenever he descended to the underground chamber hosting the Antichurch of Lucifer Triumphant in exile—what those who believed in the false faith would have called a cathedral crypt—the Master almost forgot his name.

Given how many identities he possessed, he shouldn't have been surprised. Of them, only his birth name of Heinz Rothmann was important to him, but even it was less desirable than the title he had assumed. The Master of the Antichurch was not only the guarantor of eternal death to his followers. He also still had control of the fortune that he had obtained as the businessman Jack Thomson, distributed over the years in numerous offshore banks. He was also still the sole owner of the conditioning drugs and techniques developed by his unjustly killed sister and lover, and there was no shortage of government agencies around the world that would pay with the lifeblood of their citizens for those. Not only that, he still had a large number of subjects who had been through coffining and could be activated as ruthless killers with a single phone call.

But for the Master, all of that had become a secondary reality, one seen through a glass lightly. Now he preferred the darkness that the Antichurch brought, the darkness and the knowledge that life was an illusion and that only death had any substance. The great poets had always known the power of death and its inescapable triumph. That was why the Mesopotamian tradition had the hero Gilgamesh descend to the underworld, the house of dust, to see firsthand how ineluctable the death gods were. The great poets, Homer, Virgil, even the deluded Christians Dante and Milton, had sent their protagonists to the underworld—assuming, as was obvious, that Satan was the hero of *Paradise Lost*. And even the false messiah Christ was said to have harrowed hell before his supposed resurrection. Lucifer and his realm were triumphant for eternity. To think that when the Master had revived the Antichurch in Maine, his motivation was that Americans would respond more readily to a religious cult than the antireligious ideology of Nazism. Now he knew that the Antichurch had more potential for destruction than any political system. After all, the established religions in the West had been sucking innocents into their maws for centuries.

The man with the scarred cheeks looked at the manuscripts he had laid out on the table in the underground chamber. Maybe he should see it as a crypt after all—the word meant 'hidden,' and there was nothing more hidden than the original Antigospel, written by its founders' own hands. But it wouldn't be a crypt for long. Soon the Antichurch and its primary lessons, that death governed all things and that human beings were naturally violent, would be known across the world.

But something was missing. The Master corrected himself—not something, but someone. He needed a senior disciple, a helper he could depend on. People capable of what the Antigospel required were very rare—even fully coffined subjects could not be relied upon in the most testing circumstances. He had encountered one with true potential, though: the Englishman, Matt Wells. The Master now understood that blaming Wells for killing his sister was a mistake. By that act, the crime writer, who had immersed himself deep in death's philosophies and experienced the persecution of merciless killers, was the ally he needed. The problem was, Wells was nowhere to be found.

But that would soon change, he was certain. The murders in the northern cities would see to that. Matt Wells would become one of the nameless, as had the Master. And then the will of Lucifer would sweep across the land like the flames of hell itself.

Eleven

I was checking reports of the Hitler's Hitman murders on the internet, when I heard Karen groan.

'What is it, my love?' I asked, going over to the sofa.

'I don't know, Matt. Help me up.'

I got her into a sitting position.

'I have to go to the bathroom.'

After she was on her feet, I took her arm.

'No, I'm all right,' she said, gently pulling free. She stopped before she reached the door. 'Oh, Matt.'

I was over there immediately.

'I think…' She moved a hand to her nether regions. 'No, it's all right. I thought my waters had broken.'

I took a couple of deep breaths and watched her walk on slowly. Then I called the midwife, who cheerfully told us to hang in there. I could cheerfully have throttled her, but Karen just laughed when she reappeared in the cream nightgown that she'd obtained through Julie Simms.

'Let's listen to more of that nice music,' she said.

I put the second Monteverdi disk on and went over

to join her on the sofa. We held hands until the music stopped. Karen asked me to put the first one on again, saying that *Orfeo* would always remind her of this time.

Later in the evening, after I'd made us toasted sandwiches, she dropped into an uneasy sleep. I turned the TV on, but it was too late for any fresh news. I leaned my back against the sofa and followed Karen into the land of dreams.

Not for long. Her stifled scream woke me.

'Ah!' she gasped. 'The contractions are starting, Matt.' Her face constricted and I felt nauseous. The sight of the woman I loved in pain was hard to bear.

I called the medical center and was told to calm down and wait until the contractions became more regular. All I could do was hold Karen's hand and occasionally mop her brow with a damp towel. I lost track of time and my mind seemed to go into some kind of primitive passive mode to cope with the waiting and the uncertainty. I couldn't remember much about my daughter's birth.

Eventually I managed to get the midwife to send a car over. When we arrived at the medical center, it was quiet, being that it was now five in the morning. The rooms that had been set up as a temporary delivery and neonatal ward were empty and cold. I asked for the heating to be turned up.

The midwife was a jovial Latina woman. 'Don't you worry, Mr. Wells,' she said. 'We'll take good care of your wife.'

'Partner,' I corrected. 'Wife-to-be.' When she took off her tunic to change into surgical scrubs, I saw she was wearing a green army shirt. I wondered how many midwives the U.S. military had on its books.

'Whatever,' she said, with a smile that displayed gleaming teeth. 'We don't discriminate. My name's Angela, by the way. You can call me Angel.' At least she wasn't hung up on formality like the psychologists.

We sat on either side of Karen's bed. She was mostly in control, but the layer of sweat on her forehead was a giveaway. Angel kept an eye on the monitors and from time to time ran her hands over Karen's belly and below. The hours passed. The obstetrician, a Japanese-American called Kitano, looked in around 8:00 a.m. He was in uniform and bore the insignia of a lieutenant colonel. I'd got pretty good at recognizing people's ranks since we'd been in the camp.

'Everything good, Sergeant?' he asked.

'Yes, sir,' Angel confirmed. 'Contractions are every two minutes, nil dilation so far.'

'Very well. You know where to find me.'

'Yes, sir,' Angel acknowledged. 'Reading medical journals in the colonel's office, sir,' she added, after he'd gone.

That didn't reassure me. Kitano had been brought in from an army hospital in Chicago and I could have done with more signs of his commitment to Karen's case.

I tried to take Karen's mind off the pain by talking. She answered briefly, but her mind wasn't engaged so I let her be. I even dropped off for a couple of hours, my head resting on the foot of her bed. It wasn't quality sleep, though at least I didn't dream. No nocturnal journeys through the underworld—the pale-faced Dr. Brown would have been disappointed.

The contractions eventually got more frequent and Angel's eyes and hands busier. Kitano came in a couple of times and examined Karen. He made no comment, which irritated me.

'Don't worry, Matt,' Angel said. 'Your lady's doing real well.'

I smiled at Karen. She looked like she had run a marathon, her blond hair damp and lank, her face lined. But she smiled at me bravely.

'Well done, my darling.' I kissed her on the cheek.

'What, nil by mouth?' she quipped, then gasped as another wave of pain broke over her.

I put my lips to hers. 'Hang on,' I said. 'Not long now.' I sat back, holding her hand. It went limp when the contraction passed. She was exhausted. How much longer was this going to last?

When it happened, there was no warning. Angel had checked Karen's dilation and had her hands on the bump. Then her eyes opened wide when she took in the monitors. She immediately hit the panic button and a loud alarm started to sound every few seconds. Karen moaned and her hand reached for mine. Angel was pressing buttons and unhooking cables.

'What is it?' the obstetrician demanded, arriving at speed. There were two auxiliaries with him, big guys.

'No heartbeat from the fetus in the last thirty seconds,' Angel said.

'O.R.,' Kitano ordered. 'Now!'

The auxiliaries laid hands on Karen's bed and pushed it toward the door.

'Matt!' she said, as my hand came away from hers. 'What's happening?'

I followed them down the corridor. Kitano took a set

of scrubs from a nurse and pulled his white coat off, dropping it on the floor.

'What's happening?' I repeated, my heart thundering.

'Don't worry,' Angel said. 'We know what we're doing.'

'Matt!' Karen wailed. 'Help me!'

The big man at the front of the bed crashed through the doors to the operating room and the others followed. I was stopped by a male nurse.

'Sorry, sir. You'll have to wait outside.'

I had no option—wait was all I could do. I strode up and down the corridor, never going too far from the doors to the theater. My mind was bucking like a mustang stung by a horsefly. I couldn't hold on to any thought for more than a few seconds. Was Karen in pain? What were they doing to her? Why had the baby's heart stopped? Would he be harmed? Would his brain be damaged? Eventually I realized I was panting. I stopped walking to get my breathing under control.

That didn't help. All that happened was that the possibilities hardened in my mind. Karen was being operated on. At best, she'd be denied the natural birth she wanted. At worst, her life was in danger—as might be that of Magnus Oliver Wells. I cursed myself for allowing her to make decisions about his name. An atavistic superstition about tempting fate overcame me and I staggered against the wall.

'Karen, I love you, I need you,' I whispered. 'Come back to me. Bring him back.'

Then a cruel fear lanced into me. The Rothmanns. Whatever Dr. Rivers said, the Nazis' conditioning process could be doing this to Karen. If she'd been harmed, if the birth of our son had been jeopardized, I would seek Heinz Rothmann out and make him pay.

That cold fury was all that sustained me until Kitano came through the doors, pulling a white coat over his bloody scrubs.

Peter Sebastian was in an FBI plane that had taken off from Ronald Reagan Washington National Airport a quarter of an hour earlier. He was feeling pleased with himself. The Director had approved his plan, had even congratulated him on it, and had authorized him to fly immediately to the camp in Illinois.

Sebastian had always counted himself a devious operator. He wouldn't have reached the illustrious level he had if he hadn't known how to outflank the competition and cover his ass, but recently he'd exceeded his own expectations. At this rate, he'd have a shot at deputy director within the next couple of years. After that, even director would be within his range.

Then again, he thought as he sipped black and unsweetened coffee, he had to pull this scheme off. If there were any more hate-crime murders, if the so-called Hitler's Hitman killer continued to run rings round him, the Director would be forced to replace him. You were only ever as good as your current cases, and Sebastian was running at 0-4. Still, that had its own advantages. Desperate measures were necessary and had been green-lighted. This was exactly the kind of situation that Sebastian flourished in.

A call came through on the secure phone. It was Arthur Bimsdale.

'No sign of the suspect Gordy Lister, sir. Major Carstens has circulated the description to the whole of the Philadelphia force.'

'Have you considered sending it to law enforcement at the previous scenes?'

'Already done, sir. All four have got it out to their homicide departments and to the people on patrol.'

'Very good, Arthur,' Sebastian said. Bimsdale was beginning to shine, which might be problematical.

'Em, where are you, sir?'

'That's classified, Special Agent.' Sebastian looked out of the cabin window.

It was already dark, the only lights those of another aircraft in the distance.

'I see, sir. What are your orders?'

Sebastian had thought about that. 'Get back to D.C. I'll be in touch.'

'Yes, sir.' Bimsdale paused. 'There's something else, sir.'

'Spit it out,' Sebastian said impatiently. One thing that his assistant had still to learn was to be more forceful.

'Gordy Lister. I've accessed his file. He has a brother.'

'Is that right?' Once again Arthur had surprised him. 'What about him?'

'He lost his legs in a car accident thirteen months ago.'

'Where's this going, Special Agent?'

'Well, I've run a check on him. Michael John Lister. He worked as an electrician, sir. Standard household repairs, that sort of thing. Except he recently bought a fully converted Jeep Grand Cherokee and moved into a condominium outside Tallahassee, Florida.'

'Well, well,' Sebastian said, surprised again. 'I don't suppose you've talked to this Michael Lister.'

'He's known as Mikey, sir. No, I haven't. What do you think about surveillance by the field office down there?'

'I think it's less than likely that Gordy Lister will show, but it's definitely worth a shot. Good work, Arthur.'

They concluded the call shortly afterward. Sebastian was satisfied. Bimsdale was like a dog with a fresh bone, which had distracted him from the issue of Matt Wells. When they'd spoken earlier in the day, his assistant had asked why the Englishman was so important. What would he say now that Sebastian was on his way to make Wells a major player in the investigation?

He looked out into the darkness again, the murk that lay over the eastern states. Desperate measures was right. If his plan misfired, the deleterious influence of Heinz Rothmann would spread across the land like a plague. Americans had always been prey to political extremists. Even more were attracted to religious fundamentalism. Rothmann's combination of Nazi ideology and a perversion of Christianity could unleash a wave of violence much worse than the four murders he had so far inspired. There was no doubt in Sebastian's mind that Rothmann was behind the killings, no doubt at all. The fact that the Nazi had pioneered a successful brainwashing technique made the situation even more dangerous, even if Dr. Brown's process might negate it. That was why Matt Wells, with his history of conditioning, was such a vital link.

Peter Sebastian found himself thinking about what the Englishman was going through. He had been informed that Karen Oaten was in the medical center. Matt had been through the birth of a child before, although the FBI man had no idea how he had coped. Neither did he know how the writer's relationship with his ex-wife had been. He found it hard to imagine that Matt had been more in love with her than he was with Karen. Here was a couple that lived for each other, and their shared experiences at the hands of the Rothmann twins had clearly made the bond between them even stronger.

Sebastian thought back to the births of his own children. Astrid's had been straightforward, over in a couple of hours, while Roy had been reluctant to emerge into the world and had reduced his wife Emma to a groaning wreck. Which reminded him—he should call Emma and tell her that he wasn't going to get home much in the immediate future. Since the Hitler's Hitman murders started, he had seen very little of his family, returning home to Glenmont outside D.C. only to pick up fresh clothes and eat hurried meals. Astrid and Roy didn't care. They were only interested in hanging out with their friends and indulging in the strange pursuits of modern youth. Emma should have gotten used to the demands of his job, but she had stopped being supportive in recent years, preferring the company of her female friends, even on the limited occasions he was around. Maybe she had a lover. Maybe she thought he had one, but he had never been tempted—not even by his previous assistant, Dana Maltravers. She had been some woman. Her concealed background and prolonged betrayal of the Bureau meant that she would be in federal prison for a very long time.

As the jet began its descent to the airport at Rockford,

northwest of Chicago, Sebastian thought of Matt Wells again. He put his hand into the pocket of his suit and felt the box that contained the engagement ring he had procured. It would be the least he could give the Englishman.

Twelve

Kitano looked at me briefly, and then at the floor.

I felt like I was about to faint and throw up at the same time. My vision blurred and my ears rang as if I had suddenly been immersed in freezing, muddy water. I felt a hand on my arm.

'Mr. Wells,' the obstetrician was saying, 'do you need to sit down? Mr. Wells?'

My senses recalibrated themselves.

'Tell me what happened,' I said, pulling away from him. I knew his hands had done terrible things. 'Tell me!'

Kitano looked over his shoulder. Two soldiers were watching me.

'Leave us,' the surgeon ordered.

'Tell me,' I said, my voice hoarse.

'Mr. Wells, you should sit…' He broke off, realizing that he was in danger. 'All right, have it your way. I'm very sorry, we did what we could, we really tried very hard.' He looked away. 'I'm so sorry.'

'My…my son…is he…' I couldn't bring myself to say it.

'I'm afraid so. The umbilical cord was wrapped twice around his neck. We were as quick as we could have been, but...'

I tried to slow my breathing down, but had lost power over my body.

'When...when will Karen...Karen come round?' I asked, leaning against the wall.

'You don't understand, Mr. Wells,' the obstetrician said, his face sagging. 'Your wife...your wife didn't survive the operation.'

My knees quivered and I slid to the floor. Karen? No, it wasn't possible. She couldn't be... I couldn't even *think* the word. No, he was mistaken. What did he know? He wasn't a proper doctor, he was in the army. Karen was just resting, she'd come round soon.

'I want to see her,' I said, getting to my feet with difficulty. 'I need to see her now.' I stumbled toward the doors that led to the operating theater.

'Mr. Wells,' Kitano said, alarm in his voice. 'You can't go in there. Your wife...'

I turned back toward him, tears cascading down my face. 'She's not my wife!' I screamed. 'She's my partner. We're getting...we're getting married *after...*'

This time my legs gave way as if I'd been shot. I heard a loud crack and then dived gratefully into the void.

People who thought Philadelphia was quaint had their heads up their asses, Gordy Lister thought—or they hadn't been to the southern part of the city, where he had found a cheap hotel. This was urban blight in a big way, the kind of place the *Star Reporter* would have described as 'Yuksville, U.S.A.' He looked at the copy of the paper that he'd picked up for old times' sake at a convenience store. He had worked his way up from gofer to senior editorial consultant, the latter meaning Heinz Rothmann's fixer—a position he still occupied, though the working conditions were kind of different. The paper looked exactly the same as it used to, the new owners knowing a winner when they saw one. They'd got it cheap, as well. The government had closed down as many of Rothmann's companies and blocked as many of his accounts as they could. Much good it had done them. His employer was still doing what he wanted.

Lister looked through the dirty gauze curtain at the dilapidated tenement across the street. Laundry was hanging from wires strung across window frames and the piercing voices of the poor rang out in several unfamiliar languages. He caught glimpses of people wearing scant clothing despite the chill. The fools had given everything they had, sold their futures to get here. Did they really think it was worth it? What kind of shit-holes had they come from?

Gordy Lister thought back to his own childhood in a trailer park outside Oklahoma City. His father had been a drunk, who rarely showed up. Even though she was hardly a looker, his mother turned tricks while he and Mikey played at the other end of the trailer. Often the door swung open and they saw more than was good for them. Mikey had grown up a hopeless fanny hound, at least until the accident. Not that being legless cramped his style much, or so he claimed on the telephone. Apparently some women were turned on by his stumps.

Ah, Mikey, he thought. You'll be the death of me. If Rothmann finds out I've been calling you and sending you money, I'll be the Antichurch's next sacrifice.

But what can I do? You're all I've got since AIDS took
Mom, not that I cried many tears about that vicious
bitch. Pop's liver swelled up and his skin turned yellow
before he died screaming in the emergency room. Who
else is there? Certainly not that murdering bastard Rothmann. He keeps me close because he needs me, but the
moment he finds someone who can do what I do without cracking wise, he'll have a hole dug for what's left
of me.

Lister took a slug from the bottle of cheap bourbon
on the bed and opened his laptop. It was time for the
morning report. He still had his writing skills, honed
by years at the *Star Reporter,* one of the top six supermarket tabloids, with but a passing acquaintance with
the truth. Reporters were encouraged to let their imagi-
nations loose. 'Governor Dates Alien' had been one of
his breakthrough stories. It cost the leader of a Western
state his job when it turned out that the alien in question
was a) an illegal from Guatemala, and b) a hermaphro-
dite. The photos of the weird genitalia had cost a lot, but
no one cared about that. Circulation soared and Gordy
was on his way to the tenth floor in Washington. He
looked out of the window again. Philadelphia was the
nearest he'd been to D.C. since Rothmann's organization
had been ripped apart by the Englishman Matt Wells.

Maybe that would be the way to distract Rothmann
from the absence of on-the-spot information about the
professor's murder—say that he'd seen Wells behind
the police line.

Gordy Lister flexed his fingers. No, it was too risky.
His boss would lose his cool and do anything to find
Matt Wells, even compromise the most precious of his
plans. After all, as well as screwing up the plot to kill

the President, the Englishman had killed Rothmann's twin sister. It seemed there was nothing fiercer than a Nazi whose closest relative had been murdered—so much for Hitler's followers being heartless beasts. Then again, it would be Wells who would end up heartless if Rothmann laid hands on him.

Lister laughed. 'Matt Wells was involved in the decision to let me go in D.C.,' he said under his breath. 'That was a big mistake—no one's seen him since the cathedral massacre. The Feds probably took him to Gitmo. Rothmann's been scanning the internet every day for sightings of him, but there's been nothing. That makes fingering the limey easy. I could say I saw him with that shithead Sebastian and leave the Kraut to draw his own conclusions.'

He tapped out a few lines, then stopped. His lower jaw took a dive. Even he was amazed by this flight of his imagination—what if the Feds had done some conditioning of their own? What if they were using Matt Wells as the Hitler Hitman to frame Rothmann? It wasn't so crazy. From what he'd learned, the victims had been mutilated and treated in ways that hinted at the Antichurch's rituals. There were Nazi slogans and insignia at the scenes. Was that what this was? One enormous setup?

He didn't really buy that, but it would give his boss something to chew over, thus getting him off his back. It would also justify this bullshit trip to Philly.

Yeah, Gordy Lister thought. *Job done.*

Karen was sitting on a blanket in a wide field, the sun beating down. Insects buzzed lazily about the bright green grass and clover. In the distance a wide river swung round a bend, the trees on the far bank dipping their leaves in the blue-brown water. Swallows were zipping to and fro on the southerly breeze.

Magnus gurgled in her arms.

'Who's having fun?' she said, lowering her head and rubbing her nose against his. 'Who likes the sunshine?'

Our son started laughing, stretching out his little hands to grab his mother's hair.

'Ow!' she pretended. 'Little man hurting Mummy, no, no!'

I went over to them, lowering the camera.

'Oh, here's Dadda. Now you'd better watch out.'

I put my finger out and felt his hand close round it. 'Who's a strong boy?' I said, bending over and looking into his green eyes. 'So, when are you going to give me back your mother's breasts?' He stared at me and then stuck his tongue out.

Karen screamed. 'It's the first time he's done that!' she said, kissing him on the forehead. 'Clever Magnus. Silly Dadda.'

I kneeled down and put my arms round them. 'I love you,' I said. 'I always will.'

A metallic sound made me look over my shoulder. I stood up, the camera falling to the ground. A figure in black combat fatigues was walking toward us, a cap obscuring the face. There was an assault rifle, bayonet fixed, in the figure's hands.

I turned back to Karen. 'Run! Take the baby and run!'

She gave me an agonized look, and then got to her feet and took off toward the distant line of trees.

I faced our assailant. 'No!' I yelled, as the rifle was

raised to the shoulder. Multiple shots rang past me as I rushed toward him. I lowered my shoulder and took him down before he could aim at me. We fought for what seemed like a long time. Eventually I managed to tear the weapon away and toss it behind me. Then I pulled the cap off.

'Hello, Matt,' Sara Robbins said, licking blood from her lips and smiling. 'I told you we'd meet again.'

I wasn't surprised it was her. I grabbed the front of her jacket with one hand and smashed the other into her face. I kept doing that till it was a red mush, then I let her fall back, then turned and ran.

'Karen!' I screamed. 'Where are you? Karen!'

I followed the direction she had taken, looking from side to side. The grass wasn't long enough to hide her. They had disappeared.

Could she have got to the trees? How long had I been struggling with Sara?

I reached the forest. 'Karen!' I yelled, again and again.

Then I pushed past a low branch covered in fresh leaves. There she was, lying on the ground with her arms outstretched. The baby was a few feet ahead. Both were motionless.

'Karen,' I moaned, falling to my knees. 'Magnus...'

The pain that suddenly transfixed me was worse than any I had known. I looked down and saw the bloody point of the bayonet protruding from my chest.

I screamed and then an explosion of light melted my eyes.

'Matt? Matt?'

I was blind and the pain in my chest was still intense. My head was also throbbing. The voice, soft and deep and female, continued saying my name, but I didn't recognize it.

'Pull it out,' I heard myself say. 'Pull it out!'

I felt dampness on my eyes, a cloth or the like. Then it was withdrawn and I found I could open them. Faces swam into view.

'Pull it out! Please...'

A honey-colored face that I'd seen before came close to mine. 'It's Angel, Matt. The midwife.'

My chest was in agony. 'Pull it out,' I pleaded.

'Pull what out, Matt?'

'My heart,' I said. 'My heart. Pull it out.'

Angel's eyes brimmed with tears. 'Oh, Matt.'

A man in a white coat moved in front of her. 'Mr. Wells? My name's Jimson. I'm the doctor looking after you. Do you remember what happened?'

I stared at him. 'Of course I do. Karen and I were having a picnic. It's the first time we'd taken the baby on one. We...' I broke off as I had flashes of Sara Robbins in black, a rifle in her hands. And a bayonet. 'Karen,' I said. 'Where is she? Where's my son?'

'Calm down, Mr. Wells. I gave you a sedative. You've been...you've been dreaming.'

Something clicked and my world seemed to recon-figure itself. 'That's a relief....' I said.

Dr. Jimson nodded. He was a handsome man in his uniform, a colonel, no less. I remembered the other doctor, the one with blood on his tunic. Kitano. He told me that...

Something clicked again, this time more jagged and metallic.

'He's remembered,' I heard Jimson say. 'Get ready to restrain him.'

But I didn't move. I just said dully, 'Karen's dead. Our son, as well.' A bitter taste filled my mouth and the pain in my heart got worse. 'Isn't that so?'

He looked at me and then nodded. 'I'm very sorry, Mr. Wells. My colleagues did everything they—''

'I want to see them.'

'I...I don't think that's a very good idea.'

'I want to see them. Now!'

Two big men appeared on either side of the bed and took hold of my shoulders.

'Please, Mr. Wells, you need to—'

'I want to see them!' The words burned my throat.

A face that I recognized appeared from behind one of the gorillas.

'Let him see them, Doctor,' Peter Sebastian said. 'It's what he needs to do.'

Jimson nodded. 'Very well. But he's still my patient. I need to check if he's up to it.'

I closed my eyes as he examined me. I breathed evenly, willing myself to appear normal. I couldn't feel my heartbeat; there was only the knifing pain.

After some time, I felt electrodes being removed from my chest and I opened my eyes. The big men had stepped back.

'Can you sit up, Mr. Wells?' Jimson asked.

I found that I could. One of the auxiliaries pushed a wheelchair forward.

'I don't need that.' I pushed my feet downward and put my weight on them. My legs felt weak, but I could take a few steps.

'Let him walk,' Sebastian said.

I looked at him and felt relief. At least someone

understood. Angel knelt down and slipped a pair of slippers onto my feet.

'Follow me,' the doctor said, heading toward the door.

I moved forward.

'Would you like me to come with you?' Sebastian asked.

I shrugged. Whatever happened, I was going to see them alone. He could tag along as far as the last door if he wanted.

Fortunately, nobody spoke during the short walk. Angel was in the group, probably because she felt bad about what had happened. I didn't feel anything except the pain in my heart.

Jimson led us through a door. There were desks and other office furniture, and another door across the room. A sign said Authorized Admittance Only and there was a key card panel.

'Mr. Wells,' he said, his eyes avoiding mine, 'Dr. Kitano had to perform a Cesarean section. You...you should be aware of that.'

I understood the warning—don't look down there. 'I'm going in on my own,' I said, extending my hand, palm up.

The doctor exchanged glances with Peter Sebastian, who nodded, and gave me a plastic card.

'I'll be here, Matt,' Sebastian said, his expression grave. 'Anything you need, anything at all.'

I walked away from them and inserted the card into the locking device. I pushed the door and let it close after me. The room was cold. The first two aluminum tables were shrouded by white sheets. The one on the left was almost flat, a tiny object lying near the top. The outline of an adult was on the right. I stepped up to that table first and drew the sheet back slowly. Karen's face was peaceful, the furrows labor had created on her forehead now gone. Her skin was gray, as were her lips, and her hair was limp. I stood by her for a time, my fingers on her chill brow. The pain in my heart had increased even more and I was struggling to stay upright. Tears drenched my cheeks and obscured my vision.

After a while, I went to our son. I pulled the sheet away gently and looked at the small body that was still curled as it had been inside Karen. It was swaddled in white, the face a deep, unnatural blue. His hair was dark brown and there was a lot of it. His nose was flat and his lips an even deeper shade of blue. He was beautiful. I picked him up and kissed him on the forehead. Then I took him to his mother, pulling down her shroud and setting him gently on her chest. Her arms had already stiffened, but I managed to get them around him. I stepped back to take in the sight of them together. I kissed them both for the last time, and then I covered them carefully with the sheet.

When I opened the door, the group in the other room looked away, apart from Peter Sebastian. He stepped toward me, but he didn't make it in time.

I saw the floor approach rapidly. Then everything, even the pain in my heart, was gone.

Thirteen

The Soul Collector. Sara Robbins considered the name she had given herself the last time she had been in the U.K. It struck her now as ludicrously over the top, despite the fact that it had been a tribute to her brother, who had called himself the White Devil. She had been influenced by the occult back then. Not that she believed in any of the Satanic stuff, but her sister had. And Matt Wells had killed her, just as he'd been responsible for the White Devil's death. She would never forget that, no matter how much time passed or how much the circumstances changed—and no matter what her expensive Upper West Side shrink said.

She glanced around the chairs outside the Brooklyn Heights café. It was the kind of place that pandered to its customers by putting gas heaters on the terrace in winter, even on days like today, when the sun was bright and there wasn't much wind. A pair of well-dressed young women at the table in front of her discussed their boyfriends, listing their inadequacies and squealing with laughter. They both had leather laptop cases and were obviously in good jobs. Sara was tempted to lift one of the bags. When she had worked on a newspaper in London, she had often picked people's pockets on the Underground and slipped shop goods into her pocket—nothing major enough to be missed, but she was good at it, she never got caught and it was fun. The chaos that the loss of her laptop would bring to the airhead was delicious to imagine, but Sara decided against it. As ever, she was keeping a low profile.

In the years she'd been on the run, she had changed her name and appearance frequently, paying for the best hair and facial treatments, the best documentation and bureaucratic apparatus necessary to establish false identities. The wallet in her bag contained a New York State driver's license in the name of Colette Anne Olds, born Utica, 10/3/1971. The photo matched the way she looked: short blond hair, blue eyes (courtesy of contacts) and features that bore little resemblance to how she used to look. Her nose was thicker, her lips fuller and her cheekbones almost as prominent as Joni Mitchell's. If Matt Wells sat down at the table, she was certain he wouldn't recognize her, at least not immediately. She had worked on her voice as well, developing a New York accent bought and paid for. And the kicker—if necessary, she could change the way she looked with one visit to a luggage locker in Grand Central Station. The suitcase there contained wigs, a range of colored contact lenses and two changes of very different clothes.

As befitted the neighborhood, Sara/Colette was wearing boho chic—designer jeans, Manolo Blahniks and a vintage sheepskin jacket. The dark red beret she had found on the sidewalk—it was new and couldn't have been there long. When a ditzy-looking waitress with a bare belly and pierced navel emerged, she ordered another double espresso and looked up and down Montague Street. There was no sign of the man she was waiting for, but he was only a few minutes late. She picked up the newspaper she had been reading and turned to the story about Hitler's Hitman. There had been a feeding frenzy when the newspaper hacks convinced themselves that the deaths were connected and that, therefore, a serial killer was on the loose. The last murder, the good-looking professor in Philadelphia, was under the microscope. He had written about Mussolini in less than flattering terms. Did that means no academic specializing in extreme-right politics was safe? Dr. Jack had been a ladies' man, as confirmed by students and faculty members. Did the previous victims have significant sex lives? Research was ongoing. He had been killed ritualistically. According to what rite? No one was clear about that, but there was no shortage of so-called experts with opinions—certain tribes of American Indians had dispatched their victims that way; the Nazis treated traitors in such a fashion, an idea strengthened by the apparent presence of Nazi slogans and symbols, unconfirmed by the various police departments; the killer wasn't interested in politics, he was a zombie controlled by a powerful Voodoo priestess, proclaimed one supermarket tabloid.

Sara took a sip from the cup that the waitress had laid on the table with a fake smile. There were even a few reporters who had connected the murders to the Occult Killings in Washington at the beginning of the autumn. Much of it was imaginative guesswork. She knew for a fact, a costly fact, that the Justice Department had restricted the flow of information about those deaths. Still, she didn't know exactly how Matt Wells was involved in the Rothmann conspiracy, but his subsequent disappearance, and that of his partner Karen Oaten, suggested they were working with the FBI, not least because the Bureau had denied all knowledge of their whereabouts. From what she'd been able to discover, Heinz Rothmann was the son of a Nazi and he was committed to reviving the aberrant German ideology. That made him a major suspect for the recent killings.

'Hey, doll, is this seat taken?'

Sara watched as the thin, dark-skinned Hispanic slid down opposite her. 'You're late,' she said, frowning.

'My mother told me never to apologize.' The man smiled, displaying teeth even whiter than her costly crowns.

'I'll bet she did. Still, it could have been worse.'

He looked up from the menu. 'Meaning?'

She returned the smile, but hers was icy. 'I could have ripped your eyes out, Havi.'

Xavier Marias ran a shaky hand over his shaven head. 'Calm down, pretty lady.' He raised a hand to the waitress. 'Hey, over here. Margarita, no salt.'

'It's ten in the morning,' Sara observed.

'What do you expect? You scare me shitless.'

'Good.'

'What's this about, anyway?' He took his cell from a pocket in his tan leather jacket. 'I prefer to spend my Saturday mornings in bed with Elena.' He caught her gaze. 'I also prefer not to meet my clients in person. Even when they fail to carry out instructions.'

'Relax, Havi. We're just two friends chilling out.'

'Uh-huh.' He leaned forward. 'So, are you going to tell me?'

The Soul Collector smiled. 'Tell you what?'

He sighed. 'Why you didn't terminate your last commission.'

'Oh, that. Come on, Havi, it wasn't fair. The guy deserved a chance to make things right.'

'Are you out of your fucking mind? Have you any idea how much shit I've had to eat over this?'

'You're looking very good on it.'

'Ha. I ought to drop your ass in the river.'

'But you're not going to do that.'

The broker saw the change in her—suddenly his client was a wild animal ready to pounce. 'Eh, no. No, I'm not. But don't you ever pull a stunt like that again, okay?'

The Soul Collector held his gaze. 'Don't give me bullshit contracts again.'

Havi took a hit from the margarita that had been placed in front of him. 'Hey, are you okay? You look…I dunno…kind of shitty.'

'Why, thank you, good sir. Modesty prevents me saying how you look.'

There was an uneasy silence.

'Now what?' the Soul Collector said, her eyes on the gray water below.

'Now I go back to Elena and—' He broke off, his eyes wide. 'Jesus, woman, don't…do that.'

Under the table, she dug her fingernails harder into the denim above his knee. 'Give me another job. Now.'

The broker wiped sweat from his brow. 'All right,' he said, in a loud whisper. 'Let me go.'

The Soul Collector squeezed hard once more and then sat back. 'I'm all ears.'

'All fuckin' fingers, you mean,' Havi muttered, taking an envelope from his pocket. 'I don't know what you're so fired up about. I got you what you wanted.'

His client opened the envelope and ran her eyes over the sheet of paper inside. 'Well, well,' she said. 'Not before time.' She looked up and smiled. 'Thank you, Havi. As so often, a pleasure to do business with you.' She got up and left without looking back.

Xavier Marias drained the rest of his margarita and called urgently for another.

I woke up feeling like I'd been run over by a tank. I sat up, my mind in a swirl. Then I remembered what I'd seen on the mortuary tables—the inert remains of my family—and realized I was a lot worse off than an accident victim. For a start, I was still alive.

I looked around the room, taking in the hospital fitments and plain décor. There was nothing I could use to self-harm, unless I twisted the sheets and hanged myself. That wasn't such a bad idea. I got up, my knees almost giving way, and started to pull off the bedding. I had only got as far as the top sheet when the door opened and a big guy came in.

'Put it down,' he ordered.

I thought about that, then launched myself at him. I had a flash of doing combat training with a tall soldier, but whatever drugs I was on had seriously compromised my skills. The gorilla grabbed my wrists in one hand, spun me round and pushed me back to the bed.

'I can give you another sedative, Mr. Wells.'

I looked round. Colonel Jimson had come in. Behind him, a male nurse was holding a metal tray, on which lay a full syringe.

'But I don't think you really want that,' the medic continued.

He was right. They had me cold, no matter what I tried to do. I relaxed and the auxiliary let me go. I sat down amongst the demolished bedding and lowered my head. Karen and Magnus weren't there anymore. I couldn't see them. That was some kind of relief, but I immediately felt guilty.

'Would you like something to eat?' Jimson asked.

Initially, the idea of eating seemed so trivial, so irrelevant given what had happened, that I almost laughed. Then I realized that I was ravenous.

'Bacon and sausages,' I said, swallowing a rush of saliva. 'Scrambled eggs, toast, coffee.'

The doctor nodded to the male nurse, who walked out. 'The drugs have that effect. Apart from that, how are you feeling?'

'How do you think?'

He glanced at the soldier, who was still near the bed. 'All right, Corporal, you can go.'

When we were alone, Jimson came closer. 'Are you up to receiving visitors? Mr. Sebastian told me to inform him the second you were awake.'

I looked at him. It seemed not all military men were by-the-book assholes.

Then again, remembering my trainer's name, Quincy Jerome, I realized I already knew that. 'Thanks. I appreciate it. I want to see him, too.'

'Okay. Have your breakfast first.'

I did and, to my surprise, I felt better after it. Then I was stricken by remorse again. Karen and our son were dead and all I cared about was filling my stomach. Human beings were nothing more than animals.

Actually, they were much worse. Animals didn't experiment on each other. Animals killed to eat, not for specious religions and ideologies. Animals weren't immoral and malevolent.

Peter Sebastian came in and expressed his sympathy. If I hadn't suspected that he was a highly devious operator, I'd have bought his performance. It wasn't that he didn't feel sympathy, I knew that. But I also knew he had other reasons to see me. That didn't bother me—in fact, it could work to my advantage.

'Food okay?' he asked, inclining his head toward the tray.

'You think that matters right now?'

'I imagine not. Christ, Matt, it's an awful thing.'

'It's down to Rothmann, isn't it?' I said, clenching my fists without thinking about it.

'It's too early to say. The pathologist is—' He broke off, suddenly ill at ease.

'I know what he's doing,' I said, with more bravado than I felt. Fortunately Karen and Magnus didn't appear before me. 'Is Rivers working on it, too?'

Sebastian nodded. 'And Dr. Brown. I gather her process was effective.'

'So they said. Let's hope it put paid to the Rothmanns' shit once and for all.'

'Yes.'

The way he was looking at me made me suspicious. 'What's going on? What are you keeping from me?'

'Nothing, Matt,' he said, a shade too quickly.

'What's going on? You're working some scheme, aren't you?'

'It's…it's a bit unusual,' he said, with an unusual lack of confidence.

'You're going to let me out, aren't you? All the training I've been doing, the extra sessions with Rivers, Dr. Brown's process. What's the catch?'

'I don't know if it is a catch, judging by what you said earlier.' He was more composed now, back on home ground. 'We want you to find Heinz Rothmann.'

I had to laugh, though I wasn't even mildly amused. 'That would be the Heinz Rothmann who tried to turn me into a killer? The Rothmann whose sister I killed and who would like to cut me to pieces in return?'

He nodded. 'Yes, that same Heinz Rothmann whose conditioning program may have robbed you of Karen and your son.'

'Despite the fact we were assured by you people that it wouldn't affect them.' I blinked hard before going on. 'I used to write crime novels, remember? What's important is the characters' motivation. Why has the FBI changed its story on Karen's pregnancy risks and become suddenly so keen on finding that German piece of shit?'

'Actually, he has an American passport,' Sebastian said, like a teacher correcting a pupil.

'Maybe he does, but that doesn't mean shit.'

'In any case, your question is besides the point. The Bureau has been looking for Rothmann ever since he disappeared.'

'Uh-huh. You wouldn't recently have come to the conclusion that he's behind these Hitler's Hitman murders, would you?'

'Obviously the presence of his confederate Gordy Lister at the scene in Philadelphia was suggestive.' He smiled slackly. 'Good catch, by the way.'

'Your people would have got it when they went over the footage.'

'I wish I had your faith.'

'Any further sign of Lister?'

'No. We've circulated details to the investigating teams at the other locations, but there have been no positive hits.'

I went over to the wardrobe.

'What are you doing?' Sebastian asked.

'Getting dressed. I want to be out of the camp today.'

There was a pause. 'Matt, I've no idea how long this might last. What do you want to do about...'

I stopped fastening my shirt buttons. 'About Karen and Magnus? Nothing for the time being. Can...can they be kept here?'

'I imagine so. But what about the funerals?'

'That's what I'm saying to you, Peter. Afterward. Until I nail Rothmann, I can't think about that.' I pulled on my jacket and turned to face him. 'You haven't asked about my terms.'

He raised an eyebrow. 'You tried to kill the President and you've got terms?'

'Fucking right I have,' I said, losing my cool. 'I want a lawyer. Right now!'

Sebastian stepped back as if I'd spat in his face.

'Just kidding,' I said, without a trace of a smile. 'Sergeant Quincy Jerome. I want him to watch my back.'

'But he's regular army.'

'Fix it. You weren't planning on putting Arthur Bimsdale on that detail with Sara Robbins out there, were you?'

He shook his head vaguely. 'Is that it?'

'I'll need to be armed.'

'Even with the sergeant in tow?'

'Yes. Fix that, too.' I headed for the door. 'I have things to pick up from the apartment.'

'Matt,' Sebastian said, 'Wait.' He was fumbling in his jacket pocket. 'I got this for you. I understand you might not want it now....'

I opened the blue velvet box and looked at the ring.

'Platinum and three diamonds,' he said. 'As per instructions.'

'It's good. But you keep it 'til this is over.' I managed to suppress the tears until I had passed him.

Fourteen

Dr. Lester Rivers wasn't the kind of man who hit things when he was angry, but the conference room table nearly received a pounding.

'No, Mr. Sebastian, this is not acceptable. I cannot agree.'

The FBI man stared at him stonily. 'Your professional opinion is noted, Doctor,' he said. His hands stayed away from the open laptop in front of him.

Rivers noticed that and wondered exactly what was going on. The Bureau paid his salary and funded his research center, but he had never been treated like a junior employee before. Usually a team of scientific officers reviewed his work and the atmosphere on their visits was cordial. Copious notes were taken and he was later sent copies of their reports. But ever since Matt Wells and his unfortunate partner had arrived, Peter Sebastian had run the show, despite the fact that he was a violent crime investigation specialist, not a scientist. Many things, it seemed, weren't written down.

'Mr. Sebastian,' Rivers said, glancing across the table at Alexandra Brown. 'My work with Matt Wells has shown that the conditioning he underwent was complex and profound. Although we have been able to access many of the trigger sequences, it is very likely that he is still subject to control.'

Sebastian raised a hand. 'You used the word *we*, Doctor. Let me bring in Dr. Brown at this point.' He turned to the female scientist. 'What's your feeling about releasing Wells?'

Alexandra Brown kept her eyes off Rivers. 'Extrapolation from trials suggests that my process has been highly effective. I consider the Rothmann conditioning no longer operational.'

This time Rivers did bring his hand down hard on the table. 'Extrapolation from trials? Wells was the first human subject you treated. You can't extrapolate from rats and monkeys or computer simulations. Besides, you were brought in here over my head.'

'Yes. By me,' Sebastian said firmly. 'Dr. Brown's work has been well received by other scientists.'

'But its long-term effects are unknown,' Rivers countered. 'What if there are triggers at a deeper level of Wells's subconscious? He might turn into an even more deadly killer.' He glared at the FBI man. 'And recently you've allowed him to sharpen his combat and firearms skills, again without my approval.'

Peter Sebastian stood up and closed his laptop. 'Your approval was not necessary, Doctor. I am responsible for Wells.' He turned to go.

'I don't suppose you're at all concerned about his state of mind after the death of Karen Oaten and the baby. Grief and the associated emotions can have a major effect on rationality.'

'On the other hand,' Dr. Brown put in, 'it can increase

empathy and certain forms of acuity, which may actually enhance the subject's efficacy.'

'Will you listen to yourself, woman?' Rivers scoffed. 'This is a distressed human being we're talking about, not some automaton.'

Spots of red appeared on Alexandra Brown's cheeks. She looked to Sebastian for support.

'Please calm yourself, Dr. Rivers,' the FBI man said. 'That kind of language is inappropriate.'

'Is it?' the scientist shouted. 'Well, try this for size. I'm going to send a formal complaint about your handling of Matt Wells to the Office of Professional Responsibility.'

Peter Sebastian sighed and walked back to the table. He opened his laptop and tapped on the keys. 'Please come here,' he said, eyeing each of the scientists. When they stood on either side of him, he hit the keys again. 'This is a confidential authorization. You are at liberty to check its authenticity by calling headquarters and quoting the reference number at the top.' He gave a tight smile. 'You understand there may be disciplinary consequences if you do so?'

Doctors Rivers and Brown read the document in silence, the document that authorized Sebastian to determine the status of Matthew Wells as he saw fit, signed by the Director of the FBI.

I was lying on the sofa in the apartment, my face buried in the cushions. Karen's scent was still on them. I breathed it in over and over again. Then I caught a glimpse of her. She had her back to me and was wearing a white surgical gown. She was in a narrow passage and she started to move downward, the lower part of her body disappearing.

I heard myself call her name and she stopped. When she turned, I could see that she was carrying a bundle in both arms. It, too, was shrouded in white. Our son. Karen looked at me sadly but she didn't speak—she had lost that ability, it seemed. Then she continued walking and was gone.

Great sobs tore from my chest. I tried to stifle them with a cushion, wishing that I could find my way back to them, the ones who had been taken from me. Then I saw another face—the imperious features of the Nazi, Heinz Rothmann. The implication was clear. I had to kill him to get Karen and Magnus back.

'Hey, my friend.' The soft voice took me by surprise and I raised myself from the sofa.

'Quincy.' I wiped my eyes with my arm. 'I'm sorry…'

'Don't be, man,' he said, coming up to me and putting his arm round my shoulders. 'Jesus, you must be suffering.'

I felt the need to sit on the sofa again to maintain that last link with Karen. I couldn't speak for a while.

'What's this I'm hearing? They're letting you out?'

I nodded.

'You're gonna work?'

'There isn't anything to keep me…keep me here.'

Quincy Jerome squatted in front of me. 'You need to take it easy, my friend. Let it sink in. Come to terms.'

I appreciated his words, but they were meaningless. I had a mission. Peter Sebastian might have thought he was going to use me, but he had that wrong. I was going to take him for all he was worth.

'Listen, Quincy, I don't know how much you've been told about—'

'Jack shit,' he interrupted. 'All I know is you want me to watch your back. Which is fine by me, even if my CO's ass is on fire about it. Your man Sebastian has friends in high places.'

'I don't think he's got friends anywhere, but he gets the job done.' I filled him in on Rothmann and his probable link to the Hitler's Hitman killings. He'd picked up a fair amount about the latter from the media coverage. 'I've got to do this, Quincy,' I ended. 'For...for Karen and our son.'

'Count me in, my friend.'

'It'll probably be bloody.'

'Sounds like that Nazi asshole deserves to lose every drop of his blood.'

He was right about that. I got up and started to collect clothes and other stuff. I took the laptop, too. It had a wireless connection, which would be useful. Now all I needed was weapons. I mentioned that to Quincy.

'I was told to go to the armory,' he said, unzipping one of his bags.

'Hey,' I said, belatedly realizing what was different about him. 'You're not in uniform.'

'That's what I was told,' he said, running his large hands over the black clothes he was wearing.

'You look like a special forces operative.'

'Don't complain. I've got more of the same in your size.'

It seemed Sebastian had thought of everything. Quincy started laying out weapons on the table. There was a Glock 19 semiautomatic pistol, a combat knife in a sheath, a pair of vicious-looking brass knuckles and a length of plastic-covered wire with a loop at each end.

'I've never used a garrote,' I said, picking it up.

'It's simple,' the sergeant said, taking it out of my hands and whipping it round my neck before I could move. 'See what I mean?'

I could have buried my elbow in his belly, but I wasn't up to brawling. My legs were still unsteady from the sedatives.

When he'd removed the garrote, I went back to the table and picked up the Glock. 'Where are the clips?'

'I've got them. They told me not to hand them over to you till we're out of the camp.'

'Come on, Quincy. I'm not going to shoot anyone.'

He studied me thoughtfully. 'I reckon they're worried about suicide.'

'After what I told you about Rothmann? I'm going to kill that fucker. What happens after that, I don't know.'

Quincy took a clip from his pocket. 'All right, man. Just don't get me busted.'

I checked that it was full and slapped it in.

There was a knock on the door. It opened before I could say anything.

Peter Sebastian walked in and immediately focused on the Glock. 'I hope that isn't loaded, Sergeant.'

'No, sir,' Quincy replied.

Sebastian accepted that. I put the pistol in my belt and started gathering up the other weapons.

'Thanks for having the tracking cuff taken off my ankle,' I said.

'No problem.'

'You haven't planted a bug under my skin, have you?' Rothmann's people had done that in the Maine camp.

Sebastian shook his head. 'Listen, Jerome, we need to stop using ranks when we address each other. I don't want us to stick out like cocks in a Hamburg nightclub.'

Quincy and I exchanged glances.

'My friends call me Quincy,' the soldier said.

'Do they?' Sebastian's tone made it clear he didn't see himself as one of them. 'Those fatigues won't exactly do for undercover work.'

Quincy shrugged. 'I figured you'd be taking us to the mall.'

Sebastian ignored that. 'Are you ready to go, Matt?'

'Just about. Can you get Special Agent Simms to box up what's left?'

He nodded. 'All right, let's hit the world outside.'

Before I went, I passed by the hi-fi and picked up the CD Karen and I had listened to. Our son would have heard Monteverdi's *Orfeo,* too. I wasn't going to leave that behind.

Mikey Lister was in seventh heaven. Not only had the hooker brought the grass he'd asked for, but she was a stunner—Cuban, a beautiful deep bronze color, and a rack to stop the traffic. She said she was called Lucky, but he didn't believe that for a second. After this, he was going to take that nickname himself.

She was in the shower now, so Mikey went through her clutch bag. There wasn't much in it—some keys, cigarettes, condoms, gum. There was a man's billfold containing over five hundred dollars and a credit card in the name of L. Sanchez. Maybe she was called Lucky

after all. He thought about lifting a couple of the fifties
he'd given her, but decided against it. His brother Gordy
had stepped up to the plate recently and, for the first
time in his life, his bank account was healthy. Maybe
losing his pins hadn't been so bad after all. His smarmy
shit-sucker of a lawyer had nailed the driver who had
hit him for major damages. So a hooker a week was no
big deal anymore.

Then again, he thought, looking at the uneven stumps
that protruded from his boxers, he was stuck in the chair
till he croaked. He did an hour on crutches every day,
but they made his arms hurt. Artificial legs were out
of the question. He had too little of the real ones left.
At least Lucky didn't mind. Some of the girls could
hardly disguise their horror. That made him so mad that
he made them blow him, so the bitches' faces were up
close and personal with the stumps.

'I leave now,' said Lucky, emerging from the bathroom in the least clothing that the cops would let her get
away with on the street. Girls in the Tallahassee area
weren't what Mikey would call shy and retiring when
it came to what they wore, but this one beat them all.

'See ya, doll,' he said, sticking his finger between
her legs.

She slapped his arm. 'We finished now, doll.'

Mikey Lister watched her go. Had she just given him
attitude? He pushed the wheel toward the door and got
there before it slammed behind her. He grabbed the
golf club he kept for emergencies and rolled down the
driveway.

'Hey, Castro quim, get a load of this!' he yelled,
closing on her spectacular rear.

Lucía Sanchez sidestepped the chair and Mikey

trundled past, bouncing onto the road. 'Get back here, bitch!' he yelled, swinging the club.

'Screw you, gimp!' she screamed back, as she got into her scarlet Bonneville.

Mikey watched her accelerate away, still in the middle of the street. He looked around, but there was no one outside. Just as well, he thought. He wasn't in the mood for whining from his tight-assed neighbors. About thirty yards away he saw a dark blue Crown Vic that looked familiar. Was it the same one that had been across the road from his place yesterday? Was he being watched?

He pushed the chair to the side of the road and thought about that. He didn't know what Gordy was up to these days, but it sure wasn't legal. He didn't have that paper job anymore and he'd begun calling from different places each week. He'd also told Mikey not to talk about him, not that he did. Mikey had always thought Gordy was a pathetic runt and he'd given him hell when they were kids. Maybe Gordy had someone watching him to make sure the cops weren't doing surveillance, too. Screw that.

Mikey Lister set off down the street, the golf club across his thighs.

'Hey, peeper,' he shouted, 'you want some of this?' As he got nearer, he saw the driver's head rise from the back of the seat and heard the engine start. 'Yeah, that's right, get the fuck outta here!'

The Crown Vic pulled away, leaving Mikey in the middle of the road. He stayed there until it turned the corner and disappeared.

'Yeah, Mikey,' he said. 'Way to go!' Maneuvering the chair, he pushed himself back toward the driveway of his building. The sun was beating down on the back of his neck and he could hear the cry of seagulls in the distance. Some place, he thought. Sunshine in the middle of winter. It sure beat the shit out of Oklahoma.

The pickup that had turned into the street ahead of him had large chrome bull bars. Mikey pulled into the side and gave it the benefit of his professional eye. 'Nissan Frontier,' he said to himself. '2003 or 4. Those bars are new, though. Hey, is that a woman driving? Come on, bitch, take off your cap.' He imitated the action.

The blonde obliged. Her hair was short and she looked good. Then she jerked the wheel to the right and floored the gas pedal.

Mikey Lister flew out of his wheelchair and headfirst into the trunk of a nearby palm tree. The last thing he saw was the set of the woman's lips. It looked like she was in pain.

Fifteen

Peter Sebastian drove us to the airport outside a town called Rockford. Quincy Jerome and I were in the back of the SUV. I looked out through tinted windows at the world I'd been excluded from for what seemed like years. It was icy cold and there were few people around. The exhaust fumes from vehicles hung in the air like ghosts unable to take corporeal form. Northern Illinois did not look in any way inviting.

'If you don't mind me asking,' Quincy said, 'what's the plan?'

I flexed my fingers. 'We find Heinz Rothmann and I get rid of him.'

Peter Sebastian glanced into the mirror. 'Partially correct. We need to find Rothmann, but I want him brought in, like any other felon.'

'So I'm an officer of the law now, am I?' I asked ironically.

'But if you have to use extreme force to defend yourself,' the FBI man continued, 'then so be it.'

'Uh-huh,' Quincy said. 'That applies to me as well, does it?'

'You're a soldier,' Sebastian said. 'You're trained to fire back if you're attacked, no?'

'You sure this is aboveboard?' the sergeant asked. 'I don't want to find myself in a court accused of murder.'

'Not going to happen,' Sebastian said emphatically. 'As for legitimacy, I can show you an authorization signed by the Director of the FBI.'

'Maybe later,' Quincy said, glancing at me.

I didn't respond to his look. All I cared about was nailing Rothmann.

'Where are we going?' I asked, as we arrived at the airport.

'D.C.,' Sebastian replied, showing ID at a gate. 'I want to review the murders. Then we'll come up with a detailed plan.'

I didn't buy that. The FBI's head of violent crime was about the most structured person I'd ever met. We wouldn't just come up with a plan, he'd have several carefully structured strategies already.

We were waved past the terminal building and through a gate in the security fence. Sebastian drove into a hangar and stopped next to an executive jet.

Quincy Jerome let out a low whistle. 'Cool. Never been on one of these babies.'

Neither had I, but I didn't feel any exhilaration. It was like my emotions had been streamlined—everything was directed toward finding Rothmann.

A few minutes later, we were in the air and arcing upward through a thick cloud cover. Quincy had his eyes glued to the porthole, until a tray of food arrived from the galley. When Sebastian sat down opposite me, I leaned forward and spoke to him in a low voice.

'I presume you've publicized the fact that I'm in circulation.'

He shook his head. 'We're not telling the media anything as that would provoke a feeding frenzy. But we will pass the word to some of our informers in the criminal underworld.'

'So I'm the bait.' I gave him a cold smile. 'Don't worry, I can see the attractions of that idea. But what if he doesn't come after me?'

'You killed his beloved twin sister, Matt. Trust me, he's going to come after you.'

I sat back. 'So why are we going to D.C.? Why don't we go somewhere easier for him to target?'

Sebastian thought about that. 'Got a suggestion?'

'I have, actually. You remember Mary Upson?'

'The woman who got you out of Maine.' His memory was as sharp as I had expected. 'Her mother was involved with the Antichurch of Lucifer Triumphant.'

'Correct. Maybe we can kill two birds with one stone. You can interrogate the old woman about the cult and I can find out what Mary.didn't tell me.'

'They were both interviewed at length after the cathedral massacre. The mother denied any involvement with either the Antichurch or Rothmann. Besides, your relationship with Mary Upson didn't exactly end happily, Matt.'

'True. I'll try to make it up to her.' The fact was, I was in pure manipulation mode. Rothmann would have been proud.

Sebastian looked up from the notes he was making. 'How do we let Rothmann know where you are?'

'We won't have to. If you give Mary's mother a chance, she'll find a way to get in touch with him.'

'Smart, Matt. Okay, I'll talk to the Maine State Police and find out if the women are still living there.'

'Sparta, that was the name of the town.' It was the first place I'd reached after I escaped from the Roth-manns' camp.

'I know,' he said testily. 'I went there to catch you.'

I watched him as he went to the front of the cabin and picked up the phone.

'I haven't been to Washington since I was a kid,' Quincy Jerome said, taking Sebastian's seat.

'Don't hold your breath, big man. We're rerouting.'

'Where to?'

'Probably Maine.'

'At this time of year? Shee-it.'

'Even worse than Illinois, eh?'

'You know where I'm from?' he said, shaking his head. 'Mobile, Alabama. That's about as different from Maine as you get.'

'I'll take your word for it.' I feigned exhaustion and closed my eyes. I didn't feel like talking. I liked Quincy, but often he made me laugh and I didn't want to do that anymore. I tried to think of Karen and our son, but they wouldn't come to me. My memory seemed to be working fine when it came to other things, but their faces—even Karen's—had gone. If this was what grief did to you, I could do without it. I wanted to see them and weep.

'Matt?'

My shoulder was shaken and I snapped awake.

'You've been out for over an hour,' Peter Sebastian said. 'Mary Upson and her mother—'

'Nora Jacobsen.'

He nodded. 'They've moved to Portland—Maine.

Not Oregon, fortunately. We should be there in an hour and a quarter.'

'You realize there's a serious drawback to this plan,' I said, after I'd gulped down a bottle of water.

'What's that?'

'Sara Robbins.'

Sebastian studied me impassively. 'She'll see that you've been released, sure. But how could she know you're in Portland?'

'Trust me, she'll find out. It wouldn't even surprise me if she was working for Rothmann.'

'Then we really will kill two birds with one stone.'

Quincy Jerome leaned across the aisle. 'Who's Sara Robbins?'

'You do *not* want to know,' I replied. 'On second thoughts, you have to know.'

By the time I'd finished telling him about the Soul Collector, we had almost reached Portland.

Abaddon had been given that name by her brother. As far as she was concerned, that was who she was. The family was from Atlanta, but she had lived in St. Louis for the last five years, mainly because it was centrally located and had good flight connections. She often worked on both east and west coasts, as well as plenty of places in between, so a hub was essential.

She looked out of the window in the roof of the converted warehouse in Laclede's Landing. The apartment had been an expensive buy because the area was a historic district, but that hadn't been a problem. She liked the view of the Mississippi, the pair of bridges on one side and the open space around the Jefferson National Expansion Memorial on the other. She wasn't so keen on the 630-foot-high Gateway Arch. Modern architecture and art didn't cut it for her, and the stainless steel parabola always struck her as a monument to American vanity.

Abaddon broke a couple of eggs into a glass, added salt, pepper and Tabasco, and drank them down. That would keep her going till dinner, which she would eat at Connolly's, an Irish pub that did great burgers and stews. Tonight she was celebrating. Connolly's was a young people's hangout and if she was lucky she would find a willing guy. She corrected herself. Luck had nothing to do with it. Although she was forty, she kept herself in good shape and her hair was still black as ravens' feathers. A man she lived with for three weeks—the most she'd ever managed—had told her that she had witchy looks. She reckoned he was right. She'd inherited her father's dark hair and complexion, as well as other attributes. The genes behind her mother's meekness and mousy hair had been outmuscled in a big way.

The only problem about St. Louis was that she wasn't close to the Antichurch down south. Sometimes she managed to attend rituals on the way to and from jobs; other times she flew down specially. She didn't make it every week, but she'd been given a dispensation. As long as she was there at least once a fortnight her soul remained bound to Lucifer. She couldn't imagine life without that. Then again, she hadn't been able to conceive of life without the old man until the catastrophe happened. The family had been devastated, but had managed to keep the Antichurch going, despite the efforts of the heretic. Abaddon had done what she could to avenge the lost faithful, but the enemy had always been untouchable.

Now, at last, the time had come. True, Abaddon had to do things the way her employer wanted, but that wasn't a problem. She would do anything to get a shot at the heretic, kill anyone and never count the cost. It was what she lived for, what she wanted more than anything in the world. And she knew that the great god beneath the earth was on her side. There was nothing worse than a traitor. Now the enemy would pay for his sins against the Antigospel of Lucifer.

Abaddon opened her laptop and checked her employer's secure site. Apparently Matt Wells had been released by the Feds. He could lead them to the enemy, but first she was to deal with someone else. The woman who stared out at her from the blurred photograph had short blond hair and prominent cheekbones, and she looked to be in good physical condition. As she read through the file, she felt the tingle throughout her body that always came when she was put up against a worthy opponent. This target was nothing less than a demon. She had killed at least fifty-six people, and those were only the confirmed victims— it was estimated that she was responsible for dozens of other deaths, in the U.S. and abroad. Her original name had been Sara Robbins, but later she was known as the Soul Collector. Her brother had been a vicious serial killer. Even more interesting, she had been Matt Wells's lover. Nobody seemed to know her current name. Finding her was the first part of the job. The second was to take her out.

She looked toward the Gateway Arch, glinting red in the late afternoon sun, and smiled. This was going to be some contest. Abaddon versus the Soul Collector. The angel of the pit versus the killer who culled spirits.

Assassin versus assassin. Pro versus pro. There could be only one winner. The heretic might even get caught in the cross fire.

We were in an office borrowed from the Maine state cops on the outskirts of Portland. Peter Sebastian had just finished with the major in charge, making it clear that the FBI was boss now. While he was doing that, I caught the news on a TV high up in the corner. There was more about climate change than I remembered before we'd been cut off from all news media in the camp. There was a high-profile gathering of international leaders at the UN in ten days and special correspondents were stressing how important it was that progress be made on the issue.

Quincy Jerome sat at the conference table, looking like a fish who wished he was back in the water. In the past I'd have kept him company, but I didn't have the urge anymore. There was a job to be done and being friendly was irrelevant. Besides, he'd been taken aback by what I told him about Sara. Soldiers didn't expect to be attacked by attractive women. I made sure he had no illusions—she would pick up my trail, it was only a question of time. But I found that I didn't care anymore. Nailing Rothmann was all that mattered.

Sebastian came over. 'I've got surveillance on the Jacobsen house. Both she and Mary Upson are there.'

I stood up. 'Let's go then.'

'Not yet. I'm waiting for some essential material from D.C. We'll interview them tomorrow morning. They aren't going anywhere.'

I looked at him doubtfully. 'You'd better hope they aren't. They're our only leads.'

'Apart from Gordy Lister. Look at this.' He handed me a printout.

'Jesus, this came in hours ago. How come you only got it now?'

Sebastian pursed his mouth. 'I didn't. I was informed this morning. I thought you had enough going on.'

I glared at him. 'Don't do that again. I'm the tethered goat here. I need to know what's happening.' Sebastian nodded, so I went back to the paper. 'This Mikey Lister was what? Gordy's brother?'

'Yes. I'm embarrassed to say that our Jacksonville field office had him under surveillance, near Tallahassee. I thought Gordy might show up there after we spotted him in Philadelphia. The hit-and-run driver was gone before our people could react. There will be disciplinary proceedings.'

'"No witnesses,"' I read. 'In broad daylight?'

'Apparently.'

Quincy Jerome stirred. 'Are you sure it was an accident?'

'Of course not.'

'Who would have wanted him dead?' I asked.

'I don't know.'

'Maybe someone else trying to find Rothmann thought Gordy's brother might be able to help,' I suggested.

'So why kill him?' Quincy asked.

Sebastian and I exchanged glances.

'You'll learn a lot if you pay attention, Sergeant,' the FBI man said, shaking his head.

'I thought we were done with ranks,' Quincy countered.

That almost made me smile. Then the door opened

and Special Agent Bimsdale appeared, carrying a couple of heavy bags.

'There you are,' Sebastian said. 'Have you got the insertion tools?'

The little man nodded and started unpacking his bags on the table. He handed a couple of long, thin boxes to his boss.

'Right, gentlemen,' Sebastian said, with a tight smile. 'Arm or leg?'

'I'm a leg man myself,' Quincy said, grinning. Then his eyes opened wide. 'Just what the hell is that?'

Sebastian had stripped the wrapping from an evil-looking, stainless steel probe. 'Surely you didn't think we were going to abandon you? There's a GPS implant and signaling system in each of these.' He stepped toward Quincy. 'Come on, pull up your pant leg.'

I watched as the big man obliged. Bimsdale swabbed a patch of his calf, then Sebastian pressed the button on the insertion tool. Quincy blinked once.

'Didn't hurt then?' I said, rolling up my shirtsleeve.

'You kidding? Hurt like hell.' Quincy Jerome smiled. 'But I got no problem with pain.'

I didn't enjoy the next five seconds.

Sixteen

Sara Robbins was in her apartment in Brooklyn, looking at the screen of her laptop. She spent a lot of time
doing that on the days when work didn't call her away.
The flight from Miami had arrived at 6:00 p.m. Since
getting home, she'd been after him. Sometimes she felt
like she was looking for a needle in a very large hay-
stack, but she had made herself keep the faith. The
systems she used were state-of-the-art and Matt Wells
wouldn't stay out of sight forever.

As the computer ran the complex algorithms, she
found herself thinking about the hit in Florida. She
hadn't been told the target's name, only his address
and a description. The fact that he was in a wheelchair made him hard to miss, but she'd covered herself
all the same. Killing people without identities wasn't
something the Soul Collector did. Havi was unaware
of that—there was no reason he should know she was
so fastidious. It hadn't taken her long to find out the
target's name. It was on the rental agreement for the
condo. Then she had run into problems—no one of
that name and description had been treated for serious

spinal or leg injuries anywhere in the U.S. in the last five years. She sent the photo to a seriously expensive identity recognition site that had been set up by a geek who had hacked into every archive bank he could and bingo, there he was—Michael Anderson Lister, born Oklahoma City, 3/12/1978, electrician, with an address outside his birthplace. According to his health insurer, he had shattered both legs in a car accident nearly thirteen months ago and had undergone extensive surgery and rehabilitation, the latter being withdrawn after it became clear that prosthetic limbs were not an option. There was no record of criminal activity and no connection to ongoing investigations. That had been enough to satisfy her and she had left to carry out the hit.

And now everything had changed. The word among the informants she paid was that Matt Wells had been released from FBI custody. Now she had to find him. The formulas continued to check local law enforcement sites around the country, as monitored by her network of hackers. Some of them could get into the FBI's system, too, but she had found that wasn't worth it, as the encryption codes took too long to decipher and illicit access was spotted quickly. State police sites were much less secure, and they also provided up-to-the-minute information. If the FBI took Matt out of lockdown, the likelihood was they would be using him to find Heinz Rothmann, given the murders going down. If they took him to any of the scenes, local law enforcement would be involved and, if she was lucky, some eagle scout would note his presence, not least because anything the FBI did in other people's jurisdictions tended to be logged in detail.

She sat back and watched the streams of data tumble down the screen. If there was a match within the parameters she'd entered, the flow would stop and the machine would ping like a microwave that had incinerated dinner. So far, it had been as silent as her conscience. That set her back to thinking about the man she'd killed in Florida. Lister. There was something familiar about the surname. She booted up her older laptop and inserted a memory stick—it held everything she had found about Matt Wells's involvement in the Washington Occult Killings and the subsequent massacre in the National Cathedral. Within five seconds, she had a match.

According to Washington D.C. Metro Police records, Gordon David Lister had held a senior post at the *Star Reporter,* a supermarket tabloid, and had disappeared after Jack Thomson, owner of the paper and son of Nazi doctor Nikolaus Rothmann, had vanished from his cabin cruiser on the Anacostia River.

The Soul Collector ran another check and confirmed that Gordon Lister was the brother of the man she'd killed in Florida. What she wanted to know now was, who had ordered the hit? Predictably, Havi wouldn't tell her, saying only that her next job was on the secure site they used. But she could see no reason for Rothmann to have done away with his accomplice's sibling. It was much more likely that someone was putting the squeeze on Rothmann himself. But who?

A loud ping came from her laptop. She turned back to it and looked at a small section of print ringed in red. It was part of an internal memorandum written by a Major Hexton of the Maine State Police in Portland.

In a group led by FBI violent crime Director Peter Sebastian was one Matthew John Wells, holder of British
passport number...

Sara turned off the computers and put the laptop in
the carry-on bag that she had permanently packed. The
plastic switchblade was in her underwear. She was out
of the door in less than three minutes. For once, she
welcomed the pain that pulsed and clenched across her
upper back. It would keep her mind on the job.

We had dinner on the outskirts of Portland. The diner
was obviously a law enforcement haunt as nobody was
perturbed when a uniformed cop came in and started
whispering in Peter Sebastian's ear. There was insignia
on his shoulders and a badge identifying him as Major
Jake Hexton. I nudged Quincy Jerome. Major Hexton
looked decidedly warm under the collar.

The FBI man turned to us. 'We're leaving.'

'Haven't had dessert yet,' Quincy muttered.

'What's going on?' I asked.

'Nora Jacobsen's on the move,' Sebastian said. He got
into the major's car. Quincy and I piled into the back,
which meant that Arthur Bimsdale was crushed against
the door. He bore the position without complaint.

We drove for about ten minutes, through the lights of
the city at first and then down narrow roads with only
occasional houses on either side. Major Hexton drove
skillfully, talking frequently on the radio. He killed his
lights before coming to a halt about fifty yards from a
low building with a single light outside.

'Whose place is this?' Sebastian asked.

'Isaac Morton is the registered owner,' the major replied, 'but he's been in an old folks' home for a year now.'

I recognized the green pickup parked outside. Nora Jacobsen had lent it to her daughter and me after my escape from the camp.

'Did Nora know this Morton?' I asked.

The policeman looked round at me and nodded. 'They used to keep company.'

Sebastian and I had the same thought.

'Special Agent Bimsdale?' he said.

'Yes, sir, I'm calling it up.' The young man next to me tapped the keys of a small computer. 'No, sir, there's no record of Isaac Morton being a member of the Antichurch.'

Hexton stared at Sebastian.

'Don't ask,' said the Fed.

I didn't have to. I knew that Nora Jacobsen had links with the Antichurch, though under interrogation she had claimed that she had joined when it was little more than a Maine folk memory and had left it years earlier. According to her, it had been a social club for misfits, rather than the full-blown cult Rothmann used to add force to his indoctrination plan.

'Look,' Quincy said.

Nora Jacobsen had come out of the building, which looked more like a barn than a house, and was carrying a large bag to the pickup.

The radio clicked. 'Shall we intercept?' came a trooper's voice.

'Negative,' the major replied. 'Stay on her tail.'

'You might want to tell them she can handle a shotgun,' I said, recalling my first encounter with the woman.

'My men are experienced.'

'Let's take a look inside,' Sebastian said, after Nora Jacobsen had driven off.

'We don't have a warrant.'

Sebastian looked round, his eyes glinting in the light from the dashboard. 'Major, this is a high-priority investigation. I will take responsibility.'

Hexton decided against arguing. We got out and headed for the door. Sebastian pointed Bimsdale to the door. To my surprise, the baby-faced agent jimmied the door in a few seconds.

'Was that legal?' Quincy said, under his breath.

I shrugged. 'Define your terms.' I watched as he drew his pistol and let him go ahead of me.

The interior lights came on. I was right about it being a barn—although there was an iron bed frame in one corner, the rest of the place was divided into stalls, the timber bent and cracked. There was straw on the floor and the chill air smelled of long-dead animals and their dung. It wasn't till my eyes had got used to the surprisingly bright light that I understood.

'Shit,' I said, pointing with my right arm.

What I had thought were broken posts and stanchions was actually a line of four inverted crosses, each with a rope wound around the horizontal bar and a hook at the top of the vertical.

'What the—' Major Hexton broke off as Sebastian looked up at the roof.

We all followed his gaze. They were hard to make out at first, but soon I saw the words that had been written on the uncovered boards. Each was about a foot in height, the paint faded but still red enough. I hoped it was just paint.

"'To Make Their Heaven Our Hell,'" Arthur Bimsdale read.

Silence fell in the musty old room.

'What does that mean?' the major asked, his voice wavering slightly.

'It means we urgently need to see what's in the bag Ms. Jacobsen carried out of here,' I said.

'You got that right,' Quincy said, dropping to his knees.

Lying on the floor, partially covered by straw and dust, was a curved bone. It looked like a human jaw, the lower one. Most of the teeth, though broken and discolored, were still in place. I couldn't tell how old it was but its presence, and that of the inverted crosses and the motto, suggested that the Antichurch of Lucifer Triumphant was very much alive and well.

Abaddon arrived at Logan International Airport too late for the last flight to Portland, so she rented a Grand Cherokee and headed north on Interstate 95. It was cold in Massachusetts, but at least it wasn't snowing. Although Abaddon had killed in winter conditions often enough, she didn't like them. She was a hot-blooded creature of the South, she'd told herself often enough. The North was for people without feelings.

She wasn't feeling exactly happy about this latest assignment, which took precedence over other jobs. It wasn't the first time she'd agreed to carry out surveillance, and she was good at it; but she preferred to kill. She viewed it as career progression—when she was not long out of the military and still wet behind the ears, she'd worked though all the specializations: close combat, communications, observation and surveillance, agent recruitment and handling, codes and ciphers, subversion—she was a Grade A student at them all.

Then she came to weapons training. She hadn't just been a Grade A student, she was among the best they'd ever had at the company. So going back to watching people was a demotion, even though she'd been promised that several kills, including the Soul Collector and the enemy, would follow. They'd better.

Abaddon sometimes wondered if she was wasting herself. There wasn't much of a future in her line of work. As she got older, her skills would become compromised. If she didn't screw up, she'd be able go on for a few more years. Then she would have to find something else to do. The idea of sitting at a desk horrified her. At least there were more and more opportunities in other countries these days—and employers in other areas were said to be less demanding.

Driving into New Hampshire on the near-deserted road, Abaddon went over her instructions. Undertake surveillance of house at 15 Springfield Road, Portland; identify local law enforcement and FBI operatives; identify Matthew John Wells when he arrives at house and subsequently keep him under observation for as long as possible; identify FBI violent crime Director Peter Sebastian and log his activities; ascertain if others are involved in surveillance and identify them.

It sounded as dull as a winter's day in New York: too many people, too cold and too many guns. Abaddon would do her best to keep the peace, but if anyone made a move on her, she'd do what she always did— execute with extreme prejudice.

* * *

On Major Hexton's order, police surrounded Nora Jacobsen as soon as she pulled up outside the house in Springfield Road. By the time we got there, she had calmed down, but her face was still red. State troopers had cuffed her hands behind her back and sat her in an unmarked car. Detectives had gained access to the building and were standing guard over Mary Upson. I saw her face at the window. She looked less shocked than I'd expected. Maybe she knew more about her mother's activities than she'd admitted.

'What's in the bag, ma'am?' Hexton asked, after the old woman was walked over to the pickup.

'Why don't you take a look?' she answered gamely.

I stepped forward. 'Hello, Ms. Jacobsen.'

She stared at me, and then a slack smile split her weathered face. 'I remember you. You really got under Mary's skin. Like a worm.'

'I sometimes have that effect on people.' I glanced at the bag. 'More human remains?'

She made a sound that could have been a laugh. 'If that's what you think, go ahead and look, why don't you?'

I caught her eye. 'Does Mary know?'

For a second, she lost her conviction. 'What's my daughter got to do with this? You leave her alone.'

I asked the major to have Mary brought out. Sebastian watched, apparently happy for me to be running the show because of my acquaintance with the women. Quincy was behind him, his eyes constantly moving around the scene and the buildings across the street.

'I told you, keep Mary out of this,' Nora Jacobsen said, her voice loud now.

I followed the younger woman as she came out of the house, detectives on either side. She didn't look at me until she was close. Then her eyebrows shot up and she briefly stopped walking.

'Hello, Mary,' I said, when she came up.

She studied me without speaking for what seemed like a long time. 'Matt,' she said finally. 'It's good to see you.'

I felt a pang of guilt. She had developed feelings for me during our escape that I hadn't been able to reciprocate. She had called the police on me when rebuffed, but I didn't blame her. I had taken advantage of her situation, but I had to. It seemed that she had forgiven me.

Sebastian stepped forward. 'Ms. Upson, your mother has visited a property where there is evidence of major crime.'

Nora Jacobsen snorted. 'He means the old Morton place.'

Mary looked surprised again. 'That's been deserted for months.'

'Your mother recovered that bag from the scene,' Sebastian said. 'Do you have any idea what's in it?'

'She doesn't,' Nora said, taking a step forward. One of the state troopers clamped a hand on her shoulder. 'I tell you, she doesn't.'

Mary was staring at her mother. 'Have you handcuffed her? For the love of God, she's seventy-three. What do you think she's going to do?'

'Let her go,' I said to Sebastian.

He shook his head, but gave the order to the major.

'Now, Ms. Jacobsen,' the FBI man said. 'Open that bag. Slowly, please.'

The old woman glared at him, and then took the bag from the pickup. Looking around the men, some with raised firearms, she unzipped it along its length and dipped her hand inside.

Three things happened in rapid succession. The first was that Nora Jacobsen tossed a long knife with a curved blade into the air above the bag. The second was that she pressed a button on her watch. The third was a deafening explosion in the house behind where we all stood.

Seventeen

The Soul Collector recoiled as the flash filled the lenses of her binoculars and, a moment later, her ears were battered by the explosion's report. She was on top of a four-story block about four hundred yards away, wearing thermal fleece under her dark-colored heavy-weather jacket and trousers. Flying had meant she brought no weapons of her own apart from the plastic switchblade, but that had never been a problem in the past. As smoke furled from the house and flames appeared at the windows, she watched the people in front of the building move rapidly away.

She had recognized Matt as soon as he had come into the light from the streetlamp. He looked in good shape, but his face was drawn and his shoulders sagged, as if he was carrying a heavy weight. Beside him was another person she knew: the FBI man Peter Sebastian, who had been much in evidence in news broadcasts after the chaos at the cathedral. He was in charge of violent crime across the U.S., which begged the question, what was he doing in Portland, Maine, with Matt by his side?

Sara used the high-precision binoculars to zoom in the other people who were squatting behind vehicles as the fire raged unchecked. There were police personnel in uniform, including a grizzled man wearing a cap festooned by gold braid. Despite his rank, he seemed to be taking orders from Sebastian, with Matt gesturing decisively to him, as well. Her former lover had his arm round a crouching figure in a red sweater. The blond hair was styled in a way that suggested a female. When she turned her head, Sara saw that was the case— she also saw that the woman was terrified, her mouth opening and closing rapidly as she gestured toward the house. Shortly afterward, fire engines arrived and the people behind the cars were moved farther away, out of sight.

She remained in position, trying to make sense of what was going on. She had followed a Maine State Police cruiser from the Portland headquarters to the vicinity of the house, in the hope that Matt would show up. He and Sebastian must have left before the cruiser, so she had been lucky to locate him in this manner. Since Sara didn't think much of luck, she certainly didn't want to rely on it again. That meant she had only one course of action—to get off the roof and up close and personal with Matt. She put the binoculars in her rucksack and took out the switchblade. It was time to put the surveillance skills to the test. Maybe there would be a chance to use her other more lethal abilities, too.

The Soul Collector avoided the group of rubberneckers in the street leading to the burning house and slipped into the cover provided by a line of trees. Even though her eyes moved constantly from side to side, she failed to notice the tall form crouching behind a black Grand Cherokee.

Mary Upson had been given a blanket by a fireman. She still had it round her shoulders in the interview room back at the State Police building. I pushed a cup of coffee toward her.

'It'll warm you up,' I said. The smile I gave was hesitant. She hadn't yet shown any sign of hostility to me, but she had other things on her mind. 'Have you any idea where your mother might have gone?'

She kept her eyes off me. 'I already told the FBI men I didn't.'

I'd asked for some time alone with her, though I knew Sebastian would be observing us on the other side of the glass.

'I'm not with the FBI, Mary.'

'How do I know they're not listening?' she demanded, her eyes wide. Suddenly, she wasn't the smart but naive grade-school teacher who had helped me get out of Maine in the autumn. Then again, she and her mother had been questioned at length after the cathedral debacle—that might have taught her how to stand up for herself.

'Whisper, if you like.'

She laughed bitterly. 'Whisper sweet nothings? I'm not an idiot, Matt. I know you're working with them even though you're not an agent.'

'We're trying to find a killer.' I was aware the words sounded melodramatic. I needed to personalize things. 'Your mother's a suspect.'

'What? My mother? She's a retired schoolteacher.'

'Has she been away from home in the last three weeks?'

She turned away. 'I'm not gracing that with an answer.'

'Do you watch the news?'

'Of course. We're not hillbillies up here.'

I smiled to pacify her, but got nowhere—she stared at me with undisguised dislike. 'So you know about the murders in New York, Michigan, Boston and Philadelphia?'

'Are you seriously suggesting my mother was behind those? You must be out of your mind.'

I knew Nora Jacobsen hadn't killed those people—for a start, she wasn't strong enough to have hoisted Jack Notaro to the ceiling in Philadelphia. I wasn't proud of myself, but pressuring Mary was the only way to find out whether her mother knew where Heinz Rothmann was.

'Then why did she run? Why did she blow up the house?'

'I don't know!' she screamed. 'I don't...' The words tailed away in a long moan.

'Look, Mary, there was a knife in the bag she brought back from the Morton place. The technicians will soon know if the blood on it—was human.'

She was weeping silently, her head bowed and her shoulders shaking.

'There are human remains in the old house.'

The sobs grew louder. This was going nowhere. I leaned forward and took her hands from her face.

'Just tell me, Mary. Has your mother been away from home?'

She shook her head, her eyes still down. 'Of…of course not. She…we haven't got money for traveling.'

'Okay.' I lowered her hands to the table and let them go. 'That's good.'

She looked up at me hopefully. 'Is that it? You believe me?'

I nodded. They could verify whatever Nora Jacobsen's recent movements were said to be easily enough. But she still had a link to Rothmann via the Antichurch, and her behavior suggested she had plenty to hide.

'You remember you told me about the Antichurch of Lucifer Triumphant and your mother's involvement with it?' Mary had done so when we were heading out of Maine. I'd never been sure why.

'The old cult? She didn't take that seriously.' Mary was watching me now, her eyes glistening with tears but unwavering. 'She hasn't had anything to do with it for years.'

'Are you sure?'

'Yes, I'm sure. After the FBI dragged us over the coals, she told me she wished she'd never got involved. It was in the sixties, when that kind of thing was popular. The people who ran it were hippies. Most of them are in retirement homes now. They had nothing to do with the Nazis who revived the cult recently.'

That had been Nora Jacobsen's line during questioning. She had apparently been credible enough—until last night.

'Look, Mary, this is important. It's likely that Heinz Rothmann is involved in the murders. There's no telling how many more innocent people may die. We have to find him.'

'What's that got to do with my mother?' She shook her head. 'You're crazy, all of you.'

I looked at her until she returned my gaze. 'Mary, you have to accept that your mother has been hiding things from you. Jesus, she blew up your home—what does that tell you? She's become a willing fugitive. Where do you think she is?'

'I don't know!' The scream resounded against the hard wood walls.

'All right.' I kept my voice low. 'Is there anywhere else she might have hidden things?'

Mary shook her head, and then wiped her sleeve across her eyes. Even though her face was lined and tear-stained, she was still an attractive woman. I remembered what had happened to us in the motel near West Point. She had taken me to bed and I had almost gone along with it. I caught her eye and saw immediately that she was thinking of that time, too.

'Matt,' she said softly. 'Why are you doing this?'

I felt revulsion at what I was about to hit her with, but there seemed to be no other way. She didn't deserve to be burdened by the deaths of Karen and…our son—Christ, his name had gone from me already and I couldn't bring it back, our son…

'Matt?'

I heard her voice, but I had gone elsewhere, into a silent world of shadowy figures with their arms outstretched. They were begging, not for forgiveness—they weren't sinners, they were the pure of heart—but to be remembered…

'What is it, Matt?'

I felt her touch on my hand and I came back to my vacant self.

'I…I'm sorry…' Then I took a deep breath and told her about Karen and our son—and about Rothmann's responsibility for their deaths.

Mary was crying before I finished. She got up and came round the table to take me in her arms. I felt her tears on my forehead, and my own tears running down my cheeks.

The minutes passed and I shook her off gently. She went back to her chair and wiped her eyes again.

'You…you really think my mother is in contact with him?'

I nodded.

'I think you're maybe right. But I don't know what I can do to help.'

I gave her time, feeling that I'd betrayed her again. She was a good person at heart and I was taking advantage of that.

And then she remembered.

'Fred Warren,' she said, looking up at me. 'I heard her say that name several times recently. She's begun talking to herself quite a lot, especially when she's in the kitchen…' Mary broke off as the loss of the house hit her. 'In the kitchen,' she repeated. 'I even wondered if she'd got herself a man, after all these years. Fred Warren.' She shook her head. 'I never heard of him before. Oh, and something else—there was a year as well, she would say it after the name. "Fred Warren 1943." I suppose it was the year he was born. That would make him sixty-eight. Five years younger than her, lucky woman.' She smiled sadly.

The name meant nothing to me, but I was sure that Sebastian and his people would already be working on locating the man who bore it.

* * *

Gordy Lister watched as his brother's coffin disappeared through the beige curtain. There had been three living people to send him off—apart from Gordy, a balding funeral director in a too-tight black suit, and a young Hispanic woman with a spectacular chest. Gordy didn't know what Hispanics normally wore to funerals, but he was pretty sure tight gold tops with sequins and thigh-hugging shorts weren't favored. Not that he was complaining. If she was one of Mikey's friends, then his brother had more going for him than he'd thought. Gordy had chosen the closing music himself. Mikey had always had a thing for underdressed female singers, so Lady Gaga's 'Bad Romance' it was. It was only as the song came to an end that he remembered the video that had accompanied it. The male lover had ended up burned to death. Which was appropriate for a cremation, but in even worse taste than the *Star Reporter* would have dared try.

Outside, the funeral director gave him a sharp-toothed smile and said he hoped he could be of service again in the future. Gordy wiped his brow and watched the asshole head for his corpse-mobile. This was the last time a Lister would be in Florida. It was hot, sultry and full of wrinkled people wearing not enough over their shrunken limbs.

'You Mikey's friend?' the bronze looker asked, blowing smoke past his left ear.

'Brother. You?'

'Lucky,' she said, extending her hand.

He stared at her. 'Lucky I'm his brother?'

'No, my name is Lucky,' she said, with a wide smile. 'Lucky Sanchez.'

'Oh, right. So, you a friend of Mikey's?'

'Sure.' The woman tossed her cigarette. 'Terrible thing he die.'

'Yeah.' Gordy moved closer to her. 'Say, you didn't happen to be around when he…when he was hit by that car?'

Lucky suddenly looked shifty. 'No, no. But I talk to his neighbor next day.'

'Oh, yeah?' Gordy led her under the shade of a palm tree. 'What they say?'

'Saw pickup truck come very fast, drive into Mikey.'

'See, that's strange. The police told me there were no witnesses.'

Lucky raised her smooth shoulders. 'People no talk to police.' She paused. 'You pay me for telling this?'

Gordy studied her. He was interested, and not just in her bod, but he wasn't going to show it. 'Nah, Mikey should never have been out in the road. It was his own fault.'

The woman glared at him. 'How you say that about your brother? He need fresh air like anyone else.'

'Fresh air? It's winter and it's like a sweat bath down here.'

Lucky Sanchez looked at him suggestively. 'I tell you more, you pay?'

'What more is there?'

'Hundred, okay?'

He had a stab at looking reluctant.

'Hundred and blow job?'

Now you're talking, he thought. He handed her the C-note and led her to the rental Taurus parked by the crematorium wall.

'Driver was woman,' Lucky said, as she tugged down her top. 'Short, blond hair.'

Gordy Lister grabbed hold of her breasts as she went down on him, unsure whether the lead or her mouth was giving him greater pleasure.

Quincy Jerome was sitting at the table with the rest of the guys, but his mind was far away. He hadn't the first idea how to track down this Fred Warren, so he left it to the law enforcement professionals and Matt, who seemed to be full of ideas. He was replaying what had happened over the last twenty-four hours. Never mind his first trip in a Learjet—he'd almost forgotten that.

He'd seen plenty of dead bodies in Iraq, but none of them was as creepy as the human jawbone in the barn house. The local detectives were trying to locate the rest of the body, but there was nothing in the immediate vicinity. Then there was the explosion at the house and the total destruction of everything inside. The crazy old woman had set it off with some kind of remote timer before slipping away. He had a bad feeling about what else had been in the bag she took with her—the knife she'd left behind was wicked-looking enough. And then there was Matt playing interrogator and pulling it off. The guy had hidden depths, even if he had the advantage of knowing the blonde woman from before.

But all that was nothing as compared with the upturned crosses in the barn house. They had really bothered the shit out of him and he was struggling to understand why. After all, he was Jewish, his mother belonging to a tiny group of Somalis who had ended up in Mobile. His father had been a drifter, a bluesman who showed up every few months to yell at them and

drink away his meager earnings from the road. He'd
been a Southern Baptist and he wasn't marrying no
Jew woman, not that his mother wanted a ring. She was
the mystical type and she'd instilled in her son a high
regard for things with symbolic value. He wasn't the
kind of Jew that went to synagogue often, but he stood
up for his religion when he had to—often enough when
he was a kid and before he got his stripes. He had one
big problem. Because he was both black and a Jew, he
hated racists twice as much as other people. That made
him the perfect person to take part in the hunt for Hitler's Hitman and the Nazi piece of shit who had messed
with Matt's brain, even if Matt and the cold-eyed FBI
man didn't know it—or maybe Sebastian had read his
service file.

Being Jewish also made him careful. His mother had
taught him that. He never admitted to his faith unless
it was necessary. And he never gave out his real name,
which was a lot weirder than Quincy Jerome. He'd cob-
bled that together from a high-school football player
and the maiden name of Winston Churchill's mother,
a woman his mother admired for her spirit. The down-
side of his background was that he knew more than was
healthy about evil—and those upturned crosses had
breathed malevolence to him even before the human
remains had turned up.

'How about this?' Quincy heard Matt Wells say. 'It's
not a person's name, it's a place name.'

That prompted a clatter of fingertips on keyboards.

Eighteen

There wasn't anywhere called Fred Warren in the U.S. Or Warren Fred. There were, however, numerous places named Warren and even a few named Fred. The clincher was the number.

Major Hexton wondered if 1943 referred to a road. It only took a few seconds for him to find a farm to market road in Texas. It ran between two towns called Fred and Warren, about seventy miles northeast of Houston.

'You're kidding,' said Quincy Jerome.

I pointed to the map that had appeared on Hexton's laptop. 'In the Big Thicket National Preserve.'

'The Big Thicket?' Peter Sebastian repeated. 'What exactly is that?'

'I know,' Quincy said, raising his hand. 'We went on a school trip. It's part of the Piney Woods that take up a lot of East Texas. As far as I remember, the Big Thicket's about 80,000 acres. It's got everything a nature lover could want—wetlands, pine uplands, sandylands. There are carnivorous plants, hickory, tupelo and all kinds of animals—deer, bobcats, armadillos, alligators, some real nasty hogs...'

'Oh, great,' I said. 'Southern Gothic in spades.'

Quincy grinned. 'You got that right, my man. Some of the locals are straight outta *Deliverance*.'

'It gets better by the minute,' I said.

Sebastian dropped his pen onto the yellow pad in front of him. 'Obviously because the Antichurch has got some kind of presence there.' Major Hexton kept his eyes down, no doubt hoping that the cult had a minimal following in Maine. Nothing attracts undesired attention like murderous Satanists.

'Well,' I began, 'where the Antichurch goes...'

'Heinz Rothmann and his acolytes are bound to follow,' Arthur Bimsdale completed. 'It's pretty thin.'

'You got a better idea?' Sebastian demanded. 'I didn't think so. Get on to the field office in Houston and find out about the area. In particular, if anything unusual there has attracted their attention of late.'

Bimsdale went out, his cheeks red. Sebastian might have been a good investigator, but his management sucked.

The major stood up. 'I'm going to see how things are progressing,' he said, then left at speed. He didn't want the senior FBI man to lay into *him*.

That left the three of us.

I glanced at Quincy. 'Fancy a trip to Texas?'

'Why not? It isn't too hot at this time of year. Still need your bug spray though, especially in those woods.'

'If I could interrupt your vacation planning,' Sebastian put in, 'nobody's going anywhere without my say-so.'

I gave him a tight smile. 'To coin a phrase, have you

got a better idea? I take it there still haven't been any sightings of Nora Jacobsen.'

He glanced at his laptop, then shook his head.

'No more Hitler's Hitman killings?'

Another shake, this one abrupt.

'You know the state police here aren't going to find anything.'

This time he reacted with words. 'Let's wait and see what the major comes back with. In the meantime, what exactly do you two superheroes think you're going to do down in Texas? For all you know, Nora Jacobsen might have a boy toy in the Big Thicket.'

'And I might be Jimi Hendrix's long lost twin brother,' I said, raising a smile from Quincy. 'Come on, Peter, this is all we've got.'

Mary Upson looked up as Matt came back into the interview room. Although the rings beneath his eyes were still pronounced, there was a glint in them that hadn't been there before.

'What is it?' she asked.

He sat down opposite her. 'We think we know what your mother was saying. Was she planning a trip?'

'Can't you leave my mother alone?'

'Just answer the question, Mary.'

'Yes, as a matter of fact she was. On Friday. She has a friend in Indianapolis. She goes about this time every year.'

'Did you see any tickets?'

'What? No…'

'Has she seemed different to you lately?'

Mary frowned. 'If you must know, yes, she has. Ever since we were dragged over the coals by the FBI, she's kept herself even more to herself. She was never very open, but she's gotten more secretive. I think she's going senile. That's why I gave up my job and moved back down here with her.'

'And you?' Matt asked, his tone more tender.

She ran her tongue over her lips. 'Oh, I'm all right. Out of work, bored, unhappy in love…'

He reached across and took her hand. 'You'll be okay.'

'Will I? Will you, Matt? I'm so sorry about your… your…child. It must be awful.' She paused. 'I could help.'

He tugged his hand away. 'No, you couldn't,' he said, in little more than a whisper. 'Nobody can.'

Mary Upson watched as he left the room. She had never seen anyone bearing such a weight. His shoulders were sloped and it seemed to take a great effort for him just to move his body. They could have been so good together, but fate had driven them apart. She would happily have given him a child, she still could—if only he would look at her like a woman rather than a pawn in the mad game he was playing.

'All right,' Peter Sebastian said, running a hand over his unwashed hair, 'let's go through this again.'

I was at the table with him, Arthur Bimsdale and Quincy Jerome.

'Fine,' I said. 'Mary Upson has confirmed that there's some kind of Antichurch gathering at this time of year.'

'I'm sorry,' Bimsdale said, peering at his notes. 'That's not how you reported it. She said that her mother visited a friend in Indianapolis every December.'

'Use your imagination, Arthur,' I said. 'That's what she told Mary. I'm willing to bet your salary several times over that the old woman hasn't got any friends except Antichurch members.'

'Leave that point for now,' Sebastian ordered. 'According to Major Hexton, the CSIs have found traces of human blood and tissue on one of the inverted crosses and on the floor in the barn house, though the knife Nora Jacobson pulled was clean. The jawbone we turned up has small cuts all over it, suggesting the flesh and other matter was scraped off. Identifying the person the bone came from will not be easy.'

I closed my eyes and tried to black out an unwanted vision of the mutilation being carried out. Could one elderly woman have killed and dismembered the victim on her own? Could Mary have been dissembling? If so, she was very good.

'As regards the fugitive mother,' the senior FBI man continued, 'witnesses have placed her in Portland around the times of all four Hitler's Hitman murders. Apparently she's a fixture in the markets and shops, telling people what she thinks of the way they live.'

'So what are we saying?' Quincy asked. 'She's involved in this Antichurch, but she's not our killer?'

Arthur Bimsdale laughed. 'That's quite a deduction, Sergeant.'

The big man looked on the verge of introducing Bimsdale's laptop to his head.

'Indeed,' Sebastian said, nodding at Quincy. 'If she's a follower of Rothmann, she probably is a Nazi. Judging by what we've seen here, she may well also be a murderess. But it seems she's not up for these four killings.'

'Far as I'm concerned, she's going down, whoever she killed,' Quincy said, his face set hard.

I studied him, then turned to Sebastian. 'Mary Upson. I suggest you let her go.'

He gave me a black look. 'You had the handcuffs removed from her mother, Matt. That wasn't such a good idea.'

'Keep her under surveillance. Maybe her mother will contact her, or vice versa.'

He thought about that, and then nodded. 'What did our friends in Houston tell you, Arthur?'

Bimsdale hit keys on his laptop. 'They sent a profile of the area. As the sergeant said, it's heavily wooded and treacherous ground, largely unpopulated. There are no ongoing Bureau investigations in Tyler County, and no recent buildings on the 1943 road other than private homes.'

'So if Rothmann's down there,' I said, 'he's using an existing structure.'

'Correct.' Sebastian looked at me. 'Are you sure you want to go?'

'Oh, yes.' I turned to Quincy. 'You still in?'

He grinned. 'Sure.'

'How do you want to do it?' Sebastian asked.

'No FBI planes. We'll go to Houston by commercial flight—Quincy at least five rows behind me. I'll hire a car at the airport. I want to be obvious to Rothmann's people. When I locate him, you can send your people in.'

Sebastian frowned. 'You'll be taking a big risk.'

'You put a bug in my arm, didn't you? Just make sure you've got people close by—but not too close. Quincy can take point on watching my back.'

'Not many black folks in those parts,' the sergeant observed.

'You're good at camouflage, aren't you?'

He laughed. 'Yes, sir, that I am.'

'We'll give you a locator so you can track Matt,' Sebastian said.

'What about weapons?' Quincy asked.

'I'll arrange for some to be waiting for both of you in the airport luggage lockers. You can pick the keys up from airport information.'

That seemed to cover most of the bases. I had turned myself into bait, but I didn't care. Getting to the piece of shit who killed my family was all that mattered.

Sara Robbins, currently Colette Olds, got out of the Lexus and went to the diner opposite the police head-quarters building. She was wearing a black wig and pulled a Boston Red Sox cap low over her eyes—even though she knew Matt was still in the cop shop, she wasn't taking any chances.

She bought a decaf and sat near the window. The place was full of uniformed police, but that didn't bother her. She was used to being in the belly of the beast—there was no better place for a professional killer to merge into the background.

'This seat taken?' The cop was young and fresh-faced. He was on his own, the gear on his belt shaking and jangling.

'Go ahead,' she said, giving him a restrained smile. 'Busy day?'

'Busy night, more like.' He took a slug of black coffee.

She decided to probe. 'You at that fire in Springfield Road?'

'That's right.' He looked at her quizzically.

'I saw the flames. Got to admit I did a bit of rubber-necking. What happened?'

'You didn't hear the explosion?' He was keen to impress now. 'Seems one of the residents took it into her head to blow the place up.'

She winced. 'Was anybody hurt?'

'No one, by some miracle.' The cop took a bite from his doughnut. 'We're still looking for the woman.'

'That would be Ms. Jacobsen.' The Soul Collector had done her research.

He nodded. 'You know her?'

'Not personally.'

He laughed. 'But she has a reputation.'

She went along with that. Then, out of the corner of her eye, she saw a black Grand Cherokee move forward slowly on the other side of the diner.

The driver was a well-built white woman wearing a woolen hat. It wasn't the first time she had seen the vehicle—it had been in her mirror, three cars behind, when she had driven out here earlier in the morning. Maybe it was a coincidence, but there was no point in taking a chance. Since the pain had started, she had become more prone to acting on impulse.

'Oh, no,' she groaned.

'What is it?' The young cop was the picture of concern.

'It's just…oh, never mind.'

'No, really, I'm here to help.'

Sara sighed. 'I don't know…it's embarrassing, really.'

'Whatever it takes,' said her admirer, following the direction of her gaze.

'All right, thanks, Officer. You see the Cherokee? It's been following me all week.'

The young man craned forward. 'You know the driver?'

'Well, like I say, it's embarrassing...I met her in a club last Saturday night. Em, not the kind of club you go to.'

He got her meaning, attempting to conceal his disappointment.

'We...we went back to her place, but I got frightened. You see...she wanted to do something...extreme. When I refused, she turned nasty. She found out where I live and she's been on my tail ever since. I'm...I'm frightened.'

The combination of sexual deviance and the old-fashioned damsel in distress scenario hooked the officer.

'Come with me,' he said, getting to his feet. 'We'll get this fixed.'

The Soul Collector followed him, but not too closely.

'Get out of the vehicle!' the cop ordered, when he was ten yards from the Cherokee. 'Now!'

The woman at the wheel looked at him in a way that looked lethargic to the layman, but Sara could read it was full of menace. She slowed her pace and stepped behind a pickup.

'Out of the vehicle!' her savior yelled again.

This time he provoked a reaction. The woman floored the gas pedal and the SUV roared forward. As it did so, an elderly man in a Lincoln Continental crunched into the side of the Cherokee, pushing it toward the police officer. Before the young cop could take evasive action, he was knocked into the air, landing with a crash on the hood of a pickup. His head made solid contact and he stopped moving. Cops immediately filed out the door of the diner and went to their comrade.

The Soul Collector watched as the SUV sped off, swerving out of the parking lot and accelerating up the road. She walked back to her car at normal pace and started the engine, and that's when it happened.

A line of cars came out of the underground lot beneath the police building. In the back of a Crown Victoria sat her lover, Matt Wells. This was as close as she'd been to him in a long time, and it made something in her mind click with a strange mixture of hatred and desire.

Nineteen

We took a flight to Newark and caught a connection to Houston. Neither plane was full. Quincy kept his distance. I looked around from time to time, but I didn't see anyone else I recognized. Fortunately, I managed the same anonymity. My picture had been all over TV screens and front pages after the attack on the President, and the last thing I needed was for some dutiful citizen to clamp a hand on my shoulder. I wore a Maine Forever cap low over my forehead. Sebastian was ahead of the game: he gave me a British passport with the appropriate entry visa, which listed my name as William Andrew Ronson. I memorized that. There was a credit card to go with it. Remembering the PIN code was a lot harder—I'd never been good with numbers.

On the plane to Houston, I thought about what had happened in Portland. Nora Jacobsen had got the jump on us. Sebastian was pissed off with me for getting her cuffs removed, but I had reckoned that was essential to weaken her guard—she might have let a vital piece of information slip. As it was, she and Mary had given us

a lead that had at least put us on Rothmann's trail—or
so I hoped.

I thought about Mary Upson. She had seemed gen-
uinely upset about Karen and the baby. Was that why
she told me what her mother had been saying? Was it
possible she had lived in the same house as the older
woman without realizing she was still active in the Antichurch? Could she really be so innocent? There was
a maelstrom of emotion under those soft features.

Still, Mary wasn't the most pressing problem to
come out of Maine. While we were at the airport, Major
Hexton heard about an incident in a parking lot near
police headquarters in which one of his officers had
been injured. No one was very clear about the details,
but a woman with long dark hair and a baseball cap had
been seen talking to the policeman just before a black
Grand Cherokee hit him and another vehicle before
tearing off. The interesting thing was that the dark-
haired woman had left the scene before any of the other
cops could talk to her. None of them got a good view of
her face, nor had they gotten her plates, so concerned
were they about their colleague. He had come round in
hospital, but had a bad concussion and didn't remember
what had happened.

So what *had* happened? Who was in the Grand Cherokee that had left at high speed? One report said the
driver had been another woman. Why had the dark-
haired woman also made tracks so quickly? One rapid
departure was conceivable, but two? I had noticed the
parking lot as we left. It had a good view of the State
Police headquarters building. Were the drivers there
for a particular reason—were they waiting for me? An

icy finger twisted in my gut. Could one of them have been Sara?

I took another look around the passengers. No dark-haired woman in a cap. If Sara was after us, I should tell Quincy and the others. Sebastian had provided us with cell phones, so I could call or text him when there was a signal. Then again, what good would that do? He was a professional and he knew we were heading into the lion's den. What more could he do? Besides, I thought as I emptied my bottle of water, knowing Sara was on your tail didn't reduce the chances of her nailing you. She'd have changed her identity and her appearance—like a vengeful ghost, you would never hear her coming.

Lack of sleep finally caught up with me, but I got no real rest. They were there again, the shadowy figures. The woman had one arm extended, the other holding the infant. Her mouth opened wide as she called to me, her face soaked with tears. But I could hear nothing and I struggled even to remember her name, while the baby's was long gone.

Even though it was cold in the crypt, Gordy Lister was sweating. He was exhausted after the long drive back from Tallahassee, but the Master, as he'd taken to calling himself, didn't care about that. He'd shown no interest when Gordy told him about Mikey's death, saying only that he should get back as quickly as he could, but refusing to allow him to take any of the cars. Gordy could see the point, though he'd had the hassle of wasting a fake ID to rent the Taurus and leaving it back at the depot in Houston, meaning that one of the dead-eyed bodyguards had to go and pick him up. At least he had something to tell the split-cheeked one now.

'Look at this.' The man who had been Heinz Roth-mann pointed to the computer screen.

Gordy watched as flames played at the windows of a wooden house and smoke billowed into the night. 'What is it, boss?'

'It belongs to one of the Antichurch faithful in Port-land, Maine. She detonated the safety charges.'

Gordy Lister thought the Antichurch of Lucifer Tri-umphant was for the seriously deranged, but he had kept that from the Master. 'Why do that?'

'Because she had been taken by the police. The FBI was also involved. It would only have been a matter of time until they found sacred documents and other material.'

Gordy felt a stab of concern. 'Documents that would have led to this place?'

The Master nodded.

Gordy relaxed. 'So she did good.' He tried to keep his eyes off the fresh wounds on the other man's cheeks. What was he now? Some kind of Zorro freak?

'Indeed. Of course, they are coming, all the same.'

'What?'

'Look at this.' The Master's fingers played on the keyboard.

Gordy watched as he zoomed in. 'What the fuck? That's the Englishman, Matt Wells.'

'And his FBI puppet-master Peter Sebastian.'

'What are they doing there?'

'A good question, and one which I hope our sister-in-evil will be able to answer when she gets here. She is taking a rather roundabout route. Wells may be more direct.'

'I don't get it, boss.'

'I don't imagine you do. You see, I want Matt Wells here. He belongs to me. He will do great things for us.'

'Right,' Gordy said doubtfully. 'And if the FBI comes with him in force? We're in the right state for another Waco.'

'There are other places we can go. Besides, the mid-winter rite is tomorrow. The faithful are coming from far and wide.' The Master's eyes narrowed. 'Faithful who are armed and capable of using their weapons. If the FBI wants another showdown, we can oblige.'

'Is that a good idea, boss?' Lister asked. He'd seen what happened during Antichurch rites. It was a toss-up whether there would be more blood spilt in the mid-winter blowout or in a full-on battle.

'Matt Wells is an essential part of my strategy. The fact that he is being used by the FBI shows he is important to them, but that is nothing compared with his importance to us. He is the only subject who was not fully coffined. That means that I can complete him in my own image.'

Gordy let that mumbo jumbo go. When he'd run the operation in Washington, he'd been spared the boss's more lunatic schemes—special camps, the Nazi militia, the Antichurch, the plot against the President. His main role had been to provide young people for the conditioning process. He was beginning to wonder what part he had in his boss's plans, now that he seemed to have flipped his lid in a big way.

The Master drank from a tall glass containing what Lister hoped was red wine. 'You notice there have been no more of the so-called Hitler's Hitman murders since you were in Philadelphia?'

'Yeah, well, I might know something about that.'

The other man put his glass down heavily. 'Tell me.'

'My brother Mikey, I think he was murdered. He was run down by a pickup driven by a blonde woman.' Gordy had a flash of the bronze-skinned Latina bent over his groin. 'That's not all. He was under surveillance before the hit. Probably Feds, as the local cops are much less subtle.'

'Have a drink, Gordy,' the Master said, filling another glass from an ornate carafe. 'There are several interesting points to your story. One, the killer was a blonde woman.'

Lister sipped suspiciously. 'Yeah, she had short blond hair.'

'Begging the questions, who is she and who hired her? Two, if I understand you correctly, there was no surveillance at the time of your brother's death. My condolences, by the way.'

By the way up your ass, Gordy thought. 'That's right.'

'So we are left with the interesting possibility that someone in authority pulled the surveillance to facilitate the hit, as you call it.'

'Or the guys went off for a hot dog,' Gordy said, trying to keep things simple.

The Master ignored that. 'And, third, what motivated the hit? Did your brother have any enemies?'

'Only the people whose wiring he screwed up.' Gordy felt the other man's eyes bore into him. 'Shit, no. No one who would have killed him, at least.'

The Master sat back and dabbed his lips with a napkin. 'So why was he run down, Gordy?'

'I haven't the faintest idea, boss.'

'Well, I have. Someone wants to get at you.'

Lister felt his stomach flip. 'Me? What have I done?'

The Master raised a hand. 'Don't worry, although your sins are many—not least those involving the young and beautiful twins you supplied me with—I don't think this action was aimed *primarily* at you.' He stood up and gathered his black robe around him. 'It was aimed at me.'

Gordy watched as the other man walked to the door with his head held high.

He didn't know whether to feel relieved or worried. On second thought, remembering what he'd heard about Matt Wells and the FBI's involvement, he went for worried.

I picked up my bags and then stood at a pay phone in the arrivals hall. I wasn't making a call, but looking at the other passengers at the luggage carousel. Now that I was in the real world again, despite the presence of Quincy nearby, I felt the old vulnerability that Sara used to induce. Even if she wasn't on my tail now, there was no telling when she might acquire me in her sights. I felt hollow, not just in my stomach, but in my arms and legs. She was merciless, unstoppable, an avenging demon.

I pulled myself together and scanned people as they moved toward the exit. There hadn't been many women on the flight, and those I could see fell into two groups—business types with smart clothes and leather briefcases, and students going home for Christmas. None of them looked even remotely like Sara, even assuming she had changed her appearance considerably. Then again, she could easily have disguised herself as a male. More of those were traveling business class, though many had a very Texan way of power dressing—cowboy boots under tailored suits and belts with large buckles. There were even a few outsize hats. I had to give up. Nobody looked like my ex-lover. Then again, I had no idea what she would look like when she came for me.

I went out into the main concourse and located the passenger information desk. A pretty girl with turquoise eyes handed me an envelope for Mr. William A. Ronson. Pretty soon, she'd be giving another to Mr. Jerome Quincy—Sebastian reckoned that the soldier didn't need a major change of identity. I kept my eyes to the front and headed to the luggage lockers. The key fitted the relevant lock and I took out the small bag inside. It didn't weigh much and I wondered whether going after Rothmann armed was such a good idea. He was bound to be surrounded by trained and probably conditioned personnel. I told myself to stick with the plan. Then again, turning up empty-handed was an even worse option.

I went over to the Hertz desk and picked up the SUV keys. It was a Mercedes with only a couple of thousand on the clock—nothing but the best for the FBI's brown-eyed boy. Then I took the bus to the parking lot and found the car. It was big, green and a serious gas-guzzler. Welcome to the Lone Star State.

The hotel was only half a mile away. I was on the twelfth floor, with a view of the airport lights. I showered, ordered a steak from room service and called my partner in crime fighting.

'You in the hotel?'

'That's a positive.'

'Anyone on your tail?'

'I ain't that lucky, man.'

'Are you in the bar?'

'Check.'

'Don't get drunk, Mr. Quincy.'

'No, sir.'

'Don't talk to any strange women. I'm serious.'

'Check.'

'How are you going to pay?'

'Check.'

I hung up. Quincy was a good man and I was glad to have him watching my back. But even he could only do so much against Heinz Rothmann and his band of brainwashed Nazi devil-worshippers.

Abaddon had decided that steering clear of Portland was a good idea. She drove north for ten miles, then got off the Maine Turnpike and found a quiet side road to hole up. She drank a bottle of water and ate an eggsalad sandwich that she'd bought earlier. That made her feel slightly better, but she wasn't looking forward to what she was going to have to do next. She booted up her laptop, checked the wireless connection was functioning, and then accessed the secure site. It was monitored on an ongoing basis.

666—request subject location update, she typed, hoping for a simple answer. As the seconds turned into minutes, she realized she was going to get more than that.

Commander—what happened? r u compromised?

Abaddon groaned. It was the big boss himself and, as usual, he wanted to know everything. She answered as briefly as she could, stressing the role of the woman with long black hair in the parking lot, and waited to be dismissed from the operation since she couldn't guarantee that she hadn't been spotted. Long minutes passed. She concentrated on keeping her breathing steady. Failure was not something she had experienced often.

Commander—proceed—subject en route houston tx—assume id watson georgina—meet aircraft lewiston me 1800—ditch rental, came the reply.

Abaddon clenched her fists in triumph. She was still on the case. The truth was, she'd have found a way to stay on it even if she'd been fired. She logged off and packed away the laptop. Then she got out of the Grand Cherokee and opened the bag on the backseat. She had worn gloves ever since she had picked up the SUV, so prints were not a problem. She took out the outfit that she would wear as Georgina Watson, an unironed denim shirt and patched Levi's, and took off the wig. Instead of short brown curls, Georgina, a tree-hugger, favored blond dreadlocks. She undid the buttons of her blouse and reached for its replacement.

'You know, this is private land.'

Abaddon froze, then moved her eyes up to the mirror. It showed a large man in a checkered shirt and jeans close to the rear of the vehicle. He was carrying what looked like a tire iron. Her own weapons were out of reach.

'I said, this is private land, lady.'

She left the blouse unbuttoned and turned to face him. There was a sharp intake of breath as his eyes fixed on her red brassiere and its contents.

'You…you see,' he mumbled, 'we…we get a lot of people stopping here to do the drugs they got in the city. They make a mess, scare the kids…'

The woman looked around. She hadn't noticed any buildings in the immediate vicinity. The sound of traffic on the turnpike was audible in the distance, above the cackle of starlings.

'But I don't do drugs,' she said, taking a step toward him.

The man raised the tire iron to chest height. 'They… they attacked me more than once.'

She smiled. 'Come on now, do I look like I'm going to do much attacking?' She glanced down at her front.

He laughed uneasily. 'No, ma'am, that you don't.'

Abaddon took another couple of steps forward. 'See anything you like?'

The guy was in his forties and he looked like he hadn't ever seen a woman in a state of undress before, save maybe in the movies. Lights-off-sex with the wife would be the rule. His eyes widened as she flicked off one of her straps and tugged down the cup.

Then she crushed his windpipe with the back of her hand. He died with a wet smile on his lips.

Twenty

I woke before six the next morning, in a cold sweat despite the warmth of the hotel room. They had come to me again, the ones I had lost, dressed in white like the sheets that had covered them in the morgue. My son's face wasn't blue anymore, but corpse-gray like his mother's. She had her hand stretched out to me again, her face twisted in pain and longing. And then she turned and started to walk down a rough track between trees. I knew immediately that it was the path everyone eventually had to take, the way to the land of the countless, nameless dead.

I took a shower and pulled open the drapes. It was still dark outside, the static lights of the terminal and the moving ones on aircraft shimmering through the heavy drizzle that pattered against the pane. Our plan had me leaving the hotel at eight, so that I would be in Tyler County before ten. That left plenty of time before dark to find the Antichurch's facility on the road between Warren and Fred. Quincy would keep a mile or so behind me, using the locating device to track me. He was to use his own discretion about coming to my aid if anything suspicious happened. The Bureau's Houston field office was involved, but its operatives had been told to keep their distance.

After I'd dressed, I checked the weapons in the bag I'd picked up. There was a combat knife in its sheath and a Glock 19 semiautomatic with two clips. I ejected a shell and examined it. As far as I could tell, it was the real thing. Although I didn't fully trust Peter Sebastian, I couldn't see why he would let me go into Rothmann's den firing blanks.

I logged on to the operation's secure site and read a report that Major Hexton had filed late last night. The body of a thirty-nine-year-old male had been found near the turnpike about ten miles north of Portland. His throat had been crushed. A few yards from the body was a black Jeep Grand Cherokee. The number plate squared with one logged earlier in the day by a witness in the diner across the road from police headquarters, who had come forward last night. The assumption was that the driver, a woman, had made her way to the turn-pike and hitched either north or south. A call was out for anyone who had seen or picked her up, but a lot of the traffic was interstate so drivers either might not have heard it or ignored it.

So what the hell was going on? Could this second woman have been on my tail as well? Why had she killed the man? Had he seen something he shouldn't have? That didn't feel right. Who was the woman? The last thing I needed was someone who could kill with a single blow after me. In addition to Sara, that is.

I checked out and had the Mercedes brought to the front of the hotel. I looked around surreptitiously, but there were no women apart from hotel staff in the vicinity. No sign of Quincy, either. All was as it should be.

For speed, I took I-10 to Beaumont and then headed north toward the Big Thicket. At first I thought I was back in Cajun country in Louisiana. I'd gone on a wild trip there with some other crime writers after a conference in New Orleans—we ate gumbo, drank beer, sweated buckets and made enough noise to scare off any man-eating creatures.

The forest grew thicker the farther north I got, and there was no shortage of lumber trucks—in that respect, the area was like Maine, but with more humidity and a lot more insect life. I could believe that runaway slaves and draft dodgers had made use of the Big Thicket in the old days. It struck me that the difficulty of tracking people down in the swampy terrain might have attracted Rothmann, too. Then again, there were signs of the oil industry encroaching, which would have reduced his privacy.

I made it to Warren and stopped for a cup of coffee. There was a pamphlet about the area in the diner. Apparently there were eight different vegetation zones in the Big Thicket preserve, ranging from palmetto-hardwood flatlands to stream flood plains, whatever those were. They harbored over eighty species of tree and sixty kinds of shrubs. Since I'd lived in cities on the other side of the ocean all my life, a lot of the fauna was unknown to me: loblolly pine, bluejack oak, tupelo and sundew. I breathed in and got a distinct blast of nature in the raw—swelling, burgeoning and slightly rotten. Again, just the place for Rothmann and his Nazi Satanists.

I sprayed on some insect repellent and buttoned my

cuffs. It wasn't raining anymore, but the humidity was heavy-duty. Fortunately, the Mercedes had a great air-con system. As I drove through the town, I wondered what the locals did when they weren't working. There was no shortage of churches and I remembered I was in the heartland of the Southern Baptists. Some of them believed in the reality of Satan as much as the Anti-church did, but they expected the faithful to be taken up in the so-called Rapture, while the rest of us stayed on ground level to wait for Armageddon. It struck me that the Antichurch would have found more followers down south than in sparsely populated Maine. Could that be why the annual gathering was happening here?

Then again, where was 'here'? I found access road 1943 and set off down it slowly, looking from side to side. None of the buildings looked likely candidates. Soon I came to signs on the right for the Turkey Creek Trail. According to the pamphlet, walkers would traverse a pine-hardwood forest cut with sandy knolls, then forests of loblolly and short-leaf pines, white and red oak, and others. Paradise for a nature lover, but the numerous unnumbered gravel tracks made it hell to check out thoroughly. The calls of strange birds filled the woods and I began to wonder if my boots were thick enough to repel snake bites. I was as lost for clues as Hansel and Gretel. Then it struck me that Antichurch members like Nora Jacobsen would be coming from far away and would need help to identify the hidden premises. I continued on 1943, swiveling my head until my neck began to ache. Unshaven guys with disintegrating baseball caps and dented pickups honked at me and I waved at them like a dumb tourist. Maybe I should just have asked where the devil worshippers hung out.

And then, without immediately understanding what it meant, I saw the mark on the left side of the road. It was about six feet up the thick trunk of a tree I couldn't identify. The bark had been scraped away and in the foot-square space a red cross had been painted, the upper part of the vertical much longer than the lower. The Antichurch's upturned cross. Eureka.

I got down from the SUV and took out my cell phone to send a text to Quincy.

No signal. That was hardly surprising, given the tree cover. He would be able to track me with the responder, as long as it functioned in this environment. Too bad—I wasn't going to wait. My heart rate had accelerated. I was going to find the bastard Rothmann and tear his head off. I got back into the car and drove down a narrow track. As soon as I saw a gap in the trees, I turned in and got the Mercedes as far out of the way as I could. When I opened the door, I noticed a fleshy plant where I was going to put my feet. A putrid smell rose from it, attracting flies and other insects.

It seemed I was close to the rotting heart of darkness.

Putting the pistol and knife in my pockets, I struck off through the woods, keeping the track to my right. I took cover behind a tree when I heard a vehicle approach and watched as a pair of worryingly severe guys in a pristine pickup negotiated the track. The vehicle soon vanished behind the foliage. I headed after it.

The first rustle in the bushes ahead didn't bother me. The following ones did—they got louder and shook the leaves. I stopped and pulled out the Glock. A bundle of bristles with two wickedly curved tusks on the front pelted toward me, swerving at the last moment. I found myself on my backside, breathing heavily. That must have been one of the feral hogs mentioned in the pamphlet. I laughed out loud, having not come across heavily armed suckling pig before.

I should have kept quiet. That way I might have heard what came up behind me. As it was, I turned too late and caught only a glimpse of a demon's face with fangs much bigger than the hog's.

Then I lost the light.

'Ladies and gentlemen, please welcome our most generous sponsor, Mr. Rudi Crane!'

The toastmaster gave the small man to his right on the raised table a wide and disingenuous smile. Crane did not return it. One of the many blessings that the Lord had conferred upon him was the ability to detect insincerity instantly. That had been a useful tool in his rise to the upper echelons of American business, as well as in his church. He knew exactly which senior Southern Baptists were worthy. Unfortunately, there were very few.

Rudi Crane looked out over the elite of Chicago and tried not to blink. He had started wearing contact lenses a few months earlier, and his eyes still rebelled on occasion. He knew how important it was to maintain a steady gaze, so he had disciplined himself not to react to the prompting of his nerves. As usual, his mind prevailed over his body, for which he gave silent thanks. He started out on the address he had memorized—he didn't like to refer to notes when speaking in public, nor did he allow himself to extemporize. As often happened, the words came out without conscious effort, allowing him to spend the time on more profitable conjectures. Over the years, he had come up with many important ideas while speaking, most frequently when he preached at the church he had built near the family mansion outside Birmingham. He wished he was there now, taking in the winter sun of Alabama, far away from the high society of Chicago, hypocrites all. He only contributed to their ridiculous charitable foundation because it raised his profile in the North and was essential for his business.

Rudi Crane's thoughts ran parallel to his speech for several seconds. He was explaining how Hercules Solutions had an integrated approach to every contract, and how much the company valued the work it carried out for the U.S.A. Integration was the key. The word had been misused for so many years, he reflected. Racial integration wasn't important in the modern world. What really mattered was full control of everything. Religion based on the words of great men directed the minds and souls of the people; relationships between great men led to mutually beneficial business activities; great men organized the world according to their desires and rights. He had never had the slightest doubt that he was a great man.

'My friends,' he said, moving into the section of his speech that people came to hear, 'I have been fortunate enough in my time to know many leaders, in many different fields. I have paid homage at the feet of religious leaders, I have had dealings with the kings of industry, I have known the most powerful of statesmen. When I saw the secretary of defense last weekend, he said to me, "Rudi, how do you do it? Hercules Solutions offers the best service with the best personnel for the best price. It's a miracle." I took it upon myself to correct the secretary, as only the Lord our God can bring about miracles. But it is true that Hercules Solutions takes its work very seriously, not least because we are responsible for American lives in the most dangerous parts of the world.'

As he let his voice convey the joyous message of faith-based profit and success tempered by financial and moral accountability, Rudi Crane allowed himself to revel in what he had achieved. In ten years, Hercules Solutions had become the largest private military contractor in the world, providing experienced personnel to support U.S. forces in Iraq, Afghanistan and numerous other countries. The company trained armies and police forces on every continent, as well as undertaking private security work for the world's wealthiest people. True, there had recently been legal problems in Iraq and the company had been forced to restrict its operations to nongovernment work. But in the U.S. it still trained hundreds of law enforcement officers every year. The world was one country now—wasn't that the point of globalization? It didn't matter where the profits were made.

He took a sip of water and raised his glass to his listeners, the majority of whom were drinking vintage champagne. He liked to end speeches with the emotional surge he employed in the pulpit. He exhorted them to be true to the Lord in all their thoughts and deeds. That way, their efforts would prosper and their lives would be full of joy. It always amazed him how people took his words, their expressions rapt, their eyes closed. No one was ever concerned that Hercules Solutions employed professional killers by the thousand. The Company was protected by the Lord.

* * *

Quincy Jerome had parked in a narrow space between two buildings on the eastern edge of Warren. He was watching the junction with 1943. According to the tracking device, Matt had turned off that road roughly five miles ahead and was now moving northward. The plan was that Quincy would get a text when he was to move up. He checked his cell and saw that the signal was at medium strength. If nothing had come in two hours from the time Matt turned off the road, he would go ahead regardless. A lot could happen in two hours.

A rattling Volkswagen Beetle came up to the crossroads, driven by an elderly man with a white beard. Quincy took a photograph of it, as he had with all vehicles that passed. He might as well use the time profitably. He looked at his watch. Twelve-thirty. Another hour to wait. He looked around, breathing in the air. What he'd grown up with in Mobile was different—the taste of pomegranates and pecans had never left him—but, still, this place smelled of the South, made him think he was home. He swallowed a laugh. What kind of home could a black Jew have expected to make in Dixie? He'd have been better off relocating to New York, but he'd had nothing to relocate with. When his mother died, he had sold the house and contents and taken a single bag of family mementoes back to camp.

Quincy was keeping watch on the junction, so he didn't notice the slim figure in blue denim slip up the lane behind him and take cover behind the SUV. But he did see the woman with bright yellow dreads who drove a blue LandRover Discovery up to the junction. She obviously wasn't a local, as she was consulting a map and turning her head frequently in each direction.

Quincy thought he'd parked far enough back to be invisible, but the woman suddenly stared at the gap between buildings. Then she glanced in the mirror, before spinning the wheel and moving her vehicle rapidly toward him.

He didn't like the look on her face one little bit.

Twenty-One

A pungent smell—mustard cut with burning rubber—filled my nostrils and I came round gasping for breath. White light made me immediately jam my eyelids shut again. When I reopened them, slowly, I discovered that the source of the light had been directed away from me. I tried to move, but my arms and legs were tightly secured.

A face moved into my line of vision and I blinked to clear the dampness. My eyes hadn't deceived me.

'Matt Wells,' said Heinz Rothmann, his aquiline nose as prominent as ever. Otherwise, he looked different—his head had been shaved and there was a livid scar on each of his cheeks. 'Welcome.' He smiled in the humorless way I remembered. 'I've been waiting for you.'

'Where am I?' I tried to remember what I'd been doing before I lost consciousness. Whatever he'd used to wake me up had faded and there was now a familiar metallic taste in my mouth. What was it?

'You are where no one can find you,' Rothmann said, the smile still playing on his thin lips. 'In a place where

I am the sole master.' He tapped my forearm and I felt a stabbing pain. 'You were good enough to advise us of the positioning device beneath your skin. It is currently being taken deep into the Big Thicket. In the meantime, you have been moved to another location.'

I closed my eyes and tried to make sense of what he was saying. The bastard was way ahead of me. My memory finally fired and my brain rebooted. He had lured us to the road between Warren and Fred. The inverted cross on the tree had been a setup. But that meant Nora Jacobsen had been primed to deceive us via her daughter. It wasn't so strange; Rothmann would have known that the Feds and I would go to them—there wasn't anyone else. Then I thought of Quincy—what had happened to him? Shit. Now I realized what the steely taste was. It had been in my mouth at the camp in Maine after indoctrination sessions. What else had I revealed while I was out?

'Matt?' Rothmann took hold of my chin with the latex-covered fingers of one hand. 'Come back to me.'

The command was irresistible. I opened my eyes immediately, my whole body stiffening as if I was coming to attention.

'Yes, my Führer.'

Jesus, did I say that? I really had been conditioned.

Rothmann took his hand away and stepped back. 'That's better.' He looked at his watch, a curiously old-fashioned silver thing. 'Twenty-three hours have passed since we liberated you and put you back through coffining. What do you remember?'

So I had been subjected to the drugs and the machine

that robbed people of their souls. 'Nothing,' I said, which was the truth. The fact that I was still able to reason with myself showed that the conditioning process hadn't been fully completed. Yet.

'Good,' he said. 'It is gratifying that my late sister's process has remained deep in your subconscious, waiting for enhancement. You have been good enough to describe the measures taken by the FBI's scientists to counteract the conditioning. It would appear they have been—how shall I put it?—rather deficient.'

I let him believe that. The fact was, I had no idea how long I'd be able to fight the process.

'Ah, come in,' Rothmann said, turning to his left. 'Our friend is awake.'

The familiar face of Gordy Lister came into view. He seemed to have lost weight and there were dark rings round his eyes.

'Hey, asshole,' the small man said. 'Bet you hoped you'd never see us again.'

I was submissive without wanting to be, but whatever look was on my face enraged him. He moved his hand forward rapidly and grabbed my throat.

'Whaddya know about my brother?' he demanded, squeezing with surprising strength.

I tried to place his brother, but the pain made that impossible.

'Let him go!' Rothmann ordered.

That had an immediate effect. I panted for breath.

'Sorry,' Lister said, his eyes avoiding the other man's.

'Sorry, what?'

'Sorry, Master,' the small man said, with a degree

of reluctance. So, Rothmann's megalomania hadn't decreased since I'd last seen him.

'Answer him, Matt,' Rothmann commanded.

I felt the tingling throughout my body again as the conditioning kicked in. I recited the report about Lister's brother being killed in a hit-and-run incident in Florida.

'Is that it?' Lister said, clearly disappointed.

I nodded. 'There were no witnesses.'

'No witnesses, my ass. You think people are dumb enough to talk to the Feds about a hit?'

'It was a hit?' I tried to disguise my curiosity.

'Oh, yeah. Some bitch with short blond hair deliberately ran him down. You sure you don't know anything more about it?'

I glanced at Rothmann. He was following the exchange with interest. That was hardly surprising, since an attack on Lister's brother might well have been an indirect attack on him. But I didn't care about that—what did worry me was the reference to the woman with short blond hair. Could she be—?

'I'll take that as a no, then,' Gordy said, frowning at Rothmann. 'Our boy here's going to need some more sessions. His brains are scrambled to shit.'

He was right, but not in the way he thought. My thought processes were all over the place. Where was Quincy? Had he completely lost track of me? Had Rothmann managed to cancel out the hatred I felt for him in under twenty-four hours? Was I going to be turned into one of his brainwashed killers? Had Sara been one of the women in Maine? How long would it be until she found me wherever I was now?

'Oh, by the way,' Rothmann said, 'you told me earlier

what happened to our former subject Karen Oaten and your son.' He gave a short, punctilious bow. 'My sympathies.'

That was enough to bring back everything I had felt about the Nazi fucker. I was going to rip his heart out, no matter how many times I was coffined.

Peter Sebastian had planned to spend the morning in the J. Edgar Hoover building. He got in before the Washington Beltway filled up and was surprised to find Arthur Bimsdale already installed in the office.

'Morning, sir,' his assistant said, with great enthusiasm.

Sebastian gave him a weary nod. He had quarreled with his wife the night before and ended up sleeping in the guest room, so Bimsdale's good cheer was as welcome as a cup of acid. The problem was, the young agent had come up with a potentially useful lead. They had been looking into Heinz Rothmann's companies since the massacre at the cathedral, but even the financial crime experts had been unable to identify all his backers—he had used a London-based investment bank to create an impenetrable web of foreign and offshore companies around his U.S. operations.

'How can you be sure about this?' Sebastian asked, after reading the report.

'I have a friend in Immigration. Also, I called the Willard. Sir Andrew is there until Friday.'

'I hope they haven't passed on that we're interested in him.'

'No chance. I said I worked for Senator Austiner—I saw from the latter's schedule that they're lunching on Thursday.'

Sebastian shook his head. 'I don't want to know the details. All right, Sir Andrew Frogget is chairman of Routh Limited. He's been personally involved in dealings with Woodbridge Holdings, Rothmann's holding company. The London Metropolitan Police have already questioned him at length, in the presence of FBI representatives, and got nowhere. What makes you think he'll break the banker's confidence now?'

'The recent killings. If you tell him Rothmann's involved, you'll bring him around, sir, I'm sure of that.'

'Are you?' Sebastian said icily. 'As far as I recall, we have no direct evidence that Rothmann is involved in the Hitler's Hitman killings.' On the other hand, he thought, there had been no major developments in any of the four cases and Matt Wells hadn't made contact for over twenty-four hours. Things were looking bad— maybe a bit of lateral thinking was what he needed. Bimsdale put a folder down on the desk like a poker player with an unbeatable hand.

Sebastian opened it. 'Nice, Special Agent,' he said, riffling through the color photos. 'Very nice.' They showed the Routh employee Gavin Burdett as he looked after he'd been dragged from the Anacostia River, ironically during the search for Rothmann himself. It hadn't been easy to identify him, but his brother found a small scar on his ankle. 'All right, let's give it a try.'

It wasn't much after eight when they got to the hotel. They were hoping that the English gentleman wouldn't have already left. That was confirmed by the duty manager, who looked concerned when they showed their ID, but gave them the relevant room number without delay. Sebastian told him not to let Sir Andrew know they were on their way up.

The Englishman showed neither surprise nor concern when they identified themselves and asked them
to make themselves comfortable. He was wearing a
hotel robe and had a towel round his neck. The suite
was large and luxurious.

'Lucky you caught me, actually,' he said, in the ef-
fortless drawl Sebastian had noted before in upper-class
Brits. 'I went out for a run.'

Bimsdale couldn't contain himself. 'You were cap-
tain of the Cambridge University athletics team.'

Sir Andrew smiled. 'Several decades ago.' He wiped
his patrician face and smoothed back ash-blond hair
that was longer than the average banker's. 'Now, let me
guess. You're here about Jack Thomson, also known as
Heinz Rothmann.'

'That's correct, sir,' Sebastian said, glancing at his
assistant to keep him quiet. 'Have you heard about the
murders that—'

'I do read the papers,' Frogget interrupted. 'As far
as I can gather, there's nothing to tie them to Jack. It's
all—'

'The FBI will make that judgment, Sir Andrew,' Sebastian said, reluctant to cede control of the dialogue.
'There's every chance your former client will be connected to these horrific killings.' He leaned forward
across the ornate table. 'Do you really want your bank
to be painted with the blood of innocent victims—people, I might add, who worked tirelessly against injustice
and intolerance?'

Frogget poured himself a glass of orange juice from
the tray on the table and gestured to the others to help
themselves. 'Very good, Mr. Sebastian, very good.
But I'm afraid Routh Limited has plenty of clients

with—shall we say?—unsavory profiles. Client con-fidentiality is paramount to us.'

'How about future business prospects in the most powerful country in the world?' Sebastian said, trying a preliminary scare tactic. 'Rothmann and his people tried to kill the President of the United States. Do you seriously want to go against us on this?'

The Englishman poured himself more juice. 'You really should try this—it's fresh.' He looked at them both. 'No? Very well. Listen, Mr. Sebastian. I should have our lawyer in here, but I'm willing to cut you some slack over this unannounced visit. However, once and for all, I am not able to discuss Woodbridge Holdings.'

Sebastian turned to his assistant, who took out a file and opened it in front of the Englishman.

'Good God,' Frogget said, his face whitening. 'Is this—'

'Your colleague and friend Gavin Burdett?' Sebas-tian said harshly. 'Who else? You know who killed him.'

'I most certainly do not,' Sir Andrew said, leaving the photos spread across the table.

'Or had him killed.' The senior FBI man stood up and went over to the windows. The sun was glinting on the glass of the capital's buildings. 'Sir Andrew, do you by any chance have an interest in devil worship?'

The Englishman's chin jerked up, but he did not grace the question with an answer.

'Your man Burdett did.'

'Rubbish.'

'He was in deeper with Rothmann than you think.

You know about the Antichurch of Lucifer Triumphant, of course.'

Frogget's lips twisted. 'Infantile lunacy. I can't believe Jack would be involved.'

'You'd better believe it. It's your worst nightmare. Routh Limited has been working for a Nazi Satanist.'

Sir Andrew got to his feet. 'We do not judge the political and religious beliefs of our clients.' He glanced down at the photos and shook his head. 'It won't do, gentlemen. Really, it won't. I have rights. You can't treat me like some tatterdemalion drug dealer.'

'They have rights, too,' Sebastian pointed out. 'What you've got is contacts.'

'Which I'll be certain to use. Will that be all?'

'Leave the photos of Mr. Burdett, Special Agent.'

As they approached the door, Arthur Bimsdale directed his gaze at the Englishman. 'Good day to you, sir,' he said. 'I hope you find a suitable bodyguard.'

'What bodyguard?' Frogget said, his eyes widening.

'Oh, I assumed you'd be hiring one,' Bimsdale replied. 'You see, we'll be posting on the Bureau's website that you helped us this morning.'

As they walked to the elevator, Sebastian turned to him. 'Jesus, Arthur, way to go.'

Bimsdale looked like a puppy whose belly was being stroked. 'He was in the British army,' he said diffidently. 'That would explain why the photos didn't really shock him.'

'Now you tell me.'

Abaddon had stood on the Discovery's brakes a couple of feet from the gap between the houses. The black guy at the driver's seat of the big BMW stared at her, but he looked to be in control of himself. She took the Heckler and Koch pistol from the passenger seat and opened the door. Then she caught sight of the figure moving up the narrow space between the BMW and the wall of the house to the right. There was a black balaclava over the individual's face and what looked like a Ruger machine pistol in their right hand. It only took Abaddon a moment to decide that she didn't need to be here any longer.

She pulled the door shut and shifted into Reverse. A minute later she was on the other side of Warren, in a quiet side street. She needed to do two things. First: change her appearance. That didn't take long. She removed the dreadlocks and put on a brown bob. Then she changed her clothes, putting on a floral dress. All she had to do now was find another vehicle. She fully expected to be tailing people who would be told about the Discovery, so it had to go. Her employer would understand the necessity. She looked in the mirror as a dumb-looking young white man in a dirty white T-shirt pulled up behind her in a nondescript blue pickup. Truly, the Lord Lucifer was benevolent.

Abaddon got out and gave the young man a broad smile. She hadn't buttoned her dress up all the way.

'How you doin', darlin'?' she said in a sultry voice. 'My, ain't you a big, strong boy?'

It wasn't long till they were headed out of town in convoy, heading north. The guy in the pickup was leading the way to what he said was a right pretty place for a picnic. Not that they had any food or drink. To make it convincing, Abaddon had told him she was a working girl. He said she'd be paying *him* when she saw what he had in his pants.

Half an hour later, she stopped about fifty yards down the road from the junction at the east of Warren. There was no sign of the BMW and its driver, which was good. She could only hope that the people she wanted to follow would appear at the junction. Sometimes, hope was all you could work with, hope transformed into prayer to the Lucifer Triumphant, and the friends who had been initiated into His worship.

The fool who owned the pickup she was driving didn't have any hope now, despite the fact that he was at the wheel of the best car he'd ever set foot in. The Discovery was up to its roof in the swamp and his neck wouldn't support a feather. He'd never had a chance to show her what he had in his pants. It only struck her later that she didn't know her last two victims' names. For some reason that made her uneasy, but the sensation passed in seconds. They weren't the first of her dead to be nameless.

Then she received the text message that she'd hoped and prayed for, and everything became so simple. She didn't have to follow anyone; she could head to the rite location in her own time. The Antichurch would soon return to its original, pristine glory.

Twenty-Two

The were there again, the woman and the infant, standing on the far side of a fast-moving river. She had one arm extended, the other clutching the child, and her mouth was moving, but I couldn't hear her words above the rush of the murky water. Her eyes were fixed on me and I recognized her, I knew she meant something to me—what was it? And the child? Was it mine? It seemed it might be, but why couldn't I join them, why couldn't I leap into the stream and swim across? I looked down and saw movement in the water, rapid flicks and sudden thrashes above the surface. There were creatures in it, silver-scaled with long snouts. I couldn't face them. I was afraid. I raised my head and saw that the woman and child had turned away. She was striding with her head held high, into a forest of tall, dense trees. They disappeared.

'Buna.' The word wrenched me back to myself. 'Buna.'

I kept my eyes closed and brought some order to my thoughts. I knew the voice. It was Rothmann's. Was the word a trigger? I searched my memory, flailing at a faint recollection. Buna. Yes, I knew what it was: the synthetic rubber produced by the Nazis. Dr. Rivers had told me so after I reacted to the stimulus. It was a trigger that we had neutralized. I immediately went into the zone that we had worked to reproduce. I reacted as I hoped Rothmann would expect, jerking open my eyes and clenching my fists. I tensed my entire body, realizing that I was on a bed and had been restrained.

Rothmann wore a strange gown of black material with a high collar. His eyes flicked from me to the screens in front of him. He was checking my heart rate and other vital signs to see if I was responding appropriately. I could only hope that the procedures Dr. Rivers had developed were adequate. Time passed very slowly. Eventually, Rothmann stood up and signaled to the technician beside me. The monitors were switched off and electrodes removed from my head and chest.

'Untie his bonds,' Rothmann said, sounding like a Biblical character—one whose teachings were the opposite of Christ's. He moved closer and helped me sit up. His forearms were bony, but he was strong enough.

I played up my level of befuddlement.

'Very good, Matt,' Rothmann said, in an unusually soft voice. 'You have done well. I have just one more thing for you to do today.'

I wondered what acting skills that would require. Then a short figure moved into the light.

'How'd it go?' Gordy Lister asked.

Rothmann turned and gave him a death stare.

'How'd it go, *Master?*' Lister said, dropping his gaze.

'We are ready for the test I mentioned earlier. Pass the word.'

Before he left, the small man gave me a look that was oddly sympathetic. I began to get a bad feeling about what was coming. I reckoned drastic measures were required and went into rhetorical mode.

'The National Socialist movement is not a cult,' I pronounced, 'but a racial and political philosophy grown out of exclusively racist principles. It does not have the meaning of a mystic cult, but aims to cultivate and command a *people* determined by blood. Therefore we do not have cult centers, but *people* centers. We do not have places of worship, but places for *people* to assemble and march. In the National Socialist movement, subversion by occult seekers for some hidden truth is not tolerated.'

Rothmann followed the translation of Adolf Hitler's words that had been planted in my mind during the original indoctrination process, and then nodded impatiently.

'Yes, yes, very good, but things are different now.' He stretched his arms wide and spoke to an invisible congregation. 'Cult is the basis of all we do. The Führer's ideology of discipline, racial purity and conquest is, of course, the intellectual underpinning of our work. But the keystone is our belief in Lucifer, inspirer of victories and god of baleful triumphs.'

I watched as spittle flew from his lips and his eyes shot back icy glints at the light. Something had happened to Heinz Rothmann. When I'd met him before, he had been the soulless son of a stonehearted Nazi. Now he was overflowing with the wide-eyed, utterly misdirected faith of a religious zealot. From using the Antichurch as a means to attract followers and bind the indoctrinated even more closely to his plans of domination, he had turned into a spokesman for the original force of evil.

'And now,' he said, coming out of his trancelike state, 'you will show me how dependable you are, Matt.'

He took my arm and led me out of the treatment room. The surgical gown was pulled off me by a dead-eyed young man in blue denim. I was given a black cotton outfit and shoes, and motioned to put them on.

'Ready?' Rothmann said.

'Yes, Master,' I replied, choosing that title rather than Hitler's and modeling my stance on the young man's. How many of these zombies had Rothmann produced? I had hoped that his sister's death would have left him without technical knowledge, but he must have retained some scientific personnel. He also seemed to have forgiven me for killing her—or was I about to find out otherwise?

I was led though a heavy door, and blinked in the sunlight. There was thin cloud cover, but I hadn't seen natural light for some time and it hurt. When my sight got accustomed, I realized I was standing in a wide space between tall wooden buildings that looked like barns. A decrepit tractor stood against one of the walls, all of which were in need of several coats of paint. I breathed in. The air no longer had the rank edge of the Big Thicket. How far had I been taken from it? Without the bug in my arm, I could be a long way from help. Shit.

Then I saw what was in the middle of the space and my gut took a somersault. An upturned cross of roughly hewn timber stood ten feet in the air from a heap of rocks, its horizontal ends hung with black rags and a steel ring at the top of the vertical. My gut did another vault. A naked figure was hanging by the ankles from a rope tied to the ring, its arms bound to the horizontal beam. The skin was black and, as I looked closer, I saw that the figure was male. It was Quincy Jerome.

I felt Rothmann's eyes on me.

'You know this man, do you not?'

My heart was thundering, but I got a grip on myself and tried to think straight. It was important to keep up the charade until I could come up with a plan of action.

'Yes, Master,' I said obediently. 'He is a paratroop sergeant assigned to protect me.'

Rothmann nodded. He had probably heard from Nora Jacobsen about the black man who was with me in Maine. 'And what is his name?'

I supplied that in its correct form, feeling like a traitor, but I had to buy time and playing along was the only way I could think of to accomplish that.

'What are your feelings about him?' the Master asked, as we drew closer to the cross.

'I don't like soldiers,' I said, trying to avoid Quincy's eyes. His face was swollen and bloody.

Rothmann turned and looked at me expectantly.

I took a deep breath. 'And he's black, so that makes him an *untermensch*.' I felt even more like a Judas—I had black friends back in the U.K.

The young man in blue denim stepped forward and clicked the heels of his boots. The Master nodded and his minion produced a metal baseball bat from behind his back. It was offered to me, the zombie drawing a semiautomatic pistol from his belt with the other hand. Rothmann didn't seem to be afraid of me, which meant that my performance was working. I wasn't quick enough to hit him before being shot, though.

'You know what you have to do,' the Master said, looking at Quincy disdainfully.

Out of the corner of my eye, I could see the muzzle of the pistol that was trained on me. I held the bat in a two-handed grip and did the calculation: I was too far from the gunman to hit him before he put me down. That left only one option. Keeping my eyes off Quincy's, I stepped forward, measured the blow and drew the heavy bat back past my shoulder.

The Soul Collector was in trouble. She groaned and clenched the steering wheel as hard as she could. Why now? She'd only needed a few more hours. Couldn't it have held off for a day? Wasn't she entitled to the revenge she'd been waiting so long for? Why now?

The irony that she was in a perfect position didn't escape her. Tailing Matt and his oversize black sidekick to the airport in Portland had been easy enough. She had turned herself into a seedy middle-aged man with the application of a gray wig and mustache, and some truly boring clothes. The flight to Newark hadn't been full and she had stuck close enough to hear Matt mention Houston. That flight wasn't full either, though she had to go business class. She thought she had lost Matt at the airport in Texas, but she picked him up again as she drove the Toyota Highlander she'd rented toward the exit. She'd seen which rental company he'd gone to after he'd picked up a bag from the luggage lockers, and she knew where its cars were stationed. She checked into the hotel opposite the one Matt had used and had been waiting for him in the morning, this time disguised as a dowdy woman in an oversize dress. She knew the black guy would be following Matt, but he wasn't close—presumably they had a system.

The pain started as they approached the Big Thicket. Although it had initially been in her upper back, now she felt it in her midriff. She was sweating even more than the temperature merited and she felt nauseous— she actually threw up as they drove into Warren, the bitter liquid spilling down the inside of the Highlander's door. The stink nearly made her vomit again, but her stomach was empty.

Sara had kept her distance when Matt headed down the road numbered 1943 and the plethora of tracks on each side of the road worried her. There was no short-age of turnouts, though, and Matt didn't look like he knew where he was going. He pulled up at a tree with a strange mark on it, and then turned onto a rough track through the trees. It was after she'd stopped and fol-lowed him on foot that the pain really got to her, forcing her to her knees and then into the fetal position. She recovered in time to see her former lover's unconscious form being loaded into a pickup truck by a figure in denim and a demon mask. The vehicle came slowly back up the bumpy track and she was able to attach a magnetic location finder to the rear axle.

That had exhausted her and she staggered back to the Highlander. The pickup was still in range and she followed it, keeping a mile between them and allowing other vehicles to pass her.

And now she was in a clearing in the Crockett Na-tional Forest, about forty miles northwest of Warren, waiting for the sun to go down. She had spent the pre-vious day and night in another out-of-the-way spot, in too much agony to move. The vehicle she had bugged had been stationary for all that time, so she hoped Matt was still there—it was about a mile ahead, in the depths of the woods. She presumed it was Heinz Rothmann's hideaway, although he didn't have priority. Her former lover was the number one target. She would take him down whatever the cost to herself.

The Soul Collector took another couple of painkillers. There was birdsong all around, the light falling in shafts between the trunks of trees she couldn't identify. Her back was racked again, and she recalled what the doctor had said. Apart from the cancer, she was in excellent physical condition, but she couldn't expect that to continue. She would get weaker, and would eventually need twenty-four-hour care. With the right combination of medication, she might stave off the worst effects for a month, but after that her decline would be more rapid. The bastard had actually smiled when he advised her to get her affairs in order. No doubt her manner, her refusal to accept any of what he'd said, had made him uncomfortable, even riled him.

The Soul Collector didn't care. She would be fighting to the end and she would take Matt Wells with her. That idea was all that kept her going.

Gordy Lister was standing at the edge of the space between the barns. A timber merchant had put the buildings up years back and there was a clearing of about a hundred yards outside. That made the place easy to fortify and, in recent weeks, the Master's miniature SS had put listening devices in the open ground. Anyone trying to approach except by the single track that led to the main gate would be spotted and hunted

down. The first of the Antichurch faithful had already
arrived and had been assigned one of the barns. They
were surprisingly normal-looking people, though you
wouldn't want to take them home to Mom. They had
the faraway eyes and hair-trigger temper of all religious
lunatics.

Not for the first time, Gordy wondered exactly what
he had gotten himself into. Working for Rothmann, Jack
Thomson, as he called himself at the newspaper, had
been a gas: no two days the same, plenty of cash, the
rush of wielding real power. Back then he hadn't realized how cracked the boss was, but the attack in the
cathedral had put him right. He should have hit the road
weeks ago. Maybe he would, after this ridiculous rite
was over. On the other hand, he also wanted to know
who had killed his brother, and the Master was the most
likely person to find that out. The Englishman Matt
Wells knew more than he was letting on. Then again,
the Englishman was about to beat the black guy's head
in and only a fully qualified zombie would do that.

Gordy Lister had turned his head from the men standing round the inverted cross, but at the last moment he
couldn't resist and turned it back as Wells raised the
baseball bat and swung it with wicked force.

Twenty-Three

I let out a great yell as I heaved the bat toward Quincy's head. Since he was hanging upside down, it was more like a golf shot than a baseball swing, but I'd never played either sport so I was improvising. Fortunately the sound I made didn't provoke Quincy into moving, so the metal bat thudded into the vertical under an inch from the side of his cranium. The wooden cross shook from the force of the blow, and nerves tingled all the way up my arms. I bent over, breathing heavily, and wondered what would happen now.

There was silence for longer than was comfortable. I straightened up slowly, letting the bat drop to the ground to show I wasn't interested in strike two. I must have been programmed not to carry out the execution in full.

'Very well,' Rothmann said, moving closer. 'You are willing enough, Matt Wells. We will continue your treatment after the Antichurch's great annual rite, at which your presence is required.' He gave me an encouraging smile.

I mumbled thanks, but my concern was what he would do to Quincy.

'Leave him where he is,' the Master said to the guard. 'He will be needed later.'

I didn't like the sound of that, but there wasn't much I could do. Two more denim wonder boys came up and were ordered to take me to the 'old barn.' That turned out to be a small building on the other side of the open space. The planks on its sides were buckled and its frame was uneven, but there were bars all over the windows. I was shoved inside and the door locked behind me. Solitary confinement.

There was a bed with a thin mattress in one corner of the confined interior, a large plastic bottle of water next to it. I walked around, checking the windows and walls—although the latter looked flimsy from outside, they were solid enough. Breaking out would make a lot of noise and I imagined there were guards in the proximity. The roof beams were too high for me to reach, even when I stood on the bed, and the dusty concrete for a floor ruled out digging. It looked like I'd be staying put.

I lay down on the bed and tried to get some sleep. My mouth was dry and the metallic taste lingered. I had no idea what drugs had been pumped into my system, but at least I was being given a break from the indoctrination process. I looked at the water bottle and decided against drinking, even though I was thirsty. The chances were the contents weren't pure and I didn't need any more of Rothmann's pharmacological concoctions.

I closed my eyes, but they were immediately filled with visions of the lost woman and child. I jackknifed off the bed and gazed around desperately, needing something to take my mind off them. The pain was too much to bear, and even the thought that I might be able to make Rothmann pay didn't help anymore.

Then I saw it. The book was leather-bound, the brown cover like stained wood. I hadn't noticed it before because it was in what I realized was a specially constructed wooden holder by the door, only the top couple of inches protruding. I went over and took it out. It wasn't long before my fingers began to twitch as if they had touched some kind of nerve agent. An inverted cross had been cut crudely into the soft leather.

I opened the book and read the title: *The Antigospel of the Lord Lucifer, as licensed by the Master of the Antichurch of Lucifer Triumphant.* The paper quality was good and it looked recent, although there was no date or publisher. As I flicked through the text, it became obvious that no respectable publisher or printer would have allowed their name anywhere near it. There were section headings such as 'Sacrifice of Unworthy Humans to the Lord Lucifer,' 'Children's Blood as an Unholy Sacrament' and 'The Rite of Rape.' It seemed incredible that an intelligent man like Rothmann would buy into such a crock of shit.

I turned to the section called 'The Master's Word' and began to realize that something strange was going on. Although the print and format were uniform, the style differed greatly between paragraphs. The majority were written in clumsy, old-fashioned language, with a lot of manipulation of New Testament phrases. So, the Master 'walks the fields of ruination, glorying in the light of the underworld'; 'whosoever wishes eternal life, let him know that the kingdom of hell is at hand and the powers that be are ordained of Lucifer'; 'Glory be to Lucifer Triumphant, on earth confusion, and evil will toward unbelieving men,' and so on. But other parts seemed more modern, both in language and content: 'Anyone who doubts the Master's word will live to regret it'; 'disobedience and ill discipline will be punished severely' and even, 'the Master's faithful servants must always be obeyed'—that struck me as a reference to the brainwashed killers Rothmann and his sister had created.

I read on and it became clear that, among the various subtexts, was one stressing the infallibility of the Master, which was written in contemporary English. There were references to what seemed to be a previous regime—'the false leaders'—who had diluted the Antichurch founder Jeremiah Dodds' 'fiery words, forged in the cauterizing cold of the white North.' I took that to refer to Maine, where the cult had been founded. At least, that was what Mary Upson had told me after I escaped from Rothmann's camp up there. It seemed that followers of the 'false leaders' disputed this, saying that the Antichurch had been born in the 'broken, burning South.'

The Antigospel was about as clear as a muddy brook at midnight, but meaning was less important to the faithful than the symbolic power of the language. It did seem clear that there had been more than one faction, but that Rothmann's side was in charge now. I almost felt sorry for his opponents, even though they were crazy devil worshippers. I had the strong feeling that the current Master had consigned many of them to the inverted cross and human sacrifice—which made me think about the imminent annual rite. I had heard vehicles arriving regularly, accompanied by shouts and cries of greeting.

Toward the end of the book was a list of the great rites—Beltane, All Souls' Night and so on. Most of the description seemed to be standard satanic claptrap involving obscure folk beliefs and perversions of Christian services, with a lot of violence and death thrown in. The current Master seemed as enthusiastic about that as his predecessors and opponents, stressing that 'Lucifer is at His most triumphant when his followers engage in human sacrifice and mutilation.' The annual rite, on 'the eve of the liar Jesus Christ's birthday,' was the Antichurch's greatest festival, the one that brought most glory to Lucifer. The climax, which definitely bore the mark of the Rothmanns, was a ceremony called 'self-coffining.'

I had a bad feeling about that for two reasons. One, my watch had been taken and I was unclear about dates—I suspected today was December 24th. And two, even reading the word *self-coffining* made hairs all over my body stand up and sent electricity sparking across my brain. I knew that coffining was part of the indoctrination process, but this sounded even worse. Had I been conditioned to take part in some sacred suicide pact?

Abaddon had parked in a clearing over three miles from the location she had been given and set off through the woods. The Crockett National Forest wasn't as thick as some she'd seen and she made reasonable time through the undergrowth. At least there were fewer insects here. The ground was drier and the air didn't have such a mephitic stench as the swamps farther south. It was late afternoon when she got her first sight of the cluster of buildings called Big Barns. There looked to be clear ground all around, meaning she would have to wait until dark to cross it. She scanned the area through binoculars, noting potential danger points.

She sat against a tree trunk and went through the rucksack she'd been carrying, drinking some water first and then eating two apples. A chill was coming down over the trees and she put on the black waterproof jacket tied round her waist. Checking that the Heckler & Koch machine pistol was ready for use, she put three extra clips in her pocket and slipped the pistol inside her belt next to the flashlight. That left her laptop. She considered sending a message to her employer, but decided against it—there would be time enough after the attack. Besides, she would need to work out what to tell the company. Her brother would help with that.

Abaddon thought about Apollyon. Their father, the fifth leader of the Antichurch, had given them the names, the Hebrew and Greek alternatives for 'the angel of the bottomless pit,' according to Chapter 9 of the Book of Revelation. That was the only book of the Christian Bible afforded even partial credence in the cult. Until the Enemy had stolen the Antichurch of Lucifer Triumphant's name, Abaddon and Apollyon had been heirs to the throne. Their father had died a year ago and now they were going to take back what was rightly theirs. The businessman Jack Thomson had claimed that he knew nothing of the Southern branch of the cult, saying that he was following the Antichurch set up by Jeremiah Dodds in Maine.

Trouble was, Jeremiah had fallen out with his brother Jasper, the real founder of the cult, in 1847. They had grown up in Atlanta, in the house her brother still lived in, though he didn't use the Dodds name anymore. Jasper realized Jeremiah wanted to be leader and threatened him with violence if he persisted. That made Jeremiah tremble, so he up and left for Maine, where his version of the Antichurch was taken apart by the FBI after the attack on the President.

But Jasper had been smarter. Just as bloodthirsty as his brother, he was much more careful. Using profits from his brewery, he established links with the Klan and other supremacist groups, ensuring the cult's safety as well as providing it with a steady stream of members. There was no shortage of victims, either—originally they had primarily been blacks, but recently the Antichurch had become an equal opportunity killing machine. Abaddon's professional activities had been a useful source of funds as well as expertise, though Apollyon was no slouch when it came to violence: he just preferred to spend more time playing politics in Georgia, constructing the image of a trustworthy family man and conning people. The Lord Lucifer must have been very proud.

Looking out across the open ground through her binoculars, Abaddon noticed small, uneven sections. Landmines. There would be intrusion sensors of one kind or another, too, she was sure of that. She didn't care. She had enough grenades to cause a major diversion. When the guards came running out, she would observe their access route and then mow them down.

Besides, the fools inside would be busy with their heretical version of the annual rite. Apollyon and she had agreed that they would mark their joint leadership with a ceremony on the eve of the New Year.

That year would be dedicated to the Lord Lucifer Triumphant, who would surely be delighted with the blood that was about to be spilled in his name.

They came for me when the last of the sunlight had gone from the skylight in the small barn's roof. I was sitting like Buddha, concentrating on empting my mind of superfluous material. I hoped that would include any more triggers Rothmann had planted in my subconscious, because I was going to make a move during the rite. At the very least, perhaps I would manage to do Rothmann some damage before his boys got to me.

As it happened, one of the pair who came for me was a young woman—just as unyielding as her male comrades and her blue eyes were icy.

'So, how's it going for you guys?' I asked, trying to shake them up. 'Looking forward to the human sacrifice?'

They didn't even glance at me as they latched onto my upper arms and pulled me from the barn. The space between the buildings now contained several vehicles, ranging from top-of-the-range off-road giants to rusty old pickups. There were more guards around, though most were heading in the same direction as we were.

I was taken to a door that opened at the young woman's triple knock. I found myself in a kind of multi-sex dressing room, except I'd forgotten the dress code—the faithful at Antichurch rites were naked. An undressing room, then.

Fortunately, I was allowed to keep my clothes. Perhaps I had to be formally inducted by Rothmann before I was allowed to join the pale-skinned masses—and pale-skinned was what they had been in Maine.

I was led down a narrow passage and out into what was obviously the assembly room—the interior of a large barn. There must have been fifty people in there, standing naked and in total silence. My nostrils filled with the high smell of butchered flesh and I looked at the walls. All were hung with animals that had recently been killed, their blood and entrails staining the wood and the floor below. Some were small—dogs, raccoons, rabbits—and others bulky—cows and pigs. There were even birds—hawks with their wings stretched out—and an alligator with its jaws pointing downward. The place was a charnel house in the making.

I was put in a chair at the front with guards holding a shotgun on either side, both dressed. That cut down my room for maneuver substantially—I had been considering lashing out at their bare groins. I could only hope they would be distracted by the proceedings. I looked to the front and was immediately distracted myself. There were three inverted crosses standing up from heaps of stones. Quincy was hanging from the one on my left, and a woman with her head in a sack was on the right. Both were naked and bore the signs of beating. The central cross was empty, but beside it was a coffin, its lid propped on one side. I felt my mouth go dry. Who was the box meant for?

Suddenly the faithful started screaming and wailing. The noise was deafening and I looked to my right. Even though I'd seen the masks before, when I'd been in the camp in Maine, they still made me jerk back in horror. The tall man who had appeared first, naked and with a large erection, had the head of a hyena, the pelt a greasy orange shade and the jaws studded with vicious teeth. He was slashing left and right with a short whip. To his rear came a figure in a black cloak with the head of the ugliest gargoyle imaginable, the features crushed and twisted and the eyes bulging, as if it had been pounded with a heavy hammer. The pair moved onto the raised platform in front of the inverted crosses.

Hyena-Head faced the faithful. 'In the beginning was the Master's word,' Rothmann's voice cried, 'and the Master's word was Lucifer!'

The crowd went even wilder.

Twenty-Four

Rudi Crane was at the top of the control tower of the Hercules Solutions facility known as Cedar Fort, fifty miles south of Columbus, Ohio. Although night had fallen, he was watching the exercise below with thermal optic glasses. His instructors had set the Arab troops a pretty straightforward task—the storming of a sparsely occupied bunker—and so far they were making quite a mess of it. The swarthy colonel to his left was puffing and blowing in disgust. Crane would have liked to see him take command on the ground, but that wasn't the corpulent officer's style. Only blanks were being fired, which was just as well—live rounds would have reduced the attackers to a handful.

Swinging the binoculars to his right, Crane picked up the faint glow of lights in the distance. The nearest town, not much more than a general store and a few run-down houses, was nearly ten miles to the west. On the other sides, the fort was surrounded by Wayne National Forest. His contacts in the Pentagon had provided Hercules Solutions with access to different kinds of terrain in and around the forest, making Cedar Fort the world's most attractive destination for armed forces and police departments requiring specialized training. That access was still guaranteed, despite the government's cooler approach to the company. The men in suits had to react to public pressure, largely stirred up by busybodies and unelected organizations. Deep down, they knew how essential the company was to national security.

The crackle of automatic weapons fire died down. Rudi Crane looked back at the compound below. Smoke was drifting over a lot of immobile forms. The Arab troops had been told they were all dead.

'Exercise over,' a clipped voice said in his earpiece. 'Attackers neutralized.'

'Your men are enthusiastic,' Crane commented to the colonel, who was struggling to contain his rage.

'They have disgraced the uniform of our country,' the heavy man said, stamping the floor with one of his highly polished boots. 'I will send them back immediately.'

'Don't do that, Colonel. Give us three days. I guarantee they will improve beyond recognition. But you must turn them over to my people for the whole of that time.'

Like most of his Middle Eastern customers, the colonel had refused to allow that when they arrived— he wanted to retain command. They all came around, after they'd seen how useless their men were when confronted by true professionals. Of course, the colonel would have to be otherwise occupied—Hercules Solutions had operatives who could meet any demand.

Crane went over to the elevator, after pointing the customer in that direction. He didn't need to have personal contact with the commanders, given that he knew

the men who ran their countries well. He preferred to
handle business this way, though—it showed his personal commitment to every deal and detail. The money
paid by oil-rich rulers fearful for their survival in the
modern, terrorist-ridden world made everything worth-
while.

The elevator was met at ground level by two female
Hercules employees.

Crane had already ascertained where the colonel's
tastes lay. Both women wore camouflage jackets and
skirts, the latter reaching only halfway down their
thighs. He was sure that the fat man's wife—or wives—
had to cover themselves from head to toe when they left
their homes. The colonel obviously thought he was in
some version of paradise.

He went down to the command post and swiped the
security lock to his office. Even though it was nearly
seven, his secretary was still at her desk outside. He
had brought Joanna with him from Georgia when he
moved his business and family up to Ohio ten years ago.
He knew his wife had been suspicious, but she didn't
have the nerve to complain. Not that there had ever
been anything between Crane and the buxom Joanna.
He was serious about his marriage vows—they were
an integral part of his religious beliefs. He wasn't one
of those preachers who lied and cheated, or so he told
himself every day.

Rudi Crane logged on to his computer and bypassed
the Hercules Solutions network. He wanted to know
what was going on down in Texas. It was time he had a
report. But the secure site he accessed had no new messages, and that bothered him. He felt a stir of unease.

One or other of his people should have been in touch by now.

There was only one thing to do. Rudolf Maximilian Crane got down on his knees and prayed.

The noise in the hall was deafening—wailing, chanted words, screaming. Weird music was coming from speakers hung on the walls between the animal corpses. It sounded like the cries the unfortunate creatures would have made as they stared death in the face, synthesizers and electric guitars producing a cacophony that might have raised the devil. Which, no doubt, was exactly the impression the Master was aiming at. It was working, too. The naked faithful were swaying like trees in a hurricane, their arms outstretched and their flesh shaking. Given the age of many celebrants, I chose to look to the front instead.

What I saw there was no better. Hyena-Head had started lashing Quincy's chest with his whip. I tried to get to my feet, but was immediately restrained by the guards flanking me. The figure in the gargoyle mask was concentrating on the woman, touching the breasts that were hanging toward her face. I had a feeling that it was Gordy Lister—the cloak was loose and too long. The bastard. At least he wasn't hurting her though, upside down and with her head in a sack, she must have been terrified.

Hyena-Head stopped hitting Quincy, who yelled something at him. The naked man gave him several more blows for his trouble. I was glad to see the sergeant hadn't lost his nerve, but I didn't know how I could save him from the horror that was coming. I tried to get myself into some kind of zone, but the noise of the

congregation and the stench in the air made that difficult. I stared at the empty cross, my heart thundering.
Was I going to end up there, blood rushing to my head,
vulnerable to anything the cult wanted to do? They
hadn't taken my clothes off yet, but that wasn't much
of a consolation.

Rothmann in the hyena head mask raised his whip
high and the crowd fell silent. I was ready for a sermon,
some rant about the glories of Lucifer, but he didn't say
anything. Instead, he looked toward the door at the side
of the barn. Shrieks broke out when the woman came
in. I peered at her and, stomach shrinking, recognized
who she was. She wore a black gown with her breasts
bare but, although she had a pair of long horns on her
head, she had no mask. She was carrying a knife with
a thin, curved blade. Nora Jacobsen.

I shouldn't have been surprised. The old woman had
shown how dangerous she was in Portland. But seeing
her here, features daubed in what looked like ash and
mouth set hard, still made my skin crawl. She bowed
almost to the ground in front of Hyena-Head, then put
the fingers of one hand around his erect penis. The
crowd erupted again and I wondered if I was going to
have to sit through a porn show. Fortunately, Nora Jacobsen let go after a few seconds and walked over to the
woman on the inverted cross. She crouched down and
wrenched the sack from round the prisoner's head.

I recognized Mary Upson immediately despite the
battering she had taken. Again, I was thrust back into
my seat by the guards. Before I could move, Nora
Jacobsen had cut a vertical line between her daughter's breasts, then a horizontal one under them. Blood

dripped over her face and onto the stones supporting the cross. So much for family.

Now Rothmann started to talk. 'Followers of Lucifer Triumphant! True followers, who have cast out the false leaders!'

I didn't know if he had been expecting applause or other forms of approbation, but they didn't come. The faithful were silent, their faces strangely impassive. I wondered how many of them had been brainwashed by the Rothmanns' conditioning process and how many were just old-fashioned religious lunatics.

'We gather here for the great annual rite, at which we renew our vows to Lucifer and pledge ourselves to the increase of his glory in the months to come. Your Master has already made preparations to strike a blow that will bring the misguided government of this land to its knees. With your participation, the Antichurch will gain the power it deserves.'

Again, the congregation remained silent. Perhaps they had been told in advance, but it didn't look that way because Rothmann was looking from side to side as if he was trying to elicit a response. There was a long pause before he got going again.

'And now, for the greater glory of Lord Lucifer, I bring you the new ritual that has been promised—a ritual that will bring us all closer to the life of the underworld—closer to death! Once a year, Our Lord requires self-coffining. Our sister here will give herself to Lucifer.'

There was a wave of what seemed to be discomfort across the faithful, but Nora Jacobsen wasn't waiting. She went to the empty cross, grasped it with one hand and then stabbed herself in the chest with the knife she was holding in the other. Her body dropped with a crash into the coffin that lay underneath.

Mary Upson's shrill cry split the air. Rothmann strode over to her and beat her with his whip until she was reduced to sobbing. The congregation remained quiet but, again, I sensed they were unhappy. So did Rothmann. He picked up the bloody knife that had fallen from Nora Jacobsen's hand and headed for Quincy. I was held down by the guards when I moved.

'Members of the Antichurch,' the Master yelled, 'here is an example of the races that are destroying this country. Watch as his animal heart is removed!' Then he turned to me.

I felt a tingling over my skin even before he spoke, which showed how much power he could exert. When it came, the word was almost superfluous.

'Schalk!' Rothmann screamed. 'Schalk! Execute the negro!' The crowd roared its approval.

The trigger affected me immediately. The part of me that was beyond his control—the part that still re-membered the ones I had lost—separated from my body and rose above the people in the hall. I watched as the guards allowed me to stand. I walked stiffly to the man in the hyena mask, my right hand extended. There was nothing I could do from my vantage point. I moved toward the cross from which Quincy was sus-pended. I tried to scream, tried to distract my corporeal self, but no sound came. The congregation had fallen silent. Transfixed, I raised the knife and then plunged it straight toward Quincy's defenseless throat.

Peter Sebastian had spent most of the last two hours talking to the Bureau's people in Houston. He had finally pressed the panic button at 5:00 p.m. Either Matt Wells or Quincy Jerome should have been in touch during the afternoon. He had called and sent text messages to their cell phones, but there had been no reply from either of them. He knew that the signals from their tracking implants might have been poor in the Big Thicket, so he gave Wells and Jerome a few more hours. That now looked like a mistake.

Houston's people in the vicinity had also lost contact, having held back to allow Matt and the sergeant a clear run at the Antichurch. By the time they found the tree to the east of Warren with the inverted cross carved on it, there was no sign of anyone in the vicinity. Quincy Jerome had attached a positioning device to his BMW. That led them to a clearing south of Warren. The vehicle was empty. Agents were spreading out across the area, but it was dark and there was little chance of sightings.

Sebastian had considered sending Arthur Bimsdale to Texas to keep an eye on things, but decided against that. His assistant would be of more use in Washington, especially since Sebastian himself had an urgent appointment that evening. As usual, he hadn't been given much notice. The message on the secure site that he accessed every midday was as terse as ever, providing only a time—8:00 p.m.—and a location—Room 13 in the Happy Trails Motel, a mile north of Middleburg, Virginia. He had never been there before. Checking his road map, he saw it was about thirty-five miles west of D.C. He'd allow himself an hour. Arriving late was not an option.

If Bimsdale was surprised by his departure from the office, he didn't show it. His assistant had proved

himself to be perfectly capable of working unsupervised, even if this operation was a lot more sensitive
than anything he'd dealt with in the past. It wasn't ideal,
but Sebastian had no choice. The worst of it was that
he would be turning off his cell as soon as he left the
Hoover Building, even though that was contrary to
standing orders. There were other priorities for him.

Driving onto I-66 from the Beltway, Sebastian
thought about Matt Wells. Had he blown it by using an
amateur? He still didn't think so. The fact was, Rothmann was bound to want Wells back, both to find out
what he knew and to complete the conditioning process.
The Englishman might have been aware of those fac-
tors, but he seemed only to want revenge for his family.
That was why it was so essential that they kept track of
Wells before he managed to strike at Rothmann. Sebastian himself needed to catch Rothmann to justify the
Director's faith in the operation. That was now looking
in serious jeopardy.

In the last five miles, he took a circuitous route to
the motel, stopping several times to see if he was being
tailed. He wasn't, at least as far as he could ascertain.
He had developed a talent for countersurveillance over
the years, among other things checking his car for bugs
every morning before he left home. His wife had found
him doing that once, but he'd scared her off by saying
he was looking for bombs. It was two minutes to eight
when he drove into the motel's parking lot. He parked
as far from reception as he could and took in the scene.
Number thirteen was at the end of the long building,
deliberately chosen for that reason. Resting his hand
on the butt of his Glock, Sebastian walked to the door.
There seemed to be no one around.

He knocked twice, paused, and then three times more. The door opened immediately and he went inside. The room was in darkness until the chain was applied to the door. A small light on the dresser came on.

'Peter.'

'Valerie.'

He looked at the middle-aged woman. This time she was dressed as a soccer mom, in matching blue sweatshirt and pants. Her dark brown hair was pulled back in a ponytail and she wore no makeup.

'Did they win?' he asked.

She ignored that and sat down on one of the beds. 'I've heard something that disturbs me.'

Sebastian kept a smile on his lips, hoping that the somersault his stomach had just taken wasn't obvious. If Valerie Hinton had found out about the stunt he was pulling with Matt Wells, he'd be in deep shit.

He stayed on his feet. 'What's that?'

'Sit down,' she said, refusing to allow him a dominant position and locking eyes with his. 'You've been playing hardball with Sir Andrew Frogget.'

'So?'

'So stop. Right now. That's an order.'

Sebastian looked down, aware that by breaking eye contact he had handed the field to her. He needed to find out how much she knew. 'His company worked for Heinz Rothmann—who, I would remind you, tried to take out the President and most of the cabinet.'

'Routh Limited is off-limits, Peter. I'm serious.'

'What's the CIA's interest?'

Valerie Hinton gave him a brief smile. 'That's way above your pay grade, Peter. Just do what I say. I'll leave first.'

He watched her go. During the fifteen minutes that the established protocol required him to wait before leaving, he thought about the order. The CIA had been interested in Rothmann from the beginning. He had been told to pass all his case notes to the agency as soon as the Nazi's involvement in the attack on the President was confirmed. Thankfully they hadn't used the information in a way that would implicate him—at least, not yet.

Sebastian had been working as a CIA informant for years, ever since he was caught screwing a woman with links to a drug gang in Puerto Rico. He'd have been shit-canned by the Bureau if the CIA hadn't buried his involvement, but he'd been blackmailed into keeping them advised of all his activities. So why were they so interested in Rothmann? Did they want to use his conditioning process? The Agency had a history of mind control experiments. Then again, did they imagine they could they get away with using a method developed by the children of a Nazi doctor who had worked with Mengele at Auschwitz, and had nearly assassinated the President?

The answer to that was obvious.

The real question was, could anyone stop them?

Twenty-Five

'No, Matt.' The female voice was tender, but authoritative. 'No.'

Suddenly I was reunited with my body. I stopped in midthrust, the knifepoint a few inches from Quincy's throat. I let the weapon drop to the floor.

'Karen?' I said, a wave of joy breaking over me as I turned to find her. The realization that I had remembered her name, that she was no longer one of the nameless, came at the same time as I saw Rothmann advancing toward me. He struck me several times on the face before I raised my arm to protect myself.

Karen. She wasn't here, but she had spoken to me.

'Schalk!' Rothmann screamed, tearing off the hyena mask. 'Kill the negro now!'

Bolts of electricity galvanized nerves all over my body, but my consciousness didn't rise up like it had before. The conditioning wasn't working anymore.

'Screw you,' I said, lowering my head and charging him. There was a satisfying impact and I heard the breath shoot out of his lungs. I landed on top of him, sat up and punched him on each side of his face. That didn't go down too well with his congregation. I looked up as they started to yell, and then move toward the platform with the inverted crosses. Guards in blue denim were heading my way as well, their weapons raised. I only had one option.

'Stop!' I yelled, my hands tightening on Rothmann's throat. 'Stay where you are! I can crush his windpipe in a split second.'

That arrested their progress. There were guns trained on me, but even the highly conditioned guards were hesitant. I pressed my thumbs down harder and locked eyes with Rothmann. I wanted to kill him, I wanted to join Karen wherever she was—the sound of her voice had made me even more desperate to see her again. The bastard beneath me squirmed and bucked like a dying fish, his eyes bulging. He knew exactly how serious I was.

A loud report took everyone by surprise. The guard nearest to me sprawled forward, his head an eruption of atomized bone and brain matter. More shots felled the young man and woman on either side of me. Then the barn was filled with screams and the rattle of automatic weapons fire. I had let go of Rothmann at the first shot and rolled behind him. He was gasping for breath, his hands at his throat. I could have finished him with a single blow, but I had another priority—getting Quincy Jerome and Mary Upson off the crosses. Quincy's was nearer so I went to him first, picking up Nora Jacobsen's knife on the way.

I stood on the cross's horizontal bar, avoiding Quincy's bound wrists. Bullets flew past as I reached for the rope that held his ankles. It was thick and had been dipped in something tarry, so it took me some

time to saw through the strands. When I was almost finished, I got down and started on the ropes on his wrists.
I looked at the pandemonium in front of me as I was
cutting. There were bodies on the floor. People were
on their knees clutching wounds. The guards seemed
to have taken a beating from members of the congregation, some of whom had seized their weapons and used
them against the men and women in blue denim.

I got Quincy's upper body free and pulled him away
from the cross. That broke the last strands of the rope
on his ankles and he slid to the ground in my arms.

'Keep your head down,' I said, then turned to
Mary.

To my surprise, she was already down. The black-
robed figure in the gargoyle mask was leading her to the
door, bending low and brandishing a long knife. I was
about to go after them, when a line of shots appeared
in the wooden floor ahead. I looked around desperately
for a weapon. The nearest was by the side of a dead
guard, but I was warned off that by more well-directed
gunfire. Someone wanted me to stay where I was. Who
was taking such care to tie me down, but not to hit me?
I peered out at the crowd. Someone had pulled the rear
doors of the barn open and people were disappearing
into the night.

Rothmann got to his feet unsteadily and stumbled
toward the nearest exit. He was warned off in the same
way, bullets kicking up splinters from the wooden floor
in front of him. He yelped and sank to his knees. He
didn't have the air of a master now. I found that the
desire to revenge myself on him physically had completely gone. That didn't mean I was going to let him

escape justice—assuming I myself got out of this alive.

Gradually the gunfire died down. Through the cloud of discharged smoke, I made out six people still standing. Four of them were naked, three men and a woman, one other man was pulling on the clothes he had stripped from a dead guard, and the remaining one, a woman, was fully dressed. She was carrying a machine-pistol in one hand and a pistol in the other. None of the guards seemed to have survived.

'Got any idea what's going on?' Quincy asked. He was still dazed from his time on the cross.

I shook my head. 'I think we might be about to find out.'

The man who had got dressed pointed the naked people in the direction of the various exits. They took up positions there, pulling clothes from the bodies of guards. They were all toting weapons. Then he joined the armed woman and they embraced.

'Touching,' Quincy muttered. 'Even assholes have feelings.'

I had slipped the knife under my body and was trying to get it into my pocket.

'Throw the blade over here,' the woman said, pointing the pistol at me.

I did as I was told, holding her gaze. She was tall and well-built, and she looked seriously comfortable with firearms. Her brown hair was tied back in a ponytail and she had a small rucksack on her back.

'You,' she said to Rothmann. 'Sit down and stop sniveling.'

He obeyed instantly, his hands over his now shrunken organ.

The man was also tall, with a full beard. He was carrying a shotgun and there was a combat knife in the belt he had put on.

'The Antichurch returns to its rightful leaders,' the woman said.

'Indeed, sister,' the man said solemnly, eyeing Rothmann. 'Shall we string up the heretic?'

'Of course. The true Antigospel requires that traitors be sacrificed to the Lord Lucifer.'

Rothmann made a high-pitched noise.

'Have you anything to say before sentence is carried out?' the man said to him. He had a strong Southern accent.

'I…I wish to beg forgiveness,' Rothmann said, groveling before him. 'When I revived the Antichurch, I had no idea that Jeremiah Dodds had a brother. Or that he set up his church in opposition to the original cult.'

The woman stepped forward and brought her boot down on Rothmann's right hand, making him yelp in agony. 'Jeremiah Dodds was a heretic,' she said, pressing down harder on his fingers.

'Besides, you sent people to kill us,' the man added, bringing the muzzle of the shotgun close to Rothmann's ear. 'They killed several of the faithful before we gutted them.'

'You mind telling us who you are?' Quincy asked. He was still lying prone and had lifted his head.

'Yes, I do mind.' The woman pointed her pistol at him. 'We don't pay no heed to niggers.'

I might have known that the original Antichurch would be a racist organization.

The man laughed emptily. 'Sister Abaddon, I see

three crosses. What d'you say to hanging all three of these sorry creatures up and turning their insides out?'

She smiled beatifically at him. 'That would be a truly wonderful way to celebrate the Lord Lucifer's triumph, Brother Apollyon,' she said, moving toward the rope that I'd cut from Quincy.

Her head disintegrated before she got there, the blast of the shot reaching my ears an instant later. The woman was thrown forward, her arms hooking over the horizontal bar of the cross and her head thumping against the vertical. Four more shots dispatched the people at the doors.

'Drop your weapons!'

The voice from the center of the barn was loud and clear. I watched as the bearded man complied and a figure in black combat clothes came toward us. It was a woman with short blond hair and high cheekbones.

'What the fuck now?' Quincy said, in a low voice.

My heart went into overdrive. She didn't look like she used to and she sounded like a native New Yorker, but I recognized her gait instantly.

Sara Robbins had collected plenty of souls already. And now she was coming for ours.

Arthur Bimsdale was finding his boss hard to fathom. If he'd been in charge, he'd have gone down to Texas as soon as Matt Wells and Quincy Jerome disappeared from the tracking grid. Every effort was being made by the Houston field office to pinpoint their locations, but Peter Sebastian would normally have been on the spot to concentrate the local agents' minds and coordinate their efforts. When Bimsdale had suggested he go alone, Sebastian had told him he'd be better employed handling the operation from headquarters. That was patently not the case.

His boss had returned to the office around 10:00 p.m., giving no explanation of where he had been. He had turned off his cell phone during his absence—Bimsdale knew this because he'd called him with Houston's latest negative update. Why the secrecy? Department heads, like all agents, were supposed to be contactable at all times. The look on Sebastian's face, however, had discouraged questions or comments. He received the news from Texas with a distracted air.

'Arthur, email me everything we've got on Routh Limited. Do a search on Sir Andrew Frogget, too. See if our guy in the London embassy's got any new shit.'

'New shit?' Bimsdale repeated uncertainly.

Sebastian gave him a drained look. 'As far as I recall, his record's clean. Too clean. I want to know everything about him. In particular, I want to know what his weaknesses are.' He raised a hand. 'Don't say anything, Arthur. I know he was decorated in the first Gulf War, I know he spends his weekends with underprivileged children. Now dig me some dirt!'

Bimsdale did as he was told. It didn't take him long. Ferris, the senior FBI agent in London, had picked up a hint of something rotten in the state of Frogget. Apparently his wife was suffering from depression, code in British high society for their marriage being on the rocks. On the face of it, the Routh chairman wasn't a big enough celebrity to attract the attention of the tabloid press, but he employed a notoriously devious publicity agent. That attracted Bimsdale's attention and he asked

Ferris to sniff around. An hour later, the agent called back. Nothing had ever been proved, but there was a faint rumor that Sir Andrew had paid off the parents of a twelve-year-old girl after he was found alone with her.

Peter Sebastian was less excited by that piece of news than Bimsdale expected, but he finally authorized twenty-four-hour surveillance on the knight.

After dealing with that end of things, Arthur went back to his desk and contacted Houston.

Sara Robbins had a Glock 19 in one hand and an AK-47 rifle in the other—she had taken both weapons from a sentry near the gate of the compound. She had dispatched him by cutting his throat with the plastic knife she favored. Things had worked out very well, not least because the painkillers had kicked in. On her way toward the location, identified by the bug she had attached to the pickup carrying Matt, she caught sight of a shadowy figure behind the tree line. That individual had provoked the guards by throwing a grenade into the open space in front of the buildings. When they came out to check, the intruder followed them back to the gate and killed them. Sara had been twenty yards behind, making no sound. After arming herself, she had gone toward the large barn—the intruder had stood at the door, and then slipped inside. Sara used her knife on the tires of the nearest vehicles and cautiously entered the building. She took cover behind a heap of firewood, to the rear of a group of naked people. A dead guard had been dragged there, his killer now sheltering behind an antique tractor.

It was when that individual turned to the side that

Sara recognized her profile. It was the woman from Maine—the one she had got rid of outside the diner. That wasn't too much of a surprise, though knowing who she was and who she worked for would be nice.

It turned out to be irrelevant. Sara watched the insane ritual and tried to work out what Matt was doing. He seemed to be in thrall to a naked man in a hyena mask, and almost attacked the black man with a knife. Then the shooting had started, and in the chaos that overtook the next few minutes, the bulk of the surviving congregation had thundered past Sara to the rear exit, leaving the wounded and dead behind.

Sara only recognized the tall man carrying a shotgun when he got up on the platform with the crosses. It was the beard that had deceived her. The last time she saw him, he had been clean-shaven. He had tried to kill her then and, by doing that, had signed his own death warrant—her professional standing as an assassin required all attacks on her person to be answered with maximum prejudice.

Stretching her back to dissipate the pain that had begun to bite again, the Soul Collector took aim at the woman who had been irritating her since Portland. Soon, it would be time to settle accounts with the hired gun known as Apollyon and, of course, with her former lover. The lives of the black man and of the people guarding the doors were of no consequence whatsoever.

Twenty-Six

The Soul Collector leveled the Kalashnikov at the bearded man. 'Don't even think about it, Apollyon.'

He had been stretching for the pistol in front of him, but instead straightened up and stared at the blonde woman. 'Who are you?' He turned to the motionless body on the arms of the inverted cross. 'Why did you kill my...kill my sister?'

I wasn't sure if Sara had recognized me. I hadn't seen her look in my direction once. Maybe if he went for a weapon...

'I killed her because I know what your sister, known in the business as Abaddon, was capable of,' she said, pointing the pistol at me. 'Keep still, Matt. I've got two eyes, remember?'

'Wait a minute,' Apollyon said. 'You know the business? Who the fuck...' He broke off, his jaw dropping. 'It can't be. You're the Soul Collector.' He looked like he'd just eaten a large piece of bad seafood.

Sara nodded. 'I'm glad to see my latest facial reshaping passed muster. Right, then. I don't care why you tried to take me out in Pittsburgh—I'm guessing you were pissed off I was getting all the best jobs—but you had your chance and you blew it. Personally, I'd have waited till my target was stationary, though I suppose the shot was tempting. You want to tell me what was going on here before I interrupted?'

The man called Apollyon—the name made me think of *Pilgrim's Progress,* but it was a long time since I'd read that turgid text—confirmed what I'd worked out from the copy of the Antigospel I'd read: that he and his sister were the rightful heirs to the Antichurch of Lucifer Triumphant, and that he and his companions had taken the places of members, now dead, who had been loyal to the new Master. I glanced at Rothmann, who was sitting with his knees tight together, his eyes fixed on Sara. He didn't seem to know her.

'What was your sister doing outside the compound?' Sara asked.

Apollyon gave a hollow laugh. 'She was hired to blow away this piece of shit.' He glanced at Rothmann. 'We thought that was pretty funny, considering I was going to fuck him up at the rite, but she took the job anyway. That way, we got two bites at his cherry.'

'I saw her in Maine,' Sara said. 'What was she doing there?'

'She was told to sit on that guy's ass,' he replied, angling his head toward me. 'Matthew John Wells. He's one of the Kraut's zombies. The idea was he would lead her to him, which he more or less did.'

'More or less,' the Soul Collector repeated, turning to me. 'Whose side are you on here, Matt?'

I held her gaze. 'Nobody's, least of all yours.'

She laughed. It wasn't a sound that boded well, either for me or anyone else in the barn. 'Who's your friend?'

She waved the pistol at Quincy. 'And don't pretend he's a stranger. I saw him with you in Portland.'

So she'd been on us from the beginning. I wondered how, but that wasn't important. Quincy had started to speak for himself. He rattled off his name, rank and unit.

'Very impressive,' Sara said, glancing at the bearded man. 'Your church got a policy about black people? And how about you, Heinz Rothmann?' She turned to the Master. 'Nazis view blacks as animals, don't they?'

Neither of them answered, which was a bad idea. The Soul Collector stepped toward Rothmann and stuck the muzzle of her Glock into his forehead.

'All right,' he said, his voice uneven. 'Blacks are subhumans. What do you care?'

She leaned toward him. 'I'm a professional killer. I don't have time for politics.'

'This isn't just politics, darlin',' Apollyon drawled. 'You're in the South now.'

Quincy used the distraction to spring forward, his arms outstretched and clutching at Sara. Her eyes flicked round and she loosed off two shots. He collapsed with a crash and didn't move again. I moved toward him, and then a rattle of automatic fire started from the side wall. Sara went down like a felled tree. I put my arms round my head.

After the shooting stopped, I looked up cautiously. There was no sign of the bearded man or of Rothmann. I crawled over to Quincy and laid hands on him. His chest was a slick of crimson.

'Leave him, Matt.'

Sara was sitting on the floor, the pistol pointed at me. She didn't seem to have been hit, but she was stretching her back and frowning. She got to her feet awkwardly.

'Move,' she said. 'You're coming with me.' She went over to the woman she'd called Abaddon and pulled the rucksack off her.

I glared at her, my hands wet with Quincy's blood. 'Fuck you, you murdering bitch.'

She smiled weakly. 'Good spirit, Matt. You'll be needing that. Now move.'

I followed her to the door and down the passage to the exit. I heard the roar of an engine, then a pickup careered out of the compound. Farther away, there was the sound of another vehicle.

'Apollyon must have left a friend outside,' Sara said, looking around. 'Looks clear. Come on, we'll take whatever we can.'

We went toward the gate, where there were several vehicles. The first, a large SUV, had two flat tires. The second was a small sedan. Sara told me to drive. Neither of us spoke. I was still smarting from her casual execution of Quincy, the poor bastard. I'd liked him and could have done with him watching my back.

After about a quarter of an hour on a narrow track through the dark forest, she stopped me at a clearing. There was a bulky SUV behind some bushes. This time, she got in the driver's door, after guiding me to the other side.

'Put out your hands,' she ordered, raising the Glock.

I did so with a display of reluctance, and she quickly tied my wrists together with high quality rope.

'Why don't you just kill me?' I asked, finally finding my tongue.

She smiled. 'Oh, there'll be plenty of time for that later. Right now, I've got a job to complete.'

'What's that? Putting a bullet in your competitor Apollyon's head?'

'That's not a job, that's pleasure.' She was pressing the switches on what looked like a location monitor. 'There we are.' She pointed to the screen. 'Wherever they go, we'll be on them.'

'You bugged him?'

'More correctly, I bugged the vehicle that brought you here.

'How did you know Apollyon would take it?'

'I disabled as many of the others as I could. I didn't know he was going to be here, but I always make contingency plans.'

There was something weird going on that I couldn't put my finger on. 'Who did you think would use that vehicle?'

She laughed. 'Did the crazy ritual do something to your brain, Matt? Who do you think? Abaddon wasn't the only assassin with a contract to execute Jack Thomson, aka Heinz Rothmann. I've got one, too.'

I wondered if I'd stay alive long enough to see the fucker who'd destroyed my family get his comeuppance.

Sir Andrew Frogget was enjoying himself. Not only had his Washington lawyers warned the FBI off, but he had passed an extremely successful day at Routh Limited's U.S. office. The morning was taken up with new business. The hedge funds with the closest links to the American political establishment all maintained personnel in D.C., and most had shown interest in the portfolio of recent start-ups that he had brought. Already, he had commitments for almost sixty percent of the funding required. On his return to London, he would pass the rest over to the experts, but he always liked to break the back of the work himself; he had learned in the army that commanders must undertake more than their share of the spadework.

That wasn't all the army had taught him. He thought back to the Gulf War in 1991, remembering the desert road filled with burnt-out vehicles and charred bodies. It was then that he had realized not only the U.S.'s overwhelming power, but the ruthlessness that came with it. He had engineered a transfer to Washington as military attaché and begun to build up the contacts he was still using. Many of them were involved in military operations, of course. The original directors of Routh, a collection of narrow-minded pencil pushers, had been dubious about the ethical side of such investments, but he had replaced them with people who shared his view that economic prosperity was rooted in superior firepower. The war to expel Saddam Hussein and its aftermath had illustrated the truth of that perfectly, even if the victors were less competent at rebuilding society than defeating a hostile regime.

Sir Andrew looked at his watch. His lady wife would be expecting him to call, but he wasn't going to do that. Annabel had become tiresome about his frequent foreign trips and wanted constant reassurance that all was well. He had other things on his mind, not least the progress he had made in his afternoon meetings. Even though Jack Thomson, the founder of Woodbridge Holdings, had disappeared after the massacre in the cathedral, Routh Limited had not given up on him. Some of the backers had expressed concern, but almost all were still on board, and he was convinced the others would come round. That was worth another glass of vintage Dom Pérignon.

He had just poured it when the doorbell rang. One of his local friends had loaned him his apartment in Adams Morgan for the evening, asking no questions— which was just as well. The girl who appeared on the screen by the door looked even younger than her handler said she was. Frogget's throat was dry, despite its recent lubrication by the champagne, and his heart was beating as it had done when he had led night raids into Iraq.

He slid off the chain and opened the door.

'Hello, my dear.'

The girl gazed up at him, eyes wary above cheeks inexpertly daubed with rouge.

'Come in. Have you ever had champagne?'

She batted her eyelashes at him and then took out the gum she had been chewing. 'Where shall I put this?'

Sir Andrew extended a hand to receive the sticky pink mass. 'Come and sit down,' he said, the nerves in his hand tingling as if he'd grasped a live wire.

The girl sat down on the sofa, her thin legs apart, and gazed at him impassively.

When the door was broken down ten minutes later, the knight of the realm was naked, as was his companion. Peter Sebastian and Arthur Bimsdale didn't bother to conceal their disgust.

'How can you be sure Apollyon took Rothmann with him?' I asked as Sara drove down the deserted country road, her eye flicking on and off the location monitor. 'He could easily have killed him in the forest.'

'I killed his sister. He's using Rothmann as bait to lure me out.'

'So let him go.'

'I can't do that. I have a reputation to maintain.' She glanced at me. 'Don't worry, there'll be plenty of time for me to deal with you later. You're not one of Rothmann's pathetic devil-worshippers, are you?'

'Your sister was into Satanism.'

That wasn't such a smart thing to say. She gave me an armor-piercing look.

'Don't think I've forgotten what you did to Lauren,' she said, her voice full of menace. 'But she was my *half* sister, while my brother was the real thing.'

'Who called himself the White Devil,' I said, deciding I had nothing to lose. 'And you call yourself the Soul Collector. You're the pathetic devil worshippers, not me.'

There was a thud as she hit a raccoon that suddenly loomed up in the headlights.

'I don't worship anyone, Matt,' Sara said, licking her lips as if there was blood on them. 'I just terminate people for money.'

'And gratification,' I added, trying unsuccessfully to work some give into the rope on my wrists.

'No,' she said emphatically. 'Not anymore. The excitement's worn off.' She looked at me. 'Though in your case…'

I turned to the front. She had become even more frightening since I'd last seen her—stony and pale-faced, like a devil sickening on sin.

'Oh, I almost forgot,' Sara said, with false excitement. 'You must have become a father again. Boy or girl?'

The words hit me like a sledgehammer. Bottling up the deaths of Karen and our son had been bad enough, but the idea of talking to my ex-lover about them was agonizing.

'Come on,' she said, blinking as if a large insect had just bitten her, 'do tell.'

'They're dead.'

She hit the brake and the heavy vehicle screeched to a halt. 'What did you say?'

I lowered my head. 'You heard me.'

'For God's sake, what happened?'

I tried to keep silent, but I couldn't. 'Karen…she had to have an emergency Cesarean. They…neither of them made it.' My eyes were damp, but I was determined I wouldn't cry in front of Sara. 'They think…you see, Karen and I were both…brainwashed by Rothmann and his sister. They think the drugs may have been behind what happened.'

Sara sat motionless, her hands on the wheel.

'I'm sorry, Matt,' she said, after a time. 'I really am. Nobody deserves that.'

'You fucking hypocrite. You're going to kill me.'

'I meant I'm sorry about Karen and the kid.' She paused. 'What was it, the child?'

'A…a boy.' I tried to remember the name we had chosen for him, but it was still gone.

She looked at me. 'You're going after Rothmann, too, aren't you? They let you out of…wherever…to track the fucker down.'

I nodded, keeping my eyes off her. I felt sick. Telling my ex-lover about Karen and our son seemed the worst kind of betrayal, but I hadn't been able to stop myself.

The Soul Collector slid the stick back into Drive

and moved forward, checking the monitor. 'Well, we'd better make sure our target doesn't get too far ahead,' she said, with what might once have been tenderness.

I didn't know what to think. Working with Sara meant that Rothmann had no chance of escaping, no matter how deadly the man who had taken him was. But she had killed Quincy without an iota of compunction. After she'd dispatched Rothmann, she would treat me in exactly the same way.

At least that would send me down the shadowy road to join my named and nameless dead.

Twenty-Seven

The Master, whose wrists had been bound with rusty wire, watched the driver out of the corner of his eye. The bearded man was handling the pickup with relaxed movements, his eyes glinting in the light from the dashboard. There was a curious smell in the cab, something organic but decidedly unhealthy.

'Where are you taking me?'

Apollyon glanced at him. 'Need to know basis only. Don't worry, you'll be going to meet Lord Lucifer soon enough.'

Heinz Rothmann thought about that. When he had revived the Antichurch, he had been completely cynical about it—who worshipped the Devil in the 21st century other than needy degenerates? But gradually he had come to understand the attraction of occult knowledge, despite the fact that Adolf Hitler had ultimately discounted its power. It seemed, as in many things, that Heinrich Himmler had more imagination than his Führer, with his deep interest in Teutonic lore and symbols. Since the failure of the plot against the President, Rothmann had found the Antichurch a more pressing interest than the militia of conditioned subjects he and his sister had set up.

'I am ready to meet Our Lord whenever he desires that,' he said devoutly.

Apollyon gave a hollow laugh. 'Don't be too hasty, asshole. My sister was a Mistress of Lucifer. What kind of a welcome do you think she's preparing for you in Hell?'

Rothmann saw a way to exert pressure. 'You shared power with a *woman?* There is no sanction for that in the Antigospel.'

'Not even in the one you rewrote so *your* sister could wear the gargoyle mask?'

The Master wondered how Apollyon knew about that. Security in his organization had been tight until the meddler Matt Wells had intervened. Where was *he* now? Had the female assassin dealt with him as she had Apollyon's sister and the negro? That would be a pity. He had hopes for the Englishman, hopes that could still be fulfilled, whatever Apollyon did.

The bearded man jabbed his elbow into Rothmann's ribs. 'I'm not hearing your answer, Kraut.'

'My sister...' Rothmann fought the pain. 'My sister and I were twins.'

'As if that makes a difference.'

The Master needed to divert his captor to more fertile ground. 'Do you know who the blonde woman is?'

'The Soul Collector? Sure I do. She kills for money.' The bearded man turned to him. 'Like me.'

Rothmann decided to twist the knife. 'So she killed your sister to reduce the competition?'

Apollyon reduced speed behind an eighteen-wheeler.

'Don't get cute with me, shithead. You heard what the blonde bitch said—she saw Abaddon in Maine.'

'That doesn't seem like a reason to blow her head apart.'

'What are you trying to say, asshole?'

'Simply this. The Soul Collector used to be the Englishman Matt Wells's lover. It can hardly be a coincidence that they both turned up at the barns.'

Apollyon hit the horn as the eighteen-wheeler slowed to a crawl. 'They're in this together?'

Rothmann kept as cool as he could. He knew that survival depended on sowing doubt in his captor's mind. 'Of course. This whole thing is a trap. Someone engineered it so that you and your sister would be neutralized.' He paused. 'Do you have any enemies, Apollyon?'

The bearded man swerved to the left and floored the gas pedal. Rothmann pressed back in his seat as he saw headlights approaching fast. At the last moment, Apollyon wrenched the wheel to the right. There was a horn blare from the other vehicle.

'I've been a gun for hire for eleven years,' the bearded man said. 'I've got more enemies than your false Antichurch has got followers.'

Ten minutes later, he pulled into a gas station and made a call. His face was still set hard when he got back into the pickup. Then his nostrils flared.

'What is that stink?' he said, searching under the dashboard. He found a small package loosely wrapped in silver foil and opened it. The smell immediately got worse. 'For the love of Lucifer.'

Heinz Rothmann looked at the shriveled heart. He had added a commandment to the Antigospel, requiring the faithful to keep the vital organs of their deceased loved ones. The owner of the truck had obviously been obedient. He was gratified to see that Apollyon looked physically ill. Obviously, he wouldn't be going back to remove his sister's heart.

'They've stopped,' Sara said, taking her foot off the gas. 'Just over two miles ahead, outside a place called Caluga.' She pulled up and reached toward the backseat.

I had visions of her preparing for battle. 'What are you doing?'

She laughed. 'Don't worry. I need to educate myself before I take further action. Let's see what's in Abaddon's rucksack.'

I watched as she removed the contents. There wasn't much—a combat knife, some ammunition clips and a laptop.

'Bingo,' Sara said, opening the computer and turning it on. After a few moments, her fingers started moving rapidly over the keys. 'I'm in.'

I was impressed. 'The last time I saw you with a laptop, you knew even less than I did.'

Her eyes stayed on the screen. 'A lot of things have changed since then.' She looked up. 'Including my appearance. What do you think?' She moved her head like a film star advertising shampoo.

'Em, fine.' I was trying to remember what she had looked like when I loved her, but that had gone into the void.

'Fine?' she said, in annoyance. 'The surgery cost me fifty thousand dollars.'

'It was worth it,' I said, not wanting to incite her to

further violence. I didn't tell her that her gait had given her away.

'Like the twenty grand I spent on technology skills was worth it.' She gave me a dead-eyed stare through what I presumed were contact lenses—her eyes weren't blue when we were together. 'Okay, the woman who called herself Abaddon knew what she was doing. There are no obvious files and no favorites on her internet program.'

'How about email?'

Sara gave me another hollow stare. 'Oh, thanks for reminding me.' Her fingers flew about. 'Completely empty. Either she didn't use it or she deleted all her messages.'

'In which case, they'll be in the hard drive.'

'Yeah, but there isn't time to access that now.'

I suppressed a smile. 'Did you take voice coaching from a New Yorker?'

She ignored that. After several more minutes, her fingers stopped moving.

'Shit,' she said, chewing her bottom lip. I remembered her doing that when she had a deadline from her editor on the newspaper. Our evenings together had often been interrupted by urgent stories and updates. We often ended up having wild sex after she filed. That was an unwelcome recollection. Why was it more lucid than visions of Karen?

'Wait a minute.'

I watched as her fingers hit the keys again.

'Bastard,' she said, her eyes wide. 'The fucking snake.' She sat back, her face suddenly damp with sweat.

'What is it?' Talking to her was painful, but necessary. The only way I was going to survive was by soft-ening her attitude toward me. Pretending to care about what she was going through was one way of achieving that. I imagined the ones I had lost covering their eyes and shunning me.

'My fucking broker, Havi,' Sara said. 'Abaddon had his email address buried in a maintenance file.'

'What does that mean?'

She gave me a stare that was marginally less empty. 'It means he was screwing with me.'

'Playing you off against Abaddon?'

'Maybe. I've been picking up rumors that I was the so-called Hitler's Hitman. You hear about those murders?'

'Greenwich Village, Michigan, Boston and Phila-delphia,' I said, trying not to sound too much like a Rothmann-conditioned robot.

She raised an eyebrow. 'You're very well informed.'

'What do you expect? The FBI reckoned that Roth-mann was behind them and I was their main link to him.'

She laughed emptily. 'But, of course, Rothmann had nothing to do with the killings.'

For a moment I thought she really was the mur-derer—messing with me had been her modus operandi since she'd gone on the run after the White Devil's death. Then I saw the anger on her face.

'That piece of shit,' she said, spittle flying. 'I think Abaddon did those murders and Havi set up the deal. Since then, he's been trying to pin them on me.'

'Why?'

She looked at me as if I were a small child. 'Jesus, Matt, use your novelist's imagination. If you were my broker, would you get a nice warm feeling every time I got in touch?'

She was right there. No doubt she was brilliant at her work, but she was a naked flame that attracted insects and then burned them up—I had personal experience of that. I could imagine this Havi guy might have thought he'd live longer working for other principals.

'Then again,' I said, rubbing my wrists together to restore the circulation, 'if Abaddon killed those people, she was even worse than—' I broke off.

'Even worse than me? Oh, Matt, say it ain't so.'

I remembered what she'd done to my friend Dave Cummings. She had also almost killed my mother, my ex-wife and my daughter Lucy, as well as numerous others. No matter how bad Abaddon had been, she could never have matched my ex-lover.

'Don't worry, Matt, you might still be saved. Abaddon's brother Apollyon has got an even worse reputation for savagery. Maybe he'll get me before I get him.'

I didn't find that very comforting. Apollyon was hardly likely to let me go with a pat on the back if he disposed of the Soul Collector. Besides, there was another factor.

'What about Rothmann, Sara? You've been contracted to kill him. Doesn't he take priority over Apollyon?'

She gave me a dark look. 'That deal was fixed by the scumbag Havi.' She raised a finger. 'Wait. If he's transferred my share of the advance, he's in the clear.'

I watched as she tapped away. Even though we were in what seemed to be an underpopulated part of Texas, the laptop's wireless connection was good.

No doubt Abaddon had earned enough to buy the best technology.

Sara scowled. 'The fucking bastard. Not only has he not sent anything for the Rothmann job, but he hasn't paid the balance on my last contract.'

'Whose death did that involve?' I asked, hoping she might come clean without thinking.

'Good try, Matt. Do I look like I've lost it completely?'

I was thinking about the hit-and-run incident in Florida, the one that had killed Gordy Lister's brother. If she had been hired to kill Rothmann, it wasn't unlikely that the same employer would have wanted to put Rothmann's number two under pressure. But who was that employer?

'They're on the road again,' Sara said, shutting down the laptop.

The flashing cross on the monitor had started to move.

I watched this former lover of mine as she drove on. I was thinking about the question she had asked—'Do I look like I've lost it completely?' Until she'd said that, I hadn't thought anything of the sort. But now I had begun to wonder about the sweat on her face and the tension around her eyes. Could it be that the invincible Soul Collector was finally beginning to come apart at the seams?

'I wish to see my lawyer immediately.'

Peter Sebastian was sitting across the table in the interview room from Sir Andrew Frogget, Arthur Bimsdale by his side. He looked down at the photographs that had been taken on their entry to the apartment in Adams-Morgan.

'I've already outlined the law pertaining to sexual acts with minors,' Sebastian said. 'Would you like me to send these photographs to your lawyer?'

Sir Andrew stared back, but there was less fire in his gaze than before.

'Since you've spent weekends with Mr. Mallinson at his place in the Northern Neck, you'll know his daughters Molly and Kirsten.' He glanced at his assistant.

'Molly is thirteen and Kirsten eleven,' Bimsdale supplied.

Sebastian watched as the Englishman looked away. He bided his time. The guy had medals from the Gulf War; he wasn't going to crack so easily. After several minutes, he picked up one of the photos and examined it. Frogget was in the fore as he stood over the girl, who was naked on the sofa. She had just registered the sound of the FBI team's entry to the apartment, but it looked like she was turning from Sir Andrew in revulsion.

'I imagine Lady Annabel would be interested in this,' Sebastian said. 'Have you got a fax machine at home?'

Sir Andrew smiled frostily. 'If you think that my wife will be in the least bit disturbed, you know even less about the British upper classes than your fat-arsed countrymen who hang around outside Buckingham Palace.'

Sebastian knew the investment banker's marriage was under strain, but he didn't come back on that. He wanted to see how much punishment Frogget could take.

'All right,' he said impassively. 'So you won't mind if we send the images to your old regiment?'

The Englishman blanched, but attempted to rally. 'Surely you don't believe all that crap about officers and gentlemen, Mr. Sebastian.'

'What I believe is not germane to this interview.' The senior FBI man looked at his notes. 'We can also send them over to the British ambassador. I believe you knew him at Cambridge?'

There were spots of red on Sir Andrew's cheeks now. 'I—'

Sebastian raised a hand to cut him off. 'Of course, we will have to provide your board of directors with the images. We also have the fax numbers of the *London Times* and BBC News.'

The knight's shoulders dropped.

Peter Sebastian had one last lance to pierce the bull's hide. 'We would be sure to send the photos to your London club, as well.'

All the fight had gone out of the old soldier. 'Enough,' he said, his voice cracking. 'What is it you want from me?'

'You know that very well, Andrew,' Sebastian said, deliberately dropping the title. 'I want to know every detail about the backers of Woodbridge Holdings.'

It was only as the Englishman began to spill what was a very revealing can of beans that Peter Sebastian fully realized what he had done.

Twenty-Eight

Sara kept us about a mile behind Abaddon's vehicle. There were signs to Waco on the left and Dallas on the right, but we stayed on back roads. It was difficult to make out what kind of country we were going through. All I saw were the lights of small settlements and deserted gas stations.

'Any idea where he's headed?' I asked.

The Soul Collector drew a forearm across her forehead. 'Nope. He seems to be avoiding large population centers, probably because of the weapons he's carrying.'

'You're not aware of any connection he has with this neck of the woods?'

She glanced at me. 'Killers aren't like authors, Matt. We don't have pages on Facebook or websites that advertise where we come from and where we like to spend our holidays.'

'So where do you live?' I told myself I was gathering material that could prove useful down the line, but I was actually interested in the life of the woman I had once loved. I knew she'd need some encouragement to talk. 'Let me guess. Somewhere central so you can get to both coasts quickly.' I stuck a pin in my mental map of the U.S. 'Kansas City?'

'What?' She laughed. 'Have you ever been there?'

'I have, actually. There are some good blues bars.'

'Yeah, right. Anyway, it's not great for flights. St. Louis would be better.' She paused, her brow furrowed. 'Now I come to think of it, there was talk that Abaddon was based there.'

'Maybe that's where her brother's going.'

She thought about that and then tapped buttons on the tracking device. 'Dallas to St. Louis is 621 miles, ten and a half hours. Bit of a long haul in that heap.'

'True. Then again, if he wants to keep his weapons to hand, he's hardly going to fly.'

'Mmm.' She seemed distracted.

'You haven't told me.'

'What?'

'Where you live.'

'What makes you think I even have a fixed abode?'

'Come on, Sara. I know you. Even when we were together, you kept on your own place.' I remembered the plants and wall hangings she filled the rented flat with. 'You need somewhere to shut out the world.'

'Give me one reason why I should tell you.'

'If you don't make it, who's going to water your plants?'

That off-the-cuff remark seemed to get to her. She blinked and kept her eyes on the road.

'I tell you what,' she said. 'If it looks like I'm on the way out, I'll give you my address.' She gave an abrupt laugh. 'Watch out for the booby-traps.'

I could tell she wouldn't be talking anymore. I went

back to moving my wrists surreptitiously; there didn't seem to be any slack developing. Eventually another part of my body hit the panic button.

'Em, sorry about this, but I need to pee.'

Sara looked at me as if I were a small boy interrupting the teacher.

'What? We're not all superhumans with steel bladders.'

'Evidently,' she muttered, pulling off to the side. 'Come on, then.' She went round to my door and hauled me out. There was a pistol in her other hand.

I walked into the long grass. 'You have to help me.'

She registered that I couldn't use my hands. 'Oh, for fuck's sake.' She came over and put the muzzle of her weapon against my belly, then unzipped my fly and stepped back. 'I'm not holding it.'

Overcome with relief, I smiled. 'Wouldn't exactly be the first time.'

The first shot whistled past my head and Sara shoved me to the ground. Several more rang out. I heard the bullets thud into the earth beyond us. I rolled farther into the grass, hands over my exposed dick. By the time I looked back, Sara had blasted off a clip in reply. An engine revved and a car accelerated past us. I got a clear view of the driver and the gunman.

'Are you all right?' Sara called, from the side of the pickup.

'Just about. Fortunately I'd finished peeing. You?'

'Yeah. Get over here.'

I did as I was told, keeping my head down even though our assailants were long gone.

'Did you see them?' I asked.

'A man and a woman. She was driving.'

'That's right. Any idea who they were?'

'Never seen them before. You?'

I decided there was no advantage in sharing that information with her. It might give me an advantage later. 'No. Presumably members of Rothmann's or Apollyon's cult.'

We got back into the pickup and set off again. Apollyon was still showing on the monitor and we soon caught up. There was no further sign of the car, but that didn't mean the occupants hadn't stopped and waited for us to pass. Sara was aware of that and kept looking in the mirror. I considered asking her to cut my bonds, but knew that would be a waste of breath. I needed to gain her trust before there was any chance of that.

In the meantime, I thought about the shooter. Had Gordy Lister been firing at me or at the Soul Collector? He had a look on his face that was very different from anything I'd seen before—determined, vicious, even enraged. I was pretty sure I hadn't done anything to put him in that zone. Had Sara? Or was he just so pissed off at what had happened during the annual rite that he wanted rid of us both? I thought about how he'd been before the ceremony and couldn't figure that— he wasn't a conditioned zombie or a committed devil-worshipper. Then again, maybe he'd completely fooled me and was both.

I didn't think his driver was either of those, but she could have duped me, too. Or perhaps Mary Upson had been so traumatized by the time she had spent upside down on the cross with her head in a sack that she had completely flipped. Seeing her mother's body in the coffin under the central cross would have aided that process. Then again, I had led her on when she had helped me escape from Maine and that had ended badly. I already knew the damage she could do. If she had inherited Nora Jacobsen's tendency for extreme behavior, we were in seriously deep shit.

'What is it?' Sara asked.

'Nothing. So, not Kansas City. Where *do* you live then? Omaha, Nebraska?'

She shook her head, but a smile played on her lips. Maybe I could get through her defenses after all.

Rudi Crane was on his knees in the hotel room in Washington when his cell phone rang. He ignored it and went on giving thanks to the Good Lord. Today had been a red-letter day. Both sets of meetings had ended in success. Hercules Solutions would be providing army and police training for a small but hugely wealthy Gulf oil state—the emir had himself signed the contract before lunch. The company would also be responsible for all security work for one of the world's largest oil companies. Its CEO had flown in especially to supervise the final negotiations that afternoon. The contract would be signed in London next month. Truly, the Lord was a bountiful and benevolent God.

The Reverend Crane also offered up thanks for the favorable terms he had managed to negotiate with an Israeli arms company. They guaranteed the supply of high-quality weaponry at a price that would not put undue strain on Hercules. In six months, the company would be better equipped than most nations' armies, and able to play a major role in the unrest that would soon engulf the world. It had not yet been revealed whether this would be the Armageddon that Rudi Crane had been waiting for all his sentient life but, even if it wasn't, the Second Coming of the Lord was not far off. Of course, Crane himself would be taken up to Heaven in the Rapture before the conflict started, but leaving a fully armed force to fight the Antichrist was a good legacy he could offer.

And everything had started on a small farm in West Virginia, he reflected. It was a classic American tale of greatness from small beginnings, one that Abraham Lincoln himself would be proud of. Young Rudi's parents had been dirt poor, his father a dedicated worker on the land, who had been forced to go down the coal mines to provide for his family. His mother was a saintly woman, who had been drawn to the Baptist faith despite her family's devotion to Bavarian Catholicism. Between them, they ensured that Rudi got a decent education, enabling him to win a scholarship to Bible college and start his preaching career. They had also instilled in him a deep understanding of money, in their careful management of the land and the income earned from it and the mines—his mother had taken in laundry and sewn clothes to supplement that. Investing the profits from his books and TV programs had come naturally to Rudi, and soon he was spending more time on business than preaching. He did not regret that. Clearly it was the will of the Lord.

Crane's reflections had the clarity of real life, so painstakingly had he constructed his backstory. In fact, his father had been a drunken animal, who beat his wife and young Rudi. His death, down a dry well with a sealed cover, had never been satisfactorily explained, though the local sheriff was unlikely to reopen inquiries, considering the money he had been paid. As for his mother, she had also beaten Rudi and forced him to watch her have sex with any man who could pay. After her death in a mental asylum, her records disappeared and the Director built himself a luxurious cabin in the Allegheny Mountains.

The preacher man looked at his cell phone. The call he'd missed was from Martin Mallinson, one of the D.C. lawyers he used. He couldn't begin to imagine what that slick operator would be wanting of him.

'He's stopped,' Sara said, taking her foot off the gas pedal and looking at the monitor.

I had been half-asleep. The clock in front of me showed 2:41. 'Where are we?'

The vehicle came to a halt.

'We just passed somewhere called Hutchense, sixty miles southwest of Dallas. There isn't much ahead. The next town is in ten miles. Hold on, he's moving again.'

We watched as the marker moved westward. There were no roads or settlements showing on the monitor.

'And he's stopped again.' Sara sat back and stretched her back.

'Are you all right?'

She screwed her eyes up. 'Too long in the driving seat.'

'I could have spelled you.'

'Yeah, that would have been a *great* idea.'

Despite the sarcasm, I went for broke. 'I don't suppose you fancy loosening these ropes?'

She just glared at me. 'Sure. Oh, wait, I saw what you did to my half sister.'

And then it hit me again—Christ, Quincy. She had

killed him without compunction, just as she'd killed
Dave. What was I doing cozying up to her? Then I
remembered Rothmann. The bastard responsible for
Karen's death and that of our son had priority. If Sara
could get me near him, I'd nail him and then take my
chances with her.

Sara waited for half an hour and then drove on. 'Let's
see what happening. Maybe Apollyon's stopped at a
motel.'

The area didn't seem to have many of those. Besides,
I couldn't see the assassin checking in with his cap-
tive. Then again, maybe he'd already killed Rothmann.
Though I suspected he wanted to dispatch the so-called
heretic slowly and in some grotesque Antichurch ritual
rather than in the back of a pickup.

There were very few houses on the road. This seemed
to be a deserted part of Texas, even though it wasn't so
far from Fort Worth and Dallas. It was easy to forget
how huge the state was. Over twenty million people
were swallowed up by its vastness—which made finding just two potentially very challenging.

Sara stopped by the edge of the road. There weren't
many trees around here, just open country rolling away
into the darkness.

'According to the monitor, the vehicle is three hundred yards to our left,' she said, opening her door.

I managed to hit the handle on mine and stumble
out. There were no lights at all to the left, and only a
dirt track leading away from the road we were on. The
wind blew into my face, bringing the smell of grass cut
with cow dung into my nostrils.

'Maybe Apollyon's gone to have a rest out of sight
of the road,' I suggested.

'Maybe.' Sara was checking her semiautomatic and machine-pistol. 'There's only one way to find out.'

'I'll come with you.'

She gave me a tight smile. 'You'll come with me, all right. But I don't trust you, Matt.' She came quickly toward me and wrapped a handkerchief round my mouth. 'No noise, *capisce?*'

I glared at her. I was trussed up like a Christmas turkey and about as vulnerable. She knew that and pushed me ahead of her. The words *human* and *shield* flashed up in my mind. So much for gaining her confidence.

I stumbled down the rough track in the darkness.

Ruts in the land were deep and well worn. Had Apollyon prepared a hideout nearby? I sincerely hoped we weren't anywhere near where the Texas Chainsaw Massacre was filmed.

'Hang on,' Sara whispered, putting a hand on my shoulder.

I turned and watched her look ahead. It was pitch-dark and there was no moon. I could see only a few faint stars. She nodded and I started walking again, my breath making the gag round my mouth damp. We must have gone at least a couple of hundred yards. Where had Apollyon gone?

Then my foot hit something hard. There was a loud click and we were blinded by a spotlight. I couldn't raise my hands, so I had to lower my head.

'Don't move!' came a harsh male voice.

'Do as he says,' Sara whispered from behind me. 'I'll deal with them when they come closer.'

'You at the rear! Drop your weapons!'

'Screw you,' Sara muttered.

'Final warning!'

Jesus, what was going to happen? I was sure Sara wouldn't disarm herself.

'All right,' said the voice, 'let him go!'

Let him go? Who? There was a crash of metal and I heard padding paws and a slavering noise. Narrowing my eyes, I looked ahead and saw a large canine coming straight toward us.

I did the only thing I could. I dropped my shoulder and waited for the impact.

Twenty-Nine

Peter Sebastian was sitting outside the interview room in the Hoover Building, a cup of cold coffee on the floor between his feet. Arthur Bimsdale had gone to find some food for them while Sir Andrew Frogget made his telephone call. The investment banker had insisted he talk to his lawyer, even though Bimsdale had faxed the slippery Martin Mallinson a selection of the juiciest photos of his client.

There would be some very angry people when Bureau staff started knocking at their doors. They had finally found a way into the secret world behind Rothmann's activities. Although a lot of the companies were little more than fronts, the financial crime experts would have plenty to work on.

It should have been a triumph, though Sebastian couldn't see it that way. Valerie Hinton hadn't called yet, but she would, as soon as the news got out. And then the full might of the CIA would be turned on him. Not even the Director would be able to protect him from that. Why had he done it? Partly, he was sick of being at the Agency's beck and call—it was nearly fifteen years since he'd been caught in its tentacles, and he'd had enough. But that wasn't all. There was something about this case, about the whole vicious conspiracy centered on Heinz Rothmann, that he couldn't stomach. Not only had the President nearly lost his life and a member of his cabinet been killed, but everything to do with the extended case was pure poison. The Hitler's Hitman killings showed that. Rothmann's Nazism, combined with his cynical use of the Antichurch of Lucifer Triumphant, was bad enough, but the conditioning program developed by his sister was the clincher—it had attracted big business, international investors and the CIA, and it had enabled him to place his people in law enforcement and the armed forces. If someone didn't put a stop to things now, the entire structure of government would be irreparably damaged.

That someone had to be Peter Sebastian.

He sat on the bench with his head bowed, thinking of his kids—his wife had long since written him off. Astrid and Roy were at college and had almost flown the nest. Would they remember him? Would they be proud of what he'd done? Most likely there would be a cover-up; perhaps he would even be implicated by people who were much better at the game than he was. He would be quickly forgotten by everyone who had known him, an embarrassment, one of the bad apples. Who did he think he was kidding with this pathetic act of disobedience?

Sebastian told himself to get a grip. It wasn't so bad. The Director was in on what he was doing; the Director had sanctioned his actions, despite the fact that he hadn't told him of the English knight's arrest until after it had happened. There was still room for honorable people in the Bureau, even if his previous assistant had turned out to be one of Rothmann's brainwashed automatons. But had he made a terminal mistake in using Matt Wells? Would the conditioning he'd undergone turn out to be deeper and more resistant than the scientists thought? If that was the case, Rothmann would reclaim him and Sebastian's strategy to trap him would be turned on its head. Given that Wells and his bodyguard had disappeared, Sebastian was prepared for the worst.

Arthur Bimsdale came down the corridor, carrying a tray piled high with packages of sandwiches and paper cups.

'Ham without mustard on the left, sir,' he said, bending toward his boss. 'Your coffee's next to it.' He straightened up. 'I'll give the prisoner his.'

Sebastian nodded, unwrapping his sandwich. The last thing he felt like doing was eating, but his stomach was an acid bath that needed something to work on. He managed half of it, while Bimsdale wolfed his down in under a minute.

'Here,' Sebastian said, handing over the remainder of his. 'You're obviously still growing.'

'I'm excited, sir,' Bimsdale said, with a smile. 'We're about to break the case.'

They went back into the interview room. Sir Andrew Frogget hadn't touched his sandwich, but his coffee cup was empty. He was sitting straighter than he had been and had folded his hands. Sebastian didn't like the look of that.

'Gentlemen,' the investment banker said. 'I've had a change of heart. I'm afraid our conversation is at an end.'

Then he gave a strained smile, flinched as if he'd

stepped on a live cable and pitched forward onto the table.

Sebastian felt for a pulse. There was none.

The dog hit me like a demolition ball. I was almost knocked backward, the creature's jaws going for my throat, but I had managed to brace myself just enough. I also managed to get my bound hands in between, in the process detaching the gag. After a few seconds' wrangling, the dog went after what it thought was an easier target—Sara. She brought her pistol to bear, but was slammed to the ground on her back before she could fire, the weapon dropping out of her grip. She landed on top of the gun and unable to reach it. I scrambled over the dusty ground and opened my arms to get my roped wrists round the animal's neck. I managed to exert enough pressure to pull its head away from Sara.

'Heel, Caesar!' came a commanding voice. 'Heel!'

The dog slipped its head out from my hamstrung grip and headed for its master. Before Sara or I could move, we were surrounded by men in olive drab fatigues and caps, carrying assault rifles that were all pointed at us.

'Have you finished?' came a harsh voice.

I looked round and was hit on the side of the face. A heavily built man in the same uniform, but with insignia on his headgear, raised a short stick.

'You want some more?'

'No, thanks.'

That got me a second blow, on the other side of my face.

'You learned to keep it shut now?'

I nodded. Even without my hands tied, I'd have struggled to handle him. He was carrying a lot of weight and most of it seemed to be muscle.

'How about you, bitch?'

Sara had been grabbed by a couple of gorillas. She kept quiet, having presumably decided against having her features rearranged again.

'Get them inside,' the big man ordered.

We were halfdragged, halfwalked toward a high fence with razor wire all over the top of it. A gate as wide as the largest truck was opened and we went through. There were more armed men around. Now that we were out of the spotlight, I made out a series of low buildings. There was no sign of Apollyon's pickup.

'Take the woman to block 3,' the big man commanded. 'The smart-ass is coming with me.'

I glanced at Sara as she was led away, my eyes meeting hers for an instant. She looked strangely relieved, as if she'd reached the end of a long journey. She was probably just conserving her strength and planning how to escape. As I was taken to another of the buildings, it struck me that I had completed a circular journey of sorts, too—from Rothmann's fortified camp in Maine, to the FBI facility in Ohio, to this stronghold in Texas. That realization wasn't exactly uplifting, though I had managed to get out of the two previous places, even if the cost had been high—I had a flash of Karen holding our son, but they quickly faded from view. The question was, who was in charge of this camp? I hadn't seen any signs or other means of identification.

A wooden sliding door was opened and we went inside. A long corridor stretched ahead, with doors on either side. There were letters and numbers on them, but no other features. There was a musty smell, a mixture of sweat and something oily, maybe lubricant. The floor was bare concrete. Much more basic than the Maine camp, it reminded me of the army's facility in Ohio. Was that what this was, a military installation? The insignia on the big guy's cap didn't look like any I'd ever seen before. There was a human figure with what looked like a bear's jaws over its head and a snake in each hand. That made me think of something, but my memory declined to oblige.

Another door was opened, this one on hinges, and I was pushed inside. The room was empty apart from a concrete bed on the wall. The big man and two guards followed me in, one of the latter dragging a chair. The dog called Caesar remained outside, I was glad to see.

'Sit down.' The boss man parked his ass on the chair he was handed.

I sat on the bed and held out my hands. 'Could you cut this rope, please?' I said. I reckoned that asking for help was a way of acknowledging the power he exerted over me, as well as potentially saving my wrists from further abrasion.

He thought about that, and then motioned one of the other men forward. 'Do as he says.' He grinned. 'After all, he ain't going anywhere.'

His sidekicks laughed in a way that didn't strike me as military. I thought of the militia Rothmann had set up, the North American National Revival, aka the North American Nazi Revival. These men weren't wearing its insignia, but were they in a militia like it?

'Okay, my man,' the big chief said, 'you wanna tell me what you were doing at my front fence?'

Now my wrists were free, I was no longer inclined to be polite. 'You wanna tell me what you were doing setting a vicious animal on us?'

He laughed. 'We got ourselves a live one,' he said, grinning at the guards. 'Won't do you any good, son.'

'You don't know who you're dealing with. The FBI's got me under surveillance.' That seemed as good a way as any of wiping the grin off his face, avoiding the detail that I was actually working for the Bureau.

All three of them burst out laughing.

'The *F—B—I*,' the big guy said, emphasizing each letter. 'What's that? The Fucking Bad Indians? Ain't no Indians down here no more.'

More laughter.

'And we sure don't got no Federal Bureau of Investigations.'

That killed them. I had entered a world where national institutions had as much clout as a drunken prizefighter. Then things took an even sharper turn for the worse. The door opened and the assassin who called himself Apollyon walked in.

The big man stood up and looked at the bearded man uncertainly. He had changed into olive drab fatigues, but he wasn't wearing a cap. Hanging from his belt were a combat knife in a scabbard and a pistol in a holster.

'You can go,' Apollyon said dismissively.

'You sure you'll be—'

The assassin cut the big guy off with a blunt 'yes.' Then he planted a gleaming boot on the chair and leaned toward me.

'You're Matthew John Wells and you're working for Peter Sebastian at the FBI.'

He had me there. 'Tell me something I don't know.'

'Okay, how about this? Your chances of getting out of here alive are so small that a microscope wouldn't spot them.'

I let that go. He was obviously immune to displays of bravado.

'But there is a way you can improve them.' He suddenly didn't look as pleased with himself and I wondered if he was obeying orders. 'Tell me everything you know about the blonde bitch who killed my sister.'

I thought about that, but not for long. I didn't owe Sara a thing—on the contrary, she had killed my best friend and I'd been looking for a way to dispose of her for a long time. Besides, I was a crime novelist. I was good at making things up.

'All right,' I said submissively. 'Could I have some water first?'

He went to the door and gave the order. I ran through my options quickly. If I played this right, I might get out alive. I might even give Sebastian the time to track me down. In the worst-case scenario, I'd take the Soul Collector and all the other scumbags down with me. Then it struck me. How did Rothmann fit into this setup? Had Apollyon already dealt with him as a heretic, or did the Nazi have some tie to the militia and the camp?

The bearded man handed me a warm bottle of water. I drank from it and then started to spin my tale.

The Soul Collector was in a confined room with only a concrete bed on the wall. She had been punched several times in the face and all her clothes had been ripped off. The men in fatigues had laughed at her and then left. Now she was huddled in the corner opposite the door, legs drawn up to her chest and arms wrapped around them. Was this how it was going to end? With sexual humiliation and a sordid, unreported death? She'd have struggled more, invited a beating that deprived her of consciousness, but her back had become a sea of agony. When the men saw the withered breasts and skinny frame that she had hidden beneath extra layers of clothing, they had realized how pathetic she was. In other circumstances that could have given her an advantage, but she was so exhausted by the events at the compound and the long drive, as well as the constant pretence to Matt that she was well, that she couldn't imagine landing a blow that was anywhere near lethal, for all her experience and training. For the first time in years, she felt the cold grip of fear spread throughout her body, as if it was an active part of the cancer itself.

She thought about her ex-lover. He had changed enormously. When she had known him, Matt had been bitter—his marriage had ended, his writing career had crashed, and he'd had to give up his precious rugby because of his bad knee. Her brother, the White Devil, had fed off that bitterness, but in doing so he had inadvertently unleashed a stronger, more self-reliant part of Matt's character, which his subsequent experiences with Rothmann had evidently brought to the fore. She had never known him like that, though she had realized how formidable an opponent he had become when she tried to eliminate him in London. He had nearly brought her to her knees then, and she had never returned to her home country.

And now, he was even more driven. The deaths of his lover and son had added another dimension to his profile, that of the justified avenger. She was sure he would punish Rothmann for what the conditioning process had done. The last vestiges of British reserve had been burned away.

Then it struck her that she would be a victim of that change, too. There was something cold and calculating in his eyes every time he looked at her. Certainly he had sworn to revenge himself on her, as well.

Sara looked around the vacant cell and blinked hard as another wave of pain dashed over her. Maybe this was the beginning of the final phase the doctor had talked about, not that she had allowed herself to pay attention, so convinced had she been that he was wrong. Maybe she would die before they could tear the life from her piece by piece. She shook her head. Only someone who had faith in some benevolent god or kind fate would expect that kind of ending. She had seen too many people die, often at her own hand, to imagine that death was anything but miserable suffering.

Unless Matt could save her. It seemed ridiculous to hope for salvation from the man she had betrayed and hounded, but she had seen something else in her former lover's eyes during the drive across East Texas. He still had feelings for her, even if they were compromised by what she had done. He still saw her as a human being, rather than the nameless and faceless killer she had carefully constructed. Yes, Matt would step in before they came for her. Matt would get her out.

Sara let out a sob, even though the pain had been reduced in intensity in the recent minutes. She was remembering what she had been with Matt in London, before she had walked willingly into a life of blood. They had something, but she destroyed it. She would have given anything to have it back.

Thirty

It turned out that Apollyon had done his homework. He stopped me frequently as I went through Sara's murderous career, asking questions that made it clear he knew plenty about her. Although I hadn't written a book about the Soul Collector's activities in the U.K., there had been no shortage of coverage in the media. But I probably learned more than he did from the conversation. Apparently there were grounds to believe that she was responsible for at least forty murders in the U.S., Canada and Mexico over the last two years. Given that some of them involved extreme methods and savage mutilation, I struggled to put her in any worse light.

'So the bitch and her brother killed people in the ways you used in your novels,' Apollyon said, looking at me as if I was even lower on the evolutionary scale than he was.

'They were trying to frame me,' I said uncomfortably. I could see where this was heading. I'd been given a kicking often enough at book festivals over the levels of violence in my novels….

'Yeah, but you made that shit up. What kind of twisted fuck are you, man?'

'What, writing stories about murder is worse than committing it? I never came up with anything as gross as the Hitler's Hitman killings.'

He looked away. 'My sister was only following the client's instructions.'

'Well, she had one sick client. Any idea who that was?' I tossed the question in as an afterthought—maybe I'd get lucky.

'Quit fishing, asshole. I'm asking the questions here.'

There was enough emotion in his voice to suggest he was vulnerable. He'd seen his sister die and he'd narrowly escaped death himself. Even an experienced assassin might get shaky.

'You realize she'll kill you,' I said, keeping the pressure on. 'Sara doesn't give up.'

'From what you say, she's got you in her sights, too.'

'True enough. But I don't give a shit anymore.'

'What makes you think I do?'

Stalemate—he'd lost his closest relative, too.

'What are you going to do with Rothmann?' I asked.

'You can't have him, if that's what you mean. The Antichurch has a commandment about heresy.'

'Does it involve an upside-down cross, blinding, disembowelment and strangulation?'

'Why? You want to join him?'

'Not particularly. I wouldn't mind watching, though.'

'That could be arranged. But first you've got a date with Hades.'

I felt the hairs rise all over my body. Did he mean Hades, King of the Dead, or his underground realm? There was only one thing to be said for the latter—it was where the shades of Karen and our son had gone.

Apollyon laughed. 'You look kind of eager. Just what kind of lunatic are you?'

I hoped I'd get the chance to show him in the very near future.

The duty doctor reached the interview room a few minutes after Sebastian sent for her. Confirming that Sir Andrew Frogget was dead didn't take long. Coming up with a cause was less straightforward.

'I know I have to wait for the postmortem,' Sebastian raged. 'Just give me your opinion, Doctor—' He stared at her ID tag. 'Parslow. You *are* a doctor of medicine, not philosophy, right?'

Ellen Parslow glanced past him and caught the gaze of his assistant, who looked embarrassed. 'I have medical qualifications from Yale, Johns Hopkins and the Navy,' she said, brushing back a lock of blond hair.

'So diagnose,' Sebastian ordered.

'How was he beforehand? Had he been under strain?'

'We were questioning him,' the senior Bureau man said, glancing at Arthur Bimsdale. 'It's on film if you want to take a look. He was under pressure, sure, but he seemed to be bearing up.'

Parslow looked at the younger man, who nodded his agreement. 'No shortness of breath, excessive sweating, redness of face?'

'No,' the agents said in unison.

'Do we have access to his medical records?'

'We can get that,' Sebastian said. 'He's a Brit.'

'Right. The pathologist will need to be copied.'

Sebastian raised his eyes to the ceiling. 'Obviously. Do I have to get on my knees, Doctor? Give us some help here.'

Ellen Parslow beckoned to Bimsdale and together they lifted the dead man's upper body from the table.

'Hold him there, please,' she said.

Arthur Bimsdale grimaced, but carried out the instruction.

After she'd examined the face, neck and chest, Parslow straightened up. 'I take it he'd just drunk coffee from that cup,' she said, pointing to the empty paper container.

'I…I brought him it,' the younger agent said. 'Along with something to eat.' He looked at the still wrapped sandwich that had been knocked to the floor. 'He didn't have time to…'

'I smelled coffee on his lips.' The doctor made notes on a clipboard.

'Good for you,' Sebastian said. 'So what happened?'

'The obvious candidate is heart failure. He's in good physical condition for his age, but there may have been an underlying problem—we need those records. The sudden nature of this death is interesting. You say he showed no signs of difficulty or discomfort in the period immediately before he collapsed. I would expect there to have been some signs, even minor ones. Same with other potential causes—stroke, anaphylactic shock and so on.'

'He was alone for about ten minutes before I came back with the coffee and food,' Bimsdale said. 'We checked the film before you got here. He didn't seem to have done anything to himself.'

Parslow nodded. 'That corresponds with what I'm looking at here—no signs of him having taken anything toxic. Besides, you were both in here with him for—how long?'

'At least five minutes,' Sebastian said. 'The film will show the exact time.'

'So you would have seen if he was struggling for breath or the like.'

There was a knock at the door and a pair of crime scene technicians swathed in white appeared.

'All right,' Sebastian said. 'We need to clear the area.'

'The medical examiner's on his way, sir,' one of the CSIs said.

Peter Sebastian stalked away, followed by Bimsdale.

Ellen Parslow watched them go. She'd done a course on stress management in the Navy. It looked to her that the Director of Violent Crime was in urgent need of advice in that area, not that she was going to tell the overbearing cocksucker so.

I was left alone in the cell for some time. My watch had been taken, along with my shoes and belt, and I guessed it was at least an hour. I was tired after the long, violent day, but there was no chance of me sleeping. Apollyon had obviously mentioned Hades to put the shits up me. It didn't have that effect literally, which was just as well considering the lack of facilities. My mind was working overtime. I made myself take deep breaths and tried to get into a self-protective zone. I had no doubt that I was going to have to use my combat

skills if I was to get out of the camp in one piece. I tried
to remember what Dave Cummings had taught me about
mental preparation. That made me think of Quincy—he
had reiterated much of that during our sessions. Quincy.
He was another victim of Sara's brutality. I owed her
for him, too.

At last, the door opened and a pair of large speci-
mens with buzz cuts advanced on me. My wrists were
pinned behind my back with plastic restraints and I was
led into the corridor. The concrete chilled my bare feet
and gave the soles an abrasive rub that soon became
unpleasant. At the end of the passage, we came to a
steel door. One of my guards swiped a card through the
locking device and it opened inward. On the other side
was an elevator with a steel mesh cage. We went down
what seemed like a long way. Another sealed door was
opened and we walked into the underworld.

'What the—' I broke off in amazement as the full
extent of the scene in front of me became apparent.

'Welcome to Hades,' Apollyon said, coming out of
the darkness on the right. 'In the Antichurch, we prefer
to call it Hell.'

Both names were appropriate. The underground area
beneath us was huge, with lights flashing in the distance and flares of flame blasting out all over. I made
out buildings dotted around, some low and some as
much as three stories high, but all of them in a partially ruined condition, as if a tank had driven around
firing through windows and smashing against walls.
Lengths of timber hung from some of the roofs like gib-
bets—when I looked closer, I realized that from some
of them bodies were dangling. There was a roar and
fire consumed a block in the middle distance. I could

hear screaming from it, but saw no one emerge. A black-surfaced river wound through the domain, carcasses of animals aground in the shallows. A wrecked car was hanging from a rickety humpbacked bridge in the foreground, much of the brickwork having been knocked away. The horizon in the far distance was bright red, silhouetting ramparts and uneven walls above which smoke was curling. There was a stench of rotting matter much worse than any swamp.

Apollyon smiled grimly. 'What do you think?'

'Someone's been to art school,' I replied, with a lot more bravado than I felt; I had just noticed that the pale-colored objects in the middle of the river were naked, and incomplete, human bodies.

'Hieronymus Bosch's *Garden of Earthly Delights*, right panel,' said a familiar voice.

I looked past Apollyon. Like me, Sara was barefoot and the fatigues she'd been given were too big for her. Her face was pale and drenched in sweat. What had they done to her?

'Correct,' the bearded man said, apparently gratified.

'Also, Pieter Brueghel's *Dulle Griet*, Jan Brueghel's *Orpheus*,' Sara continued. 'Plus shades of works by Michelangelo, Memling, the JS Monogrammist, Simon Marmion, Doré, John Martin...' Sara's voice faded away and her head dropped. She looked in a bad way.

'You know a lot about infernal affairs,' Apollyon said to her. 'It's a pity you can't join the Antichurch.'

I wasn't surprised that my ex-lover had educated herself about depictions of hell—after all, she did call herself the Soul Collector and her sister had been a practicing Satanist. Despite that, I was still taken aback by what I saw moving beneath us. At first I thought it was fake, some kind of model projected onto a screen, but then I realized the figures and the terrain they were moving through were real—though what did 'real' mean down here? Demonic figures with blackened faces, carrying lances and curved swords, were heading into the Hades landscape. They were followed by others, whose forms had been shaped in the imagination of Bosch—diabolical creatures with the heads of birds and fish, all armed with vicious blades and stabbing weapons. Another had the front half of a beetle and the extended rear legs of a frog, and behind it came one with a rat's head and butterfly's wings attached to its back. There was only one group missing.

'Where are the souls of the wicked?' I asked.

'Ah, you noticed,' Apollyon said. 'Where are the naked humans that the creatures of Hell will torment and feed upon?' He laughed. 'Take a guess, why don't you?'

I looked at Sara. She was nodding slowly.

'Don't worry, you can keep your clothes on,' the bearded man said. 'We'll even give you some weapons.'

One of the gorillas stepped up and dumped wooden staves in front of us, two long and two short ones.

'Oh, thanks,' I said.

'You prefer we take them back?' Apollyon demanded.

'No, that's okay.'

'All right. Now listen up. This isn't just a turkey shoot—or should I say, a turkey slash and stab.' He grinned. 'The two of you have got a genuine chance to get out of here. All you've got to do is find your way to the exit at the far side of Hades.'

'Yeah, right,' Sara said contemptuously. 'Like you're going to let us go.'

Apollyon shrugged. 'Sure I'll let you go. As long as you get past the devils and demons.'

'Oh, great,' I said. 'I take it those spears and swords are sharp.'

'You shouldn't complain. At least they aren't carrying firearms.' The bearded man turned and nodded to the big man with the badge on his cap. This time, I recognized the figure on it, one that had its own relevance to the location. Hercules, the ancient Greeks' most dynamic hero, had descended to the underworld to capture Hades' three-headed watchdog Cerberus. I hadn't seen any other characters from ancient myth in this very medieval hell.

'Right, take them down,' the officer ordered.

I was marched to a metal staircase. As I went down, I heard more footsteps. It seemed that Sara and I were going to be working together. I wasn't sure how I felt about that. Would she be watching my back or looking for an opportunity to execute me? Maybe I should have been thinking about doing that to her, but I didn't have it in me. We had enough to contend with, and I had no idea what had happened to Rothmann.

A last door was opened and we moved out onto the damp earth at the beginning of the infernal landscape.

'Hey, shoes,' I said, as my feet sank into the mud.

'Screw shoes,' the guard behind me said. 'You see any humans wearing footwear in those paintings?'

This wasn't the time or place for a discussion about realism in art. The staves were tossed a few yards in front of us.

'Follow your noses,' said another guard.

I felt the plastic shackles fall from my wrists. By the time I had picked up my wooden weapons, the door had clanged shut behind the guards. I looked over at Sara. She was rolling up the sleeves of her camouflage jacket. She drew one of them across her forehead. I noticed how thin her forearms were. Surely she hadn't given up the daily sessions in the gym that she had started in London.

'Any idea where we should head?' she asked, peering ahead.

Loud barking broke out to the right. I listened and thought I could make out three dogs. Either Caesar had a couple of friends or Cerberus was lying in wait for us.

'Let's go to the left,' I said.

'Why not? Capitalism's dead and buried, after all.'

I raised an eyebrow and set off through the mud, glancing up at the figures on the viewing platform where we had been.

'See you at the far side,' I shouted. That provoked raucous laughter. Screw them, I wasn't giving up without a fight.

As we approached the first pair of buildings, I saw a long spear wave above the roof and heard muffled commands.

We were expected.

Thirty-One

Rudi Crane was in Hercules-1, the company Learjet, en route to New York's La Guardia airport. He was working at his computer, running an eye over the balance sheets from the various divisions. He was gratified to see that activities in the Far East were coming in above projected earnings, while the Middle East was running at its usual excellent levels. Even domestic business was up, proving that some things really were recession-proof. Private security was expanding at a rate that surprised many, but not Crane. It had been obvious to him for years that an economic crash would increase the gap between rich and poor, giving Hercules a golden opportunity to ensure that customers felt safe in their gated communities, places of work and country clubs. Investments that he'd made years ago were now bearing fruit—for which, as always, the Lord was to be thanked.

Hitting the keys with two fingers—whoever would have thought that chief executives would need secretarial skills?—Crane brought up the company profile. Red dots across the globe showed Hercules facilities, while there was a mixture of red and blue on the continental U.S.—the latter color marking operations that the company financed, but kept its involvement secret for various reasons. Texas had more of those than any other state because of favorable tax and firearms legislation. There was an underwater combat training unit near Galveston and an advanced cavalry section north of Lubbock—riding skills had proved to be very useful in parts of Russia and Africa—but the preacher's attention was not focused on those blue dots. He clicked on another one and a drop-down menu appeared. The third line offered voice connection. The call was answered immediately and a clipped voice gave him an encouraging update. Praise be, everything was in hand.

'Mr. Crane?'

He looked up and smiled at the ice-blonde stewardess. She was Ukrainian and he had chosen her himself from a lineup provided by the Hercules team in that country. Unfortunately, he could never recall her name.

'Thank you, my dear.' He took the glass of tomato juice and sipped experimentally. 'Excellent. A touch less Tabasco the next time.'

The young woman bowed and stepped away.

Katya, Crane remembered. He must remember that when she came to his sleeping quarters later. In the meantime, he had to refresh his memory about the week to come. He was using the United Nations Conference on Climate Change to bring Hercules Solutions even more into the public eye, which meant a large amount of schmoozing with mercenary politicians and their hangers-on. *Schmoozing?* He banished the word from his vocabulary. It sounded Jewish. Anyway, there would be plenty of opportunity to fly the company flag, not least because he had recently begun an initiative to make all Hercules facilities and vehicles as green as possible in countries and states where that was important—not Texas, of course. It was important to give clients all the help they could get when it came to deciding on which company to use. Not that he believed in climate change. The whole thing was obviously a conspiracy by left-leaning intellectuals to jam up the wheels of business. Besides, the Lord had everything in hand. With Armageddon fast approaching, those who deserved to be saved would be taken up to Heaven. For those who remained, the state of the planet would be the least of their worries.

Before he went to the well-appointed bedroom at the rear of the cabin, Rudi Crane dropped to his knees and gave thanks for the support his plans had received from the Good Lord. Recent developments had showed that he had been right to cut loose from Jack Thomson and his Nazi fantasies. It wasn't necessary to believe in outdated ideologies, let alone debase oneself in impious devil worship. The traditions he had grown up covered things much more effectively, even if it was sometimes necessary to make exceptions: some of his best combat leaders were black; Hercules Solutions also used Jewish lawyers and accountants, and Asian bankers. Of course, none of them were candidates for the Rapture.

Crane got to his feet, holding on to the chair as the jet hit minor turbulence. When he'd been younger, he would have parted company with his lunch in such a situation, but he had trained his body to control itself.

'Oh, Katya,' he called.

Swallowing bile, the stewardess walked toward the preacher, her blouse already undone.

'Got any ideas?' I asked, as we approached the damaged building.

'Weapons,' Sara said, banging her staves together. 'Concentrate on replacing these with anything that's more lethal.' Her forehead shone in the flickering light, but her face was set hard. 'I'll take the front. You see what's round that corner.'

My mouth was dry, but my heart rate wasn't excessively rapid. I was in some kind of zone, ready to fight to the end. I had to make this good—for Karen and our son, but also for my trainers, Dave and Quincy. I glanced at Sara. I should have been paying her back for their deaths, but that could wait. Without her, I had much less chance of getting to the far side of Hades. The last I saw, she was pointing the long staff like a lance and charging the shattered door.

There were two figures waiting for me at the side of the building. I applied the long staff to the first one's rat head and hit the second with the short staff where I guessed his chin was under the demon mask. They dropped like stones. I went to the corner and looked round, pulling my head back rapidly as something came toward it at speed. I looked behind me and saw a wooden shaft quivering in the trunk of a withered tree. I ran to it and wrenched out the weapon. It had a wicked steel point like a javelin's.

I replaced the smaller staff with the spear and went back to the corner, narrowly avoiding another missile.

I went after the thrower, sprinting round the corner with a loud roar. A large man wearing a peaked cap and fatigues stepped back, then dropped the spear he was holding and raised his hands when he saw me. His face was brown and he had a mustache.

'Please, please,' he gabbled. 'They give us orders.'

I put the point of the spear at his throat. 'Tell them to fall back and drop their weapons!' I yelled, glaring at the men behind him.

The officer shouted out something in a language I didn't understand, but it had the desired effect. The men let their javelins and hooked swords fall to the ground. There were several animal and insect heads already lying there.

'Who are you?' I demanded.

'Major Mohammed Al-Haq,' the officer said, straining back from the sharp tip. 'Third Mountain Rangers Regiment, Pakistan Army.'

'Oh, yeah?' I looked through the hole in the wall, wondering what had happened to Sara. 'What are you doing here?'

'Training,' he said. 'We arrive yesterday. Tonight take part in exercise to experience mentality of insurgents armed with outmoded weapons.' He shook his head. 'Very strange costumes. I do not approve.'

Sara appeared behind the soldiers, a spear in each hand and a scimitar in her belt.

'They're Pakistani,' I said. 'Being trained, he says.'

'They need it,' she said, brandishing her weapons at the cowed soldiers.

'I hope you didn't…'

'Kill anyone? No, I don't think so. There'll be some sore heads and bellies. What's next?'

I tried to look beyond a heap of earth. There were more damaged buildings dotted about broken ground.

'If you will permit,' the major said, raising a hand to the javelin at his throat. 'I give you my word that we will not attack you.'

I glanced at Sara and she nodded, though she didn't lower her weapons.

'Why's that?'

He gave a slack smile. 'Because men defending next fortifications are from India. We would like to give them a beating.'

Jesus, what was this? International Crisis 101?

'How are they armed?' Sara asked.

'This I do not know for sure,' the major replied. 'I guess same as us.'

'All right,' I said, wondering what kind of training establishment issued participants with lethal weapons. The points and edges were very sharp. 'Try not to inflict any serious wounds.'

Sara looked at me as if I were a small child. 'Okay, you take half of the men and go left again. I'll take the center and the right.' She gave the major a steely look. 'Tell your men they can arm themselves again. If anyone tries to touch me, I'll take his throat out.' She made a rapid and extremely competent movement with one of her spears.

'I come with you, yes?' the officer said, stepping toward me.

I smiled at him. 'Good idea.' Then, when they were ready, I signaled the advance.

We were halfway across a pitted, evil-smelling no-man's-land when the first shots rang out.

Violent Crime Director Sebastian looked out over the lights of central Washington. To his left, the Capitol building stood out like an oversize wedding cake, bright and icing-white.

'Sit down, Peter,' the Director said, closing a file. 'Sorry to keep you.'

Sebastian did as he was told and looked across the desk at the wizened man who bore such a resemblance to Robert Redford that his nickname was 'Sundance.' He had been an admiral and, later, a Presidential adviser, before landing the job at the top of the Hoover Building.

'Now, what's the story with Sir Andrew Frogget?' The Director still had a Southern drawl, though it was many years since he'd lived in South Carolina. 'Was it a heart attack?'

'It looks that way. The postmortem won't be done till the morning.'

'You told the Brits?'

Sebastian nodded. 'The number two at their embassy. He said he would consult. I can't say he sounded particularly animated.'

'They don't *do* animated, Peter.' The Director steepled his fingers and looked over the points. 'Did he ask why Sir Andrew was in custody?'

'He asked if he was helping us with our inquiries.'

'Probably some British joke. Routh Limited is a major player on the world scene, though. What *was* Frogget doing in custody?'

Sebastian felt the strength of his superior's gaze. 'He was caught with an underage hooker. I took the opportunity to squeeze him about Rothmann and Woodbridge Holdings.'

'Did you now? Routh was involved, of course.'

'It was Woodbridge's main investment bank.'

'Did he tell you anything?'

'He gave us some names. We're checking them out.'

'Do you have a list?'

Sebastian handed over a printed page, which the Director scanned.

'Some more big names here,' he said, putting the sheet down. 'You had better exercise caution.'

'We will. I take it you approve the investigation?'

'Oh, certainly. Good work.' The Director looked at his computer screen and then back at Sebastian. 'Was there anything else? I have to look over my speech to the UN Climate Change Conference…. I hope your unit is running energy-efficient vehicles.'

Surprised, Sebastian stood up, but swallowed the laugh he'd been about to let loose. It seemed the Director was serious.

'Down!' I yelled, diving to the soft ground. I looked to my right. Two of the Pakistanis were lying crumpled and motionless, the rest desperately taking cover. Spurts of earth were flying up as automatic weapons fire continued to rain down.

'This is murder!' the major screamed.

'Keep them down!' I yelled back. In the distance, I could see Sara crawling forward, having jettisoned one of her spears. 'When the fire turns on us, get them to crawl back.'

The Pakistani officer nodded, his cap at an angle.

I pulled myself forward by my elbows. Before I had gone five yards, bullets began to spit into the ground around me. At least that would give the Pakistanis a chance to retreat. Ahead of me was a broken-down cart that looked like it had survived the Civil War, though only just. I took cover behind it and watched as Sara dived into a trench that ran alongside the meandering river. Spouts of water flew up from it as the defenders tried to hit her.

I crawled to the front of the cart, hearing bullets thud into the wood. The original dashboard was hanging loose at the far side. I managed to put my shoulder to the near side and detach it completely. It was about five feet long and two feet wide, and would provide reasonable protection. Now I felt like a Homeric hero behind his shield. I stuck the sword I'd picked up into my belt and lifted the board; fortunately there was a length of wood in the center that served as a grip. Taking my spear in the other hand, I stood up and made for the two-story building. By the time I got there, the wooden panel was holed and splintered, but it had done its job. Apart from a new parting in my hair and a shallow furrow in my thigh, I was unhurt. But I was pissed off in a big way, and my feet hurt like a bastard. Someone was going to pay.

I pulled myself over the remains of a window frame and threw the spear at a man in a hawk's head. It pinned him to a door at shoulder level, causing him to drop the Kalashnikov he'd raised at me. I ran forward and grabbed the weapon. He was groaning, but the wound didn't look mortal. There were ammunition clips in his pockets and I relieved him of those.

'Who are you?' I asked, as I tried to pull the door open.

'Indian Army, Sixteenth Rifle Battalion,' he gasped, trying to pull the spear out with his other hand.

'I'd leave that where it is if I were you,' I said, pulling his hand away. 'How many are you?'

'Forty plus two…three officers.'

Shit. We were seriously outnumbered. I heard bursts of fire beyond the door. After a few seconds, only one weapon was being fired. Then I heard Sara's voice.

I managed to get the door open and raise the Kalashnikov as three men in turbans charged toward me. I gave them a blast in front of their feet.

'Drop your weapons!' I ordered, watching as rifles like mine hit the uneven floor. 'Now turn round and go back the way you came.'

'No, no!' one of them gasped, his eyes wide. 'She is a demon.'

He was right there, but I reckoned I could restrain Sara. I beckoned them forward.

Sara was in the next room, swinging a pair of Kalashnikovs at a crowd of cowering Indians. Beyond her, through the shattered wall, I could see other turbaned figures making their escape, the river reaching up to their thighs. There were several men lying motionless on the ground.

'Oh, there you are,' she said, looking at me blankly. I had no idea what zone she was in, but I hoped I would never go there. Blood was dripping from her right arm and there was a crimson stain on her abdomen.

'Are you all right?'

She followed the direction of my gaze. 'Just scratched,' she said, looking round her captives again. 'These fuckers were firing live rounds.'

'I noticed. Where are the officers?'

A dark-skinned man with a huge mustache stood up slowly. 'Lieutenant-Colonel V. J. Singh.' His gaze dropped. 'My colleagues are dead.'

'What the fuck were you doing?' I demanded. 'This is supposed to be a training exercise.'

The officer held my gaze. 'Who said that? We were told that live rounds were necessary. The attackers are convicted murderers, are they not?'

I stared at him in amazement. 'You mean you signed up to kill people?'

'This is the great virtue of Cerberus Security, is it not?' he said, looking less sure of himself. 'We can give our men experience of real action.'

I glanced at Sara. 'Ever heard of Cerberus Security?'

She shook her head. 'Sound like nice people to do business with.'

Cerberus was obviously a company with a lot to hide, hence the absence of signs at the entrance to the camp. But we had other things to worry about, such as staying alive.

'Do you want to know who the people you shot at really were?' I asked the colonel, not waiting for an answer. 'Pakistani mountain troops.'

His eyes opened extremely wide. 'What? Oh, my God…' As I'd hoped, he had realized the seriousness of the situation. The neighboring countries were at loggerheads, both of them nuclear powers, and he was responsible for several Pakistani deaths. If that wasn't a de facto declaration of war, I didn't know what would be.

Everyone ducked as machine-gun fire raked the ruins from the front. Four Indian soldiers fell, two of them screaming and the others beyond that.

'Okay,' I said, crouching beside the colonel. 'You can see the shit storm you're in. Cerberus Security has obviously decided you can't be allowed to live. Either you fight back or you die.'

He looked at me gravely, then nodded. 'Sergeants, to me,' he commanded.

Two men came over, bending double to avoid the fire that continued to ring out.

I listened as he gave them orders. A third of his men were to provide covering fire, while the rest were split into three sections to storm the next line of defenses, which were silhouetted against the fiery red backdrop.

I crawled over to Sara. 'Are you all right?'

'Never better,' she said, breathing heavily.

'Stay here. I'll come back for you when we break through.'

'If you get through.' Her face was drenched in sweat. 'I'm coming with you, Matt.' She bit her lower lip till blood dripped from it. 'Just one thing. If I…if I don't make it…'

'You'll make it,' I interrupted. Now it didn't seem to matter what she'd done in the past—the fight for both of us to survive was all. I pulled myself up.

'We are ready,' the colonel said, clutching a Kalashnikov.

I nodded, my eyes still on Sara. 'Stay close to me,' I said, my mouth to her ear.

She smiled slackly. 'I always have been, Matt.'

I had just enough time to register the truth of that before the guns opened up on either side of us.

Thirty-Two

Heinz Rothmann watched as the men in fatigues and turbans charged across the open ground in three formations. It was brave, proving that *untermenschen* could sometimes fight as Aryans, but completely insane. They went down like ninepins, some screaming and others immediately caught in contorted positions. Apollyon had placed him at the front of the ramparts, with a man holding a bayonet to his back, seemingly unconcerned if he took a bullet from the men who were firing from the rear—the attackers themselves didn't have time to loose many shots. Fortunately he remained unscathed, at least until a burst rattled off the wall in front of him. He looked down and saw Matt Well's persecutor with the short blond hair point a Kalashnikov at him. He moved to his right and heard bullets thump into the chest of his captor.

He ducked down behind the low parapet, trying to understand what was happening. Another burst of fire chipped stone from the wall. The woman was still aiming at him—he could see that from a space between the bricks. Then he took a boot in the side, was knocked flat and pulled upright again.

'Hiding like the heretical rat you are!' Apollyon shouted, before letting loose fire from his machine-pistol.

Heinz Rothmann stood beside the new Master of the Antichurch, willing bullets to cut the bearded man down. He couldn't see the blonde woman anymore, but Matt Wells was leading a small group of turbaned soldiers toward the wall on the right. What was the Englishman doing in the same attack as the woman who wanted his soul?

'Stand fast, you cowards!' screamed Apollyon, shooting over the heads of defenders who were running toward the door in the huge red screen to the rear. 'Stand fast!' The assassin pulled Rothmann down as more fire was concentrated on them.

'I think…I think we're on our own,' Rothmann said.

'I've still got plenty of clips.' Apollyon slotted another into his weapon.

'I can help. Give me a gun.'

'And lose my life instantly?'

'I won't shoot you. That woman is the dangerous one. She'll kill us both.'

The bearded man dragged him over to a low wall that had been built to provide cover. 'All right. Take the pistol from my belt. Do you know how to use it?'

'Oh, yes.' Rothmann racked the Glock's slide and ducked his head as the woman came onto the roof.

Boots pounded up the stairs on the other side and clipped commands rang out.

'They're behind that wall, Matt,' the woman called. 'Apollyon and Rothmann.'

The bearded man stuck his weapon above the wall and fired in her direction.

'Not even close,' she taunted. 'You're losing your touch.'

'Apollyon!' Matt Wells shouted. 'Send Rothmann out. I'm not interested in you.'

'Maybe,' the assassin yelled back. 'But the blonde bitch is.'

'Send Rothmann out,' Wells repeated.

'Fuck you. The heretic is mine.'

Heinz Rothmann kept his head down. He was in what looked like an impossible situation, but he still had some cards to play. All he needed was the courage to make the first move. He mouthed a prayer to the Lord Lucifer and thought of his dead sister. It was time he exacted the blood price for her.

Faster than he believed he was able, Rothmann put the muzzle of the pistol to Apollyon's abdomen and fired three shots.

Peter Sebastian was no fool. When he received the summons from Valerie Hinton, he declined to meet her at the rural Maryland diner. Even if he hadn't been a devotee of spy movies, he would have known that going to a rendezvous in an out-of-the-way place with a CIA operative whose orders you've disobeyed was asking for trouble. He told her that he would meet her in a large all-night café near Union Station in half an hour. That would put her in an even worse temper, which he could work to his advantage.

Before he left the Hoover Building, he called Arthur Bimsdale into his office.

'Where are we with the list of Rothmann's backers?'

The young agent opened a cardboard folder. 'For the foreign-based companies, I've asked our local people to provide full reports ASAP.'

'Full reports, as in what illicit activities we can use to put the squeeze on them?'

Bimsdale gave him an uncertain look. 'Are you sure we should be proceeding in such a—'

'Do you want to ask the Director about that?'

'Em, no, sir.' Bimsdale looked at his watch. 'We should hear from the Far East in a few hours.'

'And the American companies?'

'There are only three. The financial crime unit is working up reports on the hedge funds Escorial and Lemas, and I've got the San Francisco field office on Tuffet and Co.'

'There are more, of course. Sir Andrew didn't give us them all.'

'Yes, sir,' Bimsdale said, closing the folder. 'If you say so, sir.'

Sebastian got up. 'I'll be out for an hour or so. You should get some sleep.'

His assistant smothered a yawn. 'Maybe I will get my head down on your sofa, if that's okay.'

'Whatever.'

As Sebastian drove the short distance to the railway station, he tried to come up with a strategy. Assuming Valerie Hinton knew about Sir Andrew's death, she was going to be seriously unimpressed. Then again, maybe he was tying his gut in knots unnecessarily. How would she have heard already? It wouldn't be the first time she had presented him with information that was classified within the Bureau. Except, in this case, she would probably have heard from her contacts in the

British Embassy. The Agency had its fingers well up the asses of all the U.S.'s allies.

Valerie Hinton had already arrived. Wearing a black hat with a low brim, she was sitting at the rear of the joint, a tall cup in front of her.

'You're late,' she said accusingly. 'And it's the middle of the night.'

'At least you didn't have to drive out to Maryland.' A waitress put a cup on the table for him and filled it with coffee.

The CIA operative waited till they were alone and gave him a piercing look. 'You owe me an explanation. What was Sir Andrew Frogget doing in the Hoover Building?'

Sebastian knew he had a little room to play hard-ball. He had no idea if Valerie had kids—he suspected she was married to the job—but even she might have a conscience. 'He was caught abusing a thirteen-year-old girl.'

Her expression didn't change. 'Who your team just happened to be monitoring.'

'No, we were monitoring *him*.'

'After I specifically told you to keep away from him?'

He raised his shoulders. 'Sometimes you have to do what seems right.'

Valerie Hinton spat the green liquid she was drinking back into the cup. 'Don't give me that shit, Peter. At all times you have to do what we tell you. Otherwise, adios career.'

'Woodbridge Holdings was dirty—brainwashing, a Nazi militia, the attempt on the President's life. Ergo, the people who backed the company are dirty, too. I wouldn't have thought the Agency would be so interested in protecting them.'

'Don't presume to think you understand what's going on here. I'll crush you.'

Sebastian stared at her dully and stood up. 'Do your worst, Valerie. I'm going ahead with this investigation.' He walked away. When he was outside, he looked back through the plate glass and saw that she was on her cell phone—probably trying to get her superior to pull strings with the Director. He had no fears there. The former admiral had told the spooks to keep their hands to themselves in the past and he had invested too much in the Rothmann investigation to pull it now.

He got into his car and put the key in the ignition.

'Put your hands on your thighs, please.'

Peter Sebastian looked around in amazement. 'Arthur?'

That was his last word. A well-honed knife cut his windpipe and his chest immediately felt like two strong hands were crushing it. He thought of Matt Wells. Had he found Heinz Rothmann, or was the bastard going to remain at large?

Then his soul went lamenting into the dark.

I heard the three shots and assumed that Apollyon had disposed of Rothmann. Then, to my surprise, the Nazi piece of shit stood up, a Glock dangling by the trigger-guard from one of his raised hands.

'Drop it!' Sara yelled. 'Now!'

Rothmann obeyed the order. There was dirt on his face, but the two livid scars were still prominent. He looked badly shaken as he came out from behind the wall. When he was in the middle of the roof, Sara went over to the low wall and looked down.

'Apollyon's dead,' she said, sounding disappointed.

I turned to Colonel Singh. He had taken a bullet to the upper arm, but his expression was triumphant. 'Keep us covered,' I said. 'And watch out for more gunmen.'

He nodded and passed on orders.

I walked into the open, the barrel of the Kalashnikov resting on my shoulder.

Sara was running her hand over Rothmann. 'He's clean.' She stepped back and leveled her machine-pistol at him.

'No!' I shouted. 'Wait!' I still wanted the bastard to pay for what he'd done to Karen and our son, but in the light of what had just happened in the Hades complex, my priorities were changing. I wanted to find out who was behind this dump and I was sure Rothmann knew.

'Matt,' he said, his voice low. 'Don't do anything hasty.' He looked over his shoulder. 'Don't allow this… individual to do anything hasty.'

Sara kicked him on the back of the knee, causing him to stumble forward. 'I'm not an individual,' she growled. 'I'm your worst nightmare.' The words were aggressive, but I could see the fight and her wounds were getting to her. There was even more blood on her tunic and her face was dripping with sweat.

'Matt?' Rothmann said, fear making his voice uneven. 'Don't let her—'

Sara emptied the magazine of her machine-pistol into the floor beneath his feet. He must have taken some ricochets, because he collapsed, clutching both ankles.

I stepped closer, raising a hand at Sara as she aimed her pistol at his face.

'Matt!' he screamed. 'Haig! Haig!'

The trigger kicked in instantly. As part of me separated from my body and rose above the roof of the ravaged building, all I could think was how smart it was of Rothmann to use a non-German word. Not least the name of the British commander whose tactics eventually defeated Germany in the First World War. Doctor Rivers would never have thought of that. I was so amazed that my attempts to gain control of myself became frantic, and the zone that I had practiced so often eluded me. Nothing.

I watched impotently as my brainwashed self swung the Kalashnikov down at speed. I fired a burst into Sara that sent her flying across the uneven surface.

Then, just as quickly, I found myself back in my body and in command of what I was doing. Either the trigger command was brief or I had fought it off somehow. I ran across to Sara and lifted the upper part of her broken body onto my thighs. It was obvious she was beyond medical help.

She gagged, blood running out of the corners of her mouth.

'You finally…you nailed me, Matt.' Her crimson lips formed into a shaky smile. 'I'm…I'm glad it…it was you.'

I looked across to Rothmann, who was still writhing around. One of the Indian troops was kneeling near him, Kalashnikov at the ready.

'Sara,' I said, leaning over her. 'I didn't mean to do it. The conditioning…'

She was still smiling. 'Of course…you meant to do…

it, Matt.' Her forehead furrowed in agony. 'It's better…
better this way.' She pulled me closer. 'Sellers and Ko-
linski, 168 Ditmars…Boulevard, Queens, New…York…
Ci…' She took a deep breath, which rattled in her throat
and chest. 'I left a file there. Tell…tell them you're my
cousin…my cousin from…Surbiton.' Her eyes closed,
and then opened again briefly. 'Get him, Matt…get
Rothmann…for…me…'

'Sara?' I put my cheek close to her mouth, but no
breath brushed against it. I rocked back on my heels
and smoothed her eyes shut with my thumbs.

I had finally put an end to my former lover, but at
the last I hadn't wanted to—if it hadn't been for the
Rothmanns' conditioning, I would probably have let
her live, but would have made sure she was arrested
for all the horrors she had committed against me and
my friends. Quincy Jerome's dead face rose up before
me again. She was a cold-blooded killer, but I had been
close to her in the past. It seemed that love couldn't just
be thrown away, no matter how much pain it brought
about.

I let her shoulders and head slide off my thighs and
slowly got to my feet. If I got out of Hades alive, I would
go and see what she'd left behind.

'Sir, sir!' Colonel Singh was saying. 'I have assem-
bled my surviving men. There are more armed men
approaching. We must go!'

I went over to the parapet and shots flew over my
head. In the distance I could see men in fatigues approaching. Cerberus Security was coming to finish us
off.

I grabbed Rothmann under his arm and pulled him to
his feet, not concerned about how much that hurt him.

Heading for the gigantic red screen that marked the boundary of Hell, I gave Sara's body a final glance. She looked at peace, whether she deserved that or not.

Valerie Hinton was standing at a pay phone inside Union Station.

'It's all right,' she said. 'Your name wasn't mentioned and neither was the company's.'

'Are you quite sure about that?' Rudi Crane's voice was less imposing than usual.

'We had a man present. He dealt with the knight before he could do any real damage.'

'He dealt with him? Won't that have left a trail?'

'Don't worry. He used a new compound. Besides, the postmortem will never be made public.'

There was a long pause. 'Very well. And you say there will be no further investigation?'

'The Director will be made to see that is not in his interest.'

'What about the lead investigator?'

'The saint who was shot full of arrows? Don't worry, he's gone to another place.'

'That is a veritable piece of good news.'

'Do you have any such news for me?'

'You mean from the Lone Star State? All is well, as far as I am aware.'

'I hope so. There are several people down there who we never want to see again.'

'Quite so. Fear not! By now, they will have started on their last journeys. Praise the Lord!'

Valerie Hinton hung up the phone and shook her head. One of the downsides of working for the Company was that you had to deal with the most objectionable people. Still, whatever it took to ensure the nation's best interests were secured.

She pulled her hat down and walked into the chill night air. There was one thing she had to do before she turned in for what would be a short night's sleep. Arthur Bimsdale had turned out to be a very satisfactory recruit. She needed to clear an evening to get better acquainted with him.

Thirty-Three

The colonel's men returned fire using the machine guns we had found. That bought us some distance from our pursuers.

Rothmann moaned as I dragged him along. One of the Indians came up and lifted his legs so at least his wounds weren't put under any more pressure—not that I cared. Looking ahead, I saw that the door was metal and there didn't seem to be a handle. Great.

'See here,' Colonel Singh said, trotting up beside me. He was holding three grenades.

'Do you think they're full charge?' I asked.

'There is only one way to find out.' He handed his Kalashnikov to one of his men and ran forward, his portly form silhouetted against the fiery backdrop. He made it to within a few yards before a burst of fire sliced across his legs.

'Shit!' I stopped to leave Rothmann with the soldier carrying his legs, then waved more of the turbaned men forward. 'Cover me!' I put down my Kalashnikov and charged to the door. Bullets ricocheted from the steel surface, whistling past me.

Colonel Singh was clutching his legs and groaning. I grabbed him by the shoulders and dragged him away, then went back for the grenades, which had spilled from his grip. There was a heap of earth about ten yards from the door and we took cover behind it.

'You play cricket, sir?' the colonel asked, extending an arm.

'Not since school. Why?'

He took one of the grenades and pulled the pin with his teeth. 'Leave to me, then. I am superb fielder.'

I took his word for it and watched as the grenade looped through the air. It exploded just before it reached the metal panels.

'Good shot!' I said.

'Not good enough.' The colonel pulled, waited and threw again.

The blast was centered on the door, but it still didn't break it. The firing behind us seemed to be increasing in ferocity.

'Last chance,' he grunted, then dispatched the third grenade.

This time the door swung open in two pieces.

'Go,' Colonel Singh said, signaling to his men. 'We will cover you.'

I wanted to thank him, but there wasn't time. I heaved Rothmann over my shoulder. It was only when I reached the door that I realized I'd left my Kalashnikov behind. A rattle of shots made me keep going.

Beyond the exit, there was a lift similar to the one on the other side. It was striking that there were no men in fatigues waiting—perhaps nobody had given us a chance against the defenders. I hit the call button. The mechanism kicked in immediately.

Rothmann was panting, even though he hadn't been carrying any heavy weights recently. I swung him to the floor, opened the door to the cage and pulled him in. The only option apart from *H* for *Hades* was *G,* which I presumed was ground level. We were there in less than a minute. I opened the door and was confronted by another steel panel, but this one had a button to the right-hand side.

The door opened onto a patch of muddy ground. The pale light of early morning was trying to break through a layer of mist. Although we were inside the compound, there was only a low wall in front of us. I picked Rothmann up again and ran toward it, levering him over. When I joined him, I saw a large yellow digger straight ahead of us, and the fence about thirty yards beyond it.

'Can…can you…drive that thing?' Rothmann asked, as I jogged toward the vehicle with him on my shoulder.

'Oh, yes,' I said, thinking of my friend Dave Cummings. He had owned a demolition company and had given me sessions on his various machines. I scrambled into the cab and hauled Rothmann up beside me. As was often the case with heavy equipment, the keys had been left in the ignition. I fired up the engine, struggled a bit to find a gear and then veered toward the fence.

'More speed!' Rothmann yelled.

'Fuck you!' I replied, the gas pedal already on the floor.

We had enough speed, though we took a long stretch of wire with us. Alarms started honking and I heard some shots in the distance, but we were clear. I stood up in the cab and tried to get my bearings. A line of trees in the distance looked like they might be alongside the road, so I headed for them. Sure enough, the SUV Sara had been driving soon came in sight through the mist. In a couple of minutes, we were there. I stopped the digger and killed the engine, then jumped down.

'Well, well,' said a familiar voice. 'If it isn't James Bond the Second.'

Gordy Lister had appeared from behind the High-lander, a machine-pistol in one hand and a snub-nosed revolver in the other. Mary Upson was at his side—at least she didn't seem to be armed, but there was blood on her shirt.

'Hold it right there!' Gordy ordered. He glanced up at the cab. 'That goes for you, too, Master.' He pro-nounced the title as if he'd just sucked a lime.

'Come over here and help me down,' Rothmann said. 'I'm wounded.'

'Like I give a shit.' The diminutive man turned back to me. 'Where's the bitch?'

I was looking at Mary. She seemed less than con-nected to what was going on—hardly surprising after what she had been through in the rite. I turned back to Lister. 'You mean—'

'I mean the blonde bitch who killed my brother.' The machine-pistol was waving around in his grip.

'Dead,' I said, pointing to my fatigues. 'This is her blood.'

Lister stared at Rothmann, who confirmed what I'd said. 'Where are you going, Wells?'

I was heading for the SUV. 'He needs to get to hos-pital.'

'Help me down, Gordy,' Rothmann said, easing his legs toward the ground and gasping. 'Now, man!'

I had opened the door in advance of moving the Highlander closer to the digger when the shot rang out. By the time I turned, Rothmann had slid to the ground, blood pumping from his head. Mary started to cry and I went over to her.

'What the fuck did you do that for?' I demanded, shading Mary's line of sight.

'He'd lost it completely,' Lister said. 'Fucking Master of the Antichurch of Lucifer fucking Triumphant. Last thing I needed was him spouting all kinds of shit about me to the Feds. Besides, if I'd never hooked up with him, Mikey would still be alive.' He paused, staring toward the camp. 'Who the hell are those guys?'

I looked past Mary's head and saw a group of turbaned troops exiting the camp by the hole I'd made in the fence.

'Indian Army,' I said.

'Say what?' Gordy ran to the car I'd seen him and Mary in before. 'Geronimo, my ass.'

He disappeared into the mist.

Jimmy Vlastos raised the blind in his bedroom and looked out over the rooftops of Astoria. It was a clear morning and the sky was pale blue, thin layers of cloud furrowing high above the planes taking off and landing at La Guardia. The sound of bouzouki music drifted up from the apartment below—his neighbors were economic refugees from the fatherland who were still homesick. Vlastos stretched his shoulders and saw an elderly woman staring at him from the opposite block. He looked down, suddenly aware of his nakedness and his half-mast morning glory. He kept his arms high and grinned at the peeper. Then he remembered the last time he'd been naked in front of a fully dressed woman.

Who was she, the blonde with the knife and the Ruger? He'd put the word out, but nothing had come back. Obviously she was a pro, but why would a pro have been hired to tell him about the scumbag who had raped his cousin Eleftheria? The more he thought about it, the more he was convinced that she had acted independently. But why? As it turned out, things had fallen neatly into place. His relationship with the Colombians had been getting problematic—they didn't like the credit he gave some customers and he was tired of being pushed around. Taking the wire cutters to Alonso Larengo's nuts had been a big risk, and letting Ria watch could have made things worse. As it was, the Colombians had been happy to get rid of the increasingly erratic Larengo, who hadn't been seen since he staggered out of the repair shop off Hazen that Jimmy had taken over for the night. He was probably in bits in the East River by now.

But Jimmy hadn't been able to get the blonde out of his mind. There was something about her, a vulnerability beneath the stone-hard exterior, that had made him want to help her. He didn't like being in other people's debt, especially since he reckoned the Colombians had actually hired her to kill him—they had hinted as much, saying that Alonso Larengo didn't have a high opinion of him. If that was the case, she'd taken a big chance. You didn't want to fuck with people who hired killers— even the brokers had been known to set up hits on hired guns who stepped out of line.

Vlastos made himself a Greek coffee, stirring the mixture in the *briki* as it came to the boil like his mama had shown him. The aroma made his nostrils twitch in anticipation and he burned his lip when he tried a sip too soon.

'*Gamoto!*' he yelled. He ran his tongue over the burnt area. But still the woman with the short blond hair and the high cheekbones stayed with him. Her easy skill with the weapons and her mastery of him should have turned him off. What the fuck was wrong with him? The bitch would have shot him without a moment's hesitation if he'd made a move. Christ, she'd shot the gun out of his hand to teach him a lesson. He should have put a contract out on her for that humiliation, even though no one else had witnessed it. What if she had talked?

But he knew she hadn't. For some reason, she had acted as his guardian angel. He couldn't forget that.

Jimmy Vlastos was in love with a ghost. For that reason, he would act on the request he had received from her by email. If killing Xavier Marias—whoever the hell he was—would improve his standing with the blonde, he'd do it in an instant.

'Come on,' I said to Mary Upson. 'This place isn't safe.' I turned to Colonel Singh, who was being held up by two of his men. 'I'm going to get help. Can you hold on here?'

'Oh, yes, sir.' He eyed the line of trees on the other side of the road. 'I am seeing a very adequate defensive position.'

I left him to it, taking Mary's arm and leading her to the Toyota's passenger door. I put the Kalashnikov on the backseat, catching sight of the rucksack that Sara had left there. The edge of Abaddon's laptop was sticking out. I started the engine and checked the sat nav monitor. The next town was less than ten miles away.

'You don't have a cell phone, do you?'

Mary shook her head. 'I wasn't wearing much on the cross, if you remember.'

'Shit, sorry.' I looked over my shoulder and pulled away. 'Are you okay?'

She raised her shoulders. 'I guess.'

'I'm sorry about your mother.'

'Yes, well, I suppose she went the way she wanted.'

I thought of the elderly woman's self-inflicted death, her body falling into the coffin. 'I'm sure she'd been conditioned.'

Mary laughed bitterly. 'I'm sure she hadn't. She'd become very strange.' She let out a sigh. 'It's me who should be sorry, Matt.' She touched my arm lightly. 'I didn't realize Gordy was going to shoot at you and that woman from the car. He fired at you in the barn, as well.'

I remembered the look on her face as she'd driven past us. 'It's all right. I imagine you thought I was responsible for your mother's death.'

She took her hand away and bowed her head. 'No, Matt, it wasn't that. I…I was jealous. You and the blonde woman looked so…I don't know…so right together, as if you'd known each other for years.'

I should have realized that Mary would have been jealous. That had been why she had betrayed me after I'd escaped from the camp in Maine.

'Who was she?' Mary asked softly. 'Where is she now?'

I told her, the answer to the former question needing rather more words than the latter. I had a flash of

Sara's body as I'd left it on the roof in Hades. What would happen to it?

When I'd finished, we were approaching the small town. Mary dabbed her eyes with the cuff of her shirt.

'I'm...I'm so sorry, Matt. Now you've lost them both.'

I tried to banish that thought from my mind, not least because putting Karen and Sara together felt disrespectful to the mother of my son. But she was right—they had all gone into the darkness and I, in my desolation, was left in the light.

'What now?' Mary asked, as I pulled up at a pay phone.

'I'm calling the FBI. You can make a run for it if you like, but you haven't got anything to hide. I won't tell them about you and Gordy.'

She looked around, taking in the clapboard houses and the almost deserted main street. 'No, it's all right. I'll back up whatever you say.'

I had a feeling it wasn't going to be that easy. There was a lot she didn't know, and Peter Sebastian would go through my story with a fine-tooth comb. I got out and headed for the phone, catching another glimpse of the rucksack. If I wanted to find out who had hired Abaddon, and who was behind the camp and the Hades complex, I needed to see what else I could find in the laptop.

Ah, fuck it, I thought. I was tired and I was hurting inside. I'd turn the computer over to the Feds and let them work it out. Mary was right. It was time to be straight. There had been too many secrets and lies.

* * *

Arthur Bimsdale had been lying on the sofa in Peter
Sebastian's office, completely unconcerned by what
he had been ordered to do with his boss, when his cell
phone sparked into life. He glanced at the clock on the
wall. 7:20. It was time to start the first working day
of his new life. Five minutes later, he had registered
the news from Texas, spoken to the Acting Director of
Violent Crime (an over-the-hill bureaucrat who hadn't
even gotten into the office yet), and arranged a Bureau
plane to fly him to Waco. He would be picked up there
by an agent from the Dallas field office, which was li-
aising with the Houston team.

In the car to the airport, Bimsdale ran through what
had happened in the last twelve hours. Although he had
begun to realize that Sebastian was acting inappropriately, the speed with which events had taken place had
come as a surprise. The secret training given to CIA operatives working inside other government agencies had
stressed that nothing might happen for long periods, but
also that everything could change in the space of a few
hours. When he'd been recruited at Yale by the Agency
(he'd never got used to calling it the Company, as the
old hands did), he had been happy to be included in the
so-called Double Helix branch—operatives whose first
loyalty was to the CIA, but who would take career positions elsewhere. He was never bothered by the idea that,
technically, he was a turncoat. The country's security
took priority over all other considerations.

He looked at the Potomac as it slid seaward under
the George Mason Memorial Bridge. That water was
where Peter Sebastian's grip on the Rothmann case had
begun to loosen. If the Nazi conspirator had been found

after jumping from his boat into the Anacostia River, things would have been very different. The attack on the President would probably have gone ahead—it was unclear whether the conditioning program developed by Rothmann's sister could be reversed on the spot, and Rothmann himself might have refused to give such a command. But subsequently, if he had been in custody, so many complications could have been avoided. The Agency would have found a way to take charge of Rothmann, probably arguing that he was technically a foreigner because his father had been illicitly allowed into the U.S. (by the CIA itself, but never mind—there had been orders from the White House). He would have revealed all he knew about the conditioning program, whether he wanted to or not—modern truth drugs were very effective—and his infantile Antichurch would have been terminally disrupted.

As it was, Sebastian had been reduced to using the clearly unstable Englishman, Matt Wells. From the little he had been told earlier, there had been a slaughter at a facility that should never have come to light and Heinz Rothmann was dead, which was hardly the optimal result. It was unclear whether Wells had killed him as threatened. He should never have been employed to find Rothmann, given what had happened to his partner and their son.

Arthur Bimsdale sat back in his seat as the terminal loomed, aircraft speeding skyward like his career.

Thirty-Four

After I spoke to the special agent in charge in Houston, I went back to the SUV and booted up the laptop—fortunately its battery still had some juice. I had realized I couldn't just let things lie. I remembered that Sara had mentioned her broker, Havi, who had been in contact with Abaddon.

'What are you doing?' Mary asked.

'Trying to find out who was behind the Hitler's Hitman killings.' Sara had left a file on the desktop containing her broker Havi's email address. I considered sending him a message, but I reckoned he'd be too smart to let me get anywhere near him. I could hardly ask who had contracted Abaddon and expect a straight answer. Then I had another thought. I checked that the wireless connection was functioning and sent a message to my friend Roger van Zandt, a computer expert, in London—my memory was as erratic as ever, unable to provide my dead son's name, but full of less essential data. I asked Rog to find out if a mailing address had been registered for the email account. It was a long shot but, even if Havi had given a bogus address, Rog might be able to follow the routing to the real location.

'Why are you doing this, Matt?' Mary asked, when I shut down the computer. 'Surely the FBI can handle things from here.'

I'd thought about that. In principle, they could, but Rothmann had managed to get his niece close to Peter Sebastian, so I wasn't convinced. There was also the fact that I was on my own, with nothing else to do with my life. I hadn't been able to avenge myself on Rothmann and I felt seriously unfulfilled—someone still had to pay for what had happened to Karen and our son.

Mary touched my hand. 'Matt, you have to let them go.'

I wasn't impressed that my feelings were so obvious, but she was right. I could still see the ones I'd lost, but their faces were blurred and they no longer came close. Soon the darkness would swallow them up completely. I had no idea how I'd cope then.

I forced myself back to the small town in Texas, which was showing more signs of activity now. I had a decision to make. Either I handed the laptop over with the rest of the gear, or I kept it from the FBI. I looked at my watch. It was nearly 8:30. The advance guard from the Dallas office would be arriving at the camp soon. I decided on a compromise.

A mile before the turnoff, I stopped. I put the computer in the rucksack and stashed it behind a tree at the roadside.

'I presume I didn't see that,' Mary said, with a weak smile.

'You presume right, if you don't mind.'

'Of course I don't, Matt. After all we've been through...'

That was some kind of invitation. I didn't respond. Mary was a good woman, but I had nothing to give her.

We came over the rise of a low hill and saw a line of stationary vehicles with flashing lights. There was a roadblock in front of them. I stopped and identified myself and Mary. We were told to get out of the vehicle by a uniformed police officer. There was a clutch of plainclothes officers at the junction.

'Is that yours, sir?' the officer asked, pointing at the Kalashnikov in the backseat of the Highlander.

'I borrowed it.'

The next few hours passed in a blur of questions, familiar and unfamiliar faces, and body bags. Colonel Singh, temporary dressings on his legs, seemed to be in pretty good spirits, even though he had lost at least half his men. He eyed Major Al-Haq belligerently when the Pakistani troops passed close by, but both kept their real disapproval for the men from the camp. Not many of them were unscathed, though I saw the bulky man who had taken orders from Apollyon pass by under guard, one arm drenched in blood. He was still wearing the cap, but the badge had been removed—I wondered by whom. I remembered the figure holding the snakes— Hercules, the invincible warrior who had descended to Hades. What was the significance of that?

'Mr. Wells.'

I looked round. 'Special Agent Bimsdale.'

He took in the scene. 'Quite a major incident.'

'You could say that. You should call the CIA. Someone needs to keep the peace between those Indians and Pakistanis.'

The young man gave me a curious look. 'I've been receiving updates on the plane. I'm satisfied that we can handle everything.'

His tone attracted my attention—suddenly he seemed more authoritative.

'Where's your boss?'

'Back in D.C.'

'I'd have thought Sebastian would be down here like a shot.'

Bimsdale twitched his lips like a debater who had won a point. 'Oh, I see.' He smiled enough to show the edges of his pearly teeth. 'You don't know, of course. I'm sorry to tell you that Peter Sebastian was murdered last night.'

'What?'

'I'm afraid so. His car was found in the northern suburbs with him inside. He'd been killed with a knife.'

Every alarm in my body had gone off. The timing of the senior FBI man's death was pretty striking, but that was nothing compared with the way Arthur Bimsdale was reporting it. He sounded like a newsreader trying and failing to emote with earthquake victims in a distant country.

'What was it?' I heard myself say. 'Robbery gone wrong.'

'That's what the police are working on, I believe.' Bimsdale gave me a look that suggested his grief had been short and shallow. 'A great loss, of course, but life goes on.'

That did it. As far as I was concerned, all bets were off. I would give the FBI whatever would be corroborated by other witnesses, but the rest I would keep to myself. Something was very wrong. I still needed to play ball, though, so I told him about the compound of barns to the east.

When I'd finished, Bimsdale looked confused. 'I don't understand how you and the Soul Collector woman ended up here,' he said, nibbling the end of an old-fashioned wooden pencil.

'We followed the car containing the assassin Apollyon and Rothmann. Sara—the Soul Collector—had bugged the pickup they were in.' I thought about Rothmann. He'd been at the rear of the Hades complex with Apollyon and had looked shit scared, but not particularly surprised. Had he been there before? If so, that suggested he and whoever was behind the murders in the northern cities had perhaps been close. Was the person I was after a former collaborator of Rothmann's? Had he or she been put off by the Nazi's full-blooded espousal of the Antichurch and decided to get rid of him?

'Okay,' Bimsdale said, putting away his pencil and notebook. 'We need to get you out of here, Matt.'

I was instantly suspicious. 'Why's that?'

'Well, you'll be much more comfortable in our Dallas field office.'

That sounded like bullshit, but I wasn't in a position to do much about it. Then the special agent's cell rang. He answered, straightened up as if he was on parade, narrowed his eyes in puzzlement and then handed it to me.

'This is the Director of the FBI,' said a nasal voice, which I'd heard on the news bulletins more than once. 'Mr. Wells, I have only just found out about your involvement in this case. I view it as a serious misjudgment by the late Peter Sebastian and would like to meet with you as soon as possible to discuss it. You could fly up to Washington on the Bureau plane that took Special Agent Bimsdale to Texas. Is that acceptable to you?'

I confirmed that it was and handed the phone back to Bimsdale. Washington was a lot closer to New York than the Lone Star State and I wanted to retrieve whatever Sara had stashed in Queens. With luck, the Director would have patted me on the back and sent me on my way by the evening.

I watched as Sebastian's former assistant ate what looked like several crows before terminating the call. 'It seems you're leaving us,' he said, red spots on his cheeks.

'Yeah. Can Mary Upson come with me as far as D.C.?'

'Certainly not. She needs to be formally interviewed.'

It was only as the Bureau car pulled away that I started to wonder exactly what the Director wanted with me.

Was he the fire to the Texan frying pan I'd just survived?

The Reverend Rudi Crane was in the master bedroom of the Hercules Solutions apartment on Central Park West. To his right, the picture window provided a vision of sylvan splendor in the midst of the metropolis, but he paid no attention to that. He drank his hot water and ate his oatmeal, reveling in a rare morning spent in bed. It had been justified by the rigorous activities of the previous night. He had promised the striking stewardess—what was her name again?—a hefty pay increase, and he was seriously considering making her his secretary, even though his wife would smell a regiment of rats if that happened. He would just have to play the affronted husband, appalled that his spouse of thirty-four years could think badly of him. Then they would pray together and everything would be forgotten.

Lord be praised, it was a beautiful day, even though the New York atmosphere was filled with all sorts of hydrocarbons and aerial poisons. That was why he was here—to fly the flag of Hercules at the United Nations Climate Change Conference that began tomorrow. He would be the only CEO and chairman of a private security contractor present and he planned to make the most of that. He had a list of meetings as long as the Ukrainian girl's leg, including a panel with the prime minister of Upper Congo—he needed to check the atlas about that country's precise location, though he knew very well that diamonds were its chief export—and the defense minister of Burma, which had a new name that he could never remember. Contracts were in the offing and he meant to close the deals with a brisk shake of his god-fearing hand.

Crane glanced at his gold Rolex. 12:20. He had to get ready for lunch. He was meeting his bankers in a low-profile restaurant near Wall Street. He knew they would have preferred a glitzy Midtown place, but he liked to play the penny-pincher with them and they knew not to cross him on that. There would be the usual veiled objections to his expansion plans in what the financial establishment perceived to be unreliable, if not downright dangerous places. They had acted that way about Iraq and Afghanistan, and he'd proved them enormously wrong. The same would be the case with the new countries he was targeting. The Lord his God was a bountiful god—if only the acolytes of Mammon could appreciate that, their working lives would become much easier.

It was an advantage that the man he would be talking to after the lunch was a business associate. That way, no one would be surprised when he stayed behind. But they wouldn't be talking finance. No, Xavier Marias might have been a highly talented economic forecaster by day, but it was his out-of-office profile that Rudi Crane valued more. On reflection, it was hardly surprising that a man who had learned how to survive in the shark-infested waters of Wall Street would have become one of the most efficient assassination brokers in the country. The plan to track down his former associate Jack Thomson by framing him and his vile Antichurch for the Hitler's Hitman killings would not have been possible without Havi's input, although Crane himself had kept a close eye on the proceedings. Havi had found the assassin and engineered the hits. He had even provided a second assassin to ensure that Thomson didn't escape. This afternoon, Crane expected Havi to confirm that the Nazi devil worshipper had been liquidated and that his conditioning program was in safe hands. That would be good news to rival the Gospels, indeed.

The confirmation last night that Sir Andrew Frogget had not mentioned the involvement of a Hercules subsidiary in Thomson's Woodbridge Holdings had been very welcome. In fact, it had led directly to his chastisement of the stewardess. She had accepted the punishment for comporting herself provocatively. Not that he had sex with that woman, oh, no. No bodily fluid of his had entered any orifice of hers, at least for longer than a few seconds—there was a spittoon by the side of the bed, naturally. He had no sin to confess, as he had been thinking of his wife throughout: thinking how horrified and disgusted she would have been if she could have seen them, she the vegetarian, who would never put anything in her mouth that hadn't been peeled or sliced.

I spent most of the flight to Washington asleep. For a change, I had no dreams—that wasn't a wholly enjoyable experience, as I didn't see Karen and our son. Had they finally been swallowed up by the ground beneath? Then I remembered, and my stomach clenched hard. The bodies of my loved ones were in cold storage in the camp in Illinois. Sooner or later, I'd have to decide what to do with them. Not now. I had to find out who was behind the murders and the Hades complex. After that, I'd concentrate on them. The idea that I would have to dispose of their mortal remains terrified me.

Then I had another thought. How had Mary Upson found her way to the Antichurch rite in Texas? Had she evaded the surveillance that Peter Sebastian put in place after her mother disappeared in Maine? She didn't have the skills to pull that off herself. Had Sebastian let her go to see where she was headed? If so, he had effectively set her up as bait. I wondered what else he might have been capable of. But why would Mary have gone to Texas? Did she know more about the Antichurch than she'd let on, after misleading them?

A trio of men in suits was waiting for me outside the plane after we landed at Reagan National. One of them introduced himself, but I immediately forgot his name. He ran an eye over me and suggested that I might like to change clothes. I was handed a couple of suit bags and ushered to a washroom in the executive lounge. There was a dark blue suit and accoutrements that I wouldn't be seen dead wearing in one bag. Fortunately, the other contained a pair of casual trousers and a green herringbone jacket, along with a pair of smart but solid boots and a pale blue shirt. Everything fitted, which showed that someone had done their homework—of course, there was no shortage of information about me in the Bureau's files. I left the silk tie untouched.

A long car with dark windows took me to the center of the city.

'The Director will see you as soon as we arrive at the Hoover Building,' my escort said, glancing at his watch. 'I have orders to take you to your hotel afterward.'

Rain began to fall as we crossed the Potomac, picking holes in the surface of the gray-green water. I remembered Rothmann's escape from the boat nearby. Now he was dead, taken out by one of his sidekicks. My urge to kill him had been a waste of time and emotion. Karen and our son were still lost to me. So was Sara. She could be seen as another victim of the Rothmanns' conditioning, but that didn't get me off the hook. I still felt sick that it had been my finger on the trigger.

I was whisked up to the top of FBI headquarters in an executive lift and ushered straight into the Director's spacious office. The tall, distinguished-looking man with white hair whom I had seen on TV rose from behind a huge desk and came to meet me.

'Mr. Wells,' he said, with a Southern accent, 'I am so glad to meet you. Please come and sit down.' He led me to a three-sided square of leather-covered sofas. 'Would you like something to drink or eat?'

'Water's fine.'

He poured me a glass from the cut-crystal carafe on the central table. 'Mr. Wells, I—'

'What really happened to Peter Sebastian?' I interrupted, determined not to let him run the exchange.

To his credit, he didn't look either surprised or irritated. 'Ah, what a tragedy that was,' he said, his cloudy blue eyes meeting mine. 'It seems he was the victim of a robbery.'

'You really believe that?'

Now he did look taken aback. 'That's what the police and our people are surmising, Mr. Wells. Do you have evidence to the contrary?'

'Evidence, no. Suspicion, plenty. He gets killed on the same night as Heinz Rothmann and the assassin Apollyon? It looks to me like somebody's tidying up.'

The Director nodded. 'I can see that logic. Do you have any idea who that somebody might be?'

'That's your area, isn't it? Do we know who owned the camp in Texas yet?'

'Yes, a company called March Violet Partners. It's based in Liberia.'

'What a surprise. The partners' names are presumably straight out of a mystery novel.'

'So it would appear,' he said dolefully. 'We are, of course, interrogating everyone on the scene.'

I thought of the man with the badge that had gone missing from his cap, but I wasn't going to share that with him. I still didn't know why he had summoned me.

Either the Director was a mind reader or he wanted to change the subject. 'Mr. Wells, there are two reasons

I invited you to Washington. The first is that I thought you would appreciate seeing one of the survivors of the Antichurch massacre.'

My heart missed a beat. Who could that be?

'Sergeant Quincy Jerome of the Airborne Division is in Walter Reed hospital.'

Jesus, Quincy.

'He underwent an emergency operation, but he is out of danger. One of his lungs collapsed.'

I nodded, suddenly doubtful of my ability to speak without breaking down. Only now did I realize how much I'd needed some good news.

'You will be driven to the hospital in the evening,' the Director continued. 'Secondly, I know how much you have been through, Mr. Wells, and I don't just mean in the past days. Allow me to offer my sincerest commiserations, and those of the entire Bureau, for the deaths of your wife and son.'

I didn't correct him over Karen's status. I would have married her if she had survived and would always think of her as my wife.

'In gratitude for your help in closing the Rothmann case, I would like to invite you to accompany me to New York tomorrow. I have to attend the UN Climate Change Conference, but we will arrange a press conference afterward. The White House has instructed the Justice Department to drop all charges against you regarding the attack on the President at the cathedral here, and I would like the opportunity to clear your name in public.' He sat back and regarded me with an encouraging smile. 'As you'll understand, that will also give me the opportunity to blow the Bureau's trumpet after the successful end to the operation in Texas.'

I could see he would want to do that, with Rothmann and the others dead. It all seemed very quick, but if that was what the White House wanted, who was I to stand in its way? More to the point, I would be in New York, where I could get hold of Sara's treasure trove, if that was what it turned out to be.

'Thank you,' I said, trying to sound more impressed than I was. I hadn't trusted Peter Sebastian that much, but I found myself wishing he was still alive.

Thirty-Five

M<small>Y</small> FBI shadow Simonsen, whose name I saw on his ID tag before we left the Hoover Building, took me to a plush hotel not far from the White House. He checked me in using a Bureau declaration of my identity and a credit card with my name on it.

'Two-thousand-dollar-a-day limit,' he said, handing the piece of plastic over with what looked like disapproval. 'I'll be back at 6:30 to take you to the hospital.'

I went up to the room, which had a good view of the surrounding buildings but not much else, and took a shower. Then I headed out and located a café with a bank of computers. There were a lot of messages in my in-box, all of which I disregarded except Roger van Zandt's. He had traced the email used by Sara's broker to an apartment block in south Manhattan. I added him to the list of things to be done in New York. Then I went on the internet and did a search for 'Hercules.' Bingo. Third from the top, after a TV series and a thrash metal band, was Hercules Solutions, a company described as having 'private security and military expertise.' I logged on to its website, which had numerous bells, whistles and links—and a corporate logo with an image of the ancient hero gripping a pair of snakes that looked very like the one I'd seen on the big guy's disappearing cap badge. The bottom line was that H.S. was a world leader in the provision of security for individuals, businesses and sovereign states; it also ran training courses at all levels and had compounds in several U.S. states and foreign countries. Were these the people behind the Hades complex? I clicked about the site, but found no locations in Texas—the nearest camp, 'a fully integrated firing range, physical training and operations center,' was in northern Oklahoma. Going back to the home page, I saw a picture of a smiling, middle-aged man, whose face was smooth as a baby's and whose brown hair looked like it had been dyed a dozen times. He was the company's chairman and CEO, and he was also a Baptist preacher—the Reverend Rudi Crane. I'd have moved quickly on, having a severely limited tolerance for men of the cloth, but I noticed a link to his forthcoming engagements. Tomorrow he would be attending the UN Climate Change Conference in New York—Hercules Solutions being committed to the most economical and sustainable use of resources in all its global activities.

Things were coming together at a frightening rate. I did a search for March Violet Partners. The Director had been right. The company was registered in Liberia but, unlike the H.S. site, there were minimal links and very little information was given out, although one of its subsidiaries was Cerberus Security. The holding company was involved in international trade and consultancy, but it didn't say in what commodities and services. There were few references to it elsewhere, and nothing linking it either to Texas or to Hercules Solutions. Perhaps I'd have to ask the Reverend Crane himself. Maybe the Director could introduce us. I had no doubt that they would know each other.

'Good coffee?' Special Agent Simonsen asked when he picked me up outside the hotel. There was a hint of a smile on his thin lips.

'I only drink tea,' I lied. It didn't surprise me that I was being watched. The Feds could check what I'd been doing on the computer, but it would take time and I had the feeling that everything would come to a head in New York soon.

The hospital was a military one, a lot better organized and staffed than the facility in the camp where Karen and our son had died. I pushed them from my thoughts, feeling like a traitor—the only way I would get through this was by focusing on the worrying number of targets I was gathering.

'Quincy,' I said, as I approached the tube-festooned, monitor-haunted bed in the single room where he lay. 'How goes it?' His upper body was swathed in bandages.

He looked up with initial bewilderment, and then recognized me. 'Matt,' he said, his voice rough from the feeding tube that had been inserted down his throat. 'You okay?'

'You should see the other guys. What about you?'

'I'll live,' he said, frowning as he tried to move an arm. 'Got a smashed shoulder on one side and a collapsed lung on the other. They say I'll come through.'

'Shit, I'm sorry, Quincy,' I said, wiping his forehead with a tissue. 'I didn't think Sara…would…' I let

the words trail away as guilt flooded through me. Of
course I knew she would kill him; that was what she
did. I should have tried to stop her.

'Forget it, man. What happened to her?'

'I…I killed her. Rothmann's dead, too, not by my
hand. He killed the hit man Apollyon.'

'Jeez, I missed a big show.' He took a ragged breath.
'Matt, I—'

I raised a hand. 'Don't talk, Quincy. You need to rest.
I'm just glad to see you alive and doing well.' I leaned
closer. 'Listen, did you ever hear of a company called
Hercules Solutions?'

'Shit, yeah,' he gasped. 'I…I was seconded…to them
in… Iraq. They…they were cowboys. Paid… a fortune
and killed anything that moved, 'specially after some
of their people got…taken out.'

'They're run by a reverend.'

'Yeah, I met him out there….'

'Really? What's he like?'

Quincy coughed painfully. When he finished, I saw
that a smile had formed on his lips. 'He…he makes
like he's full of love for everyone, but he still lives and
breathes the old South. I didn't tell you I was Jewish,
did I? So…so I made sure my Star of David was obvious. He…couldn't get out of shaking my hand, but he…
looked like he wanted to spit in my face.'

It had never occurred to me that Quincy might be a
Jew. Knowing that, I was even happier that he had escaped from the coven of racist shitheads with his life.
I put my hand on his forearm. 'Okay, my friend, that's
enough. I'm going to go now.'

'No, Matt, I—'

'Shh,' I said, stepping back. 'I'll see you in a day or two.'

I heard his voice again as I reached the door. He was calling my name. A nurse brushed past, shooting me a furious look. I felt bad that I'd disturbed him, but at least I knew what kind of scumbag Rudi Crane was. How much good that would do me, I couldn't tell. Then I thought of the Indian and Pakistani troops in the Hades complex. Had the color of their skins led to them being treated as cannon fodder? That wouldn't have surprised me at all.

The Bureau plane landed at La Guardia at ten the next morning. The Director sat opposite me during the flight and tried to get me talking about Rothmann. I brushed him off without being rude and looked through the early editions of the newspapers. They all carried stories about the climate change conference to be hosted by the UN at its headquarters. The world's main players would be there, but most attention was being paid to the Russians and Chinese, both of whom had indicated that they were finally prepared to make cuts in their emissions. This chimed with the U.S.'s new approach to the issue. Although the President wasn't attending the first sessions, he would be at the Secretary-General's dinner in the evening, while the secretary of state and several other cabinet members would represent the U.S. during the day. Writers were supposed to have big egos, but I still wasn't sure why the Director had asked me along. Maybe he thought my presence alongside him would arouse media interest in advance of the evening press conference.

We were driven to a hotel on East 42nd Street, only a short walk from the UN complex. Rain was pouring down and Simonsen handed me an umbrella. I was glad it didn't bear the letters FBI in bright yellow—I still had mixed feelings about the Bureau, given that my family died on its watch. We met in the lobby shortly afterward and I was handed a laminated UN tag with my photo and name and a bar code underneath.

'Right, are you ready to talk the talk?' the Director asked.

His use of the slang expression surprised me. He was wearing a suit that must have cost several thousand dollars, as well as a putrid yellow tie. I had again declined the suit I'd been given and stuck to smart but casual, no tie. I had nothing to prove, at least not on the sartorial front.

Security at the glass tower on the East River was tight and even the Director's group had to pass through several scanners. Although there were armed personnel outside the building, there was no sign of weapons inside. That was reassuring, though I was sure the security detail was carrying concealed handguns. At least there wouldn't be a rerun of the Washington Cathedral massacre, where members of the armed forces conditioned by the Rothmanns had fired automatic rifles into the crowd. Then again, why would anyone want to disrupt a climate change conference? Even the automobile lobby had begun to accept there was a problem. If a private security firm like Hercules Solutions could play the eco card, surely there was hope for the world.

Which reminded me. Where was the Reverend Rudi

Crane? I wanted to have a look at him. I glanced round and was surprised by the person who had appeared behind me.

Crane led his group of executives toward the elevators in the UN building's entrance hall. The security checks had been adequate, although he would have advised even more care if H.S. had handled the work. You could never tell what kind of demented terrorist might sneak into a gathering like this—the place was full of former communists: Muslims, Africans with a grudge against the civilized world, even misguided Europeans who thought the U.S. was the devil. They were benighted sinners, all of them.

Crane told himself to keep his breathing steady. He had struggled to do that sometimes in the field, resulting in costly reprisals against militias in Iraq and the Taliban in Afghanistan. His personal rule was that the body count always had to favor H.S. or its subsidiaries, even if the numbers of enemy dead were inflated by noncombatant women and children. Some people called them collateral damage, but he preferred the company jargon, 'fertilizer.' Those people weren't human beings, they were animals, put on earth for the benefit of their betters.

Entering the large conference hall, he took a deep breath. Even here, there was a hint of the high smell you got in underdeveloped countries, that mixture of sweat, excrement and death. It filled his nostrils and almost made him puke. Good Lord, give me strength, he prayed silently. It wasn't the first time he had made that request today. The news from Texas had been bad.

At least his supervisor there had managed to convince the FBI that he had been kidnapped by the 'foreigners' who ran the camp—who were now supposedly on the run. As instructed, he had mentioned March Violet Partners—much joy might they have of that carefully constructed ghost. The fact that Thomson/Rothmann/ the Master was dead, as were the assassins, was positive. No trails led back to him, as long as Xavier Marias held his well-paid tongue.

Cameras clicked ahead of him and people crowded around men in dark suits. One group had almond eyes and off-white skin—the Chinese: communist hypocrites who were doing their best to destroy American power. The others were mainly fair-haired, with high cheekbones and greedy eyes—the Russians: no longer communists, but liars and thieves whose former soldiers-turned-mercenaries were H.S.'s biggest competitors. How could anyone entrust degenerates like those with personal, corporate or national security?

If there was any justice, the Lord would smite them all with his glorious thunder, but Rudi Crane knew praying for that would be sinful. Maybe he would be lucky—it would hardly be the first time; maybe some individual or group with a justified grievance would take action.

He looked around the international crowd in expensive suits and curious national costumes, but didn't see any likely candidates. Then he caught sight of a familiar figure. The Director of the FBI was striding purposefully toward the Russian delegation. But who was that man behind him, wearing inappropriately informal clothes? Surely he had seen images of those features very recently.

* * *

The nurses were still angry with Quincy Jerome's visitor. The patient had been upset all evening, pressing the call button frequently and repeating the name 'Matt' over and over. He had become delirious and had been given medication. When he woke in the morning, he started the litany again.

What could it be that he wanted to tell the Englishman so much?

Thirty-Six

Gordy Lister had been in a bar north of Malvern, Arkansas, when he saw the TV news. So the useless idiots who called the shots were gathering in the Big Apple to save the planet—kinda like hiring Jesse James to crack down on bank robbery or General Custer to improve relations with the Indians, screw that Native American bullshit. He drained his Bud and ordered another, thinking of the time not too long ago when he'd been a bigshot newspaper man and had drunk ultradry martinis every night. Thanks to his loony tunes ex-boss, that had all gone up in smoke. He'd been lucky to slip away from the scene in Texas. He'd dumped the sedan on the outskirts of Texarkana, shaved his head, bought a suit and tie, and rented a car using one of the credit cards and fake driver's licenses he always carried. There would be more changes in his appearance and transport in the days to come.

He watched as the wide-eyed anchorwoman with her neatly sculpted hair and her glinting marble teeth turned to the economy. That was another thing he'd been screwed on—after the self-proclaimed Master had gone AWOL, all Gordy's accounts had been blocked and he'd been reduced to stealing from the donations of the deluded faithful. Fortunately, the transfers he had made to the bank in Tahiti hadn't been nailed, but they weren't much use to him here. Fuck Jack Thomson. Fuck Heinz Rothmann. Fuck the Master. Shooting him was the best thing he'd ever done.

Familiar faces appeared on the screen above the bar and Lister paid attention.

What the—? The Director of the FBI was boasting about the Bureau's success in tracking down the fugitive businessman Jack Thomson, the mastermind behind the massacre in Washington National Cathedral that had so nearly cost the President his life. He would be hosting a press conference after attending the climate change conference in New York tomorrow and details would be given there. In the meantime, he could say that the Hitler's Hitman killer had been identified as a professional assassin, in part due to the sterling work of the English writer Matt Wells, who was no longer a suspect in the attack on the President.

Gordy Lister rocked back on his stool. That bastard. Wells was *the main reason* everything had turned to shit. If he hadn't escaped from the camp in Maine and got to Rothmann, life would still have been peachy— his former boss's plans to rip apart American society and bring back Nazism had been crazy, but he'd have been in a good position to make the most of them. The madman wouldn't have got so obsessed with the Antichurch if he'd been able to stay in Washington and play Führer.

Not only that: Wells had been involved with the blonde bitch who had killed Mikey. And now the fucker was going to be paraded in front of the cameras, modestly accepting the praises of the FBI Director? No way.

He ordered a shot of Wild Turkey and thought about the dead Nazi. Sure, the Kraut was as cracked as a mirror in an earthquake zone, but he'd been good to him—cool apartment, luxury cars, plenty of tight young snatch. The limey bastard Wells would tell the Feds all about Rothmann's sidekick. Every law enforcement professional in the country would be looking out for Gordy Lister, no matter how many changes he made to the way he looked. Unless…

In the back pocket of his pants, he kept a small, leather-covered notebook.

He'd never been good at remembering numbers, but when he saw them written down he always knew what they were, meaning he didn't have to add names or other identifying symbols. On page thirty-seven was a number that Rothmann had given him a couple of months back. His boss had given him to understand that the white-haired former admiral had been an early conditioning subject—apparently it hadn't taken fully, though Rothmann still thought a certain trigger could provoke an 'interesting' response. All right—it was time to see what form that response might take.

Gordy went out into the parking lot and made the call. He recognized the respondent's tones immediately and spoke the trigger, 'Erfurt'—he'd never had any trouble remembering words. There was silence, and then the person said, 'I am at your command.'

Gordy swallowed a laugh. This was a gas. 'The United Nations Climate Change Conference,' he said, impersonating his former boss as best he could. 'Dis-

pose of people antagonistic to our ideology.' That was
the kind of tortuous language Rothmann favored. 'And
dispose of Matt Wells after use.' Then he passed on the
necessary word and he cut the connection.

Now he felt even better. Killing the Master had left
him with a small piece of guilt that might have grown
in the future. Not anymore. Vengeance for the both of
them was his! He got into the rental car and headed
north. He could get a flight in St. Louis that would
connect with others for destinations much farther to
the west. Winter in the South Seas would be balmy,
sexually stimulating and light on Feds. From there, the
world was his oyster, clam and abalone.

'Hello, Arthur. What are you doing here?'

Bimsdale gave me a searching look. 'I could ask you
the same question.'

'Ask your boss,' I replied, turning away. Maybe Sebastian's former assistant had heard about the press conference and wanted to be part of it. Then I thought of his
ex-boss. I was still unsure about what had really happened to him. And why would Bimsdale have broken
off the investigation in Texas to come to New York?

The question slipped away as the Director led me
toward the Russians, a couple of whom I recognized: a
shifty specimen who had gone from the KGB to become
energy minister and a tall guy with overgrown eyebrows
who was reputed to be the richest oilman in the world.
The FBI chief was being effusive in Russian. He then
raised his hands, apparently asking them to stay where
they were, and moved to the Chinese delegation. He
didn't know their language, but his arm and head movements were easy enough to interpret—he was herding

them toward the Russians. Another man whose face I knew from the TV arrived: the President of the European Union. In the distance, I recognized Rudi Crane. He was surrounded by men in sharp suits, while he himself—ever the preacher, apparently—was wearing a simple black combo. It struck me that he would be ideally placed to cause trouble; according to the Hercules Solutions website, he had hundreds of ex-special forces operatives working for him. All the same, he looked pretty harmless, a soft smile on his lips.

And then things started to get strange. I experienced a couple of lightning flashes in my brain and heard a babble of voices, which was rapidly reduced to one, that of a ranting, high-pitched speaker in a language I couldn't understand, but whose meaning was somehow apparent. We are surrounded by enemies…neighboring states that have been historically hostile toward us… Slavic subhumans who wish to trample us underfoot… yellow-skinned barbarians interested only in rape and plunder…we will crush them all…

I came back to myself, my fists clenched hard. What was that? Some remnant of Rothmann's conditioning that had been prompted by the sight of the various ethnic groups? I stepped closer and watched the delegates as they shook hands, reluctantly at first and then with increasing enthusiasm. The Director looked gratified, not least when the secretary of state appeared, wearing the expression of someone whose thunder has been well and truly stolen. And then the former admiral turned to me, beckoning me closer. He bent forward till his lips were only a few inches from my ear.

'Keep them together and don't allow anyone to interfere, Mr. Wells,' he said, his voice steady but euphoric. 'Chanak, I say. Chanak.'

The sentient part of me was immediately separated from my body, aware of the subtlety of the trigger but unable to resist it.

Chanak, a Turkish town that had played a strategically significant role during the Gallipoli campaign of the First World War, a campaign orchestrated by German commanders, resulting in the defeat of British Empire and French forces by the Ottoman Turks.

I watched as my body pushed the Russians and Chinese closer. Arthur Bimsdale remonstrated and I threw him several yards through the air. He came back at me, throwing me over his shoulder with a skillful judo move. I got to my feet, planted my elbow in another FBI man's gut, and lowered my shoulder. I rammed Bimsdale into the group of shocked statesmen. Security personnel approached and I rendered them harmless with karate strikes, head butts and punches.

Then I saw Arthur Bimsdale shoving through the crowd, trying to get to the Director, whose hands were moving inside his jacket. Instantly I understood what he was doing. He must have brought the undetectable chemical components of a bomb through the security checks and was now mixing them. At the same time, he was shouting to the politicians in Russian and in English to stay close, and that he was in control of the situation. Some on the outside of the circle had broken away, but there were still over a dozen in close range.

I had been trying to get my conscious self into the protective headspace that Doctor Rivers and I had worked on, but without success. This trigger must have been buried deep, giving it greater power over my actions. I tried again and again to break free. I roamed around the statesmen, keeping them in a ring around the Director and fighting off anyone who tried to intervene.

And then Karen came to me. She rose up like a goddess, dressed in a long white robe. She was cradling our son in her arms and there was a tender smile on her lips. She looked at me, looked into my eyes, and I heard her voice. She spoke words of love that brooked no argument and I heard myself respond to them. Love beyond death…

In a blur of movement, I found myself back in my body and back in control. Now I was pulling the Russians and Chinese away, shouting at them to run. Ahead, I saw the Director look up, his eyes wide. Arthur Bimsdale was behind him, still struggling to get past the confused statesmen. I pushed myself between the Russian energy minister and the European President. The Director was right in front of me, his hands holding two white plastic bottles. One of them was almost empty. A beatific expression came over the old man's face as he held it toward me.

What was he saying? Too late, I saw a wisp of smoke or fumes escape the container as I threw myself over him in the best smothering tackle I had ever made.

There was a flash and a bang, and I went speedily to another place.

'You lose,' he had been saying. 'They'll miss you.'

Thirty-Seven

Rudi Crane was across the conference hall. He had been watching the FBI Director's diplomatic activities and wondering what the former admiral was doing. He knew him, of course—had known him when he was still in the Navy and Hercules Solutions was nothing more than a small operator trying to muscle into the private security business. There had been rumors that the admiral was a CIA man, but that seemed unlikely, given his present position. When the group of statesman became a herd of confused sheep, with the Englishman Matt Wells running around like a sheepdog, Crane had got even more curious. Then fighting broke out and he decided to keep his distance, signaling the retreat to his executives. He didn't want the company to be part of any unpleasantness, an approach subsequently justified by the muffled explosion which brought chaos to the entire area.

Retiring to the entrance hall, where no one was being allowed in or out, Rudi Crane thought about what he had witnessed. Had someone made an attempt on the FBI Director's life? Certainly, Wells had been behaving strangely. Could one of the foreigners have brought explosives into the UN's neutral domain?

The only thing to be said for the episode was that it could be spun for the good of security companies like his. If Hercules Solutions had been handling matters, no one would have been allowed to smuggle explosives in. It struck him that the whole thing might be a welcome distraction from what had gone on in Texas. Although there was nothing to tie H.S. with the camp down there, he didn't like loose ends. The FBI would be working on the bodies of the assassins he had hired and, no doubt, their identities would eventually be uncovered. There was no link to him, but he would have preferred a tidier ending to his strategy of disrupting Jack Thomson's activities and gaining possession of the conditioning program. Who knew what had happened to that? He suspected his former collaborator would have made sure law enforcement wouldn't find it. There would be other government agencies after it, as well.

He took a seat in the entrance hall and watched as media people ran past, cameras and hairstyles wobbling. On reflection, he didn't regret the so-called Hitler's Hitman killings—the name had been suggested off the record to a journalist by one of his PR people. The assassin had followed their instructions and Thomson had been duly pressured. The unknown quantity had been Matt Wells. He had never expected the FBI to use a murder suspect in an investigation, especially not one with a grudge. Had the Director known about that? The fact that the lead investigator, Peter Sebastian, had been found dead was, at the very least, convenient for some people.

No, he would go back to the apartment and pray for

a better day tomorrow. He should have known that cuddling up to politicians would be a waste of time. Hard-hearted businessmen were much easier to deal with.

Which reminded him: he needed to sign off on that stewardess's promotion—what was her name again? She had the soul of a sinner, but her mouth was a miracle.

To my surprise, I came round quickly. I was still lying on top of the Director and the same besuited legs, both vertical and horizontal, were in my close vicinity. There was a foul smell in the air and Arthur Bimsdale's hair had been scorched. Otherwise, he seemed okay. He sat up as I studied him, my eyes stinging, and looked toward me.

'Are you all right?' His voice sounded tinny.

'Yeah.' My own voice was weird. I was probably lucky I could hear anything.

'What about the Director?'

I put my hands on either side of the old man's head and levered myself off him. His face and hair had turned black in the blast, most of which had been directed back at him when I crashed into him.

'Chemical bomb,' Bimsdale said redundantly. 'The proportions must have been slightly off. We were lucky.'

'He wasn't.'

The Director's blue eyes were wide open, the whites crisscrossed by broken blood vessels. A piece of sharp plastic from one of the containers had penetrated his throat. Now I was standing, I realized that the clothing on the upper part of my body was drenched in arterial blood. People all around were gasping and raising their hands to their mouths.

I took off my jacket and accepted a blanket from a paramedic.

'What happened to you?' Bimsdale asked.

'Trigger,' I said, in a low voice. 'I fought it off.'

'Good for you. And the Director?'

I stepped aside to allow the paramedics to attend to the dead man. 'Something similar, I'd guess. He spoke the word that nailed me.' I thought back to what the Director had come out with as I overpowered him. 'They'll miss you.' What had he meant? The people of the world? My friends?

The next three hours were a tedious succession of statements to various law enforcement agencies—UN, NYPD and others—and a trip to hospital for a check-up. I was given the all clear, though I was to see a doctor if my hearing didn't improve within a week. I had numerous aches and pain across my body, the result of my fights with Bimsdale and others before the explosion, but none of them were important. When I was escorted out of the hospital by Special Agent Simonsen and his sidekicks, a battery of camera lights flashed on and the vultures let loose their questions—'How does it feel to be a hero?', 'Was the FBI Director a North Korean agent?' and 'Are you going to write a book about this?' were three of them. A headache had settled over my ravaged brain, so I kept quiet. That only made them more interested.

'Do you want to freshen up?' Simonsen asked.

I nodded.

'Back to the hotel then.' He led me to a waiting car.

'Jesus,' he said, as we were driven away. 'Imagine if

the Director had managed to take out the cream of the Russian and Chinese governments.'

'Don't forget the President of Europe.'

'Oh, yeah, he was there, too. Good moves, my friend. You ever played gridiron?'

'Rugby league.'

'What's that?'

I waved a hand feebly and sat back. The buildings of New York moved by, the rain still teeming down. Was that really it, the end of the affair? I felt a wave of exhaustion crash over me, which was hardly surprising, considering my physical and mental exertions and the lack of sleep recently. But that wasn't the whole story. While I'd been on Rothmann's tail and fighting through the Hades complex, even when I'd been with the Director, I'd been able to keep the ones I'd lost at the back of my mind. I couldn't do so anymore. I could see them again, clearer than ever, Karen holding our son and smiling sadly as they hovered forever out of reach. Was this what the rest of my life was going to be? The prospect nearly made me jump out of the car.

'Are you okay?' Simonsen asked.

I raised a hand again, unable to speak. My eyes filled with tears. At first I thought I could pass that off as a result of the explosion, but then I gave up. I wasn't going to be able to hide what had happened to Karen and the baby anymore. Well, maybe a bit longer—Simonsen was a nice enough guy, but I didn't feel like opening up to him, especially with another agent in the front seat.

'Home away from home,' Simonsen said, as we approached the hotel reception. I had only just realized that the Chrysler Building was down the street and was trying to get a look at it. The rain and mist cut off the upper part of glass and steel tower.

Simonsen came with me to the thirty-second floor. 'I'll be outside,' he said, with a tentative smile.

'You don't have to do that.'

'Acting Director's orders. You're a celebrity now.'

I tried to raise an eyebrow, but that hurt. 'I presume the press conference isn't going ahead tonight.'

'Not the one the admiral set up. But stand by for one about today's fun and games.'

'Have I got a choice?'

He laughed. 'Sure. You're not one of us.'

'You got that right.' I opened the door and went inside, pulling the blanket from around my shoulders and dropping it on the floor. Then I looked up and saw them.

Karen and our son were framed by the window and behind it was the top half of the Chrysler Building, pointing to the sky like a rocket on the launch pad.

I fainted.

I came round for the second time that day. This time I was lying on a carpeted floor rather than a dead body. Two women were on their knees beside me. One of them was Special Agent Julie Simms, Peter Sebastian's sidekick from the Illinois camp, and she looked guilty as sin. The other was Karen.

'Have I died?'

'And gone to heaven,' Karen said.

'The other place, more like. I've already been there.' I got myself into a sitting position, aided by the FBI agent. Karen was holding the baby on her lap.

'Magnus,' I said, his name finally coming back to me.

'Magnus Oliver Wells,' she confirmed.

I closed my eyes, took a deep breath and opened them again. They were still there.

'How did…' My voice broke and my eyes filled with tears. This was getting to be a habit.

'Shh,' Karen said, kissing me on the forehead. 'Would you like to hold him?'

Suddenly that was the thing I most wanted to do in the world. I let her place him in my hands and then lifted him up. He was awake, green eyes wide and fixed on mine. He had a lot of brown hair.

'Magnus,' I said softly, kissing his forehead in turn. 'I'm…I'm your daddy.'

I heard Karen sob and I don't think Julie Simms was far off joining her. I held my son close and breathed in his priceless scent. He made a noise and I moved him outward again. He blinked and then smiled broadly. He was the only one whose eyes stayed dry.

After Karen had put her arms around me and we had communed silently as a family for the first time, I kissed her on the lips and pushed her back gently.

'You look fantastic,' I said, and she did.

'We've been well looked after.' She glanced at Special Agent Simms, who was now standing against the wall.

'I'll leave you,' Simms said, picking up her jacket.

'Oh, no you don't,' I ordered, provoking a squeal from Magnus. 'Shit, sorry.' I handed him to Karen, who laughed lightly.

'Don't blame Julie. She was only following orders.'

'I've heard that somewhere before.'

'Let her go,' Karen said, opening her blouse and putting the baby to her breast. 'I'll tell you what happened.'

The door closed behind the special agent before I could say anything.

And so Karen told me—how she had given birth normally, the panic having been faked by the medical team and had then been given something to make her sleep. When she came round, she was told by Julie Simms that Peter Sebastian had taken me to Washington for pre-trial meetings. The TV and laptop were removed and she didn't receive any newspapers, so she had no idea what happened in Maine and Texas. Then, a couple of days ago, they had been flown to Washington and lodged in a Bureau house for the night, before being brought up to NYC that morning.

I held Karen and Magnus while she was talking, my mind filled with conflicting images—the pair of them in the camp morgue, their skin cold and blue; the voices I had heard calling me, the visions of them disappearing down the road of no return. This was not the time to share that with her—maybe that time would never come. I looked at my son's face again. He hadn't been the baby in the morgue. They must have used some other poor mother's dead child. What had Peter Sebastian done? I'd known he was devious, but I'd never have thought he could go so far to convince me of Rothmann's guilt. Then I followed that line of thought. They'd been brought to New York this morning, after his death. There was only one person who could have ordered that—the dead Director. He and Sebastian must have been working together. Did Sebastian know about the former admiral's conditioning? If he did, he had paid the price. But Sebastian hadn't deserved that—for all he'd done, I still had some respect for him. Seeing Karen and our son had made me more compassionate, it seemed.

'Matt?' Karen said softly.

'Sorry,' I said, coming out of my reverie.

'It doesn't matter, whatever you've done. We're together now.' She kissed me. 'Forever.'

She was thinking of Rothmann, assuming I'd killed him. I didn't want to tell her about what had happened to him now, or what I'd done to Sara.

I heard voices outside the door, and then heavy footsteps going down the corridor. There was a knock on the door. I went over and looked through the spyhole.

'Arthur,' I said, after I'd opened up. 'Your hair still looks like it's standing to attention.'

He smiled. 'I know—I can't get it to lie—' He broke off and stared at Karen in astonishment. Any thoughts I'd had of his being part of Sebastian's scam disappeared. I gave him a rundown.

'I can't believe it,' he said, walking over and examining the baby. 'Well, congratulations. May I?' He pulled an armchair toward the door and sat down.

'Of course.' I went over to Karen. 'You know, I couldn't have put this in a novel.'

He laughed. 'No, you couldn't.'

'Drink?' I asked, trying to locate the minibar. I needed one myself.

'No, thanks. I'm not staying.' He paused. 'Neither are you.'

I turned toward him, my heart making a break for my mouth. To my left, Karen made a smothered, high-pitched noise. Arthur Bimsdale was screwing a silencer into the barrel of his service pistol.

'What the—'

'Be quiet,' he ordered, waving me closer to Karen and Magnus with the weapon. 'This won't take long. When I said I couldn't believe it, I meant I couldn't believe that my esteemed former chief managed to conceal this stratagem from me.'

'Exactly who are you working for?'

'Ah, that would be too easy. What I will tell you is that I had no idea about the ex-Director's allegiances, either.'

'He and Sebastian were working together,' I said, trying to buy us time. I'd seen Bimsdale in action and I knew I couldn't reach him without being shot. Maybe I'd have to do that to save the others, but I was still looking for another option.

'Apparently so,' he agreed. 'But now, I'm afraid, your usefulness has run its course, Mr. Wells. It will look like you lost your mind and tragically killed your family. Rothmann's fault, of course.'

'Let them go,' I said, looking at Karen. 'She won't say anything. Will you?'

'We're not going anywhere,' she retorted. 'We're staying together forever, remember?'

I glared at her, but she stayed where she was.

'Touching,' Bimsdale said, leveling the pistol at my chest. 'And, indeed, correct.'

'Why?' I demanded. 'There's no reason to kill us.'

'I don't write the script,' he said casually. 'If you want my opinion, I'd say my principals feel you're more trouble than you're worth.'

'Zig!' I yelled. That was the call for a rugby move

that I'd told Karen about when Sara had been after us in London—both of us made a rapid move to the left. That took us out of the pistol's immediate line of fire. Taking advantage of the momentary surprise, I dived forward, trying to get my body as horizontal and low as possible. Bimsdale knew what he was doing, because sitting down made his position more secure.

There was a spit and I felt a tug on the back of my shirt. Then my head crashed into his midriff. The air blasted from his lungs and the pistol was flung out of his grip.

Bimsdale let out a yell. I looked round as I wrapped my arms round him. Karen must have hit him. But where was the baby? The agent slipped one of his arms from my grip and backhanded her in the face, sending her spinning backward. I shoved myself up his body and then stopped. Something very sharp was piercing my back.

'It's…a…switchblade,' he said, panting as I increased pressure on his chest. 'I…found it…on the Soul… Collector's…body.'

'Matt!' Karen screamed.

'Let…me go,' Bimsdale gasped.

I kept shoving with my legs, the chair now up against the wall. The pain in my back became almost unbearable, but I wasn't going to let him harm my family. Behind me, I could hear Magnus crying and Karen moaning.

'You're about…to die,' Bimsdale said, pushing hard against me.

Then I saw his wooden pencil. The end with the eraser had been forced out of his jacket pocket. I remembered a story Dave Cummings had told me about an SAS friend, who had been in a similar situation. This was for Dave.

Ignoring the blinding pain, I moved my head toward Bimsdale's jacket and got my teeth around the pencil. He realized what I was doing, but couldn't do anything about it except continue sticking me with the knife. I pulled my head back as far as I could, and then smashed my loaded mouth forward.

There was a muffled shriek and I felt the pain in my back recede slightly. Karen was suddenly close, removing Bimsdale's hand but leaving the blade in me—she'd been trained for such situations.

'You'll be all right, Matt, darling,' she said, but the tone of her voice, as mournful as an autumn sunset, gave her away.

The last thing I saw was Arthur Bimsdale's face. The pencil had gone through one of his nostrils and deep into his traitorous brain. The last thing I heard was the conjoined wail of my wife and son.

Epilogue

I lost a kidney and a fair amount of self-respect. After all, Arthur Bimsdale was a lanky kid without special forces training. I should have taken him out with my hands rather than a primary school writing implement. I expressed that feeling to Karen and she dispatched me to the Ice Age with her eyes. After a week in hospital, I was allowed out to make it up to her. I did, somehow managing not to split my stitches.

We spent a week in an FBI apartment looking over the East River. I even managed to tag along on short walks with Karen and Magnus. I could have taken a taxi to the lawyer's office in Queens that Sara had told me about, but I decided against it. Given her record, whatever she'd stashed there would be a contemporary version of Pandora's Box. I was still puzzled by her physical condition—the sweats and the pain she seemed to be affected by—but didn't ask to see the postmortem. Sara's life was over and so, I decided, was her influence on mine. I could also have checked out the address that Roger had found for the email account of my former lover's broker, or passed it to the FBI. As it

happened, neither was necessary. On our penultimate
day in New York, there was a report in the papers of a
murder. An economist by the name of Xavier Marias
was found near that address, his throat cut. Nothing
seemed to have been stolen from his person and there
was no indication of who the killer might have been.
Sara had somehow got at her broker from beyond the
grave. That was another reason to avoid her stash—what
else might be waiting for me there?

We were flown to Washington by Bureau jet. Ethan
Simonsen was seriously embarrassed over the Bimsdale
affair, but I told him to lighten up. As it was, he stuck
to us tighter than superglue. We were put up in a smart
hotel near the Hoover Building while I was questioned
at length. I told them more or less everything I knew.
You should always keep something to yourself—in this
case, I kept back much of what Sara had told me about
her activities. They weren't germane to the case and,
since they had never caught her, they had no claim to
title. We visited Quincy several times. I had the feeling
he might have known that Karen and Magnus hadn't
died, but I didn't encourage him to come clean. It was
irrelevant now.

I never knew Sir Andrew Frogget, but I had come
across his sleazy sidekick Gavin Burrows. The postmortem on the Routh Limited chairman was inconclusive.
There were small traces in his bloodstream of a chemical compound that had never been seen before, but it
was deemed to be irrelevant. I immediately thought of
spies and dirty tricks. Obviously the CIA or their foreign equivalents would be interested in Heinz Rothmann. I let that go—I didn't need any more hassles.
That was also why I'd left Hercules Solutions to the

Bureau. As for Arthur Bimsdale, it was assumed he had been conditioned by Rothmann, though the chances of Peter Sebastian having had a second assistant who had been turned struck me as being even more minimal than those of Great Britain becoming the best rugby league team in the world. Besides, I had other things on my mind: baby shit, breast-feeding and its psychological effects on fathers, baby shit...

We were eventually cut loose by the FBI and given tickets for a flight to London. I didn't have many plans. That was because Karen did. She was going back to work, taking the baby with her until she stopped feeding him, which would be a tester for the Metropolitan Police. I was vaguely thinking about writing a book, but not about our experiences. Perhaps a kids' story, one with no monsters—and no nameless dead. Rothmann and his sister had stolen the identities of all the people they had conditioned, and their father had been responsible for hundreds of anonymous deaths at Auschwitz. It was beyond me to bring any of those victims back.

There was still the small matter of our wedding. We had some time before the thirty days after Magnus's birth that Karen stipulated. Maybe we'd slip off to Nevada before we went home. Julie Simms managed to find the engagement ring Peter Sebastian had bought. I considered sending it to his grieving family, but decided against that. He owed us big time.

In the evening, after Magnus dropped off, Karen and I listened to Monteverdi's *Orfeo* again. The mythical singer had gone to the underworld to find his dead wife, but had lost her on the way back to the sunlight.

I wasn't ever going to let go of Karen and our son.

* * * * *

Acknowledgments

My sincere thanks to: the MIRA teams around the world and, especially, to Adam Wilson, prince among editors; my admirable agent Broo Doherty; and the excellent people at MIDAS PR, London.

My gratitude and love to the family and friends who have acted as this author's support system. Particular thanks to Sofka Zinovieff for lunches and listening.

And a belated public vote of appreciation to the dedicated people who give their time and energy to supporting crime fiction in different ways—an incomplete list includes Declan Burke, Sharon Canavar and the Harrogate Crime Festival team, Michael Carlson, Barry Forshaw, Maxim Jakubowski, the Jordans, Calum Macleod, Adrian Muller and the Crime Fest team, Mike Ripley, Chris Simmons, Mike Stotter, Richard Thomas, David Torrans, Len Wanner—anyone I've carelessly omitted can look forward to the next book.

Finally, as has been customary in the Wells series (not that anyone has commented), a Neil Young title for my beloved Roula and children to ponder: 'Only Love Can Break Your Heart'…

International bestselling author

PAUL JOHNSTON

Having been brutally targeted by the "White Devil" serial killer, crime writer Matt Wells knows what it's like to look evil in the face and survive. He's rebuilt his life—but with a disciple of his tormentor still at large, he has never stopped looking over his shoulder.

When mystery writers start dying and his best friend is found murdered, Matt realizes his paranoia is well-founded. Now he must use all his resources to orchestrate the psychopath's end. But as cryptic clues to the next victims mock him, it is chillingly clear that his dance with the devil has only just begun....

THE SOUL COLLECTOR

Available wherever books are sold.

"...entertainment, fire-and-brimstone style."
— *LA Times* on *The Death List*

MIRA®

www.MIRABooks.com

MPJ2566

A FAST-PACED CRIME NOVEL FROM

RICK MOFINA

Tilly's mother Cora pleads for mercy but the kidnappers are clear: if they don't get their $5 million back in five days, Tilly dies. If anyone contacts police, Tilly dies.

After disappearing from his life without a trace decades ago, Cora frantically reaches out to her brother, Jack Gannon, a journalist. Cora tells him about the shameful mistakes she's made—but she guards the one secret that may be keeping her daughter alive.

Meanwhile, a Mexican priest hears a chilling confession from a twenty-year-old assassin, haunted by the faces of the people he's executed. He seeks absolution as he sets out to commit his last murders as a hired killer.

Time is running out...

In the U.S. and Mexico, police and the press go flat out on Tilly's case. But as Gannon digs deeper into his anguished sister's past, the hours tick down on his niece's life and he faces losing the fragment of his rediscovered family forever.

IN
DESPERATION

AVAILABLE WHEREVER BOOKS ARE SOLD

MIRA®

www.MIRABooks.com

MRM2948R

The
Don Pendleton's
Executioner®
TOXIC TERRAIN

Mad cow disease is making life crazy for The Executioner!

AgCon, the largest distributor of cattle feed in the Midwest, is controlled by retired officers of China's PLA, who have perfected a fast-acting prion to cause mad cow disease. It's up to Bolan to shut down the operation—before they are able to poison the country's food supply and cause an economic tailspin like never before.

GOLD EAGLE®

Available May wherever books are sold.

www.readgoldeagle.blogspot.com

GEX390

From the author who brought us the chilling suspense novel *While Galileo Preys*

JOSHUA CORIN

Esme Stuart is reeling from the gradual disintegration of her marriage.

She stumbles upon a website and message board tailored to assist anarchists and murderers, and soon finds herself entangled in the FBI manhunt to track down the site's mysterious webmaster, Cain42.

But can Esme find Cain42 before his deadly plan unfurls?

BEFORE CAIN STRIKES

On sale now!

MIRA®

www.MIRABooks.com

MJC2933R

REQUEST YOUR FREE BOOKS!

2 FREE NOVELS
FROM THE SUSPENSE COLLECTION
PLUS 2 FREE GIFTS!

YES! Please send me 2 FREE novels from the Suspense Collection and my 2 FREE gifts (gifts are worth about $10). After receiving them, if I don't wish to receive any more books, I can return the shipping statement marked "cancel." If I don't cancel, I will receive 4 brand-new novels every month and be billed just $5.74 per book in the U.S. or $6.24 per book in Canada. That's a saving of at least 28% off the cover price. It's quite a bargain! Shipping and handling is just 50¢ per book in the U.S. and 75¢ per book in Canada.* I understand that accepting the 2 free books and gifts places me under no obligation to buy anything. I can always return a shipment and cancel at any time. Even if I never buy another book, the two free books and gifts are mine to keep forever.

191/391 MDN FDDH

Name	(PLEASE PRINT)

Address	Apt. #

City	State/Prov.	Zip/Postal Code

Signature (if under 18, a parent or guardian must sign)

Mail to the **Reader Service:**
IN U.S.A.: P.O. Box 1867, Buffalo, NY 14240-1867
IN CANADA: P.O. Box 609, Fort Erie, Ontario L2A 5X3

Not valid for current subscribers to the Suspense Collection or the Romance/Suspense Collection.

Want to try two free books from another line?
Call 1-800-873-8635 or visit www.ReaderService.com.

* Terms and prices subject to change without notice. Prices do not include applicable taxes. Sales tax applicable in N.Y. Canadian residents will be charged applicable taxes. Offer not valid in Quebec. This offer is limited to one order per household. All orders subject to credit approval. Credit or debit balances in a customer's account(s) may be offset by any other outstanding balance owed by or to the customer. Please allow 4 to 6 weeks for delivery. Offer available while quantities last.

Your Privacy—The Reader Service is committed to protecting your privacy. Our Privacy Policy is available online at www.ReaderService.com or upon request from the Reader Service.

We make a portion of our mailing list available to reputable third parties that offer products we believe may interest you. If you prefer that we not exchange your name with third parties, or if you wish to clarify or modify your communication preferences, please visit us at www.ReaderService.com/consumerschoice or write to us at Reader Service Preference Service, P.O. Box 9062, Buffalo, NY 14269. Include your complete name and address.

Don Pendleton's Mack Bolan.

Kill Shot

Homegrown radicals
seek global domination!

The terror begins with ruthless precision when the clock strikes noon, gunfire ringing out in major cities along the East Coast. At the heart of the conspiracy, sworn enemies have joined for the nuclear devastation of the Middle East. As blood spills across the country, Bolan sights his crosshairs on their nightmare agenda.

*Available June
wherever books are sold.*

Or order your copy now by sending your name, address, zip or postal code, along with a check or money order (please do not send cash) for $6.99 for each book ordered ($7.99 in Canada), plus 75¢ postage and handling ($1.00 in Canada), payable to Gold Eagle Books, to:

In the U.S.
Gold Eagle Books
3010 Walden Avenue
P.O. Box 9077
Buffalo, NY 14269-9077

In Canada
Gold Eagle Books
P.O. Box 636
Fort Erie, Ontario
L2A 5X3

GOLD EAGLE ®

Please specify book title with your order.
Canadian residents add applicable federal and provincial taxes.

www.readgoldeagle.blogspot.com

GSB142

PAUL JOHNSTON

32778 MAPS OF HELL   ___ $7.99 U.S. ___ $9.99 CAN.
32566 THE SOUL COLLECTOR   ___ $7.99 U.S. ___ $8.99 CAN.

(limited quantities available)

TOTAL AMOUNT $ _____
POSTAGE & HANDLING $ _____
($1.00 for 1 book, 50¢ for each additional)
APPLICABLE TAXES* $ _____
TOTAL PAYABLE $ _____

(check or money order—please do not send cash)

To order, complete this form and send it, along with a check or money
order for the total above, payable to MIRA Books, to: **In the U.S.:**
3010 Walden Avenue, P.O. Box 9077, Buffalo, NY 14269-9077;
In Canada: P.O. Box 636, Fort Erie, Ontario, L2A 5X3.

Name: _____
Address: _____ City: _____
State/Prov.: _____ Zip/Postal Code: _____
Account Number (if applicable): _____

075 CSAS

*New York residents remit applicable sales taxes.
*Canadian residents remit applicable GST and provincial taxes.

MIRA®

www.MIRABooks.com
MPJ0411BL